PRAISE FO

"A whip smart cat and mouse game . . . the characters, plot, and pacing are all on point. I dare you to put it down!"

—**Samantha Downing,** *USA TODAY* **bestselling author of** *My Lovely Wife*

"A world-class whodunit that has everything a thriller lover is looking for: a killer premise, an earth-shattering crime, a true-crime podcaster with everything to lose, a cast of shady characters, and twists around every corner."

—**Heather Gudenkauf,** *New York Times* **bestselling author of** *The Overnight Guest* **and** *The Perfect Hosts*

"*A Killer Motive* is sharp, fast-paced, and kept me reading long into the night."

—**Lauren Ling Brown,** *USA TODAY* **bestselling author of** *Society of Lies*

"A twisty, compulsive, heart-pounding read!"

—**Daniel Kalla, bestselling author of** *High Society*

"*A Killer Motive* is a deadly cat and mouse thriller with a singularly cruel villain and layers of secrets."

—**Robyn Harding, internationally bestselling author of** *The Drowning Woman*

"*A Killer Motive* is my kind of book: harrowing, believable, and steeped in emotion."

—**Carter Wilson,** *USA TODAY* **bestselling author of** *Tell Me What You Did*

"*A Killer Motive* kept my heart pounding page after page. Gripping, twisty, and unpredictable, it is undoubtedly her best book yet. If you want a stay-up-all-night thriller, read this book."

—Sydney Leigh, author of *Peril in Pink*

"A tightly paced thriller and clever mystery that will keep you guessing until the end. The perfect novel for true-crime fans!"

—Laurah Norton, author of *Lay Them to Rest* and host of *The Fall Line: True Crime* and *One Strange Thing*

"Gripping from the get-go, *A Killer Motive* takes you hostage. A must-read psychological thriller."

—Rick Mofina, *USA TODAY*, *Globe and Mail*, and *Toronto Star* bestselling author

"Packed full of twists and tension, *A Killer Motive* consumed me until I'd turned the last page. The ending packs a wallop, and you won't see it coming!"

—Sarah Pekkanen, #1 *New York Times* bestselling author

A KILLER MOTIVE

ALSO BY HANNAH MARY McKINNON

Only One Survives
The Revenge List
Never Coming Home
You Will Remember Me
Sister Dear
Her Secret Son
The Neighbors

For additional books by Hannah Mary McKinnon visit her website, hannahmarymckinnon.com.

A KILLER MOTIVE

HANNAH MARY McKINNON

/||MIRA

/// MIRA

ISBN-13: 978-0-7783-8767-1

A Killer Motive

Copyright © 2025 by Hannah Mary McKinnon

All rights reserved. No part of this book may be used or reproduced in any manner whatsoever without written permission.

Without limiting the exclusive rights of any author, contributor or the publisher of this publication, any unauthorized use of this publication to train generative artificial intelligence (AI) technologies is expressly prohibited. Harlequin also exercises their rights under Article 4(3) of the Digital Single Market Directive 2019/790 and expressly reserves this publication from the text and data mining exception.

This is a work of fiction. Names, characters, places and incidents are either the product of the author's imagination or are used fictitiously. Any resemblance to actual persons, living or dead, businesses, companies, events or locales is entirely coincidental.

For questions and comments about the quality of this book, please contact us at CustomerService@Harlequin.com.

TM is a trademark of Harlequin Enterprises ULC.

Mira
22 Adelaide St. West, 41st Floor
Toronto, Ontario M5H 4E3, Canada
MIRABooks.com

HarperCollins Publishers
Macken House, 39/40 Mayor Street Upper,
Dublin 1, D01 C9W8, Ireland
www.HarperCollins.com

Printed in U.S.A.

For Rob—the love of my life
(Thank goodness we said yes before you saw the
internet search history for my books)

The one who wins plays best.
—German proverb

SIX YEARS AGO

CHAPTER 1

STELLA

My pulse thudded in my neck like Morse code. A steady *tap-tap* loosely translating as *come on*. Shoving my hands under my thighs, I slid farther down the passenger seat and peered over the dashboard toward the darkened house at the end of the street.

For ten minutes I'd willed the motion-activated porch lights to stay off. Hoped the heavy living room drapes with the silver ring print I'd been mesmerized by as a kid would remain closed, allowing us to stay undetected.

Tap-tap.

Already 9:47 p.m. Where was he?

The cloudless Maine sky had long transitioned from bright blue to bubble-gum pink before enveloping our corner of the East Coast in a blanket of rich black velvet. A cool breeze drifted through the open car window, providing a welcome break from the searing early August temperatures.

Rain was on its way for Portland and beyond tomorrow, which would be a welcome relief. For now, the sound of buzzing cicadas filled the Friday night air while this summer's hottest anthem played on a radio somewhere in the distance.

The classic smell of freshly cut grass invaded my nostrils, conjuring memories of picnics in the park, running through sprinklers, and hands sticky from melting strawberry Popsicles.

Like those lazy days years ago, tonight would be perfect. All I needed was for my brother to show up.

"Do you think he changed his mind, Stella?" Jeff said, his voice a gentle rumble.

Glancing at my boyfriend, I took in his dark blond hair, straight nose, and the sculpted stubble accentuating a set of epic cheekbones. I let my gaze sweep across his toned biceps and chest. Underneath the faded-but-somehow-still-fitted Alanis Morissette T-shirt was a set of rock-hard abs I couldn't wait to run my hands over again. Part of me almost wanted Max not to show up so we could go straight home.

I reached for Jeff's hand and gave it a squeeze. "No, he's too excited for the party. I bet he's waiting for Mom and Dad to fall asleep in front of the TV."

Jeff laughed. "Way to make them sound ancient."

My parents were fifty-one. I was about to reply that compared to Jeff's twenty-four years and my twenty-two, that *was* ancient, but the sight of Max emerging between a pair of fir trees stopped me. With a mischievous grin on his face, he speed-walked toward us, his hands tucked into the pockets of a *Simpsons* hoodie.

I smiled at my baby brother. *Baby* was slightly unfair considering his eighteenth birthday was under two weeks away, but I'd forever tease him about being four years younger. Max didn't mind. He knew that from the moment I first saw him in the hospital, swaddled in a bunny-print blanket, his plump cheeks rosy red, I vowed I'd be the best big sister in the world.

Tonight, my solemn promise meant busting his grounded ass out of his minimum-security prison, aka our parents' house, so he could join Jeff and me at what would be the coolest party of the weekend. Lighthouse Beach was a twenty-five-minute drive from Deering, the Portland neighborhood where Max and I had grown up, and now I couldn't wait to get going.

Max slid into the back seat of Jeff's old red pickup truck. I turned around, laughing at my brother's beaming face and the perpetual impish twinkle in his green eyes, which looked so much like mine.

"We were about to leave," I deadpanned. "Thought you'd chickened out."

Max snorted. "As if."

"Are we picking up Kenji?"

"He's at his girlfriend's so he'll meet us at the beach," Max said, before jokingly adding, "He'd better, considering he's taking off next week. Some best friend he is, leaving me behind."

"Hey," I shot back with mock indignation. "I thought *I* was your best friend."

"Are you two sure about this aiding and abetting?" Jeff cut in before Max could throw a good-natured sibling zinger my way. "Your mom will go ballistic if she finds out."

Max shrugged. "I don't care. She's way overprotective."

"You know her reasons," Jeff said.

We all did. Mom's older brother died when she was nine and he was seventeen. It was terrible how some asshole truck driver had run over our uncle, killing him instantly. Still, Max's rebellion tonight was fueled by the fact Mom had banned him from going to California with Kenji, saying it was too far away, and Max was too young. They'd had a massive argument about it, which led to my brother being grounded for the weekend, hence tonight's great escape.

"I told them I was heading to bed," Max said. "They never check, but I stacked my pillows under the duvet just in case. Nobody will notice."

"If they do, I'll take the full blame." I patted Jeff's hand. "Max, we'll drive you home. No after-parties with Kenji, got it? What Mom and Dad don't know can't hurt them."

"Sir, yes, sir." Max gave me a salute. "Anyway, I'll need *some* sleep. I'm volunteering at the clinic tomorrow. Woolly had a mass removed and I want to be there for him."

"Woolly?" Jeff said. "Dog or sheep?"

My brother grinned. "Giant Angora rabbit. He's awesome."

"You're such a softie," I said before letting out a whoop. "All right, let's go. Lighthouse Beach, here we come."

When I woke up a while later, I had no idea where I was until a seagull squawked in the cloud-filled sky. As I opened my eyes, the world's axis tilted, everything spinning from the Buds I'd drunk and the puffs I'd taken from a joint going around. Drugs—illicit and otherwise—had never been my thing, but the majority of the thirty people at the beach had partaken as we'd danced to EDM, our collective energy a happy high.

I sighed and stretched, reaching for Jeff, but the space next to me on the oversized fluffy beach towel was empty. It took my jumbled brain a moment to remember the argument we'd had, making me wrinkle my nose.

"We should start thinking about getting Max home," Jeff had said earlier while we'd stood by the bonfire. "It's past midnight."

"We can stay a bit longer," I said. "I'm having too much fun."

"Stella—"

"Max," I'd called over to my brother, who sat on a blanket with Kenji and his girlfriend, and another woman I didn't recognize, all of them deep in conversation. When he'd looked up, I'd tapped an imaginary watch on my wrist. "Jeff thinks we should get going."

Max laughed. "Getting a bit late for you, old man?"

"Craving cocoa and pajamas?" Kenji added with a smirk, making the girls laugh, too.

"Jeff's worried he'll turn into a pumpkin," I said.

My brother guffawed. "It's okay, Jeff, we'll roll you home. I'm good staying here a few more hours."

I gave him a thumbs-up before looking at Jeff, my grin falling when I clocked his stony expression. "You okay?"

"Thanks a lot for making me sound like an old fart," he muttered.

"Oh, come on," I said. "We were joking."

"All I'm doing is trying to stop Max from getting into a bigger fight with your mom."

"Sorry," I mumbled. "I didn't think—"

"No," he said. "Obviously not."

His words and tone were cutting, both making me bristle. I understood Jeff's reticence about bringing Max to the party. For one, he'd never been big on breaking rules. He also had a great relationship with my parents, often better than I did. Understandably, he didn't want to jeopardize that, especially considering his folks had become ill and passed away in the two years since we'd met. They'd been close, and he missed them.

Still, my annoyance bubbled over.

"There's no need to talk to me like that," I snapped.

"Wouldn't have to if you didn't make me look like an ass."

"I said I was sorry," I replied, putting a hand on his shoulder. "Look, let's forget about it and go for a walk."

Jeff shook me off. "Think I'll pass. I'm fine hanging out here."

"Seriously?" When he didn't answer, I added, "Whatever. See you later."

I'd grabbed a towel and another beer, gone for a short walk before plonking myself in the sand about a hundred yards from the bonfire. Within seconds, I'd fallen asleep.

I sat up now, wishing our argument had never happened. Instead of being mad at each other, we could've made out behind the dunes. Curled up together afterward and fallen asleep to whispers of *I love you* and *I love you more*.

As I shook the remnants of the spat away, I vowed to smooth things over with Jeff. Longing for my earlier sense of contentment to spread through me, I stood and collected the towel while reminding myself of my typically blissful existence.

I lived with my great boyfriend who worked as an EMT. My part-time job at a café came with a decent boss and flexible hours. Soon I'd enter my final year at the University of Maine, where I was studying for a bachelor of arts in communication. My ultimate dream of fund-raising for nonprofit organizations, and hopefully running one at the pinnacle of my career, was inching closer. The disagreement with Jeff tonight was a tiny blip. In no time it would be entirely forgotten.

I checked my phone. Almost 3:00 a.m. Definitely time to get Max home, just in case one of our parents checked his room after all. Dad might've been okay with my brother going to the beach party tonight, but he was loyal to Mom. If he knew Max had defied her orders, she'd find out, and Max would be grounded forever.

I quickened my pace. The once gigantic bonfire had burned itself into a pit of glowing embers, and someone had changed the music to chill-out or lounge—I never knew the difference. Most people had left the beach. A few sat in a group chatting and relaxing around the fire, and I scanned the area.

"Hey," I called out to Vivien, one of my friends from high school, who was taking out a drink from a dented royal-blue cooler. "Have you seen Jeff and Max?"

Vivien unscrewed the cap from her bottle of water and said, "Uh-uh. Not for ages."

A guy I didn't recognize, who was sprawled out on a fuchsia blanket, blinked slowly, his words slurred as he mumbled, "Max said he wanted to swim."

"Alone?" When he shrugged, a jolt of fear zapped through me, its pointy tip piercing my stomach. I shoved it away. Max knew better than to go for a solo dip, especially at night. The summer had been boiling so far, with the first week of August one of the hottest on record, but the Atlantic was frigid year-round.

Except with a few too many drinks in him . . .

I spun around, jogged to the water, hoping to see my brother curled up on the sand. Nothing. As I continued my search, I shouted his name while telling myself I shouldn't worry. I needed to take a beat and calm down.

Turning again and looking to my left, I spotted Kenji sitting twenty yards away, one arm around his girlfriend's shoulders. "Hey, Kenji. Where's Max?"

"Don't know," he replied. "Haven't seen him in a while."

"Is he with your friend?" I asked his girlfriend.

"Elle left ages ago," she replied. "Max didn't go with her."

Leaving them there, I had another look around before heading to the path that led to the parking lot. A few yards farther, I broke into a jog. When I got closer to the thick cluster of trees separating sand from pavement, Jeff appeared, walking toward me from the opposite direction, one hand pressed to his stomach.

His eyes widened when he saw me, and he grimaced. "I, uh, I think I ate too many hot dogs, and . . . Are you okay?"

"Is Max with you?"

Jeff's face seemed to redden, but another cloud covered the moon, reducing the light to almost nothing. "No, I haven't really seen him since you and I fought earlier. By the way, I'm sorry. I—"

"Never mind that now. I can't find Max. He's not on the beach. I don't know where he is."

"Probably asleep, like you were. You looked so cute. I didn't want to disturb—"

"He may have gone swimming."

Jeff frowned. "No way. Have you messaged him?"

"He left his cell at home because Mom's got him on Find My iPhone, remember? We need to find him."

"On it," Jeff said. "He can't be far. Let's split up. We'll cover more ground."

Half an hour later, as the first raindrops splattered the windshield, Jeff and I drove to Deering with Kenji close behind. My pulse no longer resembled Morse code. Instead, it was a thousand beating drums.

Max wasn't at the beach. He hadn't brought a bag or his wallet—he'd told me he'd left them on the hallway sideboard in another ploy to make Mom and Dad believe he was home—but we hadn't found his clothes or shoes. Surely that meant he didn't venture into the ocean, but nobody still at the beach remembered him leaving. No after-parties had been arranged. The people who'd left, and whom we'd managed to contact, hadn't driven Max anywhere.

"Can you go faster, please?" I whispered. "He promised he wouldn't leave without us."

Jeff squeezed my thigh. "I bet he hitched a ride. Try his phone again."

After listening to Max's chirpy voicemail, I left another message. When we arrived at my parents' house, I leaped from the car and raced up the driveway, speeding around the side of the house.

Max's bedroom was on the second floor. We'd long known how to clamber from his window to the garage roof and across to the sturdy branches of the gnarled oak tree, from where we'd lower ourselves to the ground. As I made the trek in reverse, I decided I'd give my brother such a hard time for bailing on Jeff and me, he'd think Mom was Strawberry Shortcake.

I pushed the slightly ajar window open, exhaling when I saw Max under the covers. After silently sliding into his room and tiptoeing across the carpet, I reached for my brother's shoulder, ready to shake all the living daylights out of him.

As soon as I touched Max, something felt off. His body was too soft, too squishy. Way shorter than his six-foot frame, even if his legs were bent. Then I remembered him saying he'd arranged his pillows before he'd sneaked out.

I stumbled backward and landed on my butt with a loud thud. After jumping up and taking two strides, I flicked on the overhead light, my head on a swivel as I searched the room for any indication my brother had come home.

My shoulders dropped when the door opened behind me. I turned, expecting to see Max with mussed hair, crumpled sand-covered clothes, and another cheeky grin. Except it was Mom, wearing pajamas and a bleary-eyed expression as she rubbed a hand over her face.

"Stella, what are you doing here this early?" she said, confusion taking over, her forehead crinkling when her gaze dropped to the empty bed. "Where's Max?"

I wanted to reassure her. Say everything was fine, and there was nothing to worry about, but all I could manage was a strangled whisper, my words cutting me to my core.

"I . . . I don't know. Mom, I can't find him."

PRESENT DAY

FRIDAY, JULY 25

CHAPTER 2

STELLA

After a slow and stuttering start, summer arrived with a sizzling vengeance. Today, and for at least the rest of July, Portland, like much of the upper East Coast, would apparently be more akin to Florida, sending everyone either scurrying to the beach or somewhere air-conditioned. It would be the latter for me. I couldn't remember the last time I'd buried my toes in the sand.

In the initial weeks and months after Max vanished almost six years ago, I drove to Lighthouse Beach daily and spent hours walking the shoreline. I'd searched. Hoped. Sobbed. Shouted my brother's name until my throat turned raw, my words carried away by the wind.

Six years of not seeing him. Not knowing what happened, where he was, or if he was alive. It felt like a life sentence. Of course, I'd never gone on trial for Max's disappearance, despite it being my fault. If I hadn't encouraged him to defy my mother's rules, if I'd listened to Jeff, Max would be here.

I wasn't the only one who thought so.

"Everything okay?"

Vivien's voice and gentle hand on my shoulder pulled me from the spiraling thoughts that beckoned me to the bleakest corners of my mind. As she looked at me with her stunning brown eyes, she pushed away a short auburn curl from her smooth forehead. I knew she was patiently waiting for an answer but also that she wouldn't press for one.

I gave my closest friend and business partner a breezy smile and gestured at the three-story redbrick building at the intersection of Congress and Center Streets. "Here we are."

While she shielded her eyes from the sun with one hand, a bead of sweat slithered down my spine and seeped into the waistband of my pants. We were downtown for an 11:30 a.m. radio interview about our true crime podcast, *A Killer Motive*, and the heat already felt unbearable.

Dress code didn't matter to listeners, and I knew Charlene Thornton, the host of WHMR Radio's *People of Portland* show, quite well. Still, Vivien and I needed to make a great impression, especially considering the financial stakes. I'd therefore chosen a pale blue button-down shirt and black slacks, which I wished would magically transform into shorts.

"Are we ready for this?" I asked Vivien as I lifted my ponytail and fanned the back of my neck with my other hand.

"We'll be fabulous," she replied. "Better than."

"Soon, *A Killer Motive* will be the most listened to and revered true crime podcast from coast to coast to coast."

She laughed. "I've manifested that shit into the universe so hard, it's got to come true."

"From our lips and all that. What's our main objective today?" We'd gone over my question multiple times already, but this was a pre-meeting ritual, a way to ensure focus and having the same target in mind.

"Show me the money, baby," Vivien said. "Aka raise *A Killer Motive*'s profile and get more advertisers and sponsors."

"Exactly."

"Remind me how bad it'll be if we don't. No sugarcoating. It'll serve as motivation."

I lowered my voice despite nobody being around. By saying these next words out loud, I worried I'd somehow conjure our increasingly dire prospects into immediate existence. "We can pay ourselves the bare minimum and cover expenses for six weeks. Eight at best."

This wasn't news to Vivien, but I still caught her alarmed expression, and knew it mirrored mine. My heart pinched as I thought about Max again, and his fascination with true crime. How we'd enthusiastically shared TV show recommendations right up until he'd disappeared. I wanted to make him proud when he finally came home—because he *would* come home. I refused to let myself think otherwise. If this podcast venture failed, I'd let him down.

Again.

I pulled my shoulders back. "Let's go get 'em."

We pushed open the heavy doors and headed upstairs to WHMR's offices on the top floor. Once we'd been welcomed by the receptionist, a slender assistant with a gold octopus nose piercing ushered us into a different room. When I spotted Charlene Thornton through the glass partition, nerves darted around my stomach again.

A former investigative journalist, Charlene had hosted the *People of Portland* show for five years. Every week, she interviewed local personalities about their lives and journeys.

The word *personalities* made me balk, too. I wasn't nearly as interesting as her typical guests, and it was a huge honor to be here. Spots were limited, by invitation only, and more than a little revered. CEOs, philanthropists, and politicians had gone before us. Musicians, authors, and comedians, too.

Charlene was a gifted interviewer—sharp, generous, and well-spoken. No matter how tough or challenging her questions, they were always fair, and she was consistently gracious. No doubt about it, this was a big opportunity for us.

"Charlene will be ready for you soon," the assistant said, clutching a clipboard to his concave chest. "Has either of you been on the radio before?"

"These ladies are pros," a woman with fiery red hair said as she got up from her chair by the window and walked over, arm outstretched.

I considered myself tall at five feet eight, but she had to have a good three inches on me, even in her flat shoes. Her mahogany eyes radiated a friendly warmth while her firm handshake conveyed a non-domineering assertiveness I appreciated.

"Izzy Merian, producer," she said. "Huge fan of *A Killer Motive*. I'm thrilled you're on the show today."

"Thanks for the invitation," Vivien said, head bobbing.

"You're welcome," Izzy replied. "We're going on commercial break. Follow me and let's get you settled. Grayson, can you get our guests some water, please?"

As we stepped into the on-air studio, Charlene beamed. "Stella, it's great to see you," she said as she got up, reaching for her shiny black cane before hobbling a few steps toward us.

Charlene was in her early sixties and had lived four houses away from my parents in Deering for a few years before moving to Portland's West End after her house burned down. Today, and as always, she wore her standard attire of gray slacks and a white shirt, and had styled her pristine blond hair in her signature shoulder-length bob.

Years ago, when Charlene had stopped by my parents' house to introduce herself, my impulsive brother asked why she walked with a stick. After hearing she'd sustained the injury while living in New Hampshire decades ago, Max had done some sleuthing.

Sure enough, he'd located a news article from the '90s in the *Concord Courier* about a big deal charity match featuring the Fireflies, the town's senior female soccer team. The last tackle had resulted in the captain, Charlene, suffering a severely broken leg just before the ball she'd kicked scored the winning goal.

A picture of our new neighbor had been included. She lay on a stretcher, clutching a trophy and beaming despite the undoubtable pain. I'd thought she was the kind of woman who could do anything she put her mind to, and I'd admired the hell out of her for it. I still did.

Once the rest of the introductions had been made, Vivien and I took our places opposite Charlene at the table while Izzy adjusted our microphones.

"This will be relaxed and easy," Charlene said. "I'm excited to talk about *A Killer Motive*. I was impressed to read how your work helped the cops with a few cases. It made my old journalist's heart sing."

"Thank you," I said. "The podcast's been extremely rewarding."

"Any questions before we start?" Izzy asked as Grayson set glasses of water in front of us and disappeared out the door.

"Not from me. I'm good," Vivien replied.

Nerves fluttered again as I chose my words carefully. "More of a reminder than a question. When you offered us a spot on the show, I mentioned wanting to stick to talking about the podcast, and not discussing my brother's disappearance."

"We completely understand," Charlene said. "I'm okay with the direction."

"Respectfully, Charlene, you know I don't agree." Izzy flashed us a disarming smile. "I believe if we did go there, Stella, it would help you connect with our listeners more. It'll allow Charlene to go deeper into the conversation."

I shook my head as Vivien jumped in. "We clearly stated the topic's off-limits."

When Izzy glanced at Charlene, who gave her an almost imperceptible nod, she sighed. "Okay, okay. I'm overruled. All right then. Time to roll."

This was it. A definitive make-or-break situation for *A Killer Motive*. I tried telling myself everything would be fine. This was simply a conversation with Charlene, somebody I liked and already knew.

What could possibly go wrong?

CHAPTER 3

STELLA

My apprehension eased as we got into the interview, which was slated for a half hour, including commercial breaks. True to her reputation, Charlene remained a charming, insightful host as we delved into the apparent insatiable appetite for true crime.

"Stella," she said, "you launched *A Killer Motive* three years ago with, quote, 'heaps of determination and a desire to help others.' You also mentioned you've been interested in true crime since high school. What triggered your curiosity?"

Max's and my shared love of it was the honest answer, but I went with a close second. "I've always been interested in crime fiction, but the true crime side of things was sparked when I read *I'll Be Gone in the Dark*."

"Michelle McNamara's book about Joseph DeAngelo, aka the Golden State Killer," Charlene said.

"Exactly," I replied, loving how she knew her stuff. "I've never been sucked into anything from the opening lines so fast. Ms. McNamara's dedication and research were incredible. Her work is incomparable. It's tragic how she passed before DeAngelo's arrest."

"Agreed," Charlene said. "How about you, Vivien? What drew you in?"

Vivien winked at me. "Stella. We've been friends since tenth grade. When she gave me the book a few years later, I got hooked, too. I've been fascinated by true crime ever since, although not as much in a professional capacity until I joined *A Killer Motive* two years ago."

"You have a background in media studies." Charlene gave her an encouraging smile. "Must be handy for the podcast."

"Oh, it definitely helps," Vivien said, chuckling.

"Call it instrumental," I added with a laugh. "I'm not the most tech-savvy person."

"Me neither," Charlene said. "It all moves so fast, I can't keep up. Stella, you studied communications."

As she continued talking, I wondered if she'd ask why I never returned to college after Max vanished. Truth was, I lost the ability to focus. I'd barely been able to hold on to my part-time coffee shop job because I kept bursting into tears. The new owner almost fired me when I'd sobbed uncontrollably while ringing up peanut M&M'S, Max's favorite candy.

After spending the first two years in a fog of grief, trying to investigate my brother's disappearance because I didn't think Detective Wade, who was responsible for the case, was doing enough, I hadn't uncovered anything new. Another year, and on a whim, I'd put together the voice recording about his disappearance.

In a way, it had served to triage my thoughts and let Max know I was searching for him. I never thought anyone would listen when I sent my babblings into the ether. Much less that it would lead to me repackaging the recording as my first episode of *A Killer Motive*, or how the podcast would become my regular gig. The show had saved me from imploding entirely.

Charlene's voice floated back into my ears. ". . . and you know I'm impressed by how *A Killer Motive* has helped the police. Tell us more."

My shoulders relaxed. This was an easy subject where I didn't have to bend the truth. "In our first year, a decades-old case about a deceased woman found in a suitcase under a stairwell of an apartment building was solved."

"How did this extraordinary triumph come about?" Charlene asked.

"Mainly because of the fresh burst of public interest our episode generated," Vivien said. "A new witness came forward. Someone who'd lived in the building but had moved to Singapore. One of their relatives here heard the podcast and told them about it."

"With the new information they provided, the killer was arrested, charged, and convicted," I added.

"Incredible," Charlene said. "How did it feel?"

"Like I wanted this to happen every day for the rest of my life," I answered, my throat filling with emotion as I remembered how the victim's brother had hugged me after the delivery of the guilty verdict. "The families who'd been left with more questions than answers about their loved ones were finally being heard. Nothing beats that."

"In this case," Vivien added, "we were able to play a tiny part in helping the woman's family get some of the closure they deserved."

Charlene smiled. "It was more than a tiny part, from what I read. There was another successful outcome last year, too."

"Yes, although it wasn't a cold case per se," Vivien said. "An appeal in a murder case was granted and a guilty conviction overturned after we uncovered footage on Instagram that was more than six years old."

"Considering how much gets uploaded to socials on a daily basis, I can only imagine the amount of digging that took," Charlene said. "Can you share what turned out to be so valuable?"

Eager to respond, I replied, "A video featuring the man who'd been sent to prison for the death of his girlfriend. It was a completely random recording someone else made, but he happened to be in the background, ten blocks from where she died."

"It corroborated his story," Vivien continued. "As his attorney told the judge, unless the man had a time machine, he couldn't be in two places at once."

"Social media certainly has its uses," Charlene said.

"Yes, it does," I agreed. "It led to an innocent person going free, as the death turned out to be a tragic accident, not murder."

"Excellent work, you two," Charlene said. "How do you choose the cases you spotlight?"

"Typically, we read or hear something that sparks our interest," Vivien replied.

"What might this spark feel like?" Charlene asked.

"It's hard to describe," I said, wishing Vivien hadn't made it sound so simplistic, as if only certain cases were worthy of attention. "For me, it's a gut reaction followed by a sense of anticipation and an urgent need to find out what happened. It's always coupled with the utmost desire to get justice for the victim and their loved ones. I wish we could work every case."

"Some think we're nosy," Vivien added. "Or curious, depending on how you look at it."

"I get it," Charlene said. "As a former journalist, this next question is close to my heart. How do you balance shedding light on these terrible things that have happened to people without sensationalizing them for your own benefit? After all, this is your job. *A Killer Motive* needs to generate money."

"By always being respectful and careful," I said, trying not to think about the pushback I got when I'd reposted the episode about my brother under the *A Killer Motive* brand. How I'd been called a *greedy profiteer*, a *selfish sellout*, and worse by people online.

Some of the haters had refused to believe Max existed, saying I'd invented him and his disappearance to gain *sympathy listeners*. There was evidence to the contrary, of course, but why would they bother doing research when shouting from the bandwagon they'd jumped on required no effort?

I'd almost shut the podcast down until Jeff and Vivien convinced me not to. This was why I didn't want to discuss Max on *People of Portland*. I researched his disappearance on my own time—although there wasn't anything left to dig into. No way would anyone accuse me of making money off my missing brother again, or say he wasn't real.

"We always obtain permission from the families involved before covering a case," Vivien said, and I was grateful she'd raised this point.

She hadn't understood how important it was at first, not until I'd explained how disrespectful it would be if we didn't seek their consent. Nobody wanted to see the case of a loved one badly covered or covered against their wishes. We had a duty to do right by the victims and their loved ones. Always.

"We have to be incredibly gentle in our approach, especially when we speak to the victims' families," I said. "And the families of suspects. It's easy to forget how devastating these situations are for them, too."

"Does the public ever suggest cases for you to examine?" Charlene's question was deliberate, one we'd agreed she'd ask partway through the segment.

"Absolutely," Vivien replied. "They can submit them via our website and social media, and we'd love the help of *People of Portland*'s listeners today."

"I'm sure they'd be happy to assist," Charlene said. "Tell us how."

"We've connected with the producer of *Never Coming Home*," Vivien said.

"For those of you who haven't heard of it," Charlene said, "it's the hottest fictional crime series on Netflix, and partially filmed right here in our beautiful city of Portland."

"We know the producer," Vivien added, which wasn't quite true as he was one of her contacts. I'd never met him. "As a thank-you, the person who submits the cold case we turn into an upcoming podcast episode will be invited to the set of *Never Coming Home* for the day."

Vivien had worked hard to convince me this was a good idea. The sensationalism Charlene had talked about? I hated it. Had always made it my mission to ensure *A Killer Motive* could never be accused of doing such a thing. Offering a gift to someone who submitted a cold case was uncomfortable to me, but Vivien had insisted it was a unique approach and could help boost our numbers. Reluctantly, I'd given in.

"Such a phenomenal prize," Charlene said. "Listeners, you can submit suggestions via our socials or our website, where you'll find *A Killer Motive*'s contact details, too. If you prefer, you can email them directly, just make sure you mention this show. We're also going to take suggestions live. If you have an idea for a cold case you think is a great fit for Stella and Vivien, call now."

After she'd given the phone number, we cut to a commercial break.

"You're doing great, and the social media reactions are fantastic," Izzy told us after sharing some of the details. "Let's keep it going and close strong."

Charlene spoke into her mic, her voice smooth as butter. "Welcome back to *People of Portland*. I'm your host, Charlene Thornton, and today I'm with *A Killer Motive* true crime podcast creators Stella Dixon and Vivien Ortiz."

From the other side of the glass partition, Izzy nodded and held up her index finger.

"We have our first caller," Charlene said. "Hello and welcome to the show. Please tell us your name and cold case suggestion for *A Killer Motive*."

Conrad from Bar Mills talked about the case of a badly decomposed headless adult male found in a landfill eight years ago. "I can't believe a person was decapitated and thrown out like garbage," he said. "It's disgusting. It's tragic."

We thanked him for bringing the case to our attention, but didn't share that Vivien and I had discounted working on it. We'd acquired everything we could through the Freedom of Information Act, but it had been precious little. Police hadn't been able to initiate forensic facial reconstruction. There'd been nothing left to fingerprint, and no matching record in CODIS, the Combined DNA Index System.

The victim had only worn a generic pink T-shirt, which could've come from anywhere. Genetic genealogy could potentially provide answers, and every case needed to be worked on, but the sad truth was *A Killer Motive* didn't have the resources.

The next caller wanted us to solve the infamous case of D.B. Cooper, the 1971 skyjacker who jumped from an airplane with a parachute and $200,000 in cash.

"Oh, I'd *love* to solve that one," I said, thinking it would send *A Killer Motive*'s status to the stratosphere and beyond. Sponsors and advertisers would flock to our doors. So would every TV and radio station in the country, and beyond. We wouldn't have to worry about funds for years. The number of cases we could investigate, the amount of people we could help, would expand beyond all my hopes and dreams.

Charlene announced we had time for one more. "I believe we have Liam from Augusta on the line. Welcome to the show. What's your cold case idea for *A Killer Motive*?"

"I'll start with a question for Stella." This man's tone had zero friendliness, sounding clipped and curt, bordering on rude. My guard immediately shot up.

Charlene glanced at me, one eyebrow raised, which I interpreted as, *Are we good?*

I nodded, smiled because I knew listeners would hear it in my voice, and said, "Sure, Liam. I'd be happy to answer."

"Okay," he scoffed. "Why the hell aren't you looking for your brother?"

CHAPTER 4

STELLA

My cheeks burned like I'd been slapped across the face. As I opened and closed my mouth, Liam's crystal-clear insinuation about my being a despicable sister echoed in my ears while I tried to formulate what might be considered a publicly acceptable response.

I briefly entertained telling Liam from Augusta to go fuck himself for being so ignorant, but that wasn't an option. Not when Vivien and I had to demonstrate to whomever was listening that we were worthy of advertising dollars.

If we didn't get the money, I'd still be able to pay my bills, but only because Jeff supported me financially, and we lived in the quirky Rosemont house he'd inherited from his parents, mortgage-free, after they'd passed.

Meanwhile, Vivien lived alone and had given up a full-time steady-but-loathed job in advertising to join *A Killer Motive*. The gamble had initially paid off as money flowed in, but our local sponsorship sources were almost dry because of corporate cutbacks, and she had to take more and more freelance gigs to get by. If we didn't land new funds, Vivien would have little choice but to find regular paid work elsewhere, meaning the podcast would suffer.

So, no. I couldn't tell Liam what I really thought, and had little choice but to keep calm and stay professional.

My mind sped up as I grappled with an adequate answer. Why did Liam assume I'd done nothing to find Max? Why did he care to the point of sounding furious? Did he know my brother? My parents? His name didn't sound familiar.

Would Liam believe me if I explained how my gargantuan guilt about Max disappearing from a party I'd taken him to had etched deep canyons into my soul? That I hadn't slept soundly in six years?

Then again, trying to justify myself might escalate things. I'd learned my lesson when I'd attempted reasoning with the trolls who came for me after the inaugural episode of *A Killer Motive*. No matter what I said, they accused me of turning things around and making them all about me instead of keeping the focus on my brother. Liam could do the same.

Maybe I could tell him he wasn't the first person to despise me, nor the most important. My relationship with Mom, who I knew blamed me for what happened almost as much as I blamed myself, had been plunged into a catatonic state, from which I doubted it would ever recover. Dad had been more understanding and accepting of the fact I'd busted my brother out of the house, saying it was Max's decision to leave, not mine. My father still cared for me, but he adored Mom and often leaned to her side for the good of their marriage.

Jeff, too, felt at least partially responsible because he hadn't put up more of a fight about driving Max to a party my brother had explicitly been banned from attending. Like Vivien, my husband had remained my rock, my true north. Thinking about him made my bottom lip tremble. What would Jeff say if he knew about the secrets I kept from him?

I swallowed hard, my mind spinning. Before we'd gone on-air, Izzy had said there was a five-second lag between us speaking into the microphone and it being broadcast to the outside world. "If anything goes awry," she'd told us, "I can cut things on my end."

At least two of those seconds had passed, and she hadn't given any indication of swooping in to save me. If I freaked out now, and it went on-air, I'd risk becoming a sound bite on a meme, destined to float around cyberspace forever. *Shit.*

"Liam from Augusta, are you still on the line?" Charlene's light and breezy voice whooshed into my ears as she paused and gave me a knowing wink. "It seems we got disconnected. Let's try to get him back. In the meantime, Stella, do you want to respond to Liam's question about your brother's disappearance?"

Vivien's back stiffened. She looked like she wanted to eviscerate our esteemed host, so I took a quick breath and spoke first.

"Listeners may not be aware of my personal situation," I said, my voice shaking as I hoped nobody could hear how loudly I was screaming on the inside. "My younger brother, Max, vanished from a summer beach party I took him to six years ago, not long before his eighteenth birthday. We still don't know where he is or what happened to him."

"I'm very, very sorry," Charlene said. "How devastating. May I ask . . . you said your interest in true crime dates to your time in high school, but I can't help wondering if Max's situation is related to you starting *A Killer Motive.*"

The producer, Izzy, watched me from the other side of the glass. Her face might've been filled with compassion, but I still imagined her feeling victorious about getting what she wanted. Now I had a choice—be truthful, open, and therefore vulnerable, or shut this part of the conversation down and risk being misinterpreted as dismissive and cold.

I glanced at Vivien, who silently telegraphed, *You've got this.*

"Yes, it is," I said, focusing on Charlene. "Max and I watched true crime shows all the time. Actually, one day he snapped his fingers and said *A Killer Motive* would be a great name. I never thought I'd start a podcast, not even after he disappeared. *Especially* not after he disappeared."

"Is this why you waited three years to record the first episode?" Charlene asked.

"I couldn't talk about it before," I said. "It cut too deep. To be honest, for the longest time I surrounded myself with nothing but romantic comedies. Books, movies, TV. Everything had to have a happy ending. It was all I could stomach, but then . . ." I paused. "I had to stop hiding. I needed to do more to try and find out what happened to my brother."

"In answer to Liam's question, you *have* looked for Max."

"I did everything I could think of as soon as he vanished," I said. "Spoke to everyone who was at the party, multiple times. Talked to the cops repeatedly. Went door-to-door all the way from Lighthouse Beach, where he went missing, to Deering, where Max lived—*lives*, asking if anyone saw him. I hoped the first episode, the one about Max, might jog somebody's memory, but still . . . nothing."

"What do you believe happened to your brother?" Charlene asked softly.

I sighed, shook my head. "I wish I knew. The police think he may have drowned."

"Accidentally . . . ?" Charlene said, and I knew where she was going with this.

"You're implying Max died by suicide," I said, keeping my voice even. "I'll tell you what I told the police: no way. Trust me, I've wrestled with that demon sixty thousand ways 'til Sunday, and I still can't imagine him taking his own life. Of course, some will say I'm in denial, but I really don't believe I am. I don't think he walked out on his life, either."

"I agree with Stella a million percent," Vivien said.

"Meaning an accident or foul play could've been involved," Charlene added. "Was there any indication of the latter?"

"We never found one, and I searched everywhere," I said. "I

looked for any trouble Max might've been in. Things we didn't know about. Money problems, drugs, any other conflicts he might've hidden from us." I stopped again. "My brother didn't have a single enemy. Everyone loved him."

"You've no clues at all at this point?" Charlene asked.

"Not a single one," I said. "If I had the minutest shred of evidence of someone hurting my brother, I swear I'd find Max and the perpetrator. I'd bring him to justice. Single-handedly. At the risk of sounding like a cliché, there'd be no stone left unturned. I'd go beyond the ends of the earth and back again to solve this mystery and bring Max home. No matter what it took."

Charlene gave me an empathetic look, and I sat back in my seat, suddenly exhausted.

"Thank you for being so open with us, Stella. We all hope you find Max. We truly do." She paused before switching back to her announcer-type voice. "This is *People of Portland*. I'm your host, Charlene Thornton. Today's guests were Stella Dixon and Vivien Ortiz from the excellent true crime podcast *A Killer Motive*. Be sure to check it out. Thank you for being here with us today, ladies."

"Yeah, you're welcome," Vivien said, her tone clipped, and I shot her a look.

"Thank you, Charlene," I said. "It's been a pleasure."

"Don't forget to head to our website for details about submitting cold case ideas for their show," Charlene continued. "Good luck, everyone. After a quick break, I'll be back with Timothy Collins, author of the bestselling memoir *When We Were Dead*. Don't go anywhere."

As soon as we were off-air, Izzy rushed into the room, eyes wide.

"What happened?" Charlene asked. "Who was that guy? Why did you put him through?"

Izzy waved her hands around. "I'm sorry. He suggested an

ancient case about a double homicide in Bangor. I'd never have patched him through if I'd known his real intentions."

"Are you sure?" Vivien sounded pissed. "Seems convenient, considering you wanted Stella to talk about Max."

Izzy's mouth dropped open. "No, I—"

"It's okay," I said, desperate to smooth things over. "Honestly, it's fine."

"Our listeners' online reactions *were* incredible," Izzy said. "I know it's not how you imagined closing the show, but you got a lot of awareness for your podcast. We've already had a ton of messages."

"Was my reaction okay?" I said, turning to Charlene. "Because at first I froze, then wanted to cut and run."

"Liam was an ass, and you handled it beautifully," she replied. "Really, Stella. You were so genuine. I know our audience has nothing but respect and empathy for you. I certainly do."

"Maybe some good will come from this," Izzy added. "Perhaps you'll get a useful tip."

"Thanks," I said, willing her words to come true, but still not trusting her entirely. "And thank you for being a great host, Charlene. Aside from Liam's curveball, this was a fantastic interview, and we're both grateful. Aren't we, Vivien?"

Vivien hesitated before her face broke into a smile as she got up to shake Charlene's hand. "Hopefully we can come back in the not-too-distant future."

"Definitely," Izzy said. "Charlene, we should get moving. Tim's on the line and wants to say hi before the show." She turned back to us. "Thanks again. This was amazing."

We followed Grayson, the octopus nose piercing assistant, from the studio. "I have your email, so I'll share the cold case suggestions we receive with you," he said, talking over his shoulder. "As agreed, we'll leave the competition open for ten days so anyone who didn't listen live can join in as we boost on socials."

"Sounds perfect," Vivien said. "Thank you."

"No problem," Grayson replied. "Let me know who you choose as your winner, and Charlene will give *A Killer Motive* another shout-out with the announcement. It'll get more eyeballs on your podcast. Or ears? Love the show, by the way. You're phenomenal."

"Thanks," I said, shaking his hand. "Feel free to tell Augusta's biggest asshole."

CHAPTER 5

Stella, Stella, Stella. How I enjoyed listening to you on People of Portland. *Whenever I saw your social media posts about the upcoming interview, I could hardly wait. The anticipation built so much as the day drew closer, I had to work hard to contain it.*

I was curious whether you'd talk about Max. How did you feel when Liam from Augusta demanded to know why you weren't looking for him? Did those words cut deep? Slice your heart open? Rip your insides out and spill them on the floor?

You handled it well, I must say. I was impressed, although no doubt on the inside you were a raging inferno.

Clearly you haven't given up on finding Max. The guilt about what happened must be eating you alive to the point where you're almost an empty, brittle shell, ready to break without notice.

Your comment about not leaving any stone unturned, about going beyond the ends of the earth to find him . . . I can't stop thinking about it. I need to know if it's true, how much further you can be pushed until you shatter entirely.

I guess we'll find out.

And when we do, remember you only have yourself to blame.

CHAPTER 6

STELLA

Temperatures outside seemed to have soared to new heights in the fifty minutes Vivien and I had been at WHMR. I hadn't noticed the puddle collecting under my arms, but as a gust of humid air wafted over me, a sudden gush of sweat ran down my side. I shivered.

"You okay?" Vivien asked. "Tell the truth, because that Liam guy is a total dick. I don't blame you if you're rattled. His attitude was unbelievable."

"It's all good," I said. When she looked at me, I rushed on. "Don't worry about it. Already forgotten. Honest."

She held my gaze, her eyes seemingly searching for a hint of the blatant lie I'd told. My happy expression must've covered it adequately enough. Vivien wasn't always so easily fooled, but telling her how I felt meant risking a breakdown in the middle of Portland. It wasn't something I'd do in public.

"Meet at the office to debrief?" she asked. "I've got errands to run, but I'll be there in about an hour."

"Great. See you later."

I plunged my hand deep into my bag for my keys, hoping Vivien hadn't caught the tremble in my fingers before she'd turned in the other direction. As I hurried to my Toyota, the tears I'd suppressed so far hit my eyes. I swiped at them with the back of my hand and upped my pace, refusing to let someone like Liam win.

The drive to our house in Rosemont took under twenty minutes, and I got home shortly before 1:00 p.m. By the time I'd parked in the empty driveway, I'd almost buried Liam's comments deep in the back of my mind.

I'd planned on eating the leftover tomato soup I'd prepared last night, but my appetite had vanished. After getting inside, dumping my bag, and plucking an apple from the fruit bowl in the kitchen, I popped a few walnuts into a shallow dish, added two slices of sharp cheddar, and filled my water bottle.

Armed with snacks, I headed out of the double French doors at the back and into the yard. Jeff's—or, as he always insisted—*our* three-bedroom house was the last dwelling on a dead-end street in an older subdivision. The generous lot was filled with mature, leafy trees and backed onto a ravine, providing us with ample privacy. Although we weren't far from the city, it felt rural. Neither of us could imagine living anywhere else.

Jeff's dad, Daniel Summer, a physics and math teacher, had been an avid amateur painter and bass guitar player. Because his self-confessed neat-freak wife, Yvonne, couldn't stand the mess or noise her husband made, they'd built a small studio in the backyard. It was not only equipped with a tiny bathroom but also fully insulated, heated, and air-conditioned. Daniel had created art in there to his heart's content. Meanwhile, Yvonne had kept him fed with an endless supply of blueberry muffins and slices of rhubarb pie.

When Vivien had joined *A Killer Motive,* Jeff had offered to transform the dusty studio into a brand-new office space for us. Now it held two sleek white desks with ash legs, along with pine-green fabric office chairs. In front of the floor-to-ceiling windows stood a rectangular coffee table to which we'd added an array of mini pink orchids in white porcelain vases and vibrant green succulents in glass jars.

My favorite detail by far was the trio of Jeff's father's last canvasses—colorful abstract shapes representing Portland's skyline—as well as a framed print simply saying, *Believe*.

My heart pinched as I walked across the grass, unlocked the studio door, and stepped inside, taking in the soothing scent of Vivien's lemongrass candle. She and I made such a great team. Vivien had a knack for all things tech, and her media and producing skills were off the charts. I was good at writing material, networking and liaising, and convincing complete strangers to give us a fraction of their time that could turn into hours.

For all this to disappear, for *A Killer Motive* to be relegated to a virtual *nice try, shame you didn't quite make it* shelf already filled with abandoned similar relics, would be torture. Without fresh money, this haven of creativity would be repurposed yet again, and I couldn't let that happen.

I already knew I wouldn't sleep well tonight because of the financial turmoil, but Liam's stinging words suddenly echoed around my brain again, despite my best efforts to ignore them.

Why the hell aren't you looking for your brother?

The sadistic little voice in my head sneered at me and whispered, *Because there's nowhere left to search. Because of you, Stella, Max is gone.*

Batting Liam's voice, and my own, away, I refused to let any doubt creep in through the cracks of my mind. I meant what I'd told Charlene. I'd *never* give up on Max. It didn't matter how terrified I was of what I might find. *If* I ever found anything.

My agonizing thoughts lingered as I walked to my desk. After a slight hesitation, I let my gaze drop to the bookshelf and settle on the slim red folder in which I'd saved everything ever written about Max, in print and online, since he'd vanished. The pages were scant. In desperation, I'd filled them with photos of my brother. When I'd gone door-to-door during my search for him, I'd shown them to anyone who'd listen.

After picking up the folder, I turned to the last page, which held the most recent article clipped from the *Maine Tribune* almost twelve months ago. Charlene had called in a few favors and sent the piece I'd written to one of her contacts at the newspaper, although my version ended up being heavily condensed by the journalist who'd reluctantly agreed to run it.

Despite the words appearing on the fifth anniversary of my brother's disappearance, they constituted a grand total of four lines, which could be summed up in two sentences. Max Leonard Dixon, then seventeen and from Deering, went missing from Lighthouse Beach on August 9 five years prior. Anyone with information should contact the local police.

The guy who'd edited the microscopic article had taken pity on me last year but hadn't been able to add Max's photo. When I'd contacted him last month, he'd said he couldn't write anything at all this time around because they needed the space for—he'd apologized here—more pressing stories, and, of course, advertising. None of my other contacts had been able to commit to running anything, either.

One some level, I understood. Media was a tough, competitive space. *Maine Tribune* was a business, as was *A Killer Motive*, and had to generate revenue, but the collective indifference still stung like hell.

I flipped through the folder's pages, my fingers lingering as I traced some of the photographs of my brother. He'd celebrate his twenty-fourth birthday soon. It would be a difficult day for all of us, especially me and my parents. I'd call them. Would no doubt speak to Dad, but invariably not my mother.

"It's a hard, hard day," my father would say. "I'll get Mom to phone you when she's a bit better. She'll be in touch."

Last year, over two weeks had passed before I'd heard her voice. I often missed her so much it hurt.

As the unofficial peacekeeper of our shattered family, Dad was also grieving the loss of his only son, thrown into the unfathomable situation of not knowing what had become of Max. We remained in a perpetual state of limbo, stranded on individual islands in a collective sea of despair none of us would ever swim out of. I guess the one thing Mom and I had in common was that we didn't want to escape it because it would somehow mean leaving Max behind.

My mind drifted as I wondered whether he'd still be living in Portland if he'd never vanished. He'd have graduated from his chosen engineering program by now. For years he'd talked about backpacking around South America and Australia before settling into a job.

A million questions plagued me. Would he have taken the trip? Where would he be working? Whom would he be dating? Might he be living with a girlfriend in Maine or elsewhere? What would he be like now he'd grown from a gangly teenager into a man?

Before I could contemplate the answers, Vivien bustled into the studio.

"Weren't you running errands?" I asked.

Eyes wide, she plonked her bag on her desk and practically jumped up and down as she said, "Screw that. You're not going to believe what happened."

Despite my morose mood, her infectious enthusiasm sparked my curiosity. "You'd better tell me before you spontaneously combust."

"You know Andrea Booker?"

"From Booker Media? Sure. Didn't your previous firm work with her?"

"Yeah, on the launch of her publishing division," she said, bouncing on her heels. "I met her at a conference once. She's so impressive, it scared me shitless."

"I've heard she's a tough nut."

"Ridiculously smart, too," Vivien said. "Andrea built her company from scratch and has been on those forty under forty lists multiple times. They've branched into streaming services now. She's a frigging genius." She took a breath. "Anyway . . . she called me. *Me*. About *A Killer Motive*."

"What? How come?"

"Uh, I emailed her a while ago. Suggested she check us out."

"Why—"

Vivien rushed on. "She just told me she listened to dozens of episodes. Apparently, she's had her eye on us for a while. She thought we were fantastic on *People of Portland*."

"Okay . . . that's nice, but—"

"There's more." Vivien grinned harder. "Andrea's interested in sponsoring us."

"Oh . . ."

Her face fell. "What's with the look? This is great news."

"Is it?" I said slowly. "Booker isn't a good fit. Her online outlets blow things out of proportion. They exaggerate. It's clickbait. That's never what we've been about."

"Sure, but—"

"Doesn't she have a reputation for demanding a high degree of creative input?"

"Well, yes, but—"

"Then it's a firm no."

"Stella—"

"Remember how we agreed we'd be our own bosses, no matter what?" I said. "I don't want to lose the ability to choose the cases we develop, or how we deal with them. Imagine the families we'd potentially upset with Booker's approach. No. We can't."

Vivien's joy evaporated, and she plopped herself into her chair. "We're running out of money, and time. You said so this morning. At the very least, we should hear what Andrea has to say. I told her we can meet—"

"You agreed to a meeting without discussing it with me?" I said, eyebrows raised.

She shifted in her seat, took a few beats. "If we don't turn things around, I'll have to find another full-time job. You get that means I'll likely have to quit this one, don't you?"

"Of course I do," I said. "But there's got to be another option than us being forced to make changes we don't want. We might end up with nothing."

Vivien threw her hands in the air. "We're almost at nothing *now*. I vote we—"

"No. We don't engage with Booker. As the majority shareholder, my decision stands."

"You're pulling rank? You've *never* pulled rank."

"I've never had to," I said, knowing full well this was the first time I'd ever reminded her of the thirty-seventy split of A Killer Motive Inc., the company I'd founded after starting the podcast. "I don't want you getting your hopes up, because I'm not changing my mind."

Vivien tilted her head and gently asked, "Is this about Max?"

"Why would you—"

"Because of your aversion to change," she continued, her voice soft. "I can only imagine how hard it must be to move on from what happened, but if we don't innovate with the podcast, it could destroy your future. And take mine with it."

"Mmm-hmm." I silently counted to five so I wouldn't snap at her. Move on? As if.

"Think about it," she said as she picked up her bag. "I'll give you some space and work from home for the rest of the day. Let's talk more on Monday."

I watched as she left the studio and quietly closed the door behind her. Vivien's assessment wasn't entirely wrong. Yes, I feared change. I'd started the podcast because of my brother and was afraid of things diverging from my initial *victims and families above all* vision. I had to honor Max.

What does it matter? He may never come home.

I swatted the voice away. Vivien was upset, understandably so. I had to make it up to her. Prove we could do this without Andrea Booker's money.

The next hour was spent making cold calls and follow-up inquiries with potential advertisers. It quickly became apparent either they had no cash to spare or weren't interested, at least for now.

"Call me when you've doubled your monthly listeners," the last one on my list said. "I'd be happy to talk then."

Deciding not to ask if I could borrow his magic wand, I hung up and opened my email. Grayson, the assistant at WHMR Radio, had sent a note with the subject line *Cold Case Suggestions*.

After browsing through the ideas they'd received, I cross-referenced the details with online articles and noted a couple I thought had potential. Flicking back to my email, I saw several suggestions had arrived via our website contact form, landing in the communal Gmail inbox Vivien and I had access to.

Another, similar message sat in my personal inbox. Odd. That email address wasn't listed on the website. The subject line read *AKM Cold Case*, and the sender wasn't anyone I recognized, but a random combination of numbers and letters.

I'd heard of the email provider, vaguely recalled the service offered end-to-end encryption, protecting user identity. Whatever that meant. Pretty sure all our privacy went out the window as soon as we ventured online.

I scanned the body of the message.

Dear Stella,

This is your opportunity to solve a cold case I call Blooper Beach. You're familiar with it, but here's a picture in case you don't understand.

What do you say?

Think you're ready for a real challenge?

Let's play.

AL

Frowning, I scrolled to the pasted photograph beneath.

Immediately, my head spun as the walls of the studio blurred, the entire room twisting. Vomit rose to the back of my throat. I'd seen this picture before, but we hadn't shared it widely or posted it to socials because it felt too personal, too raw. The image showed a young man sitting near a bonfire, his head back, mouth open in a gigantic laugh, beautiful green eyes partially closed.

The last photo that had ever been taken of him.

Max.

SATURDAY, JULY 26

CHAPTER 7

I knew you wouldn't have the guts to answer right away, Stella, but it's past midnight, and I'm sure you've read my email. Oh, to be invisible and sitting in your studio so I could've witnessed it firsthand.

I'm certain I made an impact. No doubt your pulse quickened when you saw that photo of Max. I like to think you gasped, your eyes widening, pupils dilating as your hand covered your mouth. I've seen those reactions before, and the intense shock is delicious to observe.

You're having trouble sleeping, aren't you? I am, too, albeit for different reasons. For me, it's the anticipation of what I'm going to do, but you . . .

I picture you lying in bed, oscillating between anger and fear, wondering who AL is, and why he sent such a provocative message. Does the name Blooper Beach ring any bells, I wonder? Perhaps I was too subtle. Maybe next time I'll be more direct, except . . .

I prefer a slow burn. There's room for more tension, more time for your dread to build.

If I asked you now to rate your fear on a level from one (completely calm) to ten (terrified out of your mind), I think you'd settle for a two. Maybe a three.

Ten is where I need you to be.

No, I'm lying. It must be beyond that. Way, way beyond. I'll get you there, I promise, but not yet. I'm an exceedingly patient person. The attribute has served me well.

It will again this time.

With you.

CHAPTER 8

STELLA

By 3:00 a.m. I was wide awake, my choppy sleep disturbed by multiple rounds of similar and eerie nightmares. On more than one occasion, Max's photo came alive. His head turned to me, his mouth silently screaming for help. I ran, arms outstretched, as I tried to reach him. Each time I got within a few inches, he vanished.

While attempting to calm my galloping heart and empty my mind, I snuggled closer to Jeff. After draping an arm over his waist, I matched my breathing to his for a while, shutting my eyes. However, the more I ordered myself to relax, the less it worked.

My irritation from being attacked by another online troll ballooned. After tossing and turning and waking Jeff twice, I got up, pulled on my workout gear, grabbed my bag, and headed to the gym.

Jeff wouldn't wonder where I'd gone when he got up for work. We both knew insomnia had plagued me for years. Whenever it did, and my imagination refused to be tamed, the scenarios about what might have happened to Max became so bleak that I caught myself thinking it might be better if my brother was no longer alive. A grueling workout, never mind if it was before dawn, was always preferable than disappearing down those treacherous rabbit holes.

The drive through the deserted streets didn't take long, and when I arrived, there were only a few other souls pumping iron this early. Thankfully, my therapist, whom I'd met here by chance, wasn't one of them. Good, because I didn't feel like talking to anybody, no matter how trivial the conversation.

I'd seen Dr. Quentin Graf for a while now. Jeff encouraged me to get counseling for years, but I'd been too stubborn. I didn't want or need anyone digging around in my head for fear of what else I'd uncover about myself to despise.

However, eighteen months ago when I'd come to the gym for one of my habitual early workouts, Max's favorite song, "Too Good at Goodbyes" by Sam Smith, popped up on Spotify.

Grief did what grief does so well, and I'd crumpled to the floor in a corner, knees pulled to my chest. Moments later, a tall gentleman came over. After kneeling a few yards away from me, he gently asked what he could do to help.

"Find my brother," I'd whispered.

"Do you want to share what happened to him?" the man asked, his voice soft, soothing. I'd looked up, was about to politely decline when I saw the warmest eyes I'd ever come across, framed by deep laughter lines. Within an instant, I'd almost wanted to bare my entire soul to this stranger but had settled for a few details.

By the end of our short conversation, I'd not only been a lot calmer, but had learned Dr. Graf was a psychologist, and added his details to my phone. Days later, we had our first session, and I'd visited him at least monthly ever since.

Shaking off the thoughts, I made a beeline for the empty mats on the far-left side. Nothing banished my anxiety or made my blood race faster than a high-intensity workout, so I set up kettlebells and plyo boxes near the battle ropes. With my earbuds in and favorite rock tunes playing, I got started and soon found a rhythm, pushing myself harder than usual.

It wasn't only my anger about Liam's phone call and AL's email driving me. Nor was it just the indelible fear about Max's whereabouts that I was trying to get a handle on. I also needed to get away from the secrets I was keeping from Jeff. The lies I'd told about us trying for a baby.

I'd always known my husband wanted kids. Jeff had been transparent about the fact since our first official date, the day after we'd met at Lézard Bleu, a legendary bar on Portland's Wharf Street, where I'd accidentally bumped into him, knocking his pints of IPA down his shirt.

After spending the evening chatting, we'd exchanged phone numbers. He'd called the next morning, and we'd gone for a walk downtown. As we sat on the wharf while eating thick slices of hot pepperoni pizza, I'd asked if he had siblings.

"I wish," he'd said. "Being an only child sucked for me. When I have kids, and if my partner's on board, I'll have a dozen."

"Twelve children?" I spluttered, almost choking on my pie. "You're not serious."

Jeff's face lit up. "Maybe not twelve. But only because I'd need a school bus to drive them around, and those bastards are hard to park. Anyway, I'm excited about being a dad one day. It'll be cool. How about you? You want kids?"

"Sure," I'd said. "Well, someday, I guess. Not for ages, though."

Jeff's desire for family also stemmed from not having any in Portland because neither of his parents had siblings, and both sets of grandparents died before he was ten. His longing for belonging had only intensified when Jeff's mother was diagnosed with terminal pancreatic cancer a few months after we met, and his father had succumbed to a massive heart attack less than a year after he'd buried his wife.

"He died from a broken heart," Jeff always said. "Quite literally."

In my former life, the one before Max vanished on my watch, I'd meant it when I'd told Jeff I saw us having babies in our more distant future. Trouble was, ever since my brother's disappearance, the mere thought of having a child of my own made me want to throw up.

I'd never told Jeff how I felt in so many words for fear I'd lose him, too. Had never dared explain I was inadequate and inept, unfit for motherhood, in case he came to the same realization: How could his wife be responsible for a baby when she couldn't take care of her brother?

"You'll be a fantastic mom," Jeff had said three months ago when we were out for our anniversary dinner. When he'd asked if I might be ready to try for a family soon, he'd sounded so hopeful, so eager, I hadn't had the heart to crush or disappoint him yet again. I'd blurted, "We can try. See what happens."

Jeff had whooped, picked me up and spun me around, his elation evident for everyone in the restaurant to see. I loved my husband and knew he'd make a wonderful father. However, when it came down to throwing out my birth control pills, I hadn't been able to. Panic set in, its thick fingers creeping up my legs, wrapping themselves around my torso and squeezing so hard I thought I'd suffocate. I couldn't have a kid. I wasn't ready. Not yet.

Instead of doing the decent thing and talking to Jeff, I'd hidden my birth control in a box of Tampax and set a daily alarm on my iPhone to take a pill. Jeff believed it was a reminder for me to eat because I tended to skip meals when I was consumed with other things.

Nobody could ever know about my birth control subterfuge. Not my therapist. Not Vivien. And definitely not Jeff. It wouldn't go on forever. It was temporary. A few months. Maybe a year. Well before my husband suggested visiting a fertility specialist because he thought there might be a problem.

As I jumped on the plyo box again, I looked at myself in the mirror, trying to ignore the spiteful voice in my head whispering I didn't deserve to be with someone as kind and patient as Jeff. That I was a horrible, despicable person. That I should tell the truth and admit I didn't want a baby, maybe *ever*. Set my husband free so he could be with a person who wanted to give him what he desired. What he deserved.

Except I didn't have the courage for that, either. I was a coward, too afraid of losing him. Petrified of being alone. That nobody else could ever want me. I lowered my eyes, not daring to look at myself as I thought about yesterday evening.

It had been Jeff's day off, and he'd been helping his best friend Owen renovate his new house. Shortly after 5:00 p.m., Jeff had come into the studio with a half-eaten muffin in one hand and a coffee in the other. I never saw him use anything other than his favorite mug, the one inscribed with *49% paramedic, 51% badass*. I'd gifted it to him a few years ago, and it still made him chuckle.

He wore a dusty pair of jeans, the sleeves of his T-shirt straining against the bulge of his toned biceps. We'd been a couple for eight years now, lived together for over six, married for four, and those muscles still made me tingle all over, exactly like the night we'd met. Jeff turned heads, and not only mine. Funny thing was, he seemed largely unaware of the effect he had on others.

"Do you realize how hot you are?" I'd asked him on more than one occasion. "In case not, it's Jason Momoa and Taron Egerton levels." Jeff would always scrunch up his face and shake his head, telling me to stop being ridiculous. Often, he'd grace my comment with a blush, making him even sexier.

He'd put his mug on my desk yesterday, scooped me into his arms and kissed me softly. His lips carried a hint of mint chocolate coffee creamer, the smell of his aftershave a blend of citrus and green tea. As we broke apart, I'd inhaled deeply and nuzzled his neck, pressing my lips on top of the cluster of freckles shaped like a strawberry.

"Congratulations," he said. "You were great on the radio."

"You listened?"

"Of course," Jeff replied. "No way would I miss my talented wife being interviewed." He gently put his hands on my shoulders and took a step back. "Liam from Augusta is an asshat."

"Agreed."

"You okay after what went down?"

"I'm fine," I'd said, keeping my tone light and immediately deciding not to tell Jeff about AL's spiteful email. From experience, I knew my husband would make it into a big deal, and I wanted to forget about it. "Are you home for the evening or going out again?"

Jeff raised his eyebrows. "Trying to get rid of me? Is your secret lover coming over?"

After I'd rolled my eyes, Jeff had pressed his hand into the small of my back before kissing me so deeply, my knees turned to Jell-O. Leaving me near breathless when he pulled away, he'd whispered, "If he doesn't kiss you like that, kick him to the curb. Where's Vivien?"

"She, uh, left for the day."

The twinkle in his eye was unmistakable. As he reached for the top button of my slacks, he leaned in and murmured, "God, I've missed you."

"I, uh, I can't," I said, pulling away. It had been a couple of weeks since we'd been intimate, but knowing he wanted to make love with the intention of getting me pregnant made it far too cruel for me to indulge frequently, never mind how much I missed him, too. "I still have to get some work done."

"Can't it wait?" he'd asked, and I'd shaken my head. "Then let's save us for later."

We hadn't, because I'd deliberately gone to bed almost two hours after Jeff.

As I took a breather from my workout, I became acutely

aware of the real thing I desperately needed to escape from today: myself. I wanted to be someone else, if only for a while. Somebody unencumbered. Light, and carefree. The person I'd been before we'd lost Max.

Knowing it was impossible, I turned up the music to drown out my thoughts, ready to push myself through another grueling round.

CHAPTER 9

STELLA

An hour and a half later, freshly showered and dressed in jeans and an azure T-shirt, I sat in my backyard studio with a giant bottle of lemon water.

Instead of being energized by my heavy-duty gym session, exhaustion took over. Years of continual insomnia had worn me down, and I wished it was time for bed despite knowing I wouldn't sleep soundly.

I gulped down some water and looked around the studio. Shortly after it had become *A Killer Motive*'s official place of business, Vivien and I had added a burgundy sofa. It lured me toward it now, and I gave in. As I sank into the plush microfiber cushions, I stretched out my legs and closed my eyes.

Perhaps I could rest a while. Half an hour, maximum, before getting back to work. Maybe I'd try the deep breathing exercises Dr. Graf had recommended, but which never seemed to stick. Inevitably, I failed at shutting off the incessant noise in my head.

I inhaled deeply. Instead of my mind clearing, it shifted to how I needed to finish fact-checking our upcoming podcast episodes and plan the week's tasks. I'd also call Vivien and apologize for yesterday, although I'd remain firm in my position about not engaging with Andrea Booker. Not yet. Not until I was desperate, which, all things considered, might not be long.

The meditation exercise felt hopeless. I'd only been lying here for thirty seconds, and my thoughts were spinning, leaping, and bounding, adding more and more to my to-do list. Not ready to quit, I tried again. This time, I let my shoulders fall away from my ears and closed my eyes, telling myself I was safe, it was okay to let go. I breathed in and out, in and out . . .

The loud cawing of a crow startled me what could've been five minutes later, but the sky seemed too bright for it to still be early morning. Sure enough, my phone said it was almost nine.

Sitting, I yawned and stretched, still tired but at least somewhat refreshed. I got up and walked to my desk, where I pressed a key on my laptop to wake it up from its slumber. When my eyes landed on the screen, my stomach heaved.

Another email from the same cryptic address that had sent me the photo of Max. I didn't want to read the message, but my fingers had minds of their own as they placed the cursor over the subject line marked *Is anybody there* . . . and double-clicked.

Dear Stella,

On *People of Portland*, you insisted you'd go "beyond the ends of the earth and back again to solve this mystery and bring Max home." You added, "No matter what it took."

I asked if you'd like an opportunity to solve the case. You haven't replied.

Either Max isn't important to you, or you don't grasp how serious I am.

To show you, you'll soon receive an extra incentive.

I'll be in touch.

Let's play.

AL

All the air in my lungs disappeared, the lemon water I'd had a few hours ago threatening to burst from my throat to make way for the rage building inside me. Who was AL? Why was he taunting me? What did he mean by *extra incentive*?

I took a beat. Both Vivien and I had received whacky correspondence and social media messages from riled listeners, conspiracy theorists, and we-know-better-than-you armchair detectives. Hell, we'd had a two-page rant from a private investigator in Texas who told us in no uncertain terms to *get off his lawn*.

AL was a troll, nothing more, but as I read his words again and scrolled to the bottom, I saw there were more.

> PS. Does your brother know his big sister is all sizzle and no steak?

The words sucker-punched me in the gut as an almost forgotten memory darted to the surface. Max had never been massively into sports, but when he was twelve, he tried flag football. He'd made the school team, and Dad and I had watched most of his games, waving gigantic foam fingers and cheering him on as loud as we could.

One Thursday afternoon, Max trotted over at halftime, face beet red, and his expression glum. "Ugh," was all he said as he collapsed on the grass.

"What's up, bud?" Dad asked.

"Xavier," Max replied, as if the name held all the answers Dad needed, before continuing with a sigh, a shrug, and the words, "He says I suck."

"What a jerk," I said. "How about I smash my—"

"Easy, tiger." Dad put his hand on my shoulder. "Which one is he, Max?"

"Number eleven on the other team."

As Max sighed again, I could see why. Unlike my brother, Xavier's growth spurt had clearly kicked in early. Towering above all the others, he could've easily played in an adult league.

"He laughed at me," Max continued, lips trembling. "Said I keep running away because I'm a wussy sissy-baby. It's true. I *have* to run away. I don't want to be crushed by a fridge."

My father ruffled Max's hair. "He may be big, but have you noticed he's slow? I think he's worried about how fast *you* are. In fact, I reckon he's scared."

"Pfft," Max scoffed. "Xavier's not scared of anything."

"Trust me." Dad sat down and put his arm around Max's shoulder. "I know guys like Xavier. He's all sizzle and no steak. Here's an idea . . ."

On the next pass, Max expertly dodged out of Xavier's way, ducking, weaving, and running like hell. He scored his first touchdown, and then did it again. The crowd went wild. I screamed so loud, I lost my voice for three days.

As we'd driven home, Max chanted his new favorite expression, "All sizzle and no steak," over and over. At one point he laughed so hard, Gatorade came out of his nose.

The day had become a distant memory to me, but Max would never have forgotten. Was AL really just a troll? This email—like AL's first—carried an insidious undertone. Threatening. Personal. Deliberately and deeply cutting. But the fact he'd used my father's exact words in his second incendiary message had to be a coincidence.

Didn't it?

CHAPTER 10

STELLA

I read AL's words again, my eyes still not wanting to believe what was in front of me.

>PS. Does your brother know his big sister is all sizzle and no steak?

Does.
Not *did*, as in past tense.
Does, meaning in the present.
I knew better than to search for clues or meaning in a message like this. I could drive myself into psychosis and beyond if I wasn't careful. As the shock from AL writing again and using such a familiar expression waned, it gave way to something else. More anger.
My fingers flew across the keyboard.

>You may think this is funny, but what you're doing is sick.
>Don't contact me again.

Engaging with somebody like AL was a *very* bad idea, but before I could stop myself, I hit Send. Another few clicks and

I'd blocked his email address. After deleting his two messages, I opened my Sent items and zapped my reply to him. Next, I emptied my Deleted folder, turning every single one of AL's spiteful words into cyber dust.

All this barely took more than ten seconds and did nothing to calm the rage building inside me. Once again, I'd spoken about my brother in public. Once again, an opinionated, conniving listener who didn't know me had decided I needed tearing down. Of course he'd never do it face-to-face. People like AL, coward that he was, would only throw virtual missiles from behind the safety of his screen, and under the guise of relative anonymity.

Deep breathing exercises were pointless now, so I jumped up and paced the studio. When that didn't work, I thought back to AL's messages, and how they'd both referenced the *People of Portland* show. Their tone gave off the same pushy and aggressive vibe as Liam from Augusta had on the phone yesterday. Was it possible the emails were from him?

Despite reminding myself I'd deleted the messages and blocked AL's email address for a reason, and I should leave things be, I brought up Charlene's contact number on my iPhone and dialed. The call went to voicemail. Too impatient, I hung up without leaving a message.

I scrolled to the *People of Portland* producer Izzy's details and tapped on the number, drumming my fingers on my thighs as I listened to it ring.

"WHMR Radio. Izzy Merian speaking."

"Hi." I forced my anger to the bottom of my stomach, replacing it with what I hoped was my friendly and professional voice. "It's Stella from *A Killer Motive*. How are you?"

"Great, thanks. You too, I hope." Izzy's warmth was audible, and I pictured her at the radio station, long legs crossed as she leaned back in her chair. "Fantastic show yesterday. We've had tons of great feedback from listeners. I gather we sent you the cold case suggestions?"

"Yes. I'm researching a few of them."

"Hopefully you'll find what you need," she said. "If not, I bet there are lots more to come. Anyway, how can I help?"

I waited a few beats, wishing I'd thought this through instead of dialing her number faster than Road Runner dodged ACME dynamite. "I, uh . . . I've had some strange emails."

"Ones we sent you? Oh, no. We generally weed those out."

"No, they didn't come via you guys. They were sent directly to me."

"I see," Izzy said, sounding relieved. "What do you mean by strange?"

As I gave her the lowdown on the messages from AL, I left out the fact he'd used one of Max's favorite expressions because I couldn't wrap my head around what—if anything—it meant. I finished with, "I think this AL creep is the caller we had, Liam from Augusta. Look at the initials. L and A. *AL*. It tracks."

"Could be, I guess." Although Izzy's voice stayed smooth, I detected more than a hint of disbelief, and anger bubbled around my stomach again.

"It's not much of a stretch. People who do these things generally aren't creative and think they're smarter than they actually are." I took a breath. "Anyway, could you please give me Liam's phone number? You must have a record of it."

"Oh, gosh, Stella, I can't—"

"But—"

"No, the privacy rules—"

"What about *my* privacy?" I asked, words tumbling out, tetchy and stubborn. "This guy was rude on the radio *and* sent two vile emails to my private address. Who's to say there aren't more coming? I want to make it stop."

"I understand."

"Do you?" I asked. "You mean how you understood I didn't want to speak about Max on your show?"

"Liam's call was unfortunate," Izzy said, her voice staying infuriatingly calm.

"Unfortunate or calculated?" I snapped. "You said there was a lag, yet you didn't cut him off. Did he really pitch a different question first, or did you put him through so you could get what you wanted?"

"Wow," Izzy said. "Listen, Stella. You don't know me, but doing stuff like that isn't my style. Please ask Charlene or anyone I've worked with. Go to my LinkedIn profile. I have tons of connections, and I invite you to speak with all of them."

The genuineness and gentleness in her voice caught me off guard. I'd expected her to push back. I'd wanted her to, so I could take my irritation out on her. Except turning the person who could potentially help into an enemy wasn't the way to go. Not if this wasn't her fault.

"I apologize," I said. "After my first podcast episode, the one about Max, I got a ton of emails and messages that turned ugly real fast. I guess I'm scarred by it all."

"I sympathize," Izzy said. "We've had our fair share of hate mail and calls to the station over the years. Putting yourself out there the way you did, being open and vulnerable, takes guts. It's not without its risks. I admire you, Stella. I truly do."

"Thank you," I said, my temper deflating. "Is there any way you can help? Could you make an exception and give me Liam's number? I'd never tell anyone. Promise."

"I can't," Izzy said, rushing on before I could beg again. "Even if I was prepared to violate the station's privacy policy, there's nothing to share. Liam called from an unknown number. Look, for what it's worth, the best way I've found to deal with people like him is to block them."

"I already have."

"Great," she said. "I'm sure this AL or Liam or whatever he's called will lose interest soon enough. Trolls thrive on getting a rise out of us. We can't let them."

After we hung up, I sank onto the sofa. Unease and doubts scaled my calves, slid into my gut, and dug in with their sharp claws, refusing to let go. The voice in my head murmured I'd best be careful. For whatever reason, and no matter who AL was, I wasn't sure he was done with me yet.

WEDNESDAY, JULY 30

CHAPTER 11

STELLA

Despite blocking AL's email address since Saturday, I'd anticipated him using a new one to send another despicable message. Each time I'd opened my email over the past few days, my stomach had twisted itself into knots. Thankfully, so far everything had remained quiet. Little by little, my nerves subsided.

On Wednesday morning, Jeff and I sat at the breakfast table. After a sixteen-hour shift the day before, he had today and most of tomorrow off. Consequently, while he happily munched his way through slices of toast and a large bowl of cereal, I picked at half a banana and barely touched my coffee.

"Not hungry?" Jeff asked. "You okay?"

I waved a hand. "A little tired, is all."

It wasn't an outright lie. Despite being less anxious than over the weekend, my sleep remained choppier than ever. I still hadn't shared AL's messages with Jeff, and unless a third email arrived, I didn't intend on doing so. My husband had already mentioned, allegedly in passing, how stress could affect the chances of pregnancy. I didn't want that subject to come up. Or for him to tell Vivien and have them both fussing.

"Are you worrying about the podcast's finances?" Jeff asked. "Because I've been thinking. We could remortgage the house."

"Oh, honey, no," I said immediately. "Absolutely not. Your salary's already supporting my dwindling income. It's an incredibly generous offer, but I could never accept."

"Stella . . ."

"No, really," I insisted. "I can't be certain we'd make the money back, and I've seen the eye-watering quotes for the roof repairs. I won't risk you losing your family home if the podcast fails."

"First of all, it's *your* home, too, and second, you *won't* fail. You'll bounce back and crush it. I know you will."

"How can you be so sure?"

"Because I believe in you, Vivien, and the podcast." He smiled, leaned back, and added, "Although if it did go belly-up, which it won't, dibs on turning the studio into my man cave. I can see it now. Barcalounger. Foosball table. A bar to stash my rum."

I laughed. "Rum? What are you, a pirate?"

"Only if you'll be my wench. What do you say?"

"Can we get a parrot?"

Jeff shivered. "Talking animals give me the creeps."

"Funny, because that makes you a big chicken."

"Ha ha. What about a gym? Think of how much time you'll save by not having to wake up at three thirty every morning to get to yours by four."

I muttered, "I don't go in early *every* day. At least not on the weekends."

Jeff grinned but didn't say anything as he set his mug down. "Speaking of weekends, how do you feel about your dad's birthday? Have you decided what you want to do on Saturday?"

I wrinkled my nose. Max's and Dad's birthdays weren't far apart, which meant we'd barely celebrated since my brother went missing. However, Dad had called last night and invited Jeff and me for lunch at his favorite Italian place with him and Mom. My initial instinct had been to fib and say we were busy, but I missed Dad. Mom too, despite the desolate wasteland of distance between us, so I'd said I'd talk to Jeff and confirm.

It had come as no surprise that when I'd mentioned Dad's suggestion to my husband, he'd said, "I'm free. It would be nice to see them."

I looked at Jeff now, taking in his expectant expression. "Let's go."

"Great." He stretched his arms and let out a yawn as I texted Dad to confirm.

"How was work yesterday?" I asked, setting down my phone. "Busy?"

"Relatively calm, for a change," Jeff replied. "Except, here's a cautionary tale for you. One of the calls was from a guy who walked down his driveway, barefoot and in shorts, carrying a heavy bag of garbage."

"Sounds like the start of a bad joke . . ."

Jeff pulled a face. "Definitely bad but not a joke. Dude didn't notice the broken bottle sticking out from the side of the bag. It slashed clean through his Achilles tendon."

"Oof, ouch," I said, wincing at the image.

"Yeah. He flopped to the ground and could barely walk."

"I'm guessing he needs surgery?"

"Plus months of rehab. Poor bastard's only twenty with a full-ride basketball scholarship for college. He cried when he found out he wouldn't be playing anytime soon."

"That's awful," I said. "Do me a favor and don't mention it on Saturday. You know how squeamish my mom can be."

Jeff put a hand over his heart. "Scout's honor. Now that you've mentioned things I shouldn't bring up . . . what about your potential collaboration with Booker? Have you thought more about it?"

I waggled a finger at him. "Uh, uh, uh. Like you said, it's off-limits."

"Stella." He gently reached for my hand. "Vivien thinks it's a great idea."

"You spoke to her about it? Did she call you?"

He shifted in his seat. "Yesterday for a quick chat. She's worried about—"

"The podcast. I know. So am I, obviously."

Jeff nodded. "You know what they say about not looking a gift horse in the mouth."

"And *you* know what they say about all that glitters not being gold."

"At least have a chat with Booker," Jeff insisted. "Maybe her being on board would be a good thing. A great one. Perhaps you could get an assistant. Wouldn't that be a relief?"

"Of course it would," I said. "It's my dream. One of many."

"Exactly. Imagine how much time you'd have to focus on your episodes, researching cases and helping people. That's the part you love, not the accounting and administrative tasks draining your energy."

Or having to deal with despicable emails.

"We're in the middle of a big local promotional push." I kept my voice light, not wanting to argue with Jeff when he was trying to help. "Let's see what comes from it all before I entertain speaking to Booker. If she's really interested, she'll still be around in a few weeks."

"Are you sure?"

"Yeah," I fibbed because I had no clue. When Jeff sighed and leaned back in his chair, I gave him a quizzical look. "What?"

"Please don't take this the wrong way."

"Nothing ever said after that sentence has been taken the *right* way."

Jeff smiled. "You know how much I want *A Killer Motive* to be successful. And you know how much I believe in you."

"But . . . ?"

"Sometimes I wish you'd started a podcast about, I don't know, gardening."

"I detest gardening."

"You know what I mean. Something that doesn't keep you—" he shifted in his seat again "—stuck in the past."

This was exactly what Vivien had alluded to. I hadn't seen her since Friday as she was working for her other gig, and although we'd chatted via text, I'd sensed some lingering tension—probably why she'd called Jeff to vent. One problem at a time, so I refocused on my husband.

"Max isn't in the past," I said quietly. "He's still out there. Missing people are found all the time. I'm not giving up on him."

"I would never suggest you do," Jeff said. "It's just . . . well . . ."

"What?"

"You dreamed of working for a nonprofit to help others."

"Which I'm doing with the podcast," I said, and with a laugh added, "Also, we're most definitely *not* making a profit."

Jeff didn't seem to appreciate my attempt to inject some humor. "But you surround yourself with people who are going through trauma and are grieving. When you tell me about the case research . . . assault, abduction, rape, murder. The other day you described, in detail, I might add, what Drano does to a corpse."

"Cleans out the pipes, that's for sure."

"See? You're making light of it, but I'm not sure it's healthy. Especially long-term."

"Investigating cases and helping people helps *me*," I said. "A lot of them are forgotten and abandoned. I can offer support and, if we're really lucky, tangible answers. What I do is important, and nothing you say can change how I feel about it."

Jeff didn't press again before apparently deciding to change tack. "How was your session with Dr. Graf yesterday?"

"He canceled," I said quickly, penning a mental note to call my therapist and apologize profusely for forgetting our scheduled appointment. "I'll see him in a few days."

"I'm glad you're continuing to talk to him," Jeff said.

"Yes, me, too."

As I got up and cleared our dishes, I didn't add that, as nice and empathetic as Dr. Graf was, what I wanted, what I *needed*, was to concentrate on the podcast. Shining light on cold cases was often a far better, not to mention more productive, treatment. I could disappear into my work. Therapy meant digging around my messed-up psyche, and I could only handle it once every few weeks.

While I stood by the sink, rinsing our plates and mugs, Jeff came up behind me. When he put his arms around my waist and his hands across my stomach, I tried not to stiffen or think about what I'd discovered upstairs yesterday morning.

I'd run out of socks and had rummaged around Jeff's drawer in our bedroom dresser to borrow a pair when a piece of red fabric caught my eye. It turned out to be a tiny onesie with a picture of an ambulance and the words *Future EMT*. Like a traitor, I'd stuffed it to the back and walked out of the room, no longer caring about my chilly feet.

"I have a call soon," I said, shoving away the taste of my rising, bitter guilt. "I'd better get at it. What are your plans for today? Will you be here for dinner?"

"I don't think so. I'm playing squash a bit later, and I told Owen I'd help with the renos again this afternoon. I have a feeling it might be a late one. Don't worry, I'll be quiet when I come home." He raised an eyebrow. "Unless you'd prefer I wake you . . ."

I gave him a kiss on the cheek. "You know I need all the sleep I can get."

As I turned, my elbow knocked my bag off the counter, spilling some of the contents over the floor as it landed upside down. Jeff knelt to pick up my scattered wallet, keys, and pens, and when he reached for the box of Tampax in which I'd hidden my birth control pills, I snatched it from his hands.

"It's okay, Stella," he said softly, clearly misinterpreting my reaction as he pulled me in for a hug. "I have a good inkling you won't be needing those much longer."

"Yeah," I said, not daring to look at him. "I'll see you later."

Dashing from the kitchen, I headed to the studio. It was almost 9:00 a.m. Vivien would arrive soon, and I needed to make a call before she got here. This was the third time in as many weeks that I'd had a near miss with Jeff almost seeing my birth control. It was time to find a better solution.

A while ago I'd researched alternative contraceptive options and learned getting an IUD was a quick and relatively simple process. It would be far more discreet, and I could basically forget about it. I'd mulled the idea over multiple times but discounted it just as often. Perhaps it was time for a discussion with my ob-gyn to see if I was a good candidate. An exploration of the option, nothing more.

I tapped on her number, spoke to the receptionist, and arranged for a consultation a week from Friday. As I hung up and glanced at the house, I saw Jeff's silhouette in the kitchen window. A freight train of remorse drove up my back and parked itself between my shoulder blades.

"I can't do this," I whispered, turning to the rear wall as I hit Redial. Not only was it utterly wrong, but if Jeff and I ever visited my doctor together, she or an assistant might bring the IUD up accidentally, even if I asked them not to, and then what would I say?

When the doctor office's voicemail kicked in, I said, "This is Stella Dixon. I need to cancel the appointment we arranged for next week. Apologies for the inconvenience. Thank you."

"Morning," Vivien said, her voice whipping me around. I'd been so focused on what I was doing, I hadn't heard her arrive. "Everything okay?"

"Yes, yeah, sure." I put my phone face down, switching it to silent in case the doctor's receptionist called back. "I was going to get my hair cut but changed my mind."

Vivien gave me a curious look. I wondered if she remembered I'd been to the salon a few weeks ago, but she plopped herself in her seat and opened her laptop before turning to me. "Are we okay?" she asked. "I hate arguing with you."

I smiled, decided not to mention her calling Jeff. "Totally fine. Promise."

"Great. Let's get to work."

We spent over two hours going over the four shows we'd recorded, then divided and tackled the new list of companies I'd come up with to approach for advertising and sponsoring money. Once we were done, Vivien offered to take another peek at the cold case suggestions *People of Portland* had generated. Maybe she'd uncover a hidden gem.

"Can I ask you something before I start?" she said, putting her hands in her lap. "You were so fantastic on the show the other day. Would you consider, maybe for part of an episode, running an update on—"

"Max?" I asked sharply.

"That's a no then?" Vivien said carefully. "Okay, I'm sorry."

"No, I'm the one who should apologize. I didn't mean to bite your head off. Again."

"Totally my fault," Vivien said. "But maybe . . . think about it. Anyway, I'm starving."

"Yeah, me, too."

"Let's go for lunch," she said. "I'll treat you before I take off to visit my folks. How about Triple Crown?"

"Great idea," I replied, grateful she'd let things drop. A relaxed lunch was exactly what we needed before she left. "I'll drive."

CHAPTER 12

STELLA

Our favorite pub was only ten minutes away, and seeing how Vivien was a huge basketball, hockey, and football fan, it was no wonder we almost always ended up here. The place had a large outdoor patio with multiple TV screens continually playing sports, and I'd never tasted traditional beer-battered fish and thick-cut fries this good.

Once we'd arrived, we grabbed our usual table outside, tucked away at the back under a midnight-blue umbrella. Because watching sports had never been my thing, I took the chair facing the pub's wooden patio enclosure. Meanwhile, Vivien sat opposite me so she could follow any game action playing on TV.

We chatted for a while about her upcoming visit to her family in Syracuse, which she was excited about because she hadn't seen them often since they'd moved a few years ago. As the server brought the menus and glasses of iced water, I noticed how Vivien kept glancing over my shoulder. She looked concerned about what was going on behind me, not entertained by the screen.

When she caught my eye, she bit her lip, exhaled, and said, "Please don't be angry."

I opened my mouth to ask what about, but she stood, arm outstretched. As I turned my head, my gaze drifted upward over a woman's lean legs, immaculately fitted dark suit, paisley shirt, and all the way up to a pair of amber eyes and long, dark hair.

"Andrea," Vivien said, shaking her hand. "What a pleasure."

My back stiffened. Andrea Booker lived in Boston. From my research, I knew she had business connections in our city, but her showing up at Triple Crown when Vivien and I happened to be here for a *spontaneous* lunch was no fluke. I wondered if Jeff knew about this.

Andrea's face lit up. "The pleasure's all mine. Thanks for suggesting this location. The Uber driver raved about the food all the way here."

As Vivien shot me a worried look, I knew my choices were limited. I could just storm out, make a scene and then storm out, or get through lunch with Andrea Booker and my so-called friend. If I went with the last option and listened to what Booker had to offer before saying no, maybe it would help get Vivien off my back about the subject for good.

Decision made, I forced a smile as Andrea sat next to Vivien. "Thanks for making the trip from Boston," I said. "Did you drive?"

"Yes, actually, I've been here since the weekend," she replied. "My wife and I are visiting coastal cottages with the kids. Owning one has been a dream of ours for a long time."

"Lovely," I said, thinking our definitions of *cottage* were separated by at least a few million dollars. "I hope you find what you're looking for."

Once Andrea's water glass was filled and we'd placed our food orders, she put her elbows on the table and steepled her fingers beneath her chin. "Vivien may have told you how impressed I was with your segment on *People of Portland*," she said. "It only confirmed what I already know. I'm a huge fan of yours and your excellent podcast."

"Thanks," I said, reminding myself of the adage about flattery not getting you anywhere, because my resolve to turn Booker down was already flagging. We needed money, and her pockets were deep. "We've worked hard to build it into what it is today."

"I can see that," Andrea said. "I understand growing the number of listeners has been a bit of a challenge recently, but we can help. It's why I wanted to meet and discuss adding *A Killer Motive* to our portfolio, so—"

"Hold on," I cut in. "*Adding?* You mean advertising on our show. Sponsoring."

Andrea frowned as Vivien turned to me. "Andrea's suggesting a far better opportunity."

"Precisely," she said. "We don't simply want to advertise. We want to invest."

"Invest?" I asked. "What do you mean?"

"Acquiring *A Killer Motive* and retaining you both as employees," Andrea replied. "I thought you—"

"Isn't it exciting, Stella?" Vivien's voice brimmed with enthusiasm. It pissed me off even more because after all the conversations we'd had, she knew damn well I wouldn't want this. Not only that. She'd clearly also told Andrea that we were struggling.

I cleared my throat, buying a few seconds to think of a reply for Andrea that wouldn't come out like an insult. As I remembered the cliché Jeff had used about not staring a gift horse in the mouth, I decided no good would come from punching it in the face either.

After a curt smile—probably more akin to a grimace—and while trying to force my expression back to neutral, I said, "What would this kind of setup involve?"

"Well, if we conclude a deal, you'll become salaried employees of Booker Media," Andrea said. "You continue running the podcast, and you have access to my company's various production, marketing, PR, admin, and finance teams."

"Gosh, that would be *so* amazing." Vivien's eyes widened. "Imagine, Stella. With Booker Media's support, we could grow our audience exponentially."

"We'd also heighten your production quality and cross-promote on other shows," Andrea added. "Plus, you'd have time to work on more material. Way more."

"Our research shows one case a week is enough for our audience," I said. "Anything beyond risks oversaturating our listeners."

"Agreed," Andrea replied. "I was thinking of monetizing it differently. We could add exclusive bonus material for paying subscribers. Short follow-ups on cases you've examined, for example. In-depth conversations with special guests such as profilers and detectives. Maybe inmates, if you can convince them, of which I have no doubt."

"It's genius," Vivien said.

"Why our podcast?" I asked. "You said yourself our numbers are a challenge."

Andrea didn't seem to notice Vivien giving me a death glare. "For me, integrity is one of the most important aspects in business," she said.

I couldn't help my laugh. "Surely you know Booker Media's reputation for sensationalism."

"I do," she replied without missing a beat or apparently taking offense. "I'm aiming to change that. Because of you, *A Killer Motive* has integrity and trustworthiness in spades, Stella. It shows in everything you do. Including what you just said. You didn't hold back and give me some hogwash answer."

"So . . . basically you'd buy us out completely?" I asked.

"You'd still get a share of the profits," Andrea replied. "The better the show performs, the better you'll do financially."

"Meaning we'll have skin in the game," Vivien added.

Andrea grinned. "A fitting analogy considering we're at a sports pub. I want all my employees to have a vested interest in the company. It's important for everyone." She smiled again, was about to continue when her cell rang. She glanced at the screen. "Would you excuse me? It's my wife. No doubt regarding our offer on a cottage."

As soon as she got up and moved away from the table, I turned to Vivien. "Did you know she wanted to buy us out?" When she didn't answer and took a keen interest in rearranging her silverware, I continued, "You ambushed me. Did Jeff know, too?"

"No, he didn't, but getting you here was the only way to make you listen." Vivien finally looked up, her eyes ablaze. "I didn't know what else to do. You keep acting as if you're the only one who cares about what happens to our business."

"Ouch, that's hardly fair."

Vivien sighed. "You might not find it fair. But it's the truth."

We sat in silence as I weighed her words. She wasn't wrong. I was fiercely protective of the podcast. Taking a step back, I could see how Vivien had poured just as many buckets of sweat equity into *A Killer Motive* as I had since she'd joined, regardless of her being a minority shareholder.

For us to fail would be devastating for her, too, and not only from a financial perspective. My stubbornness had been getting in the way of me seeing that. Trouble was, it still felt like a gigantic boulder I wasn't sure how to shift or climb over.

"Apologies," Andrea said as she slid back into her seat. "Stella, I can tell you're hesitant."

"Well . . . yes. It's not what I was expecting."

"I understand," she replied. "You started the podcast from nothing. You don't want some Bostonian interfering with what you've accomplished."

I winced a little. "Am I that easy to read?"

She reacted with a charming grin, and I found myself warming to her despite my preconceptions.

"How about this," she said. "Come to Boston on a date that works for you both. We'll tour our offices, and I'll introduce you to the team. You can speak to some of the owners of businesses we've acquired and ask them for the nitty-gritty details about what working with Booker Media really involves." She sat back, opening her arms. "We'll talk about the potential evolution of *A Killer Motive*. If you're happy with what you see and hear, we'll discuss terms."

"Awesome," Vivien said, almost jumping out of her seat, and I had to admit Andrea's suggestions sounded reasonable.

When she looked at me again, her face turned serious. "Please understand I want to put my full power behind you and *A Killer Motive* instead of another true crime podcast," Andrea said. "I guess what I mean is that when opportunity knocks, Stella, don't let someone else answer the door."

I refused to break eye contact as the words hung between us. Despite her amenable delivery, I understood Andrea would add a true crime podcast to her portfolio no matter what. Ours, or someone else's. The pressure tactic wasn't hugely surprising. Nor was it dishonest, considering her directness. Still, I hated being cornered, not to mention manipulated by Vivien to get me here in the first place, or the fact she'd spoken to Jeff in secret to get him on her side.

"We'll need time to think it over," I said, deciding I wanted an immediate moment to myself so I could collect my thoughts. I pushed away my chair. "I'll be right back."

I got up and turned to head to the bathroom, taking two steps before my eyes landed on the giant TV screen on the side of the patio. Instead of a sports game, it was the local news. I read the banner at the bottom.

Police appeal for help to find local 24-year-old man

Missing person reports always hit me hard, but this time, when a photo filled the screen, I almost tripped over my feet. Dark hair, hockey-stick-shaped scar a finger's width to the left of his Adam's apple.

The picture was of Kenji, Max's best friend.

CHAPTER 13

STELLA

Keeping my eyes fixed on the TV and as if on autopilot, I moved a few steps closer. I wanted to shout at everybody on the patio to shut the hell up so I could hear what the reporter was saying. It wouldn't have made a difference. The volume was turned too low. Despite craning my neck, I only caught a whisper of the presenter's last sentence before they cut to a segment about a leak at a wastewater treatment plant.

I pulled my iPhone from my pocket and typed *Kenji Omori* into my browser, scrolling as fast as I could. Whatever had happened to him must've been recent as the details were sparse. There was a brief piece on the TV channel's website, and I scanned through it, my eyes darting over the screen.

Twenty-four-year-old Kenji Omori from Deering had been reported missing when he hadn't returned home after work early Tuesday morning. The article included his photo along with a short physical description, plus the fact he worked at a club called Templetons in Riverside. Anyone with information was asked to contact the police.

Kenji and Max had been best friends since kindergarten. He'd lived a few streets away from us with his older sister, Ren, and their parents. The boys had been close. Loved playing board and video games, particularly *Mario Party* on Dad's ancient Wii. Three years in a row, they'd dressed up as their favorite Nintendo character duo for Halloween. At one point they insisted we call them Mario and Luigi.

For months before the fateful beach party, all Kenji and Max had talked about was going to California with a bunch of friends until Mom had taken a virtual flamethrower to their plans. Max had begged and pleaded with her. I had, too. Still, she wouldn't admit losing her brother at a young age had made her afraid to allow her son to take off.

Oh, the irony of how I'd thought she'd been overprotective given how I currently wouldn't even entertain the idea of having a baby because I was too terrified of looking after a child. Regardless, back then, neither my brother nor I could make her see reason. Not even when I pointed out if Max were going away to college instead of heading to the University of Maine in the fall, he'd be gone for much longer than a week.

"That's different," Mom had insisted. "He'd be in a controlled environment."

My brother's eyes almost popped out of his skull. "*Controlled?*" he'd shouted. "Yeah, that sounds about right. It sure seems you're controlling *me*."

Kenji had tried to negotiate with Mom, too, but all his points—whether deemed partially valid or not—had been swiftly swept aside. In the end, he didn't go to California after Max went missing but stayed in Portland, trying to help locate my brother. Since then, every year on the anniversary of Max's disappearance, Kenji posted a moving tribute on social media about his best friend, which never failed to make me cry.

He regularly texted or called to see if I had an update from the police, too. Except, as I stood on Triple Crown's patio, mouth still agape, I tried to remember the last time Kenji had been in touch. Three months? Was it closer to six?

What had happened to him? Where was he?

A sudden shudder ran through me as I recalled AL's last email. *To show you, you'll soon receive an extra incentive.*

I immediately pushed the thought away. Kenji going missing couldn't have anything to do with AL. He hadn't been serious. The guy was one of those keyboard warriors who got their kicks by winding others up with cutting, abrasive, and, above all, anonymous messages.

But then why did I feel so afraid?

My heart categorically refused to make the definitive connection while my brain screamed at me that it wouldn't be naively dismissed. All this might have something to do with Max.

Six years, and we still had no idea what happened to him. No body had been found. Foul play never entirely ruled out, at least not by me. The tingling in my spine wouldn't let me discount the fact that maybe, just *maybe*, Kenji going missing was linked to Max. To the person who called himself AL.

Head spinning harder now, I dashed to the table and grabbed my bag while mumbling an apology to Vivien and Andrea about an emergency. No clue how I got to my car or managed to back out of the parking lot without causing an accident, especially as Vivien kept calling my cell.

About halfway home, I realized I'd stranded her at Triple Crown, and she'd have to find her own way back. It wasn't enough to make me turn around. By the time I'd parked in our driveway, barreled around the house, and run up the path to the studio, I'd broken out in a cold sweat.

My chest rose and fell so fast, I could tell I was dangerously close to a full-on panic attack. It wouldn't have been the first—I'd had a few in the aftermath of Max's disappearance—so I sank onto the studio's sofa, pressed my heels into the ground, and tried to calm myself. It didn't work, and as the door opened, I bent over and vomited into the wastepaper basket.

"Stella." Jeff rushed through the door and ran over, falling to his knees in front of me. "What's going on?"

In lieu of an answer, I vomited again before grabbing a fistful of tissues from a box on the coffee table. I wiped my mouth and threw my arms around Jeff, pulling him tight.

He stroked my hair, whispering soothing words of comfort as he held me close. When I pulled away, I noticed his expression was filled with concern mixed with something else.

"What's going on?" he asked again. "I saw you run in here. What made you throw up?"

"It's . . . it's . . ."

"Is it food poisoning?"

I shook my head.

"Could it . . . could it be morning sickness?" he asked, sounding so hopeful, it tore my heart in two. When I shook my head again, he added, "Are you sure? It might be, if—"

"It isn't," I said, voice flat. "I'm not pregnant."

More fear and panic filled my body. As my shallow breathing started up again, Jeff grabbed my hand and rubbed my arm. "Tell me what happened."

"Kenji's missing," I blurted, bottom lip quivering.

"What do you mean Kenji's missing? Missing *how*? When?"

"I . . . I don't know. I was at Triple Crown with Vivien and Andrea Booker, and—"

"Booker?" Jeff said before waving a hand. "Never mind. You were at the pub . . ."

"There was a TV report. I only saw the last bit. There's barely anything online." I jumped up, pulled out my iPhone. "I'm calling the news station. I'll ask for the reporter. No, wait. I'll talk to Kenji's sister, Ren. The one who owns a gym. I can—"

"Stella, slow down." Jeff led me back to the sofa, where he gently pushed me into the seat. "Take a moment. You're obviously being triggered because of Max, but—"

"No, you don't understand. I got some emails."

"Emails?"

"From someone named AL. I think he's Liam from Augusta. The guy who called *People of Portland*." I hurriedly explained what AL's messages had contained, how he'd said I'd get an *extra incentive* to investigate Max's disappearance. "Don't you see?" I concluded. "Jeff, I think this man took Kenji."

CHAPTER 14

STELLA

"Sweetheart," Jeff said slowly. "Do you really believe that? Do you actually think Kenji's disappearance is related to Max's?"

"Yes," I whispered, before running a hand through my hair, going over the little I knew again in my mind at warp speed. "I don't know. Maybe . . . ?"

"Do you know under what circumstances Kenji went missing?" he asked. "Because perhaps he went on a massive drinking spree and passed out somewhere. Maybe he took off for a few days, forgot to tell people, and lost his phone. It happens. Chances are there's an innocent explanation, not a nefarious one. He may already be home by now."

I wanted to protest, but Jeff was right. Although books, movies, and TV made it seem like there was a killer lurking around every corner, most people who went missing weren't abducted, let alone murdered. They often came home safe and sound within a few hours or days.

"What about the call to the radio show, and the emails?"

"From a pair of assholes," Jeff said. "More than likely they're not the same person."

"Yeah, probably," I said, unsure who I was trying to convince more—Jeff or myself.

He took my hands in his, waited a while before saying, "Why didn't you tell me about those messages?"

"I didn't want to worry you."

"Stella . . ."

"I blocked AL, so I handled it. There was nothing to say."

"That's not true though, is it?" Jeff said with a hint of irritation. "I know you hold things back, but you don't need to. I'm here, and you can trust me. Shutting me out makes me worry about you because I fill in the blanks. I knew something was up."

Before I could respond, Vivien appeared in the doorway, and a round of apologies ensued for stranding her at Triple Crown. She listened carefully as I explained the reason for my swift departure. Going over the emails AL had sent to my private account made my stomach tighten again, but at least Vivien didn't give me a hard time for not mentioning anything to her before.

"You said Kenji disappeared from Templetons early Tuesday morning?" she asked. "I was there Monday night."

"What? Did you see him?" I said.

"I don't think so, but it was packed, and I haven't spoken to him in a good five years. I'm not sure I'd have even recognized him."

I grabbed my phone, zoomed in on Kenji's photo in the news article, and showed it to Vivien, but she shook her head. "I remember him from way back, of course. He practically lived at your parents' place on the weekends."

"Yeah," I said. "He, Max, and another kid hung out all the time, until that boy moved away." I paused and looked at Jeff. "I've told you Kenji didn't do well after Max disappeared, haven't I?"

"Dealt with it by acting out, right?" Vivien said.

I nodded. "Got busted for underage drinking, stole stuff from an electronics store. Then fell in with the wrong crowd. At least that's what Ren told me a while back when I ran into her. I've never talked to him about it directly. It's not my place."

"When you say the wrong crowd, do you mean a gang?" Jeff asked.

"No, no," I replied. "More like he's friends with a couple of guys who like stealing shit."

"Maybe that's why he's missing," Vivien said. "Perhaps he's with them."

"Or he pissed someone off," Jeff added.

I put my head in my hands. When the acrid smell of vomit drifted upward, roiling my stomach, I pressed two fingers over my mouth. Vivien's gaze dropped to the offending wastepaper basket, and she picked it up before swiftly disposing of the contents in the studio's little bathroom.

As she turned on the tap, Jeff lowered his voice. "I think you need to talk to Dr. Graf about what happened today."

"I agree," Vivien said over her shoulder, and I cursed Jeff for not being quiet enough. I didn't need them both on my case. They'd colluded enough already. "The reaction you had was quite extreme, Stella, walking out on us," she continued as she came back into the room.

"Are you saying that because I messed up *your* meeting?" I snapped.

Vivien ignored the overt dig. "No, Andrea was fine. We said the three of us would reconvene at a later date to be determined. Anyway, this isn't about the Booker deal. It's about *you*."

She glanced at Jeff, and although I couldn't tell what it was, I could've sworn a telepathic message passed between them. They'd known each other since I met my husband, had previously conspired behind my back for birthday, anniversary, and Christmas surprises. At one point early in our relationship, I'd even suspected Vivien had a tiny bit of a crush on him because the guy she'd been dating at the time was an ass.

While I was glad my best friend and my husband got along so well, it could have its downsides. Especially when it became two against one. And this look . . . it felt different somehow, more loaded. Just as quickly, it disappeared, making me wonder if I'd imagined it.

"I think you could be spiraling," Jeff said. "The anniversary of Max going missing and his birthday are coming up. You've barely mentioned either. Like I said earlier, I know how you keep things bottled up."

"I don't—"

"You do." Vivien patted my hand, glancing at Jeff again.

"It's fine if you don't want to talk to us," he said. "That's what your therapist's for. To help you work through this." I wanted to argue, but he pressed on with, "Think about it. That's all I'm asking. Meanwhile, I'll call Owen and tell him I can't help today."

"No need. I'm fine. Honest."

"And I'm here," Vivien added. "I'll even wait until you're back, Jeff. If Stella wants me to."

After I'd reassured him again that I was okay, Jeff hugged me and said he'd check in later. As he left, Vivien went with him to the main house to make us some tea. Frankly I'd have preferred a bottle of gin.

Watching them walk across the lawn, deep in conversation, heads getting closer and closer together, I imagined they were agreeing I'd almost lost it. Had my reaction at the pub been extreme? Neither Vivien nor Jeff had seen AL's messages. They'd heard me paraphrase them, but it wasn't the same.

On the other hand, I had been silently on edge because of the upcoming anniversary and birthday, as was the case each year. And, of course, there was my continued contraception deceit.

I sighed, called Dr. Graf and left a voicemail, asking to reschedule the appointment I'd missed. It was unlikely I'd hear from him immediately. While his practice was in an impressive colonial house in Portland's Riverton neighborhood, he didn't have a receptionist to field his calls and generally returned them in the evenings.

"Everything okay?" Vivien said when she came to the studio with mugs of chamomile tea. "Did you get ahold of your therapist?"

"Uh-huh," I said, and as casually as I could, continued with, "He had a cancellation this afternoon. Do you mind if I go?"

"Of course not," Vivien replied. "Take as much time as you need. Want me to wait?"

"I'll probably go to the gym again after seeing Dr. Graf," I fibbed. "Anyway, like I told Jeff, I'll be fine. I promise."

I gave her a swift hug before collecting my things and stepping out, welcoming the cool breeze sweeping across my cheeks.

These were lies I had no guilt over. It was common knowledge how critical time could be when someone went missing. My research on *A Killer Motive* had confirmed it over and over again.

More than a day had passed since Kenji vanished. Whether I was overreacting about his disappearance and being paranoid didn't matter. Neither did Jeff and Vivien not buying into my theory about AL and Liam from Augusta being the same person, somehow involved, and therefore a potential lead.

All that mattered was convincing the cops.

CHAPTER 15

STELLA

After hopping into my car, I opened Google Maps and headed into the city, circumnavigating a four-car pileup on the I-295 by driving via Congress Street to the Cumberland parking garage. Once I'd found a spot near the second-floor elevators, it was a quick walk to the police station.

Three other people already stood in line at the reception desk. I took my place behind a woman whose two small kids pretended her legs were a climbing frame. As they giggled and pulled faces at each other, I found it hard to stand still, too. Nervous energy coursed through my body as I bounced on my heels.

As always when it came to Detective Anthony Wade, this wasn't a meeting I felt enthusiastic about. If we'd had a better and more collaborative relationship in the past, I might've called ahead to check he was in. As things stood, I figured if he found out I wanted to see him, he'd do whatever he could to get rid of me.

Wade had worked on Max's case since the night my brother vanished. I almost scoffed out loud at the thought. *Worked* was a wild exaggeration when it came to Detective Wade. It implied he'd actively done something.

After Mom had woken my dad that fateful morning, my parents, Jeff, Kenji, and I had driven back to Lighthouse Beach to search for Max in the rain. Half an hour later, and despite the fact we hadn't yet contacted all of Max's friends to ask if he'd crashed with them, Mom had insisted we call the cops. For once, I hadn't disagreed.

They'd arrived without fanfare or flashing lights, rolling into the parking lot like they were on a Sunday afternoon drive. When an older gentleman as thin as a pencil stepped out of the car and strolled over as if he had all the time in the world, I'd groaned.

I'd met Detective Wade a few months before when the police officer he happened to be riding with pulled Max and me over for a broken taillight, and our dislike of Wade had been almost instantaneous. Max genuinely hadn't known about the damage and had apologized profusely for the oversight.

We thought the junior officer might let us go with a warning until Wade sauntered up, hooked his thumbs into his belt, and stared Max down. "You think an apology will get you out of a ticket, *son*?" he'd said before turning to his colleague. "Irresponsible and careless drivers like this one need a hard lesson."

Clearly, Wade had a tendency of trying to shove you back into the box in which he'd decided you belonged, and when he arrived at the beach, the trend continued. Three minutes into our conversation, it appeared Wade had already decided Max had drunk too much and passed out somewhere.

The detective's attitude and body language screamed that being disturbed in the middle of the night for a trip to a rainy beach where a bunch of students had previously hung out was nothing but a nuisance. Another thirty seconds, and the detective and I were at loggerheads when he dismissed bringing in the K-9 unit.

"Listen, missy," he'd said in what I would come to understand was his trademark condescending tone to anyone half his age, especially if they were female. "Let's not get ahead of ourselves. We don't call in the dogs immediately. This isn't Netflix. In the real world, those resources are finite and are currently engaged elsewhere. Now, tell me again where and when you last saw Mr. Dixon and we'll do a *proper* sweep of the area."

Yes, from the beginning, I knew Wade never took Max's disappearance as seriously as he should have. When he learned my brother had planned on going to California and fought about it with my mother, his dismissive stance solidified.

Within an instant, he appeared to surmise Max had left town of his own accord despite all of us insisting he wouldn't. Wade seemed certain my brother would call us from out West after a day or two. He continued to hold on to the belief for over a week. Although Wade ultimately acknowledged he might have been mistaken, I derived no satisfaction from his admission. Not when we'd wasted so much valuable time.

Our collaboration hadn't improved, and we'd never agreed when it came to the theories about what might've happened to Max. Wade had floated the word *suicide* on more than one occasion, despite our protests that he needed to consider other scenarios more seriously. It almost felt as if it would be more convenient for him to close the case if we'd just accept my brother had taken his own life.

"It can be hard for families to accept the truth, son," I'd overheard him say to a much younger colleague when he didn't know I was within earshot. "They miss the signs. Or refuse to see them. Part of our role is to *make* them get there."

I'd taken such offense to the way he'd emphasized the word *make*, and the way he'd become increasingly dismissive of Max's case, I'd followed him back to his house that night. After pulling in front of his Chevy Silverado, I'd leaped out of my car and had a shouting match with Wade in his driveway until he told me to leave or he'd throw me in jail.

The last time I'd spoken to the detective—whose wife had apparently packed her bags last year and moved in with her sister in Wisconsin—was about three months ago, when he reassured me Max's file was still *very much active, Ms. Dixon*. I figured the only thing active about it was how it continued attracting dust bunnies inside his creaky old desk.

I wondered what Wade would say when he saw me, and if he'd be his usual flippant self. Somehow I had to find the best way of conveying the call from Liam, the emails from AL, and their possible link to Kenji and Max. Jeff and Vivien hadn't thought much of my theories, but Wade had to. I needed him to make proper inquiries and follow up this time.

I debated asking to speak to someone else but decided against it. No matter the few decent connections I'd fostered within the local police via *A Killer Motive*, as soon as I brought up Max, they'd immediately refer me to Wade, lest they offend the old guard. Given the fact he was only a few years away from his pension, I wondered how many of his colleagues hoped he might throw in the towel early.

As the last person ahead of me moved away from the counter, I reminded myself Wade had two children older than me. He possibly had grandkids, too—I'd never thought to ask. Maybe if I appealed to his fatherly side instead of readying myself for battle, he'd listen. I took a deep breath and greeted the dimple-cheeked woman smiling at me.

"What can I do for you, hon?" Her gravelly voice and the river-deep lines in her face reminded me of my grandmother. She'd smoked two packs of cigarettes a day for sixty years and somehow still lived to seventy-five.

"I don't have an appointment," I said. "Could you please tell Detective Wade it's Stella Dixon with pertinent information about her brother's case?"

The officer's face fell. "Detective Wade isn't here. He—"

I gestured to the chairs behind me. "I'll wait. Any idea how long he might be?"

"I'm afraid you might grow roots, dear." She tapped the bottom of her pencil on a notepad filled with doodles of peonies and weeping willows. "Detective Wade retired."

"What? Why didn't anyone tell us?" I asked before waving a hand. "Never mind. Can I speak to his replacement, please?"

"Let me see what I can do. It may take a while."

"No problem," I replied. "Like I said, I'll wait."

Nearly half an hour later, a woman somewhere in her mid-to-late thirties, dressed in a no-nonsense navy-blue suit, mint shirt, and sensible black leather shoes, walked into the reception area. She had a mop of curly brown hair, and from the look in her honey-colored eyes, I sensed she didn't put up with much bullshit.

After a quick word with her colleague, the woman I gathered might be Wade's replacement looked in my direction. Instinctively, I stood as she approached, registering how tall she was. When she held out a hand, I spotted an Apple Watch along with one of those smart rings that tracked personal health metrics. Seemed overkill to me. Maybe she was a data geek, which boded well for criminal investigations.

"Stella Dixon," I said. "Thanks for seeing me."

"Detective Najwa Hadad. Good to meet you. You're here about your brother's case."

I appreciated not only the firmness of her handshake but also the fact her words had been delivered as a statement. Straight down to business. "Correct."

"You'd better come with me."

Hadad opened a door with a key card and led me through to the back. A few moments later I found myself in a small, drab interview room with scuffed gray walls, fluorescent lights bright enough to give me a headache, and two chairs pushed up against a scratched metal table.

"Can I get you something to drink?" Hadad asked, gesturing at me to sit.

"No, thank you."

Folding her lean, runner-type body into the seat opposite mine, she said, "How can I help you today, Ms. Dixon?"

"Please, call me Stella. I heard Detective Wade retired. Was it a recent decision?"

"Last month. You weren't informed?"

"No."

"My sincerest apologies for the oversight. That shouldn't have happened."

"Thank you. How much detail did he give you about my brother's case before he left?"

Hadad sighed. "Not a lot, unfortunately. He—"

"Why doesn't that surprise me?" I said with a sarcastic laugh.

"I'm familiar with your brother's case. You can share what you wanted to discuss with Detective Wade."

"It's not only about Max," I said. "It's also about Kenji Omori. Are you working his disappearance, too?"

Hadad didn't utter a word. If her silence was a cunning tactic to get me to spill my guts, it worked. I told her everything. All about the *People of Portland* radio show, Liam from Augusta's phone call, AL's emails, and my theory that they were the same person.

"Can you show me the emails?" she asked.

"I tossed them and blocked his address."

"Are they in your deleted items?"

"I emptied the folder."

"I see. If he sent anything since, it's likely in your spam."

"Let me check."

I pulled out my phone and slid my finger across the screen, bringing up my email. My junk folder was full of the usual nonsense—fake package delivery notifications, phishing expedition bank alerts, and miracle pseudo-pharmaceuticals. Nothing from AL. I found myself wishing there were because Hadad would have more to go on.

"He hasn't written again."

"I'll give you my details." She pulled a business card from her pocket and slid it across the table. "If he emails, send it straight to me."

As she stood, I felt like I had when Wade repeatedly brushed away my concerns and theories. For whatever reason, I'd expected more from Hadad, and I wouldn't let her be as dismissive as her predecessor. No way.

I planted my heels on the floor. This time, I wasn't giving up without a fight.

CHAPTER 16

STELLA

"That's it?" I said, trying to keep my tone relaxed as I crossed my arms. "Because I don't think we're done here. What about Kenji?"

If Hadad was surprised, she didn't show it but took a beat as she observed me. After sitting down again, she crossed her legs and set both hands in her lap. "What about Kenji?"

"You never confirmed if you're the detective investigating his disappearance."

"Yes, I am."

"Great. Tell me more about what happened to him."

"I'm sure you understand I can't comment on an ongoing investigation," Hadad said, tapping her fingers on the table now, her huge eyes boring into mine.

I refused to look away. "Surely you can share *something*. He was Max's best friend. There was a public appeal for assistance. I'm here. I'm the public. Let me assist."

This seemed to give Hadad pause as she offered, "Kenji was last seen at his place of work in the early hours of Tuesday morning."

"At Templetons."

"You're familiar with it?"

"Not really. It was on the news. He mentioned getting a job there the last time we spoke."

"When was this?"

"Four or five months ago, I think."

"You're in regular contact?"

"Not as much as when Max first went missing," I said, wondering when this had turned into an interrogation. She was supposed to be telling me things, not the other way around. "Like I said, he and Kenji were best friends since they were little."

"What did you and Kenji talk about?"

"What we always talked about whenever we spoke," I said. "He asked if there was an update on my brother, which there invariably wasn't because Wade barely did anything."

"I can assure you, Detective Wade—"

"I don't care about him anymore," I said before catching the terseness in my voice and checking my attitude, knowing it wouldn't do me any favors. This was my opportunity to start fresh on Max's case with a new cop. Get her on my side. "Tell me about Kenji, please."

Her eyes narrowed as she clearly evaluated how much she should share. "Templetons closed shortly after 1:00 a.m. on Tuesday morning. Kenji's colleagues left before him. He was tasked with taking out the garbage and locking up. When the staff arrived late Tuesday afternoon, the club's back door was open. Kenji's car was in the parking lot. He never made it home."

As she talked, my heart rate accelerated, and I wiped my palms on my pants. Speaking about anything related to a disappearance always did this to me, no matter how often I had these kinds of conversations for the podcast. "Are there security cameras at Templetons?"

"There's one at the front door, a couple inside, but none at the back," Hadad said. "Before you ask, there's nothing suspicious on the footage we've examined so far."

"Did anyone check the dumpsters? Maybe he fell in."

"That's a negative."

"What's your theory about where he is?" I asked.

Hadad gave me a brisk smile. "I don't speculate, Ms. Dixon. My job is to interpret and follow the evidence."

"What evidence?" I shot back, and when she didn't answer, I added, "Don't you think it's odd how my brother disappeared without a trace, and now his best friend did, too, right after I received an email saying I'll get an *extra incentive* to try to find Max?"

"An email you can't show me," Hadad said.

"I'm not lying," I said, my voice going up. "Why would I?"

When the detective spoke again, her voice became surprisingly gentle. "You see your brother's friend going missing . . . maybe you think it's an opportunity to move the spotlight."

"Onto *me*?"

"Your brother. You clearly feel Wade didn't do enough."

"It's not a feeling," I said. "Listen, I can't show you AL's emails, but they existed. As for Liam from Augusta, Friday's *People of Portland* episode is on their website. Take a listen. Better yet—" I reached for my bag, pulled out a piece of paper and a pen "—I'll give you the producer's details. Contact her or ask for the host, Charlene Thornton."

When I pushed the note in Hadad's direction, she left it in the middle of the table. "Thank you. I'll look into it."

"Will you?" I sneered, unable to help myself. "That's what *Detective* Wade said six years ago, and what did he do? Decided my brother wasn't worth the effort."

"Stella," Hadad said. "The team worked the case as much as possible. My understanding is there wasn't anything tangible to go on. It's as you said, Matt—"

"Max."

Hadad held up a hand. "My apologies. *Max* vanished without a trace. There was no indication of malfeasance." She paused again. "Stella, you said you run a true crime podcast."

"Yes, but—"

"Then you understand better than most how it's almost impossible to keep an investigation highly active under those circumstances. It doesn't mean we've given up. I promise, if there's new information about Max, we'll be all over it like cops at a doughnut sale."

I knew she'd intended to placate me with the stereotypical analogy, but all it did was piss me off. This wasn't the time for jokes. "There *is* new information. That's why I'm here."

"An irate phone call from a radio show listener and deleted emails aren't much help, I'm afraid. I wish I could do more for you, I really do."

"Have you spoken to Kenji's sister, Ren?" I asked.

"Rest assured, we're pursuing every possible avenue," Hadad said, a political stock answer if I'd ever heard one. I wanted to climb over the table and throttle her. "Now, if there isn't anything else, I—"

"You said you read my brother's case file?" I said, cutting in.

"I did, yes."

"And you're the lead detective? You've taken over from Wade."

"Correct."

"Do you know what day Max went missing?" When Hadad didn't answer, I tilted my head to one side. "Can you tell me the month?" As her cheeks made tiny movements, I shook my head. "And here I was, thinking it was only Wade who didn't care. I guess if I can't count on you, it means I'll have to look into things myself."

"Stella," Hadad said, her voice carrying more than a hint of caution. "I must warn you about not interfering with a police investigation."

"If my brother's case was *active*, I'd no doubt listen," I said, getting up. "Thanks for your time, Detective."

I figured she'd noticed the thick layer of sarcasm in my voice because she gave me a semi-smile and accompanied me to the main entrance regardless of my insistence of it being unnecessary. Once I was back in my car, I sat for a while, wondering where to go from here.

An instant later, I almost snapped my fingers as a lightbulb the size of a hot air balloon turned on in my head. I pulled out my phone and called Charlene's number, breathing a sigh of relief when she answered. We agreed to meet for coffee near the radio station. I decided to leave the car in the parking garage and walk, grateful for the fresh air after being in the stuffy room with Hadad.

Toasty Treats, the coffee shop boasting the best grilled mozzarella and tomato sandwiches in town, only had three free tables. My stomach rumbled at the smell of food, and after grabbing my order, I snagged a seat near the entrance and settled in.

Charlene arrived, pushing the door open with her cane and hobbling through. When she saw me, she said a quick hello before heading for a coffee.

"Is everything okay?" she asked when she returned and lowered herself into her chair. "You sounded stressed when you called."

"I need your help." I set my sandwich aside and launched into an explanation of what had happened these past few days.

Charlene's eyes widened. "Hold up, Max's best friend goes missing after you get a bizarre email, and this cop, Detective Hadad, doesn't think it's relevant? Are you serious?"

"*Exactly*," I replied. "I'm glad you had that reaction, because so did I."

"And you think AL's the radio caller, Liam from Augusta?" she said. "Is this why you contacted me on Saturday? Sorry for not returning your call. I was at my cottage all weekend, and when you didn't leave a message, I figured it wasn't urgent."

"Don't worry about it," I said. "I hoped you could give me AL's contact details. When I couldn't reach you, I phoned Izzy."

"Let me guess," Charlene said. "She mentioned privacy issues."

"Yeah, exactly."

"I'm not surprised. She's a real stickler for the rules. I can't blame her."

"I understand," I replied quickly. "She said she wouldn't be able to help anyway because Liam withheld his number."

Charlene looked at me. "I'll check. And do some digging into this Liam from Augusta, too. See what I can find."

"Really? You'd do that for me?"

"Of course. My investigative journalist spidey senses are tingling."

"I wish Wade's had six years ago. He botched this whole thing."

"That can't be true," Charlene said. "I met him a few times. I know he had a reputation for being abrupt and old-fashioned, but he was highly competent."

"Could've fooled me," I muttered, although it wasn't the first time I'd heard that. The problem was he only seemed highly competent in the cases he deemed worthy of his time, and I suspected Max's had never made the list.

Charlene reached across the table and put a hand on my arm. "I can't imagine what you and your family have been through. How are your parents?"

I didn't know her well enough to share the state of my fraught relationship with my mother, so I chose a neutral answer. "They're well. Health-wise, anyway."

"It must be so tough," she said. "If there's anything else I can do, please let me know. You can count on me, Stella. I'm here to help."

"Thank you," I whispered, and for the first time in ages, I no longer felt quite so alone.

THURSDAY, JULY 31

CHAPTER 17

I haven't felt this rejuvenated in quite some time, Stella. It had been a while since I'd committed a crime. Well . . . an entirely new one, anyway, and it's all because of you. You inspired me to continue what I started years ago, which means it'll soon be time for your next chapter.

It's been easy to prepare, although it wouldn't surprise you if I shared how trusting people are. From your experience on A Killer Motive, *you know how to get anyone to open up to you. And why wouldn't they? You're warm, compassionate, eloquent. Ask great questions, remain respectful. I can tell that during your conversations about another person's deceased or missing loved one, part of their story latches itself onto your soul. You genuinely care.*

I admire your dedication. We're quite alike in that way, you and I, although our methods are vastly different. It begs the question how easily you could use those attributes and instincts in less, shall we say, socially palatable ways.

I'm certain you've thought about it. Yes, you said if there was foul play involved in Max's disappearance, you'd bring the culprit to justice. No doubt having them appear in front of judge and jury isn't the only option you've considered.

You fantasize about killing whoever may have hurt your brother. Slitting their throat from ear to ear or bashing in their skull. It's natural.

We're all shades of gray. It serves no purpose pretending otherwise. The question is what we do with our darker parts—suppress or embrace. Some flow from one to the other faster than a river after a summer storm. How quickly could you flick your evil switch?

This and so much more is what I want to know about you. There will be plenty of time for me to learn every detail. And you will give me every detail.

My chosen ones always do.

CHAPTER 18

STELLA

Vivien left for Syracuse early Thursday morning. Considering how my conversation with Detective Hadad had unfolded at the police station the day before, I was glad to have the studio to myself for the coming week. As always whenever one of us was out of town, Vivien and I would stay in touch on a frequent basis, but this way I could have any necessary phone conversations without fibbing or needing to hide.

I'd meant what I'd said to Hadad yesterday. If she wouldn't properly examine the connection between Liam's phone call, AL's emails, and Max's and Kenji's disappearances, I'd do it myself. Hopefully Charlene's digging would unearth pertinent information. Frankly, I was kicking my backside for not requesting her help earlier, considering her investigative journalist expertise.

With a mug of coffee in front of me, I tried several more Google searches for Liam in Augusta, which turned out to be pointless. There were too many people in the area who shared the same first name to whittle it down to anything usable. Maybe the guy's number was unlisted. There was no way of knowing if he'd told the truth about where he lived, anyway, let alone provided his real first name.

After searching through dozens of recent posts on WHMR's website, trying to spot his acerbic tone in the comments, I gave up on that avenue, too. As it was with so many of the podcast cases Vivien and I examined, I had to accept there wasn't enough to go on.

When I was about to check my spam folder for the millionth time to see if AL had renewed contact, my anger reappeared. I hated having to wait and see if he popped up again. It made me ask myself too many questions, like if he'd really hurt Kenji, or if the timing was pure chance and I should let it go.

As I sat in the studio, I became acutely aware I'd already reached multiple dead ends on my research—which I typically excelled at—with nothing to show for it. I suddenly wished I had seen Dr. Graf yesterday rather than lying to Vivien about the session. It would've been better than my unproductive discussion with Hadad. I'd have been able to talk things through with someone else who would've properly listened, like Charlene had.

Thinking about Dr. Graf immediately made my shoulders drop from my ears. I wasn't a huge fan of therapy because of the introspection it required. However, knowing I could talk to him about anything, but leave out whatever I needed to keep to myself, still had an undeniable calming effect.

When we'd started our sessions, I'd found it a little bizarre how my therapist would learn so much about me when I barely had any details about his life, so I'd asked a few questions. Dr. Graf hadn't shared much at first, but over the course of our sessions I'd learned a few things. He'd grown up in Portland and had a daughter my age.

"Giselle lives in the UK with her partner, so I don't see them as often as I'd like," he'd said. "She's an engineer and works in green tech. I think of myself as relatively competent with all things technological, but she's a whiz kid. I'm told what she's developing now will punch climate change in the gut."

"Amazing." I glanced at the ring on his left hand. "You and your wife must be proud."

"Alas, I have to be proud enough for the both of us," Dr. Graf said, voice solemn. "My wife passed. Boating accident in Spain a few years ago."

"Oh, my gosh. I'm so sorry," I said, pulling my gigantic foot from my equally massive mouth. Dr. Graf's insistence there was nothing to forgive was yet another reminder of how compassionate he'd been since he'd found me curled up in a ball at the gym.

The urge to speak to him about what was going on grew. I'd left a message yesterday but decided to try again. I tapped on his number, elated when he picked up almost immediately.

"I was about to call you, Stella," he said. "Great minds think alike. How are you?"

"Fine." The response came automatically before I reminded myself there was little point in lying to my therapist. Dr. Graf would see through me, anyway. "Uh, no. Some stuff has happened."

"Stuff you want to talk about?"

"Yes, please. First though, I apologize for missing Tuesday's appointment. It completely slipped my mind. I'll pay for the session."

"No need," he replied. "It's never happened before, and I had a lot of paperwork to catch up on. Let's see . . . I have an opening tomorrow morning at ten, if you're amenable."

"Great," I said, surprised by how much I meant it. "I'll see you then."

After hanging up, I put my phone on my desk as movement outside caught my eye. Jeff strode across the yard to the studio. He'd come home late last night and I hadn't yet seen him this morning. When I'd returned from another early workout session during which I'd tried, and failed, to clear my head, I'd found a note on the counter saying he'd gone for groceries.

"Hey," I said as he walked in, but my smile faded at his sullen expression. "What's the matter?"

Stuffing his hands in his pockets, he rocked on his heels. He only ever did that when his patience ran dangerously low. I panicked, wondering if he'd found my birth control, but my bag was next to my feet, so that couldn't be it.

"I just hoofed it all the way to Brackett Street for those Montreal-style bagels you love. Guess who got in line behind me?" When I didn't reply, Jeff added, "Charlene Thornton."

"But . . . wait. Have you met before?"

"What? Uh, no. I don't believe so. I recognized her from the radio's website. Anyway, we got talking, and she said you saw each other in the city yesterday afternoon." He crossed his arms. "You told Vivien you were going for therapy. Did you?"

"Vivien mentioned my session?"

"I take it you mean your *fake* one?" he asked, eyebrows raised. "Yeah, she did. I texted her yesterday to ask how you were doing."

"How often are you talking about me behind my back? Why didn't you ask me directly?"

"Please don't deflect. Why did you say you were seeing Dr. Graf?"

I hesitated. Telling him now that I'd been to the cops yesterday would only rile him some more. He'd ask why I hadn't shared this with him either, at least by phone or text, and I didn't want things between us to escalate any further.

There wasn't much to say anyway, considering the outcome of the discussion with Detective Wade's replacement. Nothing had come from the meeting with Hadad. Nothing of consequence, at least.

I decided I'd tell Jeff when—if—Hadad gave me anything useful. Besides, if I explained the detective's reaction to my theory about Max's and Kenji's disappearances being linked, I had a feeling my husband would think *I told you so* and wouldn't be able to hide it.

I shrugged. "Charlene's an investigative journalist, and I needed a different perspective. Vivien set me up to meet Booker.

Then I found out Kenji's missing. The pair of you had me cornered."

"Cornered?"

"Yeah." I bit my lip before murmuring, "I needed to speak to someone else."

Jeff's stony expression softened. He took a few steps and sank to his knees. Grabbing my hands in his, he said, "I'm sorry you felt that way. We were trying to help."

"I know. I'm seeing Dr. Graf tomorrow morning. Promise. Stop worrying."

"I'll try," Jeff said, making me hope this would blow over and we'd be okay. He had no idea how much I needed him. "How are you feeling about everything that happened?"

"I'm massively concerned about Kenji. I'll contact Ren later to see if I can help. One big sister to another, you know?"

"No more weird emails?" Jeff squeezed my hand as he got up, and I shook my head. "You'll tell me if there are?"

"Yes, of course," I said, thinking I'd immediately alert Hadad thereafter, if only to prove to the detective that I hadn't invented AL to bring attention to my brother's case. The fact she'd suggested it made me grit my teeth.

"How about Vivien?" Jeff said.

I puffed out my cheeks and leaned back in my chair. "Well, I'm still pissed at her for springing the lunch on me, but I can see her point as to why she did it. I have to think about the Booker possibility. Weigh the pros and cons."

Jeff kissed me softly on the lips. "Good idea. You hungry? I left your bagel in the kitchen. I can grab it for you."

"I should stretch my legs," I replied. "Plus, you're too good to me."

"Anything for you. Listen, I'm supposed to take the truck for an oil change. Will you be okay here alone?"

After another kiss and reassurances I'd be fine, we walked to the house. Once Jeff left, I settled at the breakfast table, eating half a blueberry bagel as I scrolled on my phone for news about Kenji. No updates had been released. After debating my next move, I decided to give Hadad another chance. Maybe we'd started things off on the wrong sensible-shoe-clad foot and she'd feel more inclined to share details with me if I softened my approach. I fished the card she'd given me from my pocket and dialed.

Less than a minute into the conversation, I wondered if Hadad's predecessor had trained her in the art of policing. "There's nothing I can share with you, Stella," she said, her tone clipped. "There haven't been any developments since you stopped by. If there are, you'll be the first to know."

Yeah, sure.

Enough. Time to be proactive. No matter who disapproved.

CHAPTER 19

STELLA

After locking up the studio and the house, I headed to Nason's Corner, pulling into the parking lot of the plaza that housed Validus Fitness shortly before ten, hoping Ren had time to spare.

I hadn't known Ren as well as I'd known Kenji. She was only a year younger than me, but we'd hung out with different high school friends. Our paths had occasionally crossed at parties, although she never attended them as frequently or rabidly as I had.

Ren had been the school's star track athlete, shattering all previous records. It surprised nobody when she got a full ride to study business at Berkeley. I figured she'd stay in California, but when Kenji derailed after Max's disappearance, she returned.

For two years, she worked her butt off, putting together a business plan, getting a loan, buying out a failing gym and rebranding it as Validus. It was on the smaller side, but like Ren, it packed a punch. More than once, I'd considered moving my membership here. The only reason I hadn't jumped yet was that it didn't accommodate people who wanted to train at all hours.

After pulling open the glass door, I walked inside. Ren was on the other side of the room with a red-faced woman who rowed as if she was being chased by nautical zombies.

Meanwhile, Ren, who stood a little shorter than me, wore figure-hugging leggings and a tank top emphasizing her strong and immaculately toned body, as well as her elaborate sleeve tattoos. She'd tied her long black hair into a neat bun, and I grinned when I saw the words on her shirt—*I'd flex but I love this tank top*.

After the client was freed from her torture session, Ren gave her a round of applause, passed her a towel and water bottle, and turned in my direction. When she saw me, a look of surprise crossed her face.

"Stella, have you finally decided to join my gym?" she said, walking over. I figured her jovial tone was for the benefit of her staff and customers, because it certainly wasn't fooling me. The Samsonite-esque bags under her eyes told me she hadn't had a good night's sleep in days. "I promise you won't regret it."

"I'm sure I wouldn't." I lowered my voice. "Is there some place we can talk in private about your brother?"

Ren nodded, her face wavering. "Of course, come with me."

She led me to her office at the back, which she'd decorated with motivational posters, including one that read *When You Think About Quitting, Remember Why You Started*. I could relate.

"I'm so sorry to hear about Kenji," I said as she closed the door. "I should've called or stopped by sooner. It was a huge shock, to be honest. I wasn't sure what to think."

"Yeah, I get it. I'm not sure either."

Ren gestured for me to sit as she filled two glasses with water from a blue jug on her desk. Her laptop, two neatly aligned pens, and a paper notepad were the only other things there. Maybe tidiness gave her a sense of control.

"I appreciate you stopping by," she continued. "It must've brought back awful memories. Have there been any developments about Max?"

"It's kind of you to ask, but no. The detective responsible for the investigation retired. I met his replacement yesterday. Najwa Hadad."

"She's working Kenji's case," Ren said. "She's been very sympathetic."

"Hadad didn't tell me a whole lot," I said, wondering how

much I should share with Ren. I didn't want to upset her by telling her about Liam and AL, and especially not the *extra incentive* part. On the other hand, if the detective mentioned them to Ren, it wouldn't be fair if I hadn't warned her first. We weren't friends, exactly, but we were more than acquaintances, especially now.

I gave her a succinct overview of what had happened since the radio show, ending with, "Hadad doesn't think Kenji's and Max's disappearances are linked."

"Honestly, Stella, I can't see it either," Ren said. "Max vanished six years ago. It's been a long time. He and Kenji were basically still kids."

"True, I guess," I admitted.

"Also, remember I once told you how Kenji's *friends*, and I use the term loosely, are a bad influence? Seems the situation was worse than I suspected."

"How so?"

"My understanding was they were involved in petty theft. You know, minor stuff." Ren let out a long sigh. "Turns out my brother was boosting cars with two other guys he hung out with. Dabbled in dealing drugs, too, according to Hadad. Can you believe it? Kenji still lives with my parents."

"Do you think this has anything to do with his disappearance?"

She nodded, then shook her head, eyes glistening. "Maybe. I mean, he could've stolen the wrong person's car or sold them bad drugs. It's possible someone got to Kenji, or he took off because he was scared. I can't be sure."

"If there's anything I can do . . . If you want to talk, I'm here."

"Thanks," she replied softly as she absentmindedly patted one of the tattoos on her bicep.

"That's a cute owl," I said. "Is it new?"

"This? No, it's the first one I got. It's my lucky charm." She paused, her eyes glistening. "Kenji has the same one, only I told him to make it smaller because he'll always be my kid brother." Another pause, longer this time. "Stella, I . . . I need to know where he is."

"We'll find him, Ren," I whispered. "We will."

Ren nodded, wiped her eyes quickly, and stood. "I don't mean to be rude, but I'd best get moving. I have a few calls to make before a team meeting and another client."

"Sure," I said, getting up. "Will you keep me posted if you get word?"

Ren promised she would, and as I reached the door, she added, "How do you do it?"

I turned around to find her watching me, her cheeks now wet from tears. "Do what?"

"Cope with not knowing where your brother is."

"It gets easier with time," I lied. "Don't lose hope. It's only been a few days."

Ren nodded. "I distinctly remember saying the same thing to you."

Visiting Ren hadn't produced the results I'd hoped for, although it had confirmed Kenji might have got into trouble because of the company he kept. I tut-tutted at myself. Seemed I was in danger of treading the same path Wade had chosen when Max went missing. Taking the easy way. Assuming. Writing Kenji off without properly considering all options.

It was more comfortable to believe his disappearance was linked to him crossing the wrong person, therefore unrelated to Max's case, and AL's emails were nothing but a way for some rando to wind me up. The alternative was terrifying, but I had to be certain.

As my true crime podcaster instincts kicked in, I decided to visit the last place Kenji had been seen so I could snoop around. After finding the address online, the drive to Templetons took under ten minutes. When I arrived, I couldn't help wondering how a nightclub contained within this ugly two-story squat beige building practically in the middle of nowhere had become one of Portland's latest party place darlings.

A bit of online sleuthing, and I quickly learned Templetons was more than a club as it held a separate restaurant offering gastropub food. Their slick menu boasted hand-pressed burgers, Louisiana tofu wraps, Korean barbecue chicken bowls, and a variety of snacks, all ensuring their clientele didn't take off if they got hungry.

Apparently, the hip crowd had also been attracted by a mixture of reasonably priced quality drinks, international DJs, and extended happy hours. Easy street access and ample parking were the direct opposite of most clubs in Portland's downtown core.

With the rural setting, noise levels for the rooftop patio during the clement months weren't much of a worry, either. The closest building stood sixty yards away, with large birch trees blocking most of it from my view. What appeared to be a junkyard was located on the other side of the road, the metal fencing secured by a large set of chains.

I parked my car in Templetons's empty lot before getting out and heading to the front door. A security camera above it was pointed in my direction, and the expensive-looking wooden sign, which spelled out the establishment's name with dozens of LED bulbs, was switched off. Hopeful there might still be somebody around, I tried the door handle. Locked.

I walked along the front of the club, pushed my nose against the floor-to-ceiling windows, and cupped my hands around my eyes so I could peek inside. No movement. Stools and chairs neatly stacked on the tables, the shiny metal bar wiped clean.

I kept going and headed around the corner. There weren't any windows on this side of the building, so I scanned the area and ground as I went, searching for anything relevant, but found nothing. When I reached the back, I saw two large rusty green dumpsters. Hadad had been right—there were only a few bags inside.

When I tried the handle on the rear door of the club, it wouldn't budge either, so I stood hands on hips as I looked around, noticing that Hadad was right about something else. From what I could see, there were no cameras other than the one at the front door. The parking lot didn't have any, plus there were multiple entries and exits for cars to come and go.

If someone had driven in and picked up Kenji, it would've easily been missed. If an assailant had waited for him and pounced, they would've avoided detection, too. It was the perfect place for a crime. Or an escape.

As the breeze picked up, leaves rustled in the trees, and I shivered at the whisper-like noises. Had Kenji been in so much trouble, he'd decided to make a run for it? Could he have abandoned his car, along with his sister and his parents—his entire life—and pretended to be abducted to trick everyone, including whoever had threatened him? How could he reconcile doing that to his family when he knew how much Max's disappearance had hurt ours?

An alternate scenario was that someone had taken their revenge by making Kenji pay the ultimate price before bundling his lifeless body into their vehicle. Ren hadn't mentioned forensic evidence, but it didn't need to have been found, or to exist, for this hopefully outlandish version to have taken place. Maybe Kenji had been held at gunpoint and forced into a van. He could've been killed elsewhere or was being kept alive for whatever reason.

I rubbed a hand across my face. There were so many possibilities, and I was no closer to finding answers. These were the exact types of questions I asked myself on a loop ever since Max disappeared. I still refused to believe my brother had hurt himself, meaning his fate had either been a tragic accident or an assault. Unlike with Kenji, I'd been a hundred percent certain Max didn't have enemies.

I took one more good look around, hoping to miraculously spot a detail the police had missed. Wishful thinking. There was nothing here, so I returned to the front of the building. I wasn't sure what I'd hoped to find at Templetons, but so far this had been another waste of time.

As I was about to get into my car, a woman outside the junkyard across the street caught my eye. Thinking I had nothing to lose, I called out as I waved at her and crossed the deserted street, breaking into a jog.

"Hi," I said. "How are you?"

Crinkles appeared in the corner of her eyes. She was about fifty, her short black hair in a stylish pixie cut, her blue overalls covered in oil and grime. "Lovely day. I'm not complaining. What can I do for you?"

"This will sound strange," I said with a grimace. "I'm a true crime podcaster."

"True crime, eh?" she said with a grin. "It's my husband's long-standing obsession. Between you and me, it sometimes makes me wonder if he's planning something for me. And I don't mean a good thing. What's the name of your show? Maybe he's mentioned it."

"A Killer Motive."

She rubbed her chin. "Can't say for certain, but it could be one of his favorites."

"Awesome," I said. "I'm glad to hear it."

"You investigating a case?" She held out a hand. "Name's Poppy."

"Stella," I replied as we shook. "And yes, kind of. Did you hear about the man who disappeared from Templetons earlier this week?"

"Yeah." Poppy's expression darkened. "Saw it on the news, and the cops were here late Tuesday. Any idea what happened?"

"No, that's why I came to see if I could find anything by having a look around."

"Have you?"

"Found anything? No. Uh, do you have any security cameras pointing at the road?"

Poppy beamed. "Sure. Sent a copy of the footage to the cops already. You guys working together?"

"Not exactly," I said. "They don't want an amateur on their turf."

"Amateur?" Poppy grinned. "Hubs always says true crime podcasters are the bee's knees, and he knows what's what. Follow me. You can watch the video for yourself."

CHAPTER 20

STELLA

Poppy led me inside the building, and I was grateful to get out of the heat and into the air-conditioned reception area. The tiny room smelled of lavender and coffee, and a multitude of well-worn, different-sized metal filing cabinets lined an eggshell-color wall.

As she walked to a green Formica desk in the corner, Poppy gestured for me to follow. Once I'd taken a seat on the office chair, she leaned over and wiggled the mouse of a laptop. The screen came to life, and a few clicks later, the security camera footage appeared in front of us.

"We could do this on my phone, but you'll get a better view this way," she said, clicking another few buttons. "There you go. This is everything from Monday noon onward. You may want to fast-forward the first few hours. Templetons doesn't open until suppertime."

"Thanks, Poppy," I said.

She gave me a nod. "No worries. Got a few things to take care of. I'll leave you to it."

After Poppy had gone, I said a silent thank-you for her being such a trusting person, and settled in. Before I pressed Play, my anticipation built. I leaned in, hoping this search would return better results than the one outside.

I soon realized Poppy's camera was mounted above the junkyard's front door. It didn't cover much of Templetons's parking lot, which was a major disappointment, although I could see the club's entrance across the street well enough to not give up.

As per Poppy's suggestion, I skipped through a few hours of footage, stopping whenever I saw someone arrive. Each time it happened, I tried to make out their face when they turned their head to the side, which was frustratingly rare.

This was one of the more mundane parts of sleuthing. It could take forever. I wasn't sure what I was searching for, and if something significant didn't jump out at me, I could miss it entirely.

Half an hour of watching in fits and starts, and my fingers hit Pause when I saw Kenji arriving at the club alone shortly before 5:00 p.m. After pressing Play again, I watched at normal speed as he moved across the screen and disappeared inside the club.

I wondered if he'd had an inkling of what would go down. Had he received a threat or a warning? Been told to watch his back? Or was my other theory correct and he'd left of his own volition?

I kept trawling through the footage as more staff and then guests arrived, a steady stream of patrons entering Templetons. Some left, at which point I got a better look at them because they faced the camera.

"Anything helpful?" Poppy said as she walked in, wiping her hands on a yellow rag and setting a bottle of water in front of me.

After thanking her, I cracked the seal and took a big gulp. I hadn't noticed how thirsty I'd become. "Nothing yet. I'll keep at it, if it's okay with you?"

"Sure thing. I'll get a fresh pot of joe on the go. Want a cup?"

With a mug of some of the best coffee I'd ever tasted in front of me, I tackled the next two hours of footage. I was about to take a sip of my drink when I recognized the person on the screen. Auburn curls, toned legs, cute white lily-print dress, one I'd helped her choose. Vivien with her friends.

About an hour later, she showed up again. This time, I

watched her exit the club with someone else I knew, and whom I must've missed when she'd arrived.

Andrea Booker.

The two of them stood to the left of the main doors. Vivien swayed a little as she spoke, and at one point during their conversation, she put her hand on Booker's arm. My immediate reaction was that their exchange held too much familiarity for it to be a business discussion. But when a car arrived an instant later, Andrea shook Vivien's hand, opened the car door for her, and headed inside Templetons again.

Leaning back in Poppy's chair, I tried to decide if I'd witnessed Vivien and Andrea conspiring about our Triple Crown lunch, or if there was something more to it. I wanted to call Vivien and demand to know the truth but decided to finish combing through the footage in case anything else pertinent turned up, including about her.

Andrea left Templetons shortly after eleven with her arm around another woman. After googling photos of her, I determined she was Andrea's wife. Still unsure what it all meant, I pressed Play again. The club gradually emptied before six staff members left at 2:17 a.m., at which point I caught a glimpse of Kenji saying goodbye as he stayed behind.

I didn't dare blink in case I missed the tiniest detail, but nobody slipped in through the front door, and the section of the parking lot that I could see remained quiet. Save for the leaves on the trees swaying in the wind, there was no movement at all.

Nothing happened for ages until the screen suddenly went fuzzy. My eyes narrowed as I sped through seven minutes of static before everything returned to normal.

Once again, all stayed calm, and the only things caught on camera were a few cars driving by, and a pair of squirrels chasing each other into a bush. Nobody arrived at Templetons until late Tuesday afternoon. According to Hadad, this was when the club's team had found the back door open, and Kenji's car still in the parking lot.

Stopping the video, I went outside, where I found Poppy disemboweling a lawnmower in the front driveway, a metal tray of neatly organized nuts, bolts, and screws at her feet.

"All done?" she asked. "Hope it was useful."

"I'm not sure," I replied. "Did you notice the footage going fuzzy?"

"Can't say I did," Poppy replied. "I didn't watch it all, but it's probably a glitch. The tech warned me about wireless cameras being sensitive."

"Has it ever happened before?"

She shrugged. "Never had a reason to check."

"Can you show me any older videos so I can see if it's a regular thing?"

"I always record over the previous day," Poppy said with an apologetic grimace. "Walk around the lot first thing to make sure nothing's been broken into or stolen, then reset the recording."

"Except for Tuesday because the cops showed up?"

"Not exactly," she said. "They came here early evening. Thankfully I'd been distracted by an impromptu delivery first thing in the morning. Otherwise, they'd have nothing." She glanced over my shoulder, pointing behind me. "Speak of the devil. She's the one I gave it to."

I turned around. Detective Hadad stood in Templetons's parking lot with a uniformed police officer, their cruiser parked only a few spots away from my car. After watching them move around the building, I looked at Poppy.

"I'd better go," I said. "Thanks for your help, and the coffee."

"Anytime," she replied. "I hope you find the missing guy."

I hurried across the street and got into my car, but as I was backing out, Hadad reappeared. When our eyes met, she lifted her chin and held up a hand. No sense pretending I hadn't seen her, so I stopped and rolled down the window.

"Stella," she said, brow furrowing. "What are you doing here?"

"Same as you, presumably. Looking into what happened to Kenji."

Hands on hips, she said, "I gather it's pointless asking you to let us do our job, so hear this instead: don't jeopardize the investigation."

"Wouldn't dream of it, Detective," I replied through clenched teeth. "Have a great day."

CHAPTER 21

STELLA

Jeff's car wasn't in the driveway when I got home, so I headed to the studio, where I fired up my laptop. I hadn't checked my phone all morning because I'd been too busy watching Poppy's footage, but the first thing I opened was my email.

The sight of an empty spam folder almost made me slump onto my desk. Five days had passed since I'd heard from AL. Maybe after reading my salty reply, he'd decided to stop harassing me and had moved on to another unsuspecting and unfortunate soul to rile. Perhaps Kenji's disappearance really didn't have anything to do with the guy.

Deciding to at least try to focus on work, I glanced at my to-do list. Last night, I'd set myself the goal of completing the final round of edits on an upcoming podcast episode and contacting a list of potential sponsors—all this before noon. Given the fact I'd spent the morning in Poppy's office, I was woefully behind.

Cold calling was never fun, but it made no sense to put it off any longer. I spent the next hour either being rejected outright or emailing *A Killer Motive*'s media package, hoping it wouldn't end up in the recipients' virtual trash.

My mind went back to Vivien and Andrea outside Templetons

as I tried to interpret what I'd witnessed, and what to do about it. After playing around with the possibilities in my mind, I decided I wanted to have a conversation with Vivien face-to-face. That way, I'd get a better sense of whether she was fibbing.

Once I'd finished my latest round of prospecting, I was about to tackle the podcast editing when I noticed a new email in my spam folder. As soon as I recognized the sender's address, my jaw clenched. It was from AL.

> Dear Stella,
>
> We both already know how much you love cold cases.
> I hope you're enjoying trying to solve a red-hot one.
> Or are you still refusing to play?
>
> AL

Fury spread through me like wildfire as my fingers flew across the keyboard. First, I sent AL's note to Hadad, getting only a glimmer of satisfaction from the fact she'd see I hadn't lied. Next, I crafted a reply to AL, hoping I could provoke him into giving me more information Hadad could use to shut the asshole down.

> Is hiding behind your keyboard the only way you feel like a proper man?
> You're such a dick.
> Loser.

I sat in my chair, waiting for an answer. When nothing came in, I repeatedly refreshed my spam folder because I was ready for a fight. Finally, a new email appeared. This one didn't have a greeting or a sign-off. Only two short sentences.

Check the planter box.

Tell no one or he dies.

My breath caught in my throat as I read the words again.

Tell no one or he dies.

Who was "he"?

My heart skipped at least ten beats when my gaze snapped up and out of the window, landing on the cylindrical wooden planter box I'd bought last month. Although I loathed gardening, one Sunday afternoon I'd spontaneously decided our backyard could do with more color. Much to Jeff's amusement because I could barely keep fake flowers alive, and with multiple Pinterest photos saved on my phone, I'd visited the local garden center.

An hour later, I'd come home with a trunk full of supplies. By nightfall, I'd felt proud of the single planter box I'd filled with deep blue salvia, yellow lantana, and purple Persian shield. In fact, I'd liked it so much, I'd placed it to the left of the studio's door so I could see it from inside.

Was this the planter box AL meant? Why did he want me to check it?

How did he know I had one?

I got up. Although my body moved slowly, my pulse galloped, almost veering out of control by the time I reached the door and pulled it open. Taking a step outside, I craned my neck and looked around, half expecting someone to jump out from behind the bushes and trees.

This had to be a prank. Plenty of people owned planter boxes. He'd made a lucky guess. AL was trying—and succeeding—to freak me out. My head whipped around again, moving from left to right as I scanned the area. There—was that a face by the trees? No, only my eyes playing tricks on me.

A century seemed to pass as I took the last few steps to the planter box. Once there, I leaned over and peered inside. Nothing other than foliage, petals, and dirt.

Feeling silly, I kneeled and searched around the sides of the box before tipping the whole thing over far enough to slip my fingers underneath and examine the space. Empty. As I stood up again, relief that AL was messing with me filled my chest, but I still peered a little more closely at the roots of the flowers disappearing into the soil.

This time I saw the corner of an object I instinctively knew didn't belong.

After pushing away the loose earth, I drew a sharp breath when I saw a shred of clear plastic. Fingers scrambling, I dug deeper and gave whatever had been buried a yank. Moments later, I held a compact phone, sealed in a transparent plastic freezer bag.

My heart pounded as statements and questions collided together. AL had left me a phone. Who was he? He'd been at my house. What did he want? He knew where I *lived*. Why was he doing this?

I stumbled back into the studio, slammed the door, and sank into my chair with the bagged phone clutched in my trembling fingers. AL's email still goaded me from my computer screen, the black text on white background too bright and obnoxiously loud.

Tell no one or he dies.

I was about to reply, demanding to know who he was and what he was doing, when Jeff opened the back door of the house and stepped outside. My first instinct was to rush over and shout out what had happened, but AL's warning was already etched deep into my brain.

Tell no one or he dies.

The screen of the phone inside the plastic bag lit up with

an incoming, muted call. Unknown number. I willed my husband to walk to the garden shed, or go back inside the house, but he came toward the studio. As he got closer and the screen kept flashing, I shoved the phone inside my drawer and swiftly closed my email.

When Jeff walked in, he said, "Thought I'd say goodbye before my shift. It's my twenty-four hour one, so . . ." His face fell. "Are you all right? You look like you've seen a ghost."

I nodded quickly. "I—I'm fine. Just worried about stuff."

Jeff came over and gave me a kiss on the lips, and it was all I could do to not pull him close and never let go. "You've still got an appointment with Dr. Graf tomorrow?"

"Yes."

"You'll go?"

"Of course I will," I snapped, nerves bubbling over. As much as I wanted my husband to stay, I needed him to leave. He had to go so I could deal with AL. Except . . . how? I had to tell Jeff. He could help. We'd figure this out together. I opened my mouth to speak . . .

Tell no one or he dies.

"Sorry," I said with a fake smile. "My appointment's at ten. I promise I'll be there."

Jeff kissed me again. "Call if you need me before I'm home. Anytime. Love you."

"Love you, too."

As he went to the studio's door, he stopped and turned around. "What happened to your flowers?"

I feigned innocence. "Huh?"

"The planter box. There's dirt all over the ground. Maybe squirrels attacked it."

"Probably. I'll clear it up later."

He headed back to the house, and I forced myself to wait a while before sneaking to the driveway to ensure his truck was gone. Back in the studio, I darted to the bathroom, where I found a pair of disposable latex gloves under the sink and pulled them on. In the last ten seconds I'd decided I'd tell Hadad about this new development, and I didn't want to mess up the forensics more than I already had.

Very slowly, I opened my desk drawer and took out the freezer bag. The Nokia inside looked brand-new, and when I pressed one of the buttons through the bag, the screen sprang to life. There had been two missed calls and an alert from an app called Whisperz, which I'd never heard of.

I tapped on the icon, and a message appeared.

Congratulations. By not picking up you sealed his fate.

Just as quickly, the words disappeared. When I tapped on the screen, furiously trying to retrieve them, all I ended up with was the Whisperz logo. I tried to respond, but the app wouldn't let me.

I was immediately on my computer, bringing up AL's last email. I wanted to delete it. Get rid of it forever and never think about it again, but I couldn't. Not if there was a possibility of him having Kenji. Fingers shaking, I hit Reply.

What do you want?

A minute went by, and then another. I had to force myself to calm my breathing multiple times as my heart had landed in the back of my throat. My temples throbbed as I waited for the Nokia to ring, my eyes fixated on the darkened screen. I wrote another email.

Do you know where Kenji is?

As I was trying to decide who to contact first, Hadad or Jeff, finally the Nokia buzzed. Incoming call. Unknown number. Gathering every shred of courage I could scrape together, I slid my finger across the screen.

CHAPTER 22

STELLA

"We talk at last."

AL's voice was deep, causing a multitude of icy chills to zap down my spine. Although I heard him well enough with the phone still in the plastic bag, I didn't recognize him. I immediately went into rational autopilot mode, somehow understanding AL's cadence and tone weren't entirely natural.

From my experience conducting research for *A Killer Motive*, and from watching true crime shows, I gathered AL was using voice-altering software or a handheld device to disguise his identity. Either option was cheap, easy to use, and readily available. Highly effective and often impossible to trace, too.

"Who are you?" I said, my voice and entire body trembling. I hated myself for conveying so much weakness in three words, but this man had come to my house. He'd been in my backyard, outside the studio. Was he watching me now?

I jumped up and raced to the door, which I quickly locked before retreating to my desk. As I walked backward, I scanned the yard, eyes sweeping left and right, expecting to see a disturbing face in the leaves.

If he burst into the studio now, what would I do? I didn't have a weapon, nothing to defend myself with but my bare hands. Jeff wasn't home. I eyed my iPhone, wondering if I should call 911, but AL spoke, his icy tone freezing me to the spot.

"Don't keep me waiting again, Stella," he said. "Ever. We're not yet well acquainted. However, you'd be wise to heed my instructions or there will be consequences. Not only for you."

"Tell me who you are," I said. Despite trying to force strength and assertiveness into my voice, the words came out as a pathetic whisper. My legs buckled, and I slid into my chair. "What do you want?"

"Please, call me Anwir," he said, his tone suddenly pleasant, almost jovial.

"Are you Liam from Augusta?" I waited a few beats, but no reply came, only the sound of Anwir's breathing. Every single hair on the back of my neck stood on end. I pressed the phone to my ear, trying to detect any other noise that could provide a clue, but the guy seemed to be calling from a vacuum. "Why did you come to my house?"

"I'd have thought it obvious. To gift you the burner phone you're holding."

"Why?"

A soft chuckle caused a fresh river of ice to slide down my spine. "Do you enjoy games, Stella?"

"Do I . . . What are you talking about?"

"I love them. We're going to play together. It'll be fun."

"What do you want? Did you hurt Kenji?"

"So many questions," the man who now referred to himself as Anwir said as I detected amusement in his words. "Must be your podcast experience. Always searching for information. All in good time. First, tell me why people play games."

"What?"

"Come, Stella. It's a simple question. Why do people play games?"

"I, uh . . . for fun?"

Anwir clicked his tongue. "Some, yes, it's true. I want another reason."

"I don't know—"

"Think," he snapped. "This shouldn't be difficult."

I took a beat, tried to calm my racing pulse. "People play games to . . . to win."

"Exactly," he replied. "I love to win, but if you beat me, which I doubt, but *if* you do, you won't be the only person who'll benefit. Kenji will, too."

A gasp escaped my lips. "You took him?"

"He really, *really* wants to go home. Begged me to let him go." Anwir made a *mmm-mmm* sound. "I love it when they beg. I think it's my second favorite part."

"Have you hurt him? Please tell me he's—"

"The rules." Anwir cut me off, and my entire body stiffened as I drew a sharp breath. "All games need rules. Number one, you'll be allocated time to find our friend, which I might shorten or extend depending on how well you're doing. Fail to find him, and he'll never be seen again. Trust me when I say his body won't be discovered until and unless I want it to be."

"Why—"

"Number two," he continued. "Breathe a word about this to anyone in any way, be it verbally or in writing, and he dies. Simple enough, but in case my instruction isn't clear, this includes Detectives Wade and Hadad, and their colleagues. It means Jeff, Vivien, your parents, and your friends. It extends to Kenji's family and acquaintances. *Anyone* covers your doctors, your therapist, and your mailman. It would include your pets, if you had any. Do you understand?"

"Yes," I whispered. "I understand."

"Number three," Anwir said. "Always have the burner phone on you. Wear something with a front pocket. Keep it in there.

Answer immediately when I call. Delay, and there will be severe penalties."

"How can I be sure you're telling the truth?" I demanded. "How do I know you have Kenji and you're not some—"

"Careful, Stella. You already insulted me enough in your email. How can you afford to think I don't have him?"

"I want proof. Otherwise, I'm not doing anything."

Courage rushed back and flooded my veins. As soon as we were done, I'd go to the cops with the emails and the Nokia. Surely Hadad would take me seriously now, find out who Anwir was and if he'd abducted my brother's best friend.

"I wouldn't have expected anything other than this kind of pushback from you, Stella," Anwir said slowly. "Although, be warned. You should be careful what you wish for."

Before I could ask what he meant, I heard another voice on the other end of the line. This time, I recognized it instantly.

"Help me. Please, please help me," Kenji begged, his words filled with terror. "Do as Anwir says, or I'll die. Please don't let me die. *Please*, and . . . No, what are you doing? Don't. Please don't. Put it down. Put it *down*."

As Kenji let out a guttural scream, I covered my mouth with one hand. Tears burned the back of my eyes and rolled down my cheeks. Despite my best effort not to, I let out a sob.

"Satisfied?" Anwir asked quietly.

"Let me talk to him," I gasped. "Put Kenji on the phone."

"No, that's not possible."

"Why?" I shouted. "Put him on the phone. *Now*."

"Don't test my patience," Anwir said. "You're in no position to state any demands. I made a recording though. Playing it back to you would give me a little *frisson*, so I'd enjoy it. Would you?"

"No," I whispered, my mind grasping at another desperate possibility. "But you've proved nothing. Scammers use AI to clone voices all the time. They've tricked families into paying thousands of dollars in ransom, and—"

Anwir started to chuckle. A deep rumble at first, which suddenly exploded from his throat in a loud and lengthy guffaw. "Oh, Stella."

"Why are you laughing?" I demanded. "You think this is funny?"

"Funny? No. It's hilarious. I don't want *money*. I want—"

"I don't care what you want."

Anwir let out a bored sigh, all the laughter gone. "You're *a liar*. I hope you realize you only have yourself to blame for Kenji's predicament. After all, I gave you a chance when I wrote to you about looking into Max's case."

"Don't talk about my brother," I said, my voice a snarl as my backbone regrew. "Don't even *think* his name."

"Listen to me," Anwir said, his glacial tone slicing my insides in half. "I knew you'd react this way, so here's one more *extra* incentive for you to play. The final one."

I didn't answer, and my hand gripped the Nokia so hard, I wondered if it might turn to dust inside the freezer bag. I wanted to shout at Anwir, say I was going to the cops, but what if he was telling the truth? What if that had been Kenji's voice and petrified screams, which I already knew would give me nightmares until the day I died? What if Anwir made good on his threat, and my brother's best friend disappeared forever?

"You'll play," Anwir said. "Because if you win, not only will you get Kenji back alive, you'll also be rewarded with information about what happened to Max."

"What did you say?" I whispered. "You have details about my brother? Please, tell me what you know."

"Oh, I couldn't possibly," he said, feigning obvious dismay. "But you'd best do as you've been told. Otherwise, you'll never find out."

"You're sick," I said, teeth clenched. "You're a sick bastard who's—"

"Oof, I'm hurt, Lella."

I let out another gasp. "How do you know—"

"Max's pet name for you when he was little?" Anwir said. "I know all about you reading *The Little Prince* to him, too. It was his favorite book until he discovered *Asterix and Obelix*. Is the collection of graphic novels still on the shelf above his bed?"

My stomach heaved, threatening to empty itself across my desk. How did Anwir know my brother hadn't been able to say my name properly until he was three, or how obsessed he'd been with those books? These details hadn't been included in any of the public reports about Max going missing. Had we told the cops?

Realization slithered up my arms and over my shoulders, insisting I needed to stop and think. I could be talking to someone who knew what had happened to Max . . . or more likely the person who'd hurt him, and now Kenji, too. My deepest, darkest fears were coming true. Max hadn't had an accident. He hadn't drowned himself. He'd been taken. By the worst kind of monster.

"Tell me where they are," I said. "Please. *Please*, Anwir."

"Oh, I really do love it when they beg," Anwir replied, and my eyes flooded with fresh tears. "Remember the rules. Tell no one about our conversations. Don't share a single thing about me with anyone. If you do, you'll have another death on your conscience."

I balked at the word *another*. If the second was Kenji, then the first meant my brother. "Tell me what you did to Max. Tell me now, you motherfu—"

"Patience, Stella," Anwir chastised. "I'll be in touch soon. Win my first challenge, and you'll get information. A clue, if you will. If you lose, you'll . . ." He clicked his tongue. "Look at me, getting ahead of myself. I'll share those details with you when it happens. I don't want to spoil the surprise. Have a good day, Stella."

"Wait," I shouted. "Wait. I—"

"Keep the phone close. Put it in your front pocket. Talk soon."

I yelled his name, pleaded with him not to hang up.

Too late.

He was gone.

CHAPTER 23

STELLA

As my heart threatened to claw its way out of my mouth, my thoughts whirred, a scramble of nonsensical words I couldn't fit together into anything coherent. The studio walls inched closer, threatening to crush me alive. I forced myself to put my head down and inhale deeply, wondering if I might fall to the floor.

I'm not sure how much time passed. A few seconds. Minutes. An hour. Finally, when my breathing was no longer quite so ragged, I wiped a hand over my sweaty face and stood.

The two available options became crystal clear. I could go to the cops and tell them everything. Yes, it meant risks, but surely it was the better choice. There was no way I could give in to Anwir's demands and stay silent about the things he'd said.

But the threats about hurting Kenji . . .

The information he said he had about Max . . .

I had to keep quiet.

No. I couldn't.

Jeff already had both eyes on me. As soon as he saw me in this state, he'd know something had happened. I couldn't—*shouldn't*—hide anything of this magnitude from him. And what about my parents? We'd waited six years for a lead on Max's whereabouts. How could I entertain keeping this to myself?

Added to all this was the fact I wasn't a cop. Sure, working on *A Killer Motive* had provided me with a better than average understanding about crime, criminals, and the inner workings of the justice system, but I wasn't an expert. I didn't possess adequate know-how to deal with this situation, nor did I have access to the professional and technological resources and tools Hadad had at her fingertips. Besides, Vivien was the tech person, not me.

There was also Kenji's sister, parents, extended family, and friends, who'd been thrust into a missing person situation. When Ren had asked how I coped with not knowing what had happened to Max, she'd sought reassurance. I'd dismissed her with a placating answer. Tried to protect her from the truth. Until Kenji was found, and possibly every day thereafter depending on the result, her heart would shatter.

The anguish and despair, the not knowing, was a terrible, painful burden I'd carried for six years. I hadn't wanted to tell Ren that Max was my first thought when I woke up and the last one before I went to sleep. I didn't want her to suffer the same fate. I had to *do* something. Get the cops involved. If our situations were reversed and Anwir had contacted Ren, it was what I'd expect from her.

I tried clinging to the belief that Anwir was a crackpot, a charlatan of the nth degree. Except the things he'd shared about Max, the unforgettable terror in Kenji's voice . . . I had to take Anwir seriously until proven otherwise.

But . . . who was he?

The part of me still somehow functioning properly took over, guiding my hand to my iPhone. I watched—almost as if it were an out-of-body experience—as my fingers zipped across the screen, opened my browser, and typed *Anwir*.

The first link was a Wikipedia page about a village in the Palghar district of Maharashtra in India. My brow creased as I wondered if it meant anything. If this place was somehow significant to Anwir—perhaps where he was from.

I searched my memory, tried to recall if I knew of or had ever encountered anyone from the area, but couldn't get there. Besides, it felt simplistic. Anwir was too sophisticated to leave such an obvious clue, or to use his real identity. He wasn't named AL, or Anwir. Liam was no doubt another pseudonym. Either way, I had little to go on.

A flicker of hope flared. Charlene had promised she'd try to track Liam or whatever his name was down. She was a former investigative journalist. Should I tell her about what had happened? I wanted to but wasn't sure I dared. Not yet.

The next hyperlink went to a baby name site, and my fingers stopped moving as my eyes scanned the words. Anwir was Welsh and meant *liar*. Finally the pieces snapped together like a malevolent jigsaw puzzle. He'd signed his emails as *AL*. *A liar*. That's what he'd called me before, even emphasizing the words.

"Asshole," I shouted, cursing some more as I imagined him sitting behind his computer somewhere, congratulating himself on his ingenuity. I had no idea who he was, but the choice of pen name immediately told me I'd have to triple question everything coming from his mouth.

What else had he given me? The name *Blooper Beach*. Why did it suddenly sound familiar? When I googled it, I found it was in *Mario Party 9*, Max and Kenji's favorite Wii game. How had he known that? Or had the reference been because I'd fucked up and my brother had gone missing on my watch?

Although I wasn't surprised my research hadn't returned any actionable results, *yet*, I let out a frustrated cry. I was at another impasse. I couldn't handle this on my own. I needed to talk to the police, and it had to be now. There was no more time to waste. Afterward, I'd call Jeff, and ask him to come home.

Mind made up, I set the ringer on the Nokia to vibrate and shoved it, freezer bag and all, into my tote before removing the latex gloves. After dropping them in the wastepaper basket, I grabbed my things and headed out the door, locking it behind me.

This time the I-295 was clear, and as I drove, I called the cops to inquire if Detective Hadad was in. Once that was confirmed, I put my foot down and gripped the steering wheel so hard, my knuckles turned translucent.

The sign in front of the Cumberland parking garage announced it was closed because of water pipe maintenance. Cursing again, I kept driving, and a few turns later, I arrived at an outdoor lot across from the police station.

There weren't any free spaces. With my patience levels dangerously depleted, I circled the lot another time and turned a corner. In my haste, I didn't see the man stepping out between two parked cars until it was too late.

"Argh," I yelled as I slammed on the brakes. My reaction wasn't fast enough. I heard a thud and watched in horror as he fell to the ground in front of my car. Within a second, I'd switched off the engine and leaped out. By the time I'd raced around the hood, the man had already stood up.

"What the hell?" he said as he brushed off his pants. "Didn't you see me?"

"I'm so, so sorry." I knew I shouldn't admit responsibility for fear of getting sued, but I couldn't help it. "Are you okay?"

He didn't answer as he rubbed his elbow before pulling his Toronto Blue Jays baseball cap a little lower on his head. I guessed him to be in his midtwenties, and as I moved a little closer, the shape of his blue eyes and the smattering of freckles on his nose seemed vaguely familiar.

"Are you hurt?" I asked.

"*Yes*, I . . ." He must've reconsidered whatever else he was going to say as he waved a hand. "No, it's fine."

"I really am sorry."

The man grimaced. "That'll teach me to not look both ways. Grams always says I shouldn't have my head in the clouds."

"Do you need a doctor to get yourself checked over?"

"No insurance."

"My husband's an EMT," I said quickly. "I could call him. See if he's—"

"No, really. It's not necessary."

"Okay . . . Let me give you my details in case you change your mind." I put a hand to my chest. "I'm Stella, by the way. Stella Dixon."

"Dylan Firth."

"What's your number, Dylan?" I asked as I hastily retrieved my iPhone. Now that I knew he wasn't hurt, I needed to get this conversation done with as quickly as possible so I could go find Hadad.

Once Dylan had recited the digits, I sent him a text.

"Please let me know if you end up seeing a doctor," I said. "I'd be happy to cover the expense. Is there anything else I can do? Call an Uber to take you somewhere, maybe?"

"No, my car's over there." He pointed to an ancient silver Accord. "It's all good."

"I'm glad you're not hurt," I said. "Apologies again."

I gave him a quick wave and hopped back into my car. Once I'd carefully parked in a spot that had opened up, I darted across Middle Street and ran up the steps of the police station. When I pulled open the front door, I saw the same woman from the other day sitting behind the reception desk.

Thankfully, there was nobody else in line this time, so I dashed over. As I was about to ask for Detective Hadad, something buzzed. It took me a few seconds to comprehend it was the Nokia from Anwir inside my bag.

"Can I help you?" the woman asked with an expectant expression.

The phone kept buzzing. Anwir had instructed me to keep quiet, carry the phone with me in my front pocket, and answer whenever he called, or there would be repercussions.

I'd already disregarded his instructions, and I was at the police station, with Detective Hadad a few dozen yards away.

She could help. I had to ignore Anwir . . . except what would happen if I did?

As the woman's tone turned wary, her eyes narrowed. "Anything I can do for you?"

The buzzing of the Nokia seemed deafening now, so intrusive it practically pierced my eardrums. I spun around and rushed out of the door as I pulled the phone from my bag, cursing myself when I realized I wasn't wearing gloves and had added more of my prints to the freezer bag.

"Hello?" I whispered.

"Are you certain you want to break my rules?" Anwir's tone caused a lightning bolt of anxiety to tear through me, rooting my feet to the ground. "You know there will be consequences to your behavior. Severe and painful ones nobody will enjoy. Except me."

"How did you know—"

"Answer. The. Question," he demanded. "Are you certain you want to break my rules?"

I glanced around. "No."

"You have until the count of five to walk away from the police station and go home. Understand?"

"Yes," I replied, but still my feet wouldn't move.

"One," Anwir said. "Two . . . three—"

I hurried down the stairs. "I'm leaving. I didn't speak to anyone, I swear. Please don't hurt Kenji. *Please.*"

Stinging tears clouded my vision while I held the bag with the phone to my ear. Panic rose, rendering me hopeless and lost. Pathetic. Isolated. Terrified. The fact Anwir had known exactly where I was when he'd called hit me, and sheer horror invaded my entire body all over again.

"You're following me," I said.

"Following, tracking, watching, observing," Anwir said. "This was a test to see if you could follow a simple instruction, and you failed, Stella. Miserably."

"I'm sorry, I—"

"There's spyware on the burner," Anwir continued. "I know where it is at all times. I can listen to your conversations whenever I want. Don't try stopping me from hearing what's going on around you. Don't even think about leaving the phone in another room or stuffing it under a pillow. Make sure it's in your front pocket only from now on. Do *exactly* as you're told, or Kenji will suffer."

"But I—"

The line went dead as a fresh jolt of fear almost made me throw up. I forced myself to stand still and look around. My chest heaved when my eyes landed on a man with a purple baby buggy coming toward me. Was he Anwir? How would I know?

I scanned the street again. Three tweens twenty yards away were pointing at one of their phones. Were they Anwir? A few years ago, I might've dismissed that anyone so young could be a vicious criminal, but there'd been plenty of instances I'd come across to prove me wrong. Kids were savvy, especially when it came to tech. I watched as one of them held up their phone and they smooshed their heads together for what seemed to be an innocent selfie.

Next, I saw an older woman pulling a shopping trolley behind her, her steps slow and labored. An improbable candidate, but I suddenly understood Anwir could literally be anyone and anywhere. That thought alone got me walking toward my car, desperate for relative safety.

I quickened my pace, needing to get away from the police station in case he thought I'd changed my mind about talking to them. I couldn't risk it, not if Anwir had Kenji and details about Max. My plan to alert Hadad in person had been blown to smithereens. If what Anwir said was true, and he could listen to my conversations, I'd have to email the detective and tell her what was going on in secret. First, I needed to get out of here.

After waiting for two cars to pass, I rushed to the other side of the road. In my haste, I tripped over the curb and was about to hit the ground when a hand grabbed my arm.

"Whoa," a man said, lifting me to my feet. "Watch out."

It was Dylan, the guy I'd run into in the parking lot. He held a deli bag in his free hand, and when he let go of my arm, he took a step back. "You okay?"

"A bit clumsy today." I forced a laugh, but it sounded way too fake and hollow to be believable. I didn't have the courage to look at Dylan in case he saw through my crumbling facade. If he offered his help again, I'd burst into tears.

Without another glance, I darted to my car. As I opened the door, I glanced at the police station and saw Detective Hadad exiting the building with two uniformed colleagues. I ducked and climbed inside my Toyota, hoping she hadn't seen me. If Anwir was watching, and Hadad came over to talk to me, there was no telling what he might do.

My heart leaped a little. Would Hadad investigate AL's—Anwir's—email I'd forwarded to her? Had she done so already? Would she and her team be able to trace the IP address and see from where and whom it had come? Maybe it would be enough to help, but what if Anwir thought I'd alerted Hadad after he'd explicitly told me not to?

Willing myself not to freak out, I tried to make sense of the little I knew. A man who called himself Anwir had planted a burner phone at our studio, and—

Another glimmer of hope grabbed hold of me. We had security cameras at the front of the house. Fingers twitching, I wanted to pull out my iPhone and check immediately, but I needed to demonstrate to Anwir I was following his instructions.

My mind raced ahead. If I didn't find anything on our footage, maybe one of the neighbors' security devices had picked Anwir up. There weren't many houses on our street, but it was concrete action I could take. The more information I had, no matter how small and seemingly insignificant, the easier it would hopefully be for the cops to find Anwir once I got them involved.

Still, Anwir knew my location, said he could activate the Nokia and listen to my conversations at any time. It meant I had to be smart, and careful. Make him believe he was in control and in charge, and—

The Nokia buzzed again, and I jumped. I picked it up, and without waiting for him to speak first, I said, "I did what you asked."

"Good girl," he said. "I'll be in touch. Be ready. Tell no one, or he dies."

This time, we both knew I'd do as I was told.

FRIDAY, AUGUST 1

CHAPTER 24

I can hear you, Stella. Your muttering, and your cursing. Your fear. I underestimated how exciting this would all be from afar. I'm enjoying our time enormously. More than you, which is to be expected given our roles, but also because I know what the outcome will be.

Naturally. Because I make the rules.

You think you're going to win, don't you? Part of you, no matter how small, believes there's a chance you'll get the upper hand. I'll let you believe that for as long as possible. Almost until the end. It's what will keep you going, and I don't want you to give up.

Not yet.

I need to see you in battle. Then I want to witness all the fight leaving your body, nothing but submission left in its place. That part may take a while. Far longer than in the past. I had my reasons for not choosing someone like you before, but now I wish I had.

Good things come to those who wait, or so the saying goes.

I guess that includes me, although most would say I don't deserve it.

Do you believe everyone thinks they're the hero of their story? I don't. Assuming those who do evil consider their actions to be justified, perhaps good, is a common misconception. I'm not under any such illusion.

Is what I do despicable? Heinous? Repulsive? Monstrous?

Why, yes, Stella. Yes, it is.

That's precisely why it's so much fun.

CHAPTER 25

STELLA

At 2:10 a.m. I lay in bed, wide awake. My insomnia had grown tenfold, making it impossible to sleep more than a few minutes at a time. Jeff wouldn't be home until this evening, meaning I'd had the house to myself since returning from the police station yesterday afternoon.

The first thing I'd done when I'd pulled into our driveway was bolt inside, then check that all the doors and windows were locked. Next, I combed through our front door security camera footage, going as far back as the recordings would allow. There'd been nothing unusual over the past six weeks. No strangers other than a few delivery drivers, and all their drop-offs could be accounted for.

As darkness fell, my anxiety had morphed into a near uncontrollable beast. I leaped from the sofa at least twice an hour to recheck the doors and windows, and throughout the evening, every creak and groan had made my heart pound.

At one point I'd been certain someone was moving around in the basement. I always screamed at slasher movie characters who told their friends, "Don't worry, guys, it's nothing. I'll show you." Invariably they got slaughtered, and yet I did the same thing by tiptoeing down the wooden stairs. Thankfully, it turned out to be the protests of our ancient hot water tank, but I shoved a chair under the basement door handle anyway once I'd darted upstairs.

In a perverse way, I fleetingly hoped Anwir would come here so I could somehow incapacitate him and call the cops. Except I had no idea how I'd do that, or who I'd be up against. It was a joke to think I'd be capable of anything other than trying to flee.

I'd finally headed upstairs at around 12:30 a.m. Once I'd turned the volume all the way up on the Nokia, I'd set the phone on my nightstand to ensure I'd hear it ringing. Not that I'd needed the precaution considering I was still awake almost two hours later, wondering if Anwir was listening.

Lying in bed, I fretted about what I'd do with the device once Jeff got home. He'd ask what it was if he saw it, but Anwir's instructions about having it within reach had been clear. I fiddled around with the settings on both devices until I found almost identical ringtones. One problem solved. A million others to go.

Inspiration struck, and I tried to forward the calls from the Nokia to my iPhone, but the settings wouldn't allow it, and I reluctantly gave up.

After tossing and turning for another five minutes, I headed downstairs to the kitchen for a glass of water. Rubbing my eyes, I debated having a shot of booze, preferably lots of them, but it wasn't a good idea. I had to stay sober. Be ready for anything.

I shuddered at the thought. What would Anwir do? What might he ask of me? How far would I go to locate Kenji and find out what Anwir knew about my brother? I'd always said I'd give my life for Max's, but when it came down to it . . . would I have the guts?

Once again, I tried to figure out who Anwir was, why he was doing this, and what he could possibly know. Maybe he'd never met Max. He could be an ex-convict. Perhaps while in prison, he'd heard details about Max and was gearing up to demand money in exchange for intel. Except . . . why take Kenji? He'd clearly expressed no interest in cash. Not yet.

AL. A liar.

I couldn't trust anything Anwir said or any theories I came up with about him, his knowledge, or his motivations. As I marched from the living room to the kitchen and back again, I understood Anwir's currency wasn't money, it was information. He'd acquired details about Max that weren't public knowledge or accessible online.

I tried to remember who else knew about Max's love of the *all sizzle and no steak* quip, him calling me Lella, and his fascination with the *Little Prince* and *Asterix and Obelix* books.

Likely Detective Wade, but whether he'd bothered to listen or write it down was another story. My parents, of course. Jeff, probably. Perhaps some of Max's friends and exes. Impossible to know for sure, or whom they might have told. Perhaps I was wrong and the details, while personal, were more widely known than I thought.

With the things we shared online these days, it would be easy for someone to research our history, likes, and dislikes, especially if we or our loved ones didn't keep the security settings tight. Circumstances depending, someone pretending to know us intimately wouldn't be hard.

Then again, if Anwir hadn't hurt Max—never even met him—it was also possible he'd obtained the information in a different, more invasive way. Maybe I'd mentioned Max calling me Lella, and his favorite books, to my dad on the phone, or to Jeff. A shudder zipped down my back as I imagined Anwir listening to our conversations because he'd broken into our home to install hidden cameras.

As wild as it seemed, I couldn't discount the theory. Nothing had been out of place in the house recently, but that would've been exactly the point. Also, this was an older dwelling. Jeff's parents had never installed an alarm system, and aside from the door cam, we didn't have security. Jeff and I joked we had nothing of value to steal. An alarm system would cost more than anything anyone could take.

Now I regretted our flippancy. For all I knew, Anwir was watching me on a nanny-cam. I imagined a hooded figure in front of a screen. The only visible thing his mouth in a gigantic smirk as he saw me pacing the room with the goddamn Nokia perched on the coffee table like a coiled-up rattlesnake ready to strike.

I hated this not knowing, being unable to tell for sure if Anwir had abducted Max or he was simply pretending. If he had Kenji or it was another ruse. I had to *do* something. Take some kind of action.

While not a tech genius, I had carried out extensive research for *A Killer Motive* cases, which had led to me learning about hidden cameras, including how to locate them. I grabbed my iPhone and downloaded the best detector app I could find as I prepared myself for the hunt.

It took ages to make my way through our entire house. Room by room, I turned off the lights and slowly scanned everywhere I could think of with my iPhone, my heart pounding as I watched the screen for a telltale red dot indicating a hidden camera. The reassurance I felt when I didn't find anything wasn't enough. After I'd finished my sweep, I ordered a more professional bug detector online.

A little while later, I headed upstairs. Once I'd put my iPhone on the bedside table, and the Nokia under the bed with the volume turned up, I closed my eyes. When I tried to sleep, I bit my lip to stop myself from crying as I thought about Jeff. I desperately wanted to tell him what was going on, that I needed help, but I couldn't. Not when I risked losing my only shot at finding Kenji alive, and potentially getting details about Max.

When I woke up, it was after 7:30 a.m. I retrieved the Nokia, relieved to see there were no missed calls. As I slid out of bed, I grabbed my iPhone and opened my email. Nothing from Anwir there, either, but I'd received a text from Jeff an hour ago, asking if everything was okay.

My fingers darted across the screen. All fine. Have a good shift, hon.

I hit Send and pressed a hand over my mouth, willing myself not to cry. There'd be time to fall to pieces later, once this was all over. Until then, I had a job to do.

CHAPTER 26

STELLA

The cloudless sky promised another scorching day as I jogged across the street to our closest neighbor, Mrs. Osei, hoping to catch her before she left for work. Four visits to the surrounding houses later, and I'd struck out again.

Everyone bought my story about trying to find a porch pirate who'd stolen one of my packages, but nobody had security footage showing someone snooping around our house. Anwir must've crept into our backyard via the ravine. I hadn't found a single image of him.

As soon as I closed the front door behind me again and walked to our compact, happy sunflower-yellow kitchen, the Nokia buzzed with an incoming call, making my stomach turn.

"Having fun chasing your own tail?" Anwir said as soon as I answered, his voice filling with glee. "Did you really think your neighbors would've picked me up on their door cams? Give me some credit, Stella. I'm many things, but sloppy isn't one of them."

He didn't wait for my reply and ended the call, leaving me standing in the kitchen with my mouth hanging open. Anwir had warned me he could listen in to my conversations at any given time, but until now, I'd hoped it might be a scare tactic.

Heart thumping, I called Ren, desperate for good news, but she told me Kenji hadn't come home. Nothing new from the cops, either. "They have zero leads," Ren said. "But we're staying hopeful. We have to."

When a reminder about my session with Dr. Graf buzzed on my iPhone, I immediately considered canceling, but decided I had to get out of the house. I needed to give myself the impression I was getting somewhere, doing something—*anything*—other than hanging around with the Nokia burning a hole in my chest pocket as I waited for Anwir to make contact again.

I zipped upstairs, brushed my teeth, and splashed my face with cold water. Five minutes later I was in the car with my laptop and notebook in my bag. Not long after, I walked up the front path to my therapist's private practice in Riverton. I rang the doorbell, unsure if I could hold it together for the next hour.

"Welcome back, Stella," Dr. Graf said, opening the heavy black door. Dressed in his usual attire of corduroy pants and a polo shirt, he ushered me into the hallway, and I headed directly to the room on the right.

I'd never ventured farther into Dr. Graf's house, but if his study was anything to go by, it had to be tastefully decorated. He'd chosen an off-white paint for the room in which he spoke with his patients, a bright space with a large bay window overlooking the front yard.

The fireplace I presumed had originally been intended for wood and coal was fitted with a sleek electric insert. The teak desk held a computer screen and two framed photographs, and the blue filing cabinets on the left wall added a splash of color. The office didn't give off cozy vibes as much as a serene tranquility.

I approached the red velvet armchairs in the middle of the room. When I'd seen Dr. Graf for the first time, nervous as hell for my inaugural session, I'd joked about being grateful that I didn't have to sit on a couch in case I fell asleep.

Dr. Graf had smiled. "My father did so nightly in these chairs, so I won't judge."

Back then, his relaxed demeanor had relieved my anxiety a little, but now I wished I'd canceled today. I couldn't speak freely. Couldn't tell Dr. Graf anything about Anwir. I knew about patient-therapist confidentiality, but the Nokia sat in my front pocket. Anwir would be listening.

"You seem preoccupied," Dr. Graf said. "Would you like to share what's on your mind?"

"It's work," I said a little too quickly, fumbling for a decent fib and wishing I'd had the forethought to plan things out better. How could I turn this into a useful conversation for me? My mind spun before I settled on, "Vivien asked if I'd consider recording a follow-up episode about Max for the podcast."

Dr. Graf nodded sagely. "What's your reaction to her request?"

"Not good," I said as an idea formed about how I could get Dr. Graf's help after all. "Actually, I was thinking about suggesting we make a more general episode about people going missing under mysterious circumstances. Perhaps delve deeper into common personality traits of those who abduct and hold others captive. From what you've read, what are the broad similarities?"

Dr. Graf waited for me to finish speaking, taking his time as he crossed his legs and rearranged the notebook in his lap. I often wondered what he wrote about me during our sessions. Perhaps it was better if I didn't know.

"I'm not a criminal psychologist, or a profiler," he replied carefully. "Therefore, I'm not the best person to ask."

"Okay, but I'll bet you know more than me," I said as casually as I could. "Is it true it's generally white men?"

"Statistically, I think that assumption can be made, especially if the abductors are also serial killers," Dr. Graf replied, and I worked hard not to balk. "They tend to be between thirty and forty. Generally speaking, they often have a history of relationship issues."

"Criminal history?"

"Potentially, but not always. There could be a pattern of sexual inappropriateness or assault, but again, not always. Each case is different. Each person is, too."

"What do you think motivates these people to abduct others?" I asked, forcing my face to stay neutral, wondering if Anwir was listening.

"Power, mostly," Dr. Graf replied. "From what I've read, it seems to be the driving force whether there's some kind of sexual desire behind their actions or not. Typically, it's about control. It's often selfish and narcissistic behavior."

"Sounds accurate," I muttered.

Dr. Graf scribbled a few more words before putting the pen down. "Stella, does this curiosity stem from Kenji's disappearance?"

My brow knitted together. Kenji's story had been on the local news and social media. No wonder he'd heard about it, but how had he made the connection so fast?

"You mentioned Mr. Omori a few sessions ago," Dr. Graf said, almost as if he'd read my mind. "I recall Kenji is your brother's best friend. You were worried about him. This must be especially traumatic for you considering what happened to Max."

My shoulders sagged. "Jeff doesn't think their disappearances are linked."

"Do you?" he asked, and I wanted to blurt out I was almost certain they were, but pressed my mouth shut. "Tell me why you're hoping for a connection."

"Closure," I said, keeping the rest of the reason—finding Anwir—to myself.

"You hope if they're connected, and Kenji's found, it'll solve the mystery of what happened to Max."

"Yes, exactly."

I wished I could tell him everything. My therapist was kind and thoughtful. Though I paid him to listen, it felt as if he genuinely cared. I opened my mouth to elaborate, but the weight of the Nokia in my pocket pushed the words down my throat.

"Stella?" Dr. Graf said. "Is there more you'd like to share?"

Despite the airiness and emptiness of the room, it suddenly seemed claustrophobic, the velvet chair getting hotter and hotter, burning the backs of my legs. I pushed the feelings away, knowing I had to continue pretending this was a regular session.

"I'm still afraid of having a child," I said. "Jeff's hopeful it'll happen soon, but . . ."

For the next while, we discussed how getting pregnant and being responsible for another human freaked me out more than anything in the world. On some level I hoped Anwir was listening to the conversation. Maybe I'd appeal to his compassionate side. If he had one.

"I'm not sure I can be trusted as a mother," I concluded, and despite Dr. Graf challenging the notion, I countered with, "I may not ever be ready. It's as simple as that."

"What might happen if you talked to Jeff in detail about how you feel?"

"I'm not sure."

A few beats went by, until finally Dr. Graf said, "Judging by what you've told me, and the way you've described your marriage, Jeff loves you. His reaction might surprise you."

"Maybe," I replied. "I promise I'll consider it."

"That's a great place to start." As Dr. Graf closed his notebook, his doorbell rang. "Apologies. I'm expecting a delivery, but they assured me it would be after lunch. Please excuse me."

After he left the room, I heard him walk to the front door and greet his visitor. A few moments later, the door closed again, and as Dr. Graf headed back to his office, the Nokia buzzed in my pocket.

I jumped up as Dr. Graf entered the room, and words shot from my mouth like a tsunami. "I—I'm late for another meeting."

"That's fine, I—"

"Please charge my card as usual," I said, catching a glimpse of Dr. Graf's raised eyebrows as I grabbed my bag before bolting out of his office, throwing another apology over my shoulder.

Once I reached the front step and slammed the door behind me, I grabbed the Nokia, stabbing at the buttons, trying to answer the call. Too late. The screen had already gone dark.

"Shit," I yelled, tilting my head skyward. *"Shit."*

When the phone lit up again, I could barely whisper, "H-hello?"

"You're incapable of following simple instructions," Anwir barked. "You obviously don't care about what happens to the information I have regarding Max, or Kenji. So be it."

"Wait," I said as I hurried to my car, climbing inside as fast as I could. "Please, wait. I'm sorry I couldn't answer. I—"

"I warned you about repercussions." Anwir spoke softly now, the audible smile in his voice making him more threatening. "Now you'll both learn what they are."

CHAPTER 27

STELLA

"Poor Kenji." Anwir almost sounded apologetic. "He won't appreciate what's coming next."

"Leave him alone," I shouted. "He hasn't done anything wrong."

He tutted. "But you did. I've given you a free pass already, Stella. Twice. I can't have you thinking I don't keep my word."

"Give me another chance," I said, knowing how weak and pathetic I sounded. I couldn't help it. I *was* weak and pathetic, and Anwir knew it.

"Kenji has a finite amount of resources to get him through this situation until you find him." Anwir chuckled. "*If* you find him. However, your incompetence has cost him a day's worth of his supplies. Do you know how long it takes someone to die from dehydration?"

"Don't punish him for my mistake," I said quickly. "What if—"

"The jury's out. Some say three days. Others claim it's anywhere up to nine. Let's split the difference and say a week. That's about how long he's got right now. Do you think you'll find him in time, Stella?"

"You don't have to do this," I said. "Please."

"The thing is . . . I want to." Anwir let out a sigh. "Perhaps you can redeem yourself. Let's play a game. I might even give you another real, tangible reward if you win. A clue."

I waited for him to continue, wondering what he'd say next, and what I'd do. I'd never felt so alone.

"I call this *Guess Who: Serial Killer Edition*," Anwir said, his jovial tone returning. "Here's how it works. I give you three clues. You name the killer. Simple enough. Any questions?"

"Why are you hurting him?" I said, tears burning my eyes. I swiped at them with the back of my hand. "Kenji's a human being. A person. A *good* person. He doesn't deserve to be treated this way."

"*Good* is such a peculiar concept," Anwir said. "It all depends on perspective."

"He's a great kid. He hasn't hurt—"

"Hasn't he?" Anwir cut in. "It's as I said, *perspective*. I'm not sure the people whose cars he stole or the families of those he and his friends sell drugs to would agree with your assessment. They're probably happy he's gone. Frankly, they might be *un*happy if he returns."

"It's not his fault," I said quickly. "Kenji had a really difficult time after Max disappeared. It messed him up. Badly."

"Do you believe that triggered his behavior?" Anwir's voice sounded surprisingly gentle, and it was all the encouragement I needed to keep going.

"Yes," I said. "He lost his way. Most of us do at some point in our lives. The important thing is to get back on track." I took a quick breath, rushing on before Anwir could cut me off again. "You may have helped him," I added, trying not to clench my teeth as I tried the flattery route. "Maybe if you let him go, he'll get his act together and sort out his life."

"You truly think there's a chance of that?"

"I do. Everybody can redeem themselves. Everyone deserves a second chance."

"Including me?" Anwir asked. "Do you think I do, too, after what I've done?"

I pushed my hatred away, relaxed my tone as much as I could. "Yes. Definitely. Like I said, everyone deserves a second chance."

As the lie tumbled from my mouth, I wished Dr. Graf were here to help me say the right things. I needed more insight into Anwir's personality, and in figuring out his background. A tiny misstep on his side might offer a detail to help me discover his identity, meaning I could discreetly alert Hadad and have the authorities take Anwir down. Except I'd no doubt lose whatever information Anwir had about Max. He'd never tell if I went against his rules.

Mind speeding up, I imagined emailing, texting, or writing a letter to the detective, asking her to converse with me only in writing. Would that work? What if she told her colleagues or demanded to see me? We could meet at a neutral location, and I'd stuff the Nokia deep into my bag, ensuring any conversations would be muffled, but it was risky, especially if Anwir was following me. It might be worth the gamble if we found Kenji alive, but I couldn't guarantee it.

Another thought hit me. Anwir was stealthy. Tech-savvy. He'd known I was at the police station. Sure, he'd said there was spyware on the Nokia, and I believed him, but what if it was more? What if he'd been watching me from *inside* the building? What if Anwir was a *cop*?

My shoulders slumped. No. I needed more to go on before I alerted Hadad in case Anwir was in law enforcement and had access to her files. I had to assume he had eyes on Hadad as she was the lead investigator. Involving her in any way was too dangerous.

"Maybe it's not too late for you to sort out your life, Anwir," I said, digging deep for all the fake compassion I could find. "Let me help. You need to unburden yourself from whatever trauma has happened in your past."

"It's not possible," he said, surprising me when his voice wobbled on the last two words. "There's no way back from this, Stella. No way back for me at all."

"Yes, there is," I said, grabbing hold of the emotional wave he was riding, determined to turn things to my advantage. "There are specialists you can speak to. Lots of different programs you could try, and—"

"No." He suppressed what sounded like a sob. "They'll lock me up forever. My mother, my father, my siblings. They'll know what I've done. How could they ever understand who I've become? They'll disown me. I'll go to prison. My entire life will be over."

"Please, Anwir, let Kenji go," I whispered. "Warn him to never, ever tell anyone about you or you'll find him again. It'll work. I'm sure it will."

"I don't think—"

"*Please*. I'll destroy this phone. I don't know who you are, and I promise I'll never try to find you."

"You'd do that?" he whispered.

"Yes," I lied again, thinking back to what Dr. Graf had said. Anwir's actions could be power-related. "You're the one in control. You can decide to end this now by letting Kenji go. You're the only person who can give me and my family the closure we need by sharing the information you have about Max. Anwir . . . by helping us, you can help yourself. Doesn't that sound good?"

Another sob, not muffled this time. "Yes. Yes, it does."

"Let Kenji walk away and tell me what happened to my brother." Hoping it would give him another ego boost, I tried not to clench my teeth as I added, "I'm *begging* you."

"Okay." Anwir exhaled a stream of shaky breath. "The night Max disappeared, I . . . I . . ." He trailed off, and I could barely stop myself from screaming at him to tell me or I'd find out who he was, where he lived, and come for him in his sleep.

When he let out another sob, I didn't move as I waited for him to continue, gasping suddenly when he laughed. Cold. Hard. Condescending. A sound hacking deeper into my soul than I ever thought possible.

"I had you going there, didn't I?" he said.

"Anwir, I—"

"Jeez, I loved drama club in high school. You should've seen our production of *Oliver Twist*. Thanks for the trip down memory lane. Nice try with the armchair psychology routine. Dr. Graf would be proud." He chuckled again. "Okay, we've had our fun. Let me be clear—you're wasting your time trying to get into my head. Now, let's play."

CHAPTER 28

STELLA

"Round one, clue one," Anwir said.

"Stop," I shouted. "You said I could ask questions."

"Oh, Stella. You already did. More specifically, you said, *why are you hurting him*."

"You didn't reply."

"I'm hurting him because I want to. And because I can. Simple as that." Anwir's delivery was so frigid, devoid of emotion, this time I knew he was telling the truth, which made him even more terrifying. "Back to the game. Don't forget, if you get this right, there's a potential reward at the end. Get it wrong . . . and Kenji will be more miserable."

"But—"

"Here we go. Once a gravedigger, I also worked at a morgue, and as a truck driver." He waited for my response, but I stayed quiet. It wasn't enough to go on. "Come on, Stella, it's a huge clue. You've got nothing? Here's the next one. Fake license plates, screwdrivers, a hammer, and a knife were part of my downfall."

My mind was a jumble of thoughts competing for attention, all of them worthless. A serial killer who'd been a gravedigger and was arrested because of tools? A name flitted out from the depths of my memory, but as panic set in, I couldn't grab hold of it fast enough.

Anwir clicked his tongue. "Also known as Peter Coonan—"

"The Yorkshire Ripper," I said as fast as I could.

"Also known as . . . ?"

"Peter William Sutcliffe. He killed over a dozen women in the UK in the '70s and '80s."

"Well done," Anwir said. "See? That wasn't hard. Don't get comfortable, because it was the easiest one. Here's the first clue for round two. One of my favorite childhood hobbies was devouring my mother's romance novels."

"The Giggling Granny," I replied, heart thumping. I knew I was right. I'd recently read about the woman who wiped out most of her family with arsenic—including four of her husbands—allegedly in her quest to find true love. "Also known as Nannie Doss or the Lonely Hearts Killer."

"Color me impressed," Anwir said. "Your podcast obviously serves you well. Get ready for round three . . . They don't have a name for what I am."

"Was that a clue?"

"As ambiguous as it might seem, yes," he said evenly, almost sounding like a game show host. "Here's another. Someone called me the Robin Hood of killers."

My mind raced to connect the dots. I closed my eyes, searching for anyone who might resemble the description, but came up empty. When Anwir sighed with impatience, I wanted to snap that I needed more information, but instead I bit my tongue so hard, I tasted blood.

"Don't give up," he chastised. "How about this? I helped the FBI catch a killer."

I imagined the smirk on his face as he waited for my reply. I knew of several murderers who'd helped the authorities after they'd been caught, but it would be too precarious for Kenji if I named the wrong one.

"Tell you what," Anwir said, "I'll be generous. Take another ten seconds. Hazard a guess. It's better to try and fail than to capitulate. Time's up in five . . . four . . . three . . . two—"

"Edmund Kemper. He helped the authorities profile serial killers."

"True, but you didn't think your answer through," Anwir said, and my heart sank. "Why would someone who killed his grandparents and his mother, his mother's neighbor, and six female students be referred to as Robin Hood? Disappointing answer, Stella."

"Ted Bundy," I rushed on, immediately realizing it couldn't be him, either.

"The answer was Hannibal Lecter."

"From *The Silence of the Lambs*? He's not real."

"I never specified any of them had to be," Anwir said. "You could've used your free question at the beginning to clarify, but you wasted the opportunity."

"Let's do another round," I said. "Now I understand your rules, I'll—"

"No, I don't think so."

"Come on, Anwir," I said, fist balled. "You're obviously enjoying yourself."

"If I agree, what will you give me in return?"

"What do you want?"

"I want you to tell me a secret," Anwir said.

"A secret?"

"About yourself."

Like Hannibal Lecter and Clarice Starling. I kept the thought to myself and went with, "My mother blames me for Max's disappearance, but I know she'll never hate me as much as I hate myself."

"Pfft, it's hardly a secret," Anwir said. "You alluded to it during your first podcast episode. What else? I want something you've never told anyone."

"I don't know—"

"Make it a personal tidbit I can savor. A detail you feel guilty about and bury deep, but can't pretend isn't there. Tell me what hurts."

"I'm terrified of becoming a mother," I said.

Anwir let out a massive and obviously pretend yawn. "Yes, yes, you blame yourself for Max's disappearance, and you can't imagine having a child. Boring and predictable, and you already told Dr. Graf. Dig deeper."

"I—I always thought Mom favored Max over me," I whispered, and when I blinked, tears ran down my cheeks. I'd never told anyone this. Not even Jeff.

"Why?"

"Her brother, Bennett, got run over when he was seventeen," I replied, my voice so quiet I wondered if Anwir could hear me. "She was nine. I don't think she ever truly recovered."

"How tragic. But why would she favor Max over you because of Bennett?"

"I . . . I think Max reminded her of him."

"How did it feel, knowing you were second-best?" Anwir pressed, voice gentle.

"When I was little . . ." I stopped, didn't want to share this with my tormentor.

"Go on," he urged. "Tell me, and don't lie, because I'll know."

"When I was little," I said again, quietly, "I sometimes wished my brother would disappear so there would be space in her heart for me."

"Ah," Anwir said. "You think it became a self-fulfilling prophecy. Except Max vanishing had the opposite effect. Your mom shut you out more because you took him to the beach party."

"Yes," I whispered. "Ever since that night, I wish I could trade places with Max. I wish *I* could disappear, so I don't see how much destruction I've caused." I shuddered, unable to believe I'd shared such a personal thing. "There. Now you know a secret

I've never told anyone. Not my husband or my parents. Give me what you promised. Where's Kenji? How can I find him?"

"Are you afraid of me, Stella?" Anwir asked, but I stayed silent, my chest heaving as I tried to get myself back under control. "No need to answer. I can hear it. Underneath all your anger and desperation lies what I enjoy more than begging. *Fear.* Yours is so thick I can taste it." He took what sounded like a deeply satisfied breath. "Rusty truck nail."

"What?"

"I won't hurt Kenji, for now. Rusty truck nail is the other reward. It's your clue."

"A rusty truck nail? What do you mean? Is this something about Kenji, or Max? Give me more context. I need—"

"You *need* to *think*. Do your research. Goodbye, Stella. Good luck."

As Anwir disconnected the call, I let out a frustrated howl, slamming my palms on the steering wheel until they stung. When I looked out of the window, I saw a dog walker hugging the hedge as she passed the car, clearly freaked out.

Being observed didn't stop the rage sweeping through my body. I couldn't believe I'd trusted Anwir—AL, a liar—to give me anything useful. This was all part of his perverse game, his way of tormenting me.

Rusty truck nail.

What, if anything, did it mean?

CHAPTER 29

STELLA

As I sat in my car, trying to find my way out of the thick swirling fog muddling my brain, I realized *rusty truck nail* might not have been the only thing Anwir had given me. He'd talked about his parents and siblings in the present tense, saying they'd be disappointed if they learned the truth about what he'd done. He'd also mentioned his love for drama club in high school, and a production of *Oliver Twist*.

What if it hadn't all been lies but was partially anchored in truth? It wasn't much, and I couldn't be certain of anything, but it was a little more than I'd had before the call. If I could stay calm next time and keep him talking, maybe he'd slip up properly. As I started the car, my desperation gave way to determination.

Rusty truck nail.

I didn't know how, but it had to be important. It *had* to.

Easing out of the parking spot, I glanced at the time. It wasn't even noon, but I was exhausted. I wanted to go home, curl up in bed with the duvet pulled over my ears, and pretend none of this was happening. Except I didn't want to be home alone again. Not now.

No. I couldn't hide. I had work to do.

The hunt was on.

After pulling back over to the side of the road, I grabbed my iPhone and sent Jeff a text, saying I was going to the library for podcast research, and not to worry if I wasn't home when he got back. I was about to head off again when my iPhone lit up with an incoming call from Vivien. Grateful she hadn't used FaceTime, meaning she wouldn't see me, I answered after the third ring.

"Hey, how are you?" I hoped I hadn't injected too much fake enthusiasm into my voice. While I hadn't forgotten about seeing Vivien with Booker on Poppy's security footage, it paled in comparison to everything else. I could only deal with one problem at a time. "How's Syracuse?"

"Oh, the usual drama with my baby sisters," Vivien said. "We haven't killed each other yet, but there's ample time. How are you? I missed your voice, so I thought I'd call."

"I'm fine."

"You sure? You sound stressed."

"No, no. Everything's fine."

"Okay . . . Hey, I listened to our upcoming episodes and did a few minor tweaks. I think these might be our best shows yet. The Doyle case is particularly compelling. Our audience will love it. Your interview with the forensics consultant is amazing."

"Thanks," I replied. "Talikha's a great source."

"Yes, she is. Before I forget, did you read the newest suggestion from *People of Portland*?"

"No, I, uh, must've missed it."

"It's a Canadian case, and super odd. Get this. A woman from a rural town in New Brunswick left her house one night. Poof. Vanished into thin air. Five years later, her cousin is on business in Toronto when he spots her walking down the street."

"Wow, what a coincidence."

"That's not all. He asks where she's been, so she takes him to a coffee shop, saying she'll explain everything. Next thing he knows, she disappears out the back door after pretending to go to the bathroom. Poof. Gone again."

"She vanished a second time?"

"Yup. Three years ago. Not a trace since. I think this could be the one. We haven't explored a Canadian case yet, and we can easily drive to Saint John to meet the cousin and spend a few days there. Apparently, his best friend is a cop, and—"

"Maybe," I said, my gut feeling telling me the case missed the mark. "Let's talk about it when you get back next week."

"Stella, what if this guy pitches the idea to another show? We should grab it."

"If you want to speak to him and do some of our usual preliminary research, then fine," I said quickly. "Just remember some people don't want to be found."

"Yeah, but if we track her down, the ratings could—"

"Look into it, okay? I . . . I have a few other things to take care of. Advertising and fund-raising are still my priority."

"Which this is part of," Vivien said evenly. "When we pick the winner of our competition, Charlene and the TV producer will post an announcement on socials. If we lock in this case, I bet Booker will be happy."

"I thought you'd put her off. Told her the three of us would speak sometime."

"Yeah, but she won't hang around forever. We've got to keep her on the hook."

I pressed a hand over my eyes. "We'll talk about Booker when you get back."

"Are you sure everything's okay?" Vivien asked. "You and Jeff all right?"

Seizing the opportunity to throw her off, I lowered my voice. "Things didn't work out for us again this month."

"Oh, that sucks."

"We'll get through it." I had to work hard to swallow the lump of lies in my throat. "Anyway, I really must get going. Enjoy the time with your family."

After we hung up, I sat in the car, wishing I had the courage to tell Vivien the truth. I needed help figuring out who Anwir was and what he meant by his cryptic *rusty truck nail* clue. She would've been the perfect partner, but Anwir would hear. He'd punish Kenji for my transgression and enjoy it. How was my brother's best friend coping? How badly had he already been hurt? Was he dying of thirst right now?

I tried to detach myself from the situation as if I were working a cold case for *A Killer Motive*. The first thing I typically did was list the random bits of knowledge and information I had to see if any of it could be connected. Perhaps if I could be analytical about the situation, I'd gain perspective, make things clearer.

Filled with trepidation and a sense of renewed urgency, I drove into the city, dumped my car, and headed into the Portland Public Library. Once settled at a table away from the other patrons, I pulled out my laptop, notebook, and pen.

I spent the next two hours obsessing over the words Anwir had given me, scouring newspaper headlines and articles, losing count of the number of searches I ran. *Rusty truck nail* became my nemesis, and the more I dug, the more I could hear Anwir mocking me.

There was a cold case from the early '80s involving a Rusty Nail pub. Next came a murderous trucker character nicknamed Rusty Nail in the *Joy Ride* movie series. Did either of those mean anything? Perhaps Anwir was telling me he worked in a pub or owned a semi. Maybe the message was he loved booze and driving. Or it meant nothing at all.

Staring defeat straight in the face, I refused to give up, turning to acronym and anagram solvers next. After searching through relevant word games, still nothing made sense. At one point I looked up high school productions of *Oliver Twist*, hoping Anwir hadn't fed me a lie and something would magically jump out at me. Without anything else such as a place or a year to narrow it down, it was useless.

You need to think.

Anwir's words flashed through my mind, and I balled my fists. I *was* thinking, damn it. I was thinking so hard the screen had become a blur. My stomach growled, reminding me I'd barely eaten since this morning, and it was already after lunch.

I wasn't sure I could keep anything down, but I needed sustenance to avoid fainting in the middle of the library, and to continue with my search. Reluctantly, I got up, forcing myself to stretch my legs and clear my thoughts before I buckled down for another round.

After collecting my things, I headed across the street to a deli. As I stood at the counter clutching an egg salad sandwich and a bottle of water, my eyes dropped to the wicker basket of protein bars. When I saw the image of the rock climber on the wrapper, a story I'd read a few weeks ago tugged at the back of my mind.

Last fall, a pair of amateur, underequipped climbers had lost their way in the mountains. As nightfall approached and temperatures plummeted, one of them slipped and broke an ankle. Not much later, a torrential storm rolled in, unleashing the mother of all downpours, accompanied by thunder, lightning, and pebble-size hail.

Faced with extreme weather, injury, and a lack of food, warmth, and shelter, they'd contacted emergency services and provided their exact location by using an app called what3words. Two hours later, they were rescued.

I'd never heard of the app before. Thought it was genius how the creators had overlaid the entire world with a nine-by-nine-foot virtual grid. They'd assigned each square a unique code far easier to remember than GPS coordinates because it contained only a combination of different words.

Three words.

Words like rusty truck nail.

"Did you find everything okay today?" a woman with a sparkly butterfly hairclip asked.

My mind had sped up so fast, I couldn't get any words out. In lieu of an answer, I thrust a bill into her hands. Running from the store with my sandwich, water, and iPhone clutched in my hands, I ignored her calls of "What about your change? You gave me a fifty."

Once outside, I darted to the steps of a nearby building and sank down as I googled *what3words*. I clicked on the link, typed in *rusty truck nail*, and hit Enter, zooming in on a tiny square located at Bradley Hills State Park.

I knew this place, had hiked there with my parents and Max when we were kids, and years later with Jeff. Bradley Hills was half an hour away.

Maybe Anwir had finally given me a real clue, after all.

CHAPTER 30

STELLA

Bradley Hills was possibly the first tangible lead Anwir had provided. I couldn't ignore it, but going to a remote location alone wasn't smart. On the other hand, there was no way I could alert the cops. It would mean telling them everything. Anwir would know I was scheming if I hid the phone and he couldn't hear. And if he followed me and saw me with Hadad . . .

Even if I met the detective and showed her the Nokia, I didn't think I'd bust through her near impenetrable levels of skepticism. Anwir used Whisperz, the app that made messages vanish, and he only called from an unknown number. He never left voicemails.

If Hadad wanted her tech team to examine the burner, I'd have to give it up. Then what? Both Kenji and I would be screwed. Also, I still had no idea if Anwir was a cop, or at least cop-adjacent.

My heart pounded as I thought about the very real risk of meeting Anwir face-to-face at Bradley Hills. I debated my choices, each time coming back to the conclusion there was only one option: I had to go. However, I needed a weapon to defend myself.

Thankfully, by the time I got home, the driveway was still empty. I raced to our bedroom and swiftly changed into running shorts. Turned out none of my moisture-wicking shirts had a front pocket—not that I thought Anwir would've even considered this for a nanosecond—so I slipped into one of Jeff's before grabbing my hiking boots from the closet.

Back on the main floor, I filled a large water bottle at the kitchen sink and stuffed it into a backpack along with a light jacket. As I turned, my gaze landed on the knife block near the counter. Three steps later, I had an eight-inch chef's knife in my hand.

While wrapping it in a dish towel, I hoped taking the knife would be a precautionary measure. As much as I wanted to believe I could protect myself against an assailant, it was impossible to know how I'd respond if I were attacked.

Should Anwir come at me, I might freeze and cower, no matter how much I wanted to fight and win. I had no clue how old, strong, or agile Anwir was. If he had black belts in multiple martial arts, or if he'd be waiting for me with a gun. There wasn't time for debate. Worried Jeff would return, I dashed outside, got in my car, and headed north.

Nerves swarmed my stomach as I drove past Gorham. By the time I reached Standish, I wanted to throw up and turn the car around. I forced myself to keep driving. Ten miles later, I pulled into the empty Bradley Hills parking lot.

This lesser-known park offered a variety of scenic trails for walking, mountain biking, and cross-country skiing in the winter. The small lake attracted kayakers and stand-up paddleboarders but was rarely busy. In fact, the park's welcome hut wasn't manned. I was completely and utterly alone. The thought terrified me.

Climbing out of the car, I grabbed my supplies and opened what3words on my iPhone, trying to get my bearings. The square marked *rusty truck nail* was a mile and a half away, about fifty yards off the path. I turned my head left and right, spinning in a circle as I tried to determine if I was being watched. There was no movement save for the leaves on the trees gently swaying in the wind.

Gulping in more air to calm my nerves, I headed off. Walking in the woods alone had never bothered me, but now every few steps, I whipped around, trying to catch Anwir stalking me like a mountain lion. The sun sat high in the sky, and despite the foliage offering shade as I walked up the trail, sweat trickled down my back, seeping into my shorts.

I'd forgotten how steep the incline at Bradley Hills was. This trail led up to and around the little lake, and one of the highlights if you kept going was the view from the top of the cliffs. Maybe Anwir's plan was to lure me there and push me off.

No, I couldn't think this way. It was possible I was in completely the wrong place, or Anwir's so-called clue was nothing but a farce. He could well be tracking my every move from the comfort of his living room, highly amused by my wild-goose chase.

Another twenty minutes and I veered off the trail and into the denser part of the forest. My pace slowed as I scrambled over fallen trees and low bushes, prickly twigs and thorns scraping my bare calves.

Finally, as I approached my destination, I saw I was nearing the bottom of the sheer cliffs. The app told me to continue another thirty yards, which made no sense. Was I supposed to climb? I didn't have the equipment or the expertise.

As I inched forward, the trees cleared a little, and at the bottom of the rocky face, I saw a faded green metal door, and vaguely recalled that Bradley Hills had an abandoned silver mine from the 1800s. Although I expected the door to be locked, when I looked closer, I noticed a broken steel chain on the ground.

Maybe this was one of the old entrances to the mine. Whatever I was searching for could be inside, yards away. Ignoring my shaking hands, I took out the chef's knife and unwrapped it as my mind bellowed this was a trap. I grabbed the door handle and heaved.

The noise of screeching metal made me jump. I retreated a few steps, wielding the knife in front of me as I listened for noises inside. Nothing but still air. Creeping through the doorway, I switched on my iPhone's flashlight and took one step, and then another, continually glancing over my shoulder.

The mine smelled damp and musty, as if this was the first time in decades anyone had been inside. Shiny green moss covered the stony walls, and I shuddered when a giant centipede darted across the ground in front of me and slithered behind a rock.

I didn't think my heart could withstand the stress of venturing deeper into the mine. As I was about to talk myself into turning around because clearly this was the wrong location, my feet hit something solid. I stumbled. Before I could steady myself, I lost my balance and landed on the ground, my iPhone and knife skittering out of reach.

On my hands and knees, I fumbled for my cell and the weapon. As soon as my fingers closed around them, I jumped up and shone my flashlight on whatever I'd fallen over. A plain black sports bag sat on the ground. It looked brand-new. Barely a speck of dust.

With my heart pounding harder and blood thundering in my ears, I undid the zipper and spotted another object inside. It was about a foot long and wrapped in a plain white plastic bag. Exhaling all the air left in my lungs, I gently lifted out the white bag, opened it, and shone the light inside.

As my piercing scream echoed around the mine, I dropped the bag and the knife, barely managing to hold on to my iPhone. It had been unmistakable. The lower part of an arm. A *severed* arm. Cut an inch below the elbow and vacuum-sealed in a transparent plastic bag.

I turned and ran, trying not to go flying a second time as I burst out of the door and fled to the trail, leaving *whoever* that was behind. A dozen steps later, the Nokia buzzed.

I didn't want to answer. Didn't want to talk to the man torturing me this way. But what was the alternative? Ignore him and let Kenji pay the price? Never find out if Anwir had either hurt my brother or acquired details about who had? I couldn't stop now, and I had no doubt Anwir knew exactly how much power he held over me. I hated him for it.

Slowing my pace, I grabbed the phone and answered the call, shouting, "What did you do? I swear, if you hurt Kenji or my brother, I'm going to kill you. I'll—"

"Calm yourself," Anwir said. "After solving my puzzle, you should be proud."

Unable to hold back the tears, I sobbed, trying four times before I stuttered, "Wh-whose a-arm is it?"

"I can't tell you. Well, I could, but I won't."

"Is it Max? Kenji? Did you kill them? Tell me what you did."

"No," Anwir said. "Our fun would be over, Stella. Wouldn't you be sad?"

"I'm calling the cops—"

"I expect nothing less," he replied, sounding amused. "However, you'll keep the details of our conversations to yourself."

"I *won't*."

"You *will*. Everybody knows a person can live without an arm. Without a head, on the other hand . . ." He let out a chuckle. "I look forward to talking soon, Stella. Congratulations again. Keep the phone close."

After he hung up, I collapsed on the ground next to a hollowed-out tree stump. As my shoulders heaved, I knew calling Hadad was the only choice, but I had to be careful now that I understood with absolute certainty how dangerous Anwir was. He'd hurt someone. Cut off their arm.

The question was, whose? I had to find out if it was Max.

As I thought of a plausible cover story to give the cops about how I'd discovered the remains, I realized I'd left the chef's knife inside the mine. I couldn't leave it. Hadad would ask what the hell I was doing carrying it around. I doubted I'd come up with a believable enough reason she wouldn't see straight through.

Trying not to cry again, I slowly went back inside. When

I saw the white plastic bag, a small piece of me ached to remove the body part so I could try to determine if it was Max's. I couldn't. I was too afraid.

Once I'd located the knife, I wrapped it in the dish towel and put it in my backpack before changing my mind. Hadad might want to search my belongings, maybe my car, and if I told her she needed a warrant, an array of alarm bells would go off in her head. I didn't need the detective looking at me or my whereabouts in more detail.

When I reached the hollowed-out tree stump again, I decided to bury the knife there, hoping Jeff wouldn't notice it was missing before I had a chance to replace it. After digging a large enough hole, dropping the knife inside, and patting the earth back into place, I covered it with twigs and leaves. Once done, I pulled out my iPhone.

"Detective Hadad," I said when she answered. "It's Stella Dixon. I need your help."

SATURDAY, AUGUST 2

CHAPTER 31

You've already impressed me beyond my wildest dreams. When you so easily solved the first two rounds of Guess Who, *I had to throw you a curveball with the Hannibal Lecter reference. A little unfair, perhaps. But as they say, life is unfair.*

I love how you're a quick thinker. The various monikers were no trouble for you at all. It made me wonder what name you'd give me, if you knew about all the things I've done. Maybe we'll come up with one together. I'd like that. It'll be another game we can play.

You're smarter than all the others, by a mile. I didn't think you'd solve the rusty truck nail puzzle. I figured you'd need an almighty shove in the Bradley Hills direction, and I'd have to lead you by the tippy tip of your nose.

You proved me wrong, which I don't mind in this instance. It only serves to confirm my decision to choose you now was a thousand percent correct.

But for what's to come, Stella, you're not prepared. At all. It will be fascinating to watch you deal with the next act. If you knew what I've unleashed, you'd brace yourself, although there's nothing you can do to avoid what's about to happen. The things you're about to learn.

Will these things hurt you? Definitely.

Break you? I can't wait to see.

CHAPTER 32

STELLA

"You're sure about this, Stella?" Jeff put on the turn signal, his jaw set, expression filled with concern. His disquiet hadn't eased since we'd been at the house. It was probably why he'd gently taken my car keys from me and insisted he drive. "We don't have to go after what you went through yesterday. We can still cancel. Your parents will understand."

"No, I'll be okay." I gave him a determined nod. "I need to take my mind off things. Plus, it's for Dad's birthday."

Jeff looked like he was about to argue but must've thought better of it as he silently turned into the parking lot of Julia's Italian Eatery. This was my father's favorite restaurant ever since he'd discovered the place a decade ago. While it was a bit of a drive to the outskirts of Falmouth, the homemade soft-as-pillows gnocchi and deliciously tender meatballs were worth every mile.

Today, though, I wasn't hungry. The image of the neatly wrapped arm I'd found was permanently imprinted into my memory. I could still see the torn flesh, the gray, pallid skin. Feel the panic shooting up my throat as I'd turned and bolted for the mine's exit.

When I noticed Jeff had eased my car into a parking space, cut the engine, and was observing me intently, I tried a smile. It felt entirely wrong and grimace-like, as if I was wearing a scary

Halloween mask. Hoping he hadn't noticed, I said, "Please don't mention what happened yesterday."

"Stella—"

"Not today. Like I said, we're here to celebrate Dad's birthday. I'll share everything with them later."

"Fine, fine," Jeff said. "I still don't understand what you were doing at Bradley Hills though. Or why you went without telling me. What if something had happened to you?"

"It *did*," I said. "I handled it. Also, I told you why. Sometimes there's nothing like a walk in the forest to find inspiration for my work."

This was the story I'd told Hadad when she'd arrived. I'd kept it as simple and thus hopefully as believable as possible, saying I'd wanted fresh air to think about the podcast and had gone for a hike. When I'd needed to relieve myself, I'd veered off the path and seen the door to the mine was open, and curiosity had taken over.

"You went that far off the path to pee?" Hadad asked, one eyebrow raised with what I'd come to understand was her usual dubious expression.

"Not exactly. I got a little turned around before coming across the mine."

"You're saying finding the bag was coincidence?"

"A lucky one, if you ask me," I'd replied with such sincerity, I wanted to congratulate myself. "Who knows how long it might've been before it was discovered otherwise."

Hadad had called in the forensics team but hadn't asked to search my car. At one point she'd sat on a rock near the hollowed-out tree stump as we'd waited for her colleagues. I'd crossed my fingers, hoping I'd hidden the chef's knife well enough.

While there was no forensic evidence linking me to the severed arm, having a weapon here would've been enough to raise a whole load more questions. Ones I had no intention of answering.

"I looked into the email you sent me," Hadad said. Part of me hoped it had proved to be useful in finding Anwir, while another part worried. No doubt the prick was listening to our conversation. "The tech team hasn't had any luck tracing it."

"Oh."

"I'll give it a try as well. I have a couple of other contacts I can reach out to."

"I see. Well . . . okay."

Hadad glanced at me. "Problem?"

"Not at all," I said quickly. "I'm hoping you find the sender, but I expect you were right. It was probably some random person getting their kicks messing with me before they moved on."

"Hmm . . ." Hadad had said, still looking at me.

I'd dropped my gaze, worried what Anwir would make of Hadad's intentions of doing more digging. Why was he suddenly comfortable with me contacting the police, providing I didn't mention his name? What was he playing at? I shifted my face into what I hoped was a neutral expression as Hadad continued staring at me.

Her apparent distrust of me hadn't sat well, but I had other problems to focus on. On my way home, I'd bought an identical chef's knife to replace the one now hidden in the forest.

At home, I'd fed my husband the same lies I'd served Hadad. Although I'd tried reassuring Jeff the ordeal hadn't been a *big* deal, he'd become frustrated, borderline angry at the entire situation.

"You should've called me," Jeff had said. "You don't always have to handle things on your own. Stop shutting me out, Stella. Asking for help doesn't make you weak."

"I called the police," I said, wondering how and when I'd become so good at hiding the truth from him. "There wasn't anything you could've done."

"Except be there for you." He'd thrown his arms into the air. "Why won't you let me, huh?"

Exhausted, I'd gone to bed early but had been too wound up to rest. When Jeff had come upstairs, I'd pretended to sleep, not wanting to get into things again.

Now, as we sat in the parking lot in front of Julia's, I wasn't sure I could keep my poker face intact for the duration of the meal, let alone afterward. Jeff had the day off, wanted us to spend the afternoon together. No doubt to keep a vigilant eye on me.

I couldn't blame him, and yearned for the simplicity of a day where we could simply hang out in the backyard with a few beers, enjoying each other's company. Except there was so much I couldn't tell him. A few days ago, my biggest worry was his reaction if I confessed to still taking birth control pills and how I was considering an IUD. I wished those were my only secrets now.

It was unimaginable what my husband would do if I told him I'd been talking to a man who likely abducted Kenji, potentially hurt my brother, and lured me to the mine at Bradley Hills, where he'd left human remains for me to find. Jeff would frog-march me to Dr. Graf's office in a straitjacket. I wouldn't blame him if he did.

As I'd lain in bed last night, feeling increasingly isolated, I'd fretted about whose arm I'd found. How long would it take the cops to work it out? The more I thought about what Anwir had done to another human, the more overwhelmed I'd become. That soon gave way to fury at my helplessness. Yes, I was alone, but also pitiful. Weak. Pathetic. Exactly what Anwir wanted.

But why? And what if he hadn't hurt Max or didn't possess a shred of knowledge about his case? Could all this be to punish me for something instead? Was it all somehow related to one of the cold cases I'd worked on? Someone who'd become pissed off at my endless questions and digging? Maybe they were worried I'd expose them, and they wanted to shift my focus. But what about Vivien? She worked on the show as much as I did. Where did she fit in?

"Stella," Jeff said, pulling me out of my head. "You good? You spaced out, and—"

"All good, I swear." I reached for the door handle. "Let's get inside."

Julia's was a quaint bistro with chunky oak tables and surprisingly comfortable rattan chairs. The host greeted Jeff and me before leading us to the back, where my parents already sat.

Dad wore an immaculately pressed pale green button-down shirt, and Mom had chosen a daisy-print maxi dress. A few years ago, she'd decided to stop dyeing her hair, and her shoulder-length silver curls looked sophisticated as they sparkled under the soft teardrop pendant lights.

Mom might have been a few years shy of sixty, but from a distance, she could've passed for a decade younger. It was only when you got close and saw the sadness in her eyes that you might suspect this was someone living a nightmare. Except much worse considering she might never wake up from it. It was another reason to keep engaging with Anwir. If I got information about Max, perhaps I could give my parents the closure they so desperately needed.

Dad stood when he saw us, shook Jeff's hand, and clapped him on the back before giving me a bear hug. Mom didn't move from her seat and said a quiet hello as Jeff sat down opposite her, an arrangement he and I had discussed on our drive over.

"Happy birthday, Dad," I said, handing him a gift-wrapped bottle of his favorite Canadian rye and a large box of dark chocolate truffles. "Don't eat them all at once."

"Thanks very much. It's good to see you guys," Dad replied, his voice bubbly. He always carried the conversation, meticulously bridging the gap between Mom and me, forever trying to erase any tension. "What's new? How's work? Both busy, as usual, I presume. I'm glad you could take the time off to be here."

"Wouldn't miss it," Jeff replied as the server approached. After she'd filled our water glasses and handed us menus, she listed the specials, which I tried to focus on to stop my mind from wandering back to the mine.

As we perused the food options, the four of us talked about the upcoming football season, the weather, and Jeff's job. Thankfully he stayed quiet about the bottle in a garbage bag versus Achilles tendon incident. So far, so good. I forced myself to relax a little, pulling my shoulders away from my ears as I pretended everything was normal.

All went fine until two middle-aged women in flowy dresses and clickety-clack heels moved from the bar to a table close to ours. Judging by the volume of their voices, the full wineglasses they held weren't their first drinks.

"Did you hear what happened yesterday?" one of them said as they drifted past. "They found a head at Bradley Hills. Can you imagine? A *head*. Who do you think it could be?"

"They'll find out soon enough," the other one replied. "They'll probably use facial recognition software. I saw it on *CSI* once, and . . ."

Moving out of earshot, they continued their conversation, and Mom quietly muttered, "It was an arm. And don't they know *CSI* isn't real? If only every case was solved in no time."

Although I willed it not to, Jeff's gaze landed on the side of my head, practically burning a hole in my temple. "Stella," he whispered, leaning over. "I think you should—"

"No," I replied, my voice terse. "Not now."

"What is it?" Mom asked. "Jeff, do you know something about the arm? Were you called out to Bradley Hills yesterday?"

"It was Stella," he blurted. "She found the arm while hiking."

"*What?*" Dad said. "What happened? How did—"

"*Jeff,*" I snapped, giving him a sharp look. "We weren't going to discuss it."

"I'm sorry." He held up his hands. "I am, but I think your parents deserve to know. Especially since you're not dealing with the trauma of the discovery well, and—"

"I'm *fine*," I said. "I told you, Detective Hadad came as soon as I called."

"Detective who?" Dad asked. "Does he work with Wade?"

Balls.

There were too many lies already, too much to keep track of and plenty to trip myself up with. I had to tell the truth. "Wade retired," I said, looking at Dad, then Mom, taking in how her eyes had already narrowed so much they'd practically disappeared. "Detective Najwa Hadad replaced him. She's looking after Max's case now."

Mom drew in a sharp breath. "When did you find this out?"

"I met her on Wednesday afternoon," I replied, deciding to own up to that fact, too. I was already so far up shit creek, I'd not only lost my paddles, but also the map. How much more harm could throwing myself out of the boat do?

CHAPTER 33

STELLA

As soon as I saw my husband's face, I regretted owning up to visiting the police station on Wednesday afternoon.

"You did *what*?" he said. "Wait, was this after your abandoned lunch with Vivien and Booker? When you were supposed to see Dr. Graf but met Charlene? You never mentioned you were going to the cops."

"Because you would've tried talking me out of it," I said, frustrated by his parental tone.

"What did they say?" he rushed on. "Is there any new information?"

"No. Hadad basically shut me down when I said I thought Kenji's disappearance might be linked to Max's."

"You see a connection?" Mom's voice felt sharper than an ice pick to the throat. "Why didn't you share this with your father and me until now?"

"I . . . I . . ."

"Why do you believe they're linked?" Dad asked gently. "We spoke with Kenji's parents, and they don't think there's a connection. To be honest, neither do we."

"Call it a gut reaction," I said, focusing only on Dad as Jeff stared at me again, his gaze intense. "He and Max were best friends, and then he disappears, too. Anyway . . ." I shrugged, hyperaware of Anwir's instructions to keep my mouth shut. "Hadad told me there's no link. I obviously overreacted."

"It doesn't change the fact we had a right to know the lead detective on your brother's case was replaced," Mom said. "The police not bothering to inform us comes as no surprise, but you not sharing those details? It's classic Stella."

"What's that supposed to mean?" I asked.

"Doing whatever you want, whenever you choose," she replied. "To hell with everybody else or the consequences of your actions."

"Erin." Dad placed a hand over hers as her open barb hit me squarely in the heart, digging deep. I knew she blamed me for Max's disappearance, but this was the first time she'd come so close to saying it out loud. "That's not fair."

"Isn't it?" Mom snapped at him. "I guess it's no surprise you're taking her side."

"I'm not taking sides," he said, his voice measured. My gosh, how I wished I had his capacity for stoicism considering my blood was rocketing from simmer to boil. Dad must've noticed because he turned to me. "Finding those remains had to be terrifying. Are you all right? Do you want to tell us more?"

Mom got up, pushing her chair back so hard, it almost toppled over. "I can't do this," she said. "I won't sit here and discuss this . . . *discovery* over lunch. Howard, I want us to go home. We'll celebrate your birthday another time."

"Mom, please," I said. "Sit. We'll change the topic."

"It's too late," she said, chin raised. "My appetite's ruined, and a headache's coming on. Jeff, it was lovely seeing you. I regret it was brief."

As she turned and strode to the exit, Dad puffed out his cheeks. "Sorry, kiddo," he said. "You understand how she gets whenever there's a morbid discovery in the area. She's always expecting a call from the cops saying it's . . . you know."

"Yes," I whispered. "I know exactly. I lost Max, too."

Dad reached for my hand and gave it a squeeze. "I'll drive her home, but first, are you sure you're okay?"

"Yes. Go. No sense in you suffering her wrath and being turned to stone, too."

My father half smirked, got up, and kissed the top of my head. "We'll speak soon. Jeff, look after Stella for me."

I waited until Dad left the restaurant before turning to my husband. "Why did you tell them about the arm? We agreed we wouldn't bring it up."

"I didn't. Those two women—"

"You shouldn't have added to it," I said, my misdirected anger taking aim at Jeff because he was the only one here. My frustration needed an escape hatch. It had no place else to go. "What you did wasn't fair."

"What *I* did?" He put a hand to his chest. "Hold on, Stella. You went to the cops three days ago and didn't say a word."

"I don't have to tell you *everything*," I said, hearing how petulant it sounded, but the words left my mouth before I could stop them. "You and Vivien were belittling my concerns about Kenji's case being related to Max's. I took them to someone I thought might believe me."

"Except she told you she doesn't see a connection either," Jeff said. When I didn't answer, he added, "And for the record, I wasn't trying to make light of your feelings. Quite the opposite. I'm worried about you. Will you please accept the possibility you're spiraling? I think you have PTSD and—"

"Stop psychoanalyzing me, Jeff," I said, the volume of my voice enough to make the two women turn their heads, drinks poised midair, eyebrows raised, their posture telling me they were hungry for gossip. I tapped the side of my head, and when I spoke again, it was a terse whisper. "I already have one therapist digging around up here, thanks. I don't need you picking up a shovel and having at it."

"What's going on with you?" Jeff tried to put an arm around my shoulder, but I leaned away, trying to stay out of reach. I couldn't handle physical contact. I couldn't handle sympathy. If I tried, it would break me.

"I told you," I replied. "I'm pissed you brought up what happened, and when we're here for Dad's birthday, no less. We haven't properly celebrated in years."

Jeff shook his head. "Bull. I know you. There's more to it. You've been off for weeks, especially lately. You're distant. Preoccupied. You won't let me touch you. You pretend to be asleep when I come to bed, and—"

"There's *nothing* going on," I insisted. "Nothing you don't already know about."

"I don't believe you, Stella," Jeff said. "We always agreed honesty is one of the most important aspects of our relationship. Tell me the truth. Don't shut me out."

I pressed my lips together, willed away the tears. "There's nothing," I whispered. "I haven't got anything else to add."

"Is this about you not getting pregnant?"

"Oh my god, *no*."

"Then what—"

"Stop *pushing* me," I yelled before clamping my lips shut again.

Jeff threw his hands in the air, standing up and pulling my car keys from his pocket before dropping them on the table. "Screw it. I can't handle this right now. I don't know what else to do but give you the space you obviously want. I'll see you later."

"How will you get home?"

"Taxi. Rideshare. Whatever. Who cares?"

My cheeks burned as he stormed out, and I put my head down, blinking hard. When the server came over, I mumbled our lunch plans had been canceled because of an emergency. No way she believed me, but she was gracious and kind, insisting it was no problem before asking if I still wanted to order.

I was about to decline, but hunger pangs changed my mind. After asking for a small portion of their gnocchi and meatballs, I settled into my chair. With a furtive glance left and right, I removed the Nokia from my front pocket and looked at the screen.

No missed calls. No messages. No progress.

I hated this waiting game. Detested the fact I was at Anwir's mercy, anticipating him making a move. Things had to change. Grabbing my iPhone from my bag, I dialed Charlene's number, relieved when I heard her voice.

"Stella," she said. "How are you?"

"Not great, to be honest," I replied. "Been a rough couple of days. Have you found any details on Liam from Augusta?"

"Not a single thing," she replied, sounding as frustrated as I felt. "Believe me, I've searched. Izzy didn't fib. The number was withheld when he called. It's a dead end. I asked a few of my contacts to try, but the name's too common to narrow it down. I'm sorry."

"Me, too."

"Stella?" Charlene said. "What else has happened? Has Liam been in touch again?"

I longed to share what was going on but could only tell her part of what I'd discovered. "Did you see the report about the severed arm at Bradley Hills?"

"Yes. Shocking stuff."

"I found it."

"*What?* How on earth . . . ?"

I gave her the same fictional version of my going for a hike at the state park and heading into the mine, forcing conviction into my voice to make it sound true. "It was horrible. Today isn't much better. I had an argument with my husband and my mother . . ." I stopped, took a breath. "I'm not sure why I told you that."

"Don't worry about it," Charlene said. "We've known each other for years, Stella. We were neighbors. I hate seeing you go through this. Is there anything I can do?"

Find Max and Kenji. Help me hunt down a potential killer. Mend the relationship with my mother. Figure out how I'm going to tell my husband I don't want kids. Maybe ever.

"You don't happen to know a discreet ob-gyn, do you?" I blurted, thinking at least it would solve the issue of my birth control pills, giving me time to focus on the rest.

"Sure, I do," she said. "One of my good friends works for a local family planning clinic. She's awesome. Tell her I referred you."

As Charlene gave me the name and number of her friend, I plugged the details into my phone and thanked her profusely before apologizing again for my sudden and personal outburst.

"You're under a lot of stress, I can tell," she replied. "If you ever want to talk about anything, I'm here."

"Thank you," I whispered. "I'm grateful for your ear and perspective."

"You're welcome," Charlene replied. "Whatever's going on, maybe the answer's simpler than you think. Anyway, we'll speak soon. Don't be a stranger. I'm here whenever you need me."

Once we'd hung up, I drummed my fingers on the table as Charlene's words swirled around me. I wondered if I'd missed an obvious detail about Anwir from the beginning. Whenever I reached an impasse on a cold case I examined, I forced myself to retrace my steps and return to the start. Maybe it was time for me to do exactly that.

This whole ordeal began with Liam from Augusta's phone call to *People of Portland*. Next came the emails from AL, who had finally morphed into Anwir when he'd left the Nokia in the planter box.

It was possible Liam, AL, and Anwir were the same person, but what if Liam was one individual, and AL and Anwir another? If they didn't know each other, Liam couldn't help me locate Anwir. However, there was another scenario—they were complicit and working together.

A flutter close to excitement built in my stomach. So far, we hadn't been able to locate Liam. Didn't even know if it was his real name. But . . . if I tried again and succeeded this time, maybe Liam could lead me to Anwir.

Perhaps I could then secretly follow Anwir to wherever he was holding Kenji. If the cops arrested Anwir, I'd get Hadad to force him to share what he did to or knew about Max. Maybe he could use it to—I shuddered at the thought—negotiate a lesser sentence. Anything was worth a shot. It sure beat my current state of inertia.

As the server brought over my food, I took a few bites before pushing the plate away, too focused on what needed to be done. Neither Izzy nor Charlene had been able to help me find Liam, but I couldn't give up without one final Hail Mary.

The only other person I knew who worked at the radio station was Grayson, the assistant with the octopus nose piercing. Maybe he'd come across Liam from Augusta before, especially if he was the one fielding calls from cranky listeners. Perhaps he knew his real name.

I was good at getting people to recall things they didn't think were relevant, no matter how small a detail. And while I was reaching with all these *perhaps* and *maybe* scenarios, my experience on *A Killer Motive* told me to not give up and to get digging.

I opened the browser on my phone and navigated to the *Team* page on WHMR's website to see if I could find a direct number for Grayson so I could bypass the switchboard. A second later, I recognized a face in one of the profile pictures gazing at me.

Dylan Firth.

CHAPTER 34

STELLA

Dylan Firth. The guy I'd almost run over in the parking lot opposite the police station. Had he been following me? Was *he* Anwir? He could've panicked when he saw me near the cops and tried to stop me from talking to them by causing a fake accident.

It hadn't worked well enough—I guessed he couldn't risk getting severely hurt—so he'd called the burner as soon as I'd gone inside the building. After making threats and giving me a warning, he'd hung around long enough to ensure I capitulated. Except . . . he'd seemed so nice. So . . . *normal.* Appearances could be deceiving.

Had Dylan Firth taken Kenji? Left a severed arm for me at Bradley Hills? Had he hurt Max? Been at the beach that night? If not, how had he obtained information about Max's disappearance—unless that was all a complete lie?

To answer those questions, I needed to find out more about Dylan. According to WHMR's website, he was an intern for the station. There was no additional info other than he liked '80s rock music, fish, and craft beer. His LinkedIn profile was sparse at best, his Instagram set to private, and a general internet search of his name gave me nothing helpful.

I sat staring at Dylan's profile picture, trying to decide if our parking lot encounter had been nothing but coincidence. Speculating otherwise risked turning me into a paranoid mess who saw potential enemies where there were none, but I couldn't convince myself strongly enough this was innocent.

Returning to my internet search, I continued flicking through the results. My eyes widened when I read the origin of the name Dylan. *Welsh.* Like the name Anwir.

I cursed out loud, thinking no matter how slim the connection, it confirmed the possibility Dylan and Anwir either knew each other or were the same person. No clue if I really was looking for a serial killer, but I couldn't discount the possibility. Dr. Graf had told me yesterday that the average serial murderer was male, white, and aged around thirty to forty. I estimated Dylan to be in his twenties, but there were always exceptions to any rule. Perhaps he'd started early.

What about motive? I didn't know the guy well enough to hazard a guess. Didn't mean there wasn't one, only that I hadn't yet figured it out. I was unsure if this was the right track, or *any* track, but I needed to keep pulling on the thread, especially considering it was my only one.

After waving the server over and settling the bill, I grabbed my stuff and headed to my car. Once inside, I called WHMR, pretending to have a delivery for Dylan, and asking if he was in. Learning he'd be there for the next hour or so, I hung up and drove downtown, where I parked across the street from the radio station. My vantage point offered a perfect view of the building's front entrance, so I hunkered down and waited, telling myself not to lose my nerve.

At first, I imagined jumping out as soon as I saw Dylan and confronting him, but when he appeared three quarters of an hour later, I decided differently. I wanted to know more about the guy without him realizing I was onto him. When he got into his beaten-up faded silver Accord and pulled out, I followed.

After crossing Casco Bay Bridge, he continued to a quiet residential area of South Portland, finally stopping in front of a ramshackle bungalow. The yellow siding was faded and worn, with strips of flaky paint flapping in the breeze while the chimney sat precariously askew, a few of its bricks missing.

An array of weeds and bramble bushes had conquered the garden, spindly jagged fingers with stray food wrappers and empty plastic bags snagged on their thorns. One of the front door's panels was covered with plywood. The stoop held a collection of overflowing recycling bins.

As Dylan got out of his car with a Reebok backpack slung over his shoulder, I looked around. A tall, heavyset man pushed a lawnmower through the grass in the yard directly across the street. If my suspicions about Dylan being dangerous were confirmed, at least there was someone around. Just in case, I pulled out my iPhone and pressed 911 without hitting Dial, preparing to alert the authorities if needed. Readying myself, I opened the door and got out.

"Hey," I shouted as I jogged across the street, but Dylan kept walking up the front path to the run-down house. "Dylan," I yelled before he reached the front door, and this time, he turned around.

"Uh . . . hi, Stella," he said, surprised. "What are you doing here?"

I stayed a few steps back with my iPhone still in my hand, thumb hovering over Dial. He carried a phone, too, and as he looked at me, I kept one eye on his fingers, trying to determine if it was the device he was using to track me via the Nokia.

"You work for WHMR," I said, straining to hear my voice coming through Dylan's phone. Nothing.

"Uh . . . yeah."

"I was on the *People of Portland* show last week."

Dylan's eyes widened. It was so fast, I almost didn't catch it. Gesturing to his front door, he said, "I need to—"

Bolstered by his apparent nervous energy, I leaned in and very, *very* quietly whispered, "Anwir?"

"Huh?" Dylan scrunched up his face. "What?"

Changing tack, I said, "Did you follow me into the parking lot the other day?"

"Whoa, you hit *me*," he said, but the way his eyes darted around told me I'd rattled him. "I'm fine, by the way. Thanks for asking."

Although I didn't get the sense Dylan was dangerous, I couldn't rely on gut instincts alone. They weren't infallible. I had to remain vigilant.

As I prepared to challenge him again, the front door creaked open. A hunched-over woman with gray curls, bloodshot eyes, and a nasal cannula stuck her head outside. The crepey texture of her face made it impossible to guess her age, but when my gaze dropped to the floor behind her, I noticed a slender oxygen tank on wheels.

"Did you get my meds?" she asked Dylan, her throaty words sounding as if they required a Herculean effort to pass between her lips.

Dylan removed a paper bag from his backpack and handed it to her. "I'll be right in." After the woman thanked him, backed away, and slowly closed the door, Dylan turned to me, eyes downcast. "My grandmother. She's sick. Emphysema."

My shoulders dropped. "That's rough. Do you take care of her?"

"Yeah."

"Alone?"

"Mostly. Mom took off, and Dad's on disability. I'm trying to support us financially."

"That must be hard."

He gave a dismissive wave. "That's life, I guess."

"I guess so." As I studied him, a few pieces clicked together, and I wondered if I'd misjudged the reason for him walking in front of my car in the parking lot completely. If so, I was going to find out.

CHAPTER 35

STELLA

"Dylan," I said gently, taking a step back. "Tell me what really happened the other day."

"You already know," he said, eyes darting around again. "You hit me."

"Are you sure?" I asked. "Because I think maybe it was the other way around."

"What do you mean?" he said. "It wasn't like that. I . . . I . . ."

"Were you hoping for money?" I continued, keeping my tone soft, approachable. Nonthreatening. When his body squirmed, I added, "Why me? Was it random?"

He let out a long sigh of defeat. The sound of someone who'd been busted. "Not exactly."

"You targeted me? Why?"

"I saw you at the radio station."

"When we were on the show?"

"Yeah. Then I recognized you when you drove into the parking lot and were circling around for a space . . ." He shrugged. "It was a split-second decision. I figured you had cash from your podcast, and I thought I could sue you."

"But you didn't. You insisted you were fine."

He muttered under his breath, and when I asked him to repeat what he'd said, his face turned crimson. "Grams didn't bring me up that way. Plus, I know you. From before."

"Before what?"

"I was at middle school with your brother."

It took me a beat, but I got there. Snapping my fingers, I said, "I thought you looked familiar. You were the kid who always ate half a pound of Chicago Mix and turned one of my mother's sofa cushions orange."

"She was so cool about it. Said everything comes out in the wash." Dylan's expression was tinged with so much exhaustion, he almost appeared twice his age. "Those were good times. We all lost touch when my mom left and Dad and I moved in here with Grams. I was sorry to hear about Max going missing. Hard to believe it's been so long."

"Did you hear about Kenji vanishing Monday night?"

"Yeah. I haven't seen him in forever, but that sucks."

Before I could respond, Dylan's grandmother opened the front door again. "Honey," she rasped. "I forgot to tell you we don't have any bread. Can you be a dear and get some?"

He closed his eyes, and I thought he might cry. "Yes, of course. I'll go now."

"Thank you," she said before turning to me. "You Dylan's girlfriend?"

I smiled. "No, ma'am. I'm a . . . business acquaintance."

"Fancy," she said. "He's a good boy, eh? Hard worker."

"Definitely." I decided to push a little. Dylan might have seemed all innocent, confessing and acting like he could be trusted now, but I couldn't be certain. "Must be his Welsh genes."

"Pardon me?"

"Isn't Dylan a Welsh name?"

"No clue," she said, before coughing into her fist. "I'm a fourth-generation Portlander myself. His mom adored Bob Dylan though. Shame she didn't love her boy as much or she'd have stuck around." She coughed again, deep and throaty. "I've got to sit. Nice meeting you. Please don't forget the bread, Dylan."

"I'll be back in a flash," he said. "Then I'll make you something to eat. I think we have some soup left." After she disappeared inside, he turned to me. "I hope they find Kenji and Max. And I really am sorry about the parking lot, but I gotta leave. Grams needs to eat before I go back to work."

"At the radio station?"

"Burger joint. The internship at WHMR doesn't pay enough."

"Before you go, can you tell me what you do there?"

"Get coffee, admin work, set up meetings, field calls."

"What about when I was on the show? What were you doing then?"

He shrugged. "Izzy sent me to get sandwiches and Charlene's dry cleaning."

There was no way I could reconcile Dylan's downtrodden demeanor with Anwir's cunningness. They didn't fit. The kid worked two jobs to support his family, had deliberately walked into my car because he was broke. He hardly seemed a criminal mastermind capable of abduction and worse. The evidence just wasn't there.

I shoved my iPhone in my pocket and grabbed my wallet. After taking out a fifty-dollar bill and a ten-dollar gas station gift card I'd received a while back, I held them out to Dylan. "Have these. For your trouble."

"What?" he said. "No, I can't. Not when I almost screwed you over."

"But you didn't. You changed your mind. Take them, please."

He stretched out his arm before pulling back. "I can't. It's wrong."

I lowered my hand, assuming he was either too proud or ashamed to accept what had to seem like charity. "Good luck, Dylan. All the best to you and your grandmother."

I'd barely walked two steps before he called out, "Don't trust the woman from the show."

I turned around. "Izzy? Why?"

"Not her. The one who came with you. Vivien."

My frown deepened. "What makes you believe I can't trust my best friend?"

"The call. Liam from Augusta," he said, squirming again, looking like he might bolt inside the house and lock the door. "She gave me a hundred bucks to make it."

"She did *what*?"

"I'm sorry," he said. "She gave me a script of what to say once I was on-air. Word for word."

"But . . . how did you get through?"

"I told Vivien there was no way I could guarantee it, but she insisted I try." He winced a little. "There are tricks of the trade. Plus, I knew the kind of cold case suggestions they were looking for. Charlene and Izzy briefed us about it before you two arrived."

I could barely speak as I pointed to my throat. "Your . . . your voice—"

"I've done improv and took voice-over classes a while back," he said, shifting his tone and suddenly sounding exactly like Liam from Augusta had. There was no mistaking it. Dylan wasn't lying about this.

"Why would she—"

"I didn't ask."

Head spinning, my knees buckled as I almost sank to the ground. Vivien had asked Dylan to call *People of Portland* while we were on-air. She'd given him specific instructions on what to say. Why would she do this? What could she possibly have to gain?

I suddenly wondered if *she* was Anwir, but it didn't make sense. Or did it? She'd been at the beach party the night Max vanished, but Jeff had been there, too. So had I. It didn't mean she was involved in my brother's disappearance. Or Kenji's. But then why had she asked Dylan to make the call pretending to be Liam?

Suddenly, her possible motivation became clear. She'd pressed me on more than one occasion to record a follow-up episode about Max. She knew I didn't want to talk about him on *People of Portland*. Getting Dylan involved in this way had increased the radio show's ratings, got more ears on *A Killer Motive*.

Vivien had hoped it would make us attractive to advertisers. More sensationalist to Booker, whom she'd talked to before we'd gone on-air and seen at Templetons before she'd manipulated me into the lunch at Triple Crown.

What else had she done?

I shivered as I remembered a case I'd read about years ago. A woman who'd faked her own disappearance because she was hungry for fame. Were Vivien and Kenji in on this together? Hadad had accused me of lying about AL's emails to move the spotlight back onto Max's case. What if the detective was right, but it had been Vivien's plan? She'd said she hadn't seen Kenji in years, but I couldn't trust her. And what about the severed arm?

"Did she tell you to send me any emails?" I asked Dylan.

"Only the call. I swear."

"When, and how?"

"Three weeks ago," he said with an apologetic grimace. "She walked up to me outside the station and offered me money in exchange for the call. Half up front, half after. She Venmoed me. That's all I know."

Anger toward my so-called best friend grew in my stomach. Thrusting the cash and gift card into Dylan's hands, I said, "Take these. Call me immediately if Vivien contacts you. *Immediately*, okay?"

"I will," Dylan said. "I promise. Please don't tell Izzy or Charlene. I can't afford to lose my job. Not with the state Grams is in."

After promising I'd keep quiet if he held up his end of the bargain, I got into my car. My entire body trembled as I sat and watched Dylan drive away while I attempted to decide how to handle my newest discovery.

I wanted to call Vivien but expected her to deny it all. My only evidence was the word of someone I barely knew who'd almost screwed me over because he was broke. Hardly a reliable witness. Still, whether or not it turned me into the most gullible person on the planet, I believed him. Dylan was Liam, but not Anwir. Anwir was still out there, hiding.

As I drummed my fingers on the steering wheel, I held firm to my belief that when I confronted Vivien about the radio call and seeing Booker at Templetons, it had to be in person, once she returned from Syracuse, so I could see her reactions in real time. I'd know for sure if she was lying.

As I sank into the car seat, mind whirring with all the disconnected pieces of information I desperately wanted to fit together, my iPhone rang. When I saw my mother's number, I figured she was calling to give me an earful about Dad's disastrous birthday lunch. I let it go to voicemail, frowning when the phone chimed. Mom only left messages in emergencies.

When I listened to the recording, the urgency made me bolt upright. "Stella, call me back," she said. "Your father's being questioned by the police about what you found in the mine."

SUNDAY, AUGUST 3

CHAPTER 36

Surprise.

Bet you weren't expecting that, Stella. Not in a million years. In The Merchant of Venice, Shakespeare famously said, "The sins of the father are to be laid upon the children."

What will you do with Howard's, I wonder.

I take immense pride in my work. I suppose I feel somewhat like a sculptor, chip, chip, chipping away. But instead of the material I'm working with being stone, it's your soul.

Whatever's left of it by the time I'm done will belong to me.

I can hardly wait.

CHAPTER 37

STELLA

My world had been turned upside down all over again. The knockout punches kept coming so fast and hard, I no longer knew which was the right way up, what to do about my loss of control, or how to find steady footing again.

Sitting in the kitchen alone at an unearthly hour on Sunday morning as rain splattered across the windows, I tried to wrap my head around what had happened yesterday.

After listening to Mom's message about Dad being with the police, I'd called her immediately. "What's going on?" I'd asked, trying not to sound frantic. She'd always tended to expect the worst, but my own panic levels had shot up to almost match hers. "What do you mean, Dad's with the cops?"

"Detective Hadad came to the house to talk to him," she replied, her words thick with tears. "I don't know the details. Only that it's related to the arm you found."

"That doesn't make sense. Are they still there?"

"No. They said it would be better if they discussed things at the station downtown. I'm here now, waiting."

"Did Dad call his attorney?"

"No—"

"Why not?"

"He insisted there's no need," Mom snapped. "Your father

hasn't done anything wrong. Do you know what this is about? Have they told you more about what you found?"

"No, nothing. Listen, don't move. I'm coming over."

I'd hesitated about calling Jeff. Early on in our relationship, I'd learned that when we had an argument, he needed time to process the disagreement. However, Dad being hauled in for questioning about the human remains had changed the situation entirely.

As I shoved my feet into my sneakers, I'd called Jeff's cell. When he didn't pick up, I decided not to leave a voicemail until I had additional information. No sense having him freak out, too.

With no more time to waste, I headed into Portland and parked in the lot opposite the police station, where I'd run into Dylan. While his explanation about what happened that day seemed plausible, being back there caused doubts to resurface. I pushed them down. No opportunity to dissect them now. Other things needed my attention.

I hurried across the street. Before I reached the police station's main entrance, the Nokia rang. "Don't forget our deal," Anwir said when I answered. "You know what'll happen if you breathe a word about me. I'll be listening."

He didn't wait for a reply before hanging up. Within an instant, the nerves in my stomach swarmed like rabid bats trying to burst from my abdomen in a bid for freedom. It was exactly what I wanted to do. *Escape.* Run away and only return once this nightmare had resolved itself.

Except I was the one who had to work things through. Walking away from Anwir meant abandoning Kenji and Max. Not an option. In any case, whatever connection the cops thought they had between Dad and the arm was a mistake. A misunderstanding.

Steeling myself for what I was about to hear, I dropped the Nokia in my front pocket and walked into the police station. Mom sat in the reception area with a scrunched-up Kleenex in her hands, eyes red and puffy, mascara smudged across her cheeks.

"Stella," she said, getting up. I expected her to hesitate before hugging me, but she remained two yards away, working the tissue between her clenched hands.

"Any news?" I asked. "Have they been out to see you?"

"No, and I don't understand why we're here in the first place."

"Are you certain we shouldn't call an attorney? I can't believe Dad's talking to the cops without representation. Although . . . I suppose it shows good faith, and he has nothing to hide."

My mother leaned in and lowered her voice. "What about you, Stella?"

"Me?"

"Yes, you." She glared at me. "I don't think your father's hiding anything, but I can't say the same for you."

"What do you mean?"

"Did you really happen to stumble across that . . . that *body part* at Bradley Hills?"

"Yes. It's like I told you and Detective Hadad already. I was hiking and—"

"I know what you *said*, Stella," Mom cut in. "But I also know *you*. Something's not sitting well. What's going on? If you have information that could help your dad, you need to share it with the police. Do you hear? *Immediately.*"

She was right, of course, and I would've followed her command if Anwir's instructions weren't still ringing in my ears. I *would* tell Hadad. I'd tell her, Jeff, Mom, and Dad everything as soon as I could. But not now. Not until Kenji was safe and I had Anwir's information about Max.

"You want answers, Mom. It's completely understandable," I said gently, rushing on as she opened her mouth, no doubt to protest or to accuse me of being condescending. "I wish I could give them to you, but I don't know more than I've shared."

I forced myself to hold her gaze. Luckily, Hadad walked into the reception area, interrupting our standoff. When Mom spotted her, she rushed over.

"What are you talking to my husband about?" she demanded. "Why did you bring him here? I have a right to know."

"Mrs. Dixon." Hadad held up both hands, palms turned toward Mom as she made a distinct *calm down* gesture. I wanted to break her fingers. "I was hoping we could speak."

"Will you tell me what's going on with Howard?"

"Let's do this in private." The detective indicated the door. "Please. Come this way. We'll get you a coffee and talk properly."

"What about me?" I asked.

"We're good for now," Hadad replied before tilting her head. "I'll be in touch soon."

And with that, the two of them disappeared.

I'd gone home. Checking and rechecking that the doors and windows were locked while wondering what was happening downtown, and spinning theories about how my father was connected with the severed arm, each one more outlandish than the next.

Time dragged on. I was no closer to discovering who Anwir was. I wasn't sure if Dylan had told the truth. If he had, it meant Vivien had set me up not only for lunch with Booker but also on the *People of Portland* show with the call from Liam. How could she do that to me?

Frustrated, angry, and overwhelmed, I ignored a text from her that read, You're quiet. Everything okay? Thought more about meeting Booker soon? I'd set my phone to Do Not Disturb, ensuring only calls from Jeff and my parents came through. Exhausted, I must've fallen asleep around nine and had only woken up briefly when Jeff got home.

I hadn't been able to face getting into any more discussions or arguments with him, so I'd pretended to be asleep yet again. Now, as the sun kissed the clear skies with a touch of cotton-candy pink, I stood in the kitchen, preparing a pot of coffee.

By the time I'd eaten half a piece of toast and pushed my plate away, I heard Jeff coming downstairs. The first thing he did when he walked into the room was put his arms around me. His embrace felt so good, so reassuring, I wanted to stay wrapped in our cocoon forever.

"Why are you up already?" I asked.

"Couldn't sleep anymore without apologizing," he whispered. "I'm sorry about yesterday. I shouldn't have told your folks anything. Especially when you asked me not to. It was wrong."

"I'm the one who needs to apologize," I replied, hugging him. "I overreacted."

He kissed the top of my head and murmured, "Maybe we both did. I shouldn't have stomped off like a moody teenager, either. Have you heard from your folks? All good?"

"Not exactly . . ."

Jeff listened, eyes widening, as I told him about Dad being taken in for questioning. Shivers zipped down my back as I shared the sparse details, my mind still trying to grasp how or if any of this was connected.

"Holy hell," Jeff said once I'd finished. "I don't get it. What does a severed arm dumped in an old mine have to do with your dad?"

"That's about where I've been since yesterday," I said, blinking hard as tears slithered down my cheeks. "I'm confused. Exhausted. I can't think straight."

Jeff grabbed my hand, pulling me back in for a hug. "I wish I'd been here for you. I'm an ass. I saw your missed call and wasn't ready to talk, so—"

"It's okay—"

"It's not," he insisted. "You needed me. I wasn't there. But we'll figure this out, I promise. I'll do whatever I can to fix this."

I'm not sure how long we stayed in the kitchen, me sobbing, Jeff trying to give me the reassurance I desperately needed. I couldn't take much more of Anwir's mind games. Where would they end? When would it be over? Would Kenji still be alive? Would I? What would I learn about Max? As my thoughts kept spiraling, the sound of the doorbell made me jump.

"I'll get it," Jeff said, and a few moments later, I heard Detective Hadad's voice in our hallway, and the front door closing as she came inside.

I wiped my face with a napkin and blinked a few times as the two of them entered the kitchen. Hadad wore another of her sharp suits, hair pulled back into a loose ponytail, a brown leather messenger bag casually slung over her shoulder. She seemed well rested, immediately sparking my envy.

"Hello, Detective." I tried to smile, didn't get far, and gave up.

"Can I get you a drink?" Jeff asked, ever the ultimate host. "Water, tea, or coffee?"

"Coffee would be great," Hadad replied. "Black. Thank you, Mr. Summer."

"Please, call me Jeff."

The detective and I settled at the breakfast table while Jeff filled a mug and put it in front of Hadad before sitting next to me.

"Appreciate it," Hadad said, lifting the drink to her lips.

"Can you please tell us what's going on?" I asked, unable to wait. "Where's my dad?"

She set the mug down. "He left the station late last night."

"Why did you talk to him?" Jeff said. "Stella mentioned it's related to the Bradley Hills discovery, but it makes no sense."

The detective slowly turned her gaze on me. "We found your father's prints."

"His prints?" I asked. "Where?"

"On the sealed bag the remains were in," Hadad said. "And on the arm."

CHAPTER 38

STELLA

Whatever answer I expected from Hadad, her response wouldn't have crossed my mind in a century. It was ridiculous. Preposterous. So outrageous, in fact, that I couldn't help a laugh from escaping my mouth.

"You found Dad's prints?" I said, voice going up. "On the arm?"

Hadad nodded once. "Yes."

I searched her face, waiting for her to tell me she was kidding. Except she didn't. This wasn't a joke. Hadad was completely serious.

"This is absurd," Jeff said. "There's got to be a mistake. Your lab messed up."

"Wait," I said. "How did you know they were *his* prints?"

Hadad looked at me. "Mr. Dixon has been in the system for over thirty years."

"Huh? Why?"

The detective took a few beats. She smoothed down her shirt before meeting my eyes, her expression filling with something akin to empathy. "He was a suspect in a homicide."

This time I wondered if I'd slipped into a parallel universe where everyone spewed nonsense. "My father was accused of killing someone? I don't believe you. No. No way."

"*Suspected.* Not accused, charged, or convicted." Hadad observed me. "You didn't know."

"*No*," I said. "Whose murder?"

Hadad opened her messenger bag and retrieved a manila folder. Jeff squeezed my fingers, but my hand went limp as if all the strength had left my body. Neither my father nor my mother had ever mentioned Dad being suspected of hurting someone. Then again, *if* it was true, it was hardly a discussion my family would have over Sunday lunch. Max and I had only found out about Mom's older brother being killed when Dad had let it slip when I was twelve.

"Zachary Arlington," Hadad said, the folder still closed as she set it on the table.

"Who's he?" Jeff asked. "Did Stella find *his* arm?"

"Have either of you heard of Zachary Arlington?" Hadad asked, ignoring the questions. "Did Mr. or Mrs. Dixon mention his name?"

"No, not once," I said. "Tell us who he is."

Hadad opened the folder, took out a photograph, and slid it across the table. I found myself examining a picture of a man I figured was somewhere in his early thirties. Short red hair, almost translucent complexion. Freckles dotted across his cheeks. A thick gold figaro chain around his neck peeked out from the top of his blue V-neck knitted sweater.

"I don't know who this is," I said. "I've never seen him before."

"Zachary Arlington was your mom's boyfriend years ago," Hadad said. "They split up about a month before she and your father met. Apparently, Mr. Arlington didn't take the separation or her new relationship with Mr. Dixon well."

"What do you mean?" Jeff asked. "What did this Zachary guy do?"

"According to the police reports, he was overly jealous," Hadad replied. "He followed Erin for months. Waited outside her apartment and at her work. Made anonymous calls."

"A stalker?" I asked.

"Yes, and things escalated," the detective continued. "He left feces on her doorstep, canine and otherwise. Allegedly slashed her tires, although there was no proof he did it. Then Mr. Arlington and Mr. Dixon had a few run-ins."

"What kind of run-ins?" Jeff asked.

"Physical," Hadad replied. "The police were called at least twice when things got out of hand. Arlington had a history of intimate partner violence and often got into bar brawls, too."

"Intimate partner violence," I repeated. "Including with my mother?"

"No." Hadad drummed her fingers on the table. "At least that's what she always maintained. But she'd witnessed Arlington picking fights when they were out. Provoking. Always ensuring he got the first punch in. They were only together for three months. She told the police she ended things because he was, quote, *trouble*."

"What happened to him?" I asked. "Tell me if his arm was in the bag."

Hadad took a slow sip of coffee. "Arlington's body was found in Sebago Lake a week after his sister reported him missing thirty-two years ago. Intact. The arm doesn't belong to him."

"And Howard was cleared as a suspect?" Jeff asked.

I winced at the suggestion my father could've committed homicide. It was too ludicrous to contemplate for more than a nanosecond. Dad would never hurt anyone. Except . . . how many times had I heard people say the same thing about their loved one who'd unequivocally killed another human being?

"The case remains unsolved," Hadad said. "Mr. Dixon swore he never touched Arlington. Mrs. Dixon confirmed your father's alibi for the approximate time of death. Of course, some viewed her statement as convenient, particularly as during one of the fights between Arlington and your father, witnesses heard threats being made."

"By my dad?"

Hadad nodded. "According to one witness, his exact words were, 'If you come near me or Erin again, I'll make sure you stop breathing.'"

"Doesn't mean anything." I sat back in my chair. "People say all kinds of stuff when they're angry or scared. It's impulsive. Territorial. Most never act on it."

"True," Hadad agreed. "Although the ones threatened don't typically end up dying from blunt force trauma to the side of the head and disposed of in a lake, weighed down by rocks."

"Was there any evidence my father did that?" I demanded. "Anything linking him to the case other than a few empty threats? How about forensics? Witnesses? *Anything?*"

"No," Hadad said.

"Any evidence my mother gave him a false alibi?" I continued.

Hadad waited a few beats. "None. Like I said, Arlington's murder is a cold case. The perfect kind for *A Killer Motive*, come to think of it."

It didn't sound at all as if that thought had spontaneously popped into her head. "What are you implying?"

"Seriously," Jeff said. "What does Stella's podcast have to do with Zachary Arlington or the arm? Also, if it's not his, then whose is it? You still haven't told us."

"Has your father ever been violent, Stella?" Hadad asked, ignoring our questions again.

"Excuse me? *No.*"

"Howard's the most even-tempered man I've met," Jeff added. "He's so laid-back he's practically horizontal. The only time I've seen him upset is after Max went missing. He was a wreck. On a bad day, he still is. Otherwise, nothing fazes him. Violent? No chance."

Hadad, who seemed to have been waiting for this exact segue, turned to me. "Have you ever thought your father might be involved in Max's disappearance?"

"Are you kidding me?" I exploded, my words bouncing off the kitchen walls. "Where the hell did that come from? Dad would never hurt Max. *Never.*"

"Stella." Jeff put a hand on my back, but I shrugged him off. I wasn't done.

"He loves my brother," I continued, my eyes boring into the detective's. "And for the last time, whose arm did I find? Stop skirting the question."

"We don't know," Hadad said. "Yet. But here's another thing. I'm not sure you told the truth about how you found it." When I opened my mouth, she held up a hand. "Hear me out. You're a true crime podcaster. A self-confessed cold case junkie. So I got to wondering, what if you stumbled across Zachary Arlington's case and learned your father was a suspect."

I crossed my arms. "I told you. I'd never heard of him."

"Indulge me," Hadad continued. "Maybe you did some research into your father. Perhaps your research led you to locating the arm somehow, but not at Bradley Hills. Somewhere else. See, initial tests show the bag hadn't been in the mine for long."

"Hold on," Jeff jumped in. "Let me get this straight. You're saying Howard was a suspect in a murder three decades ago. Now you think he cut off someone else's arm, then Stella somehow found it and took it to a state park? Can you hear how ridiculous you sound?"

"When we first met, you said you don't speculate," I added, my tone glacial. "What happened? Because it seems you're doing a whole load of it now."

"The fingerprints are telling me at least part of the theory isn't ridiculous," Hadad said. "I believe you're a good person, Stella. If you found out your father had hurt someone, you'd be compelled to speak up. But I also know how difficult the relationship between you and your mother is."

"How did you—"

"You talked about it on the first episode of *A Killer Motive*," she replied. "My point is, if you pretended to find the arm by coincidence, Erin couldn't blame you for giving up your dad."

"That's not what happened," I said, my voice raised, my mind reeling. "My father didn't kill anyone. He didn't hack off anybody's arm. And he most certainly *didn't* hurt Max."

Hadad seemed to roll this around her head for a few beats, then said, "Your brother loved true crime, too. What if he stumbled across evidence linking your father to Arlington's murder, or the dismemberment of another person, and confronted your dad with it?"

"No, I—"

"Come on, Stella, tell me how you located the arm," Hadad said, tone soft. "When and where did you really find it?"

"Enough." Jeff slammed a palm on the table. I flinched. Hadad didn't blink.

"Agreed," I said, getting up. "I won't sit in my own house while you accuse my father of murder and me of whatever the hell else. I've got nothing more to say. Please leave."

Hadad blinked this time, but didn't move, not until Jeff added, "I'm sure you heard my wife. I'll show you out."

As soon as they went into the hallway, I grabbed my iPhone and called Mom, mind spinning. "Is it true?" I said, the words tumbling out before my mother had a chance to utter much of a hello. "Was Dad a suspect in your ex-boyfriend's murder?"

After a long pause, Mom said, "Yes, but he didn't do it. He swore."

"He *swore*? What do you mean? Was the alibi you gave him a lie?" When she didn't reply, I added, "Hadad told me the arm I found has Dad's prints on it. What do you know about that?" Silence. "*Mom?* Where's Dad? Is he home? I need to speak with him."

"He's resting," Mom said. "He's exhausted. This is taking such a toll on him. And me."

"Who else knew about him being a suspect in Arlington's death?" I demanded. "Did Max find out?"

"I . . . I don't think so," she whispered. "I don't know. But I have to go. I can't talk about this now. I can't."

We were so alike, she and I. Unable to properly discuss things we considered too painful, continually shutting others out, no matter the short- or long-term damage it caused.

And my father? As I sat there with the iPhone still clutched to my chest, I wondered if he, the person I'd trusted all my life, had committed unspeakable crimes. Had he killed at least one man? If so, where did Anwir fit in? Was he related to Zachary Arlington and hungry for justice? But why involve me? Why not point the cops to the mine directly? Why put the arm there in the first place? Why abduct Kenji? Why did Anwir say he had information about my brother?

Had my father hurt Max?

No. *No.* I wouldn't let Hadad plant her theory in me, a tiny seed that would grow and bloom, infiltrating everything else, clouding my judgment. Dad would never, *ever* hurt his son. Not even to protect himself.

Would he?

As unbearable and unsavory as it was, I couldn't stop thinking about the detective's words. I knew damn well everyone could kill, given the right—or wrong—circumstances. Next to money, survival was often one of the strongest motives.

What if Hadad wasn't wrong, and my brother had found out Dad was a murderer? Could my father have decided the only way for him to survive and somehow keep the rest of his family together was to silence Max . . . forever?

MONDAY, AUGUST 4

CHAPTER 39

STELLA

Jeff wasn't happy when I insisted last night that he didn't need to cancel work on my behalf. He'd begrudgingly left, but only after I promised ten times to call immediately if there were any developments, no matter how small.

Settled at my desk in the studio early Monday morning, I tried to detach my emotions from the situation as best I could. My first task was continuing a deep and thorough search about Zachary Arlington to learn about his case. I soon found out that other than what Hadad had shared with us yesterday, there wasn't much to go on.

After reading the articles written when Arlington went missing, and watching videos from the time his body was found, I couldn't locate anything more recent. It was shocking how fast he'd been forgotten, the news cycle zooming ahead to fresher stories.

Next came researching the arm in the mine. I couldn't wait for, or count on, Hadad to keep me updated. Time to activate my own sources. I looked up Talikha Chatterjee, a forensics wunderkind with the Portland crime lab, which collaborated with the Office of the Chief Medical Examiner.

Although we weren't close, I'd had the pleasure of connecting with Talikha while researching cases for *A Killer Motive*. We'd first met last year, when Vivien and I had investigated a case I'd mentioned on *People of Portland*.

A seventeen-year-old girl named Paisley had suffered a blow to the head during a college party and was found unresponsive in a shallow fountain. Her boyfriend, Jasper, with whom Paisley had been seen arguing earlier that night, was convicted of her murder.

He swore his innocence. Said he'd left the party and gone for a walk to cool off but had no witnesses to corroborate his version of the truth. His family couldn't afford an attorney, and Jasper's DNA under Paisley's fingernails had practically made the case a slam dunk.

When Jasper's mother contacted *A Killer Motive* years later, asking if we'd consider looking at the evidence, both Vivien and I had been dubious. The case wasn't cold. It seemed clear-cut enough. Still, we were curious, did our due diligence, and that was when I'd found Talikha. Turned out she wasn't convinced of Jasper's guilt, either. However, she'd been told to leave things be, that her focus was required elsewhere.

It had been enough for us to pursue the story, going over police reports and interviewing partygoers who shared details about the argument between Jasper and Paisley, but also how much in love they were. Hardly anyone believed he'd killed her. Even Paisley's parents had their doubts.

When we spoke to Jasper, he was so distraught by his girlfriend's death and his murder conviction, he'd barely been capable of putting a sentence together. Both Vivien and I thought he was telling the truth. If not, he deserved all the Best Actor Oscars.

We'd doubled down. After hours of examining party footage and videos on social media, we had nothing and were on the verge of giving up. Late one evening, Vivien was scrolling through Instagram and let out a shriek.

A guy had posted a series of time-stamped selfies and videos, celebrating the day he'd completed his first 10K run. It was the day of Paisley's murder, and there in the background was Jasper, sitting on a bench ten blocks away. Exactly at the time of

Paisley's death, which had been narrowed down to a window of four minutes.

An appeal was granted, and after a renewed dive into forensics, which Talikha led, it was determined Paisley had slipped, cracked her head on the side of the fountain, and drowned in five inches of water. An accident, not murder.

Jasper was released, *A Killer Motive* made headlines, and Talikha, who was in her early forties and loved her job more than anything in the world, had received some serious professional recognition along with a career boost. If there was anyone I could discreetly ask for information about what I'd found at Bradley Hills, it was her.

"Stella," she said, picking up almost immediately. "It's been forever. How are you? Working on another episode of the podcast, I hope. You know how much I love your show."

"Thanks," I said, her calm demeanor and praise a balm for my splintered soul. After we exchanged a few pleasantries and I asked about her ever-expanding first-edition spy novel collection, I got down to it. "Talikha, I, uh, need a favor."

"I figured this wasn't only about my latest haul at the secondhand bookstore," she said. "Hold on, I'll close the door . . . Okay, tell me how I can help. Is this about the arm?"

I exhaled. "You heard I found it?"

"Read it in the report. Figured you might call. Identifying your father's prints was a shock, too, let me tell you."

Grateful she hadn't shut me down yet, I said, "Can you say anything more about it? In strictest confidence, of course."

"Stella, with your dad's possible involvement—"

"But that's exactly it," I begged. "Please, Talikha. I can't get it out of my head. Have you been able to identify who it is?"

Talikha sighed, obviously evaluating how much she should share. "Not yet," she finally said. "DNA testing will take a few weeks. Hopefully we'll get lucky in CODIS."

"Can you tell if my dad's prints on the arm and the vacuum pack were left at the same time?" I asked. "Maybe—"

"No, we don't have the tech for that," Talikha said. "Dating fingerprints is impossible. Same as blood evidence, really, although that can be done in some rare instances."

"What about the victim's prints? Are they in the system?"

Talikha waited a beat. "There were no fingertips."

"They'd been cut off?" I let out a gasp. When I'd opened the bag, I hadn't inspected the arm closely enough to notice. I'd been too busy trying to get away.

"At the distal interphalangeal joint," Talikha replied. "Likely postmortem. Obviously, it makes it harder to identify the person. We'll try the palms. Worth a shot."

"Can you tell how old the remains are?"

"Several years," Talikha replied. "At least five. Maybe as much as fifteen. They were well-preserved, but I can't narrow it down yet. I can say the person was severely emaciated. Almost skeletal."

I put a hand to my mouth to stop myself from throwing up. The timeline meant it couldn't be Kenji, but there was no way to exclude Max. The police had his DNA. We'd given it to Wade when my brother had gone missing, and Mom, Dad, and I had provided our own for comparison purposes. How could I wait weeks to know if it was him? My heart wouldn't withstand it.

"Do . . . do you think it's my brother?" I asked, not daring to move until she answered.

"I wish I could rule it out, Stella," she said gently. "I'll let you know as soon as I can. Listen, the info I've given you so far . . . you could've noticed it when you found the arm, but this next part stays between us."

"Of course. I promise."

"There's a UV tattoo."

"What's that?"

"Basically, the same as a regular one," Talikha said. "Except they use a fluorescent dye so you can only see it under a black light. They're practically invisible otherwise."

"I've never heard of them."

"They're not as common."

"What's the tattoo of?"

"I'm not sure. Some symbol. Hold on . . ."

When my phone buzzed with an incoming text, I saw Talikha had sent me a photograph. "I know what that is," I said, my voice going up a notch. "Aries."

"As in the star sign? Are you sure?"

"Practically positive. Google it. Tell me what you think."

A few seconds later, Talikha whistled. "I'll be damned. This is great. Thanks, Stella."

"You're welcome," I said, glad to have been of use. "Thank you for confiding in me."

After we hung up, I sank into my chair. Max's star sign was Leo, and he'd never thought much of astrology. As far as I knew, he'd never wanted any ink, UV or otherwise.

Maybe the arm in the mine wasn't his, after all.

CHAPTER 40

STELLA

As I reached for my glass of water, my eyes landed on the Nokia. It had stayed ominously silent since Saturday. Why? Not that I wanted to speak to Anwir, but he'd tracked me to the police station. Surely he'd listened to my conversations. What was he waiting for?

Seconds later, my iPhone rang, making me jump. Jeff asked if I wanted to go to Owen's for dinner. When I said I wasn't in the mood, he insisted he'd stay home after his shift, meaning he'd be back before lunch.

I headed to the house for some coffee and found that my hidden camera detector had finally been delivered. After securing the doors and windows, I swept the place with the new handheld device, relieved when I didn't find anything.

Jeff would be home any minute now, but I needed another few hours to myself, undisturbed. I sent him a text saying I was heading to the library to work. At least it wasn't a lie this time.

Once there, I spent ages researching tattoo websites and scrolling through blogs and Instagram accounts, comparing pictures with the photo Talikha had sent. After a quick bathroom break and a candy bar, I pushed myself to get back to work.

Half an hour later, I found a post from almost twelve years ago. The identical UV Aries tattoo I'd been trying to find. As unease fluttered in my belly, I looked more closely at the poster's profile. He went by the handle @koolkat_dude91, and from what I could tell, he was local to Portland.

Another two clicks, and I had his name. Fynn Baumann. His last post was a photo of him giving the camera a thumbs-up as he held a giant hooked fish in the other hand. I glanced at the comments, the newest of which was dated a few months back.

Miss you brother #FindFynn

Wish we knew you're okay #FindFynn

Please let us know you're safe #FindFynn

There were dozens of older comments like this, turning the post into a virtual shrine—exactly what had happened to Max's account. Fingers scrambling, I typed *Fynn Baumann Portland missing* into my browser.

After a bit of scrolling, I learned Fynn had disappeared over a decade ago after a football game, when he was twenty-two. He'd vanished into thin air. No trace had ever been found.

Three local men. Fynn, Max, and Kenji. Anwir was the link between all three. But why? How? How could my father be connected to a—or multiple—crimes? Frustratingly, my research didn't uncover more, but I called Talikha to give her the update.

"I found something," I said, hoping the information would help her and the cops get further ahead, and she'd potentially share her findings with me. "A man named Fynn Baumann has a tattoo like the one on the arm. He's a missing person from Portland. Disappeared twelve years ago."

"How on earth did you figure this out?" she asked.

"Scoured the internet comparing pictures of the Aries tattoo," I said. "I can't be a hundred percent certain, but maybe you can positively ID him. Here, let me show you."

"Wow," Talikha said when she opened the link I sent her to the photo of Fynn's tattoo. "This could be our guy. Are you sure you're not a cop?"

"Ha, no, and please don't tell anyone I found this. Take the credit. It's all yours."

"Your secret's safe with me. This is awesome. Thank you."

When I got home, it was almost 6:00 p.m. I headed to the kitchen where Jeff stood in front of the stove, stirring a pot of boiling pasta.

"Hungry?" he asked as he came over to hug me.

I was starving, but as I dropped my bag on the floor and slid out of my jacket, which I hung on the back of a chair, I said, "Not really. I have a pounding headache. I think I'll go rest upstairs."

I knew it was unfair. Jeff's emotions were in turmoil, too, but I couldn't face him. Wasn't prepared to answer the questions he'd have or talk about my dad and how I was feeling. It was wrong to hide, but it felt a damn sight easier.

A short while later, Jeff came upstairs, and I closed my eyes and steadied my breathing until he headed into the bathroom for a shower. Just as he switched off the water, I heard a phone ringing. Loud. It wasn't Jeff's unless he'd changed his ringtone, and my iPhone, which had been in the pocket of my jeans, sat on my nightstand.

The Nokia. I'd forgotten it in the kitchen with the sound switched on.

With my heart in my throat, I leaped out of bed and dashed into the hallway, almost tripping as I barreled down the stairs. I raced to the kitchen and grabbed the phone, hoping Anwir hadn't hung up. If he had, Kenji would suffer.

"Hello? *Hello?*" I said, moving to the living room.

"Your conversations have been the highlight of my past few days," Anwir said, his voice filled with unabashed delight. All the hairs on the back of my neck stood sentry. "How must it feel to be a murderer's daughter, I wonder. How many others do you think he's killed? One? Five? Twenty?"

"Is it Fynn Baumann's arm?" I whispered. "How is my dad involved?"

"You'll find out in good time," Anwir replied. "Until then, sweet dreams, jelly bean, as your dad used to say. And all this time you thought he was such a great man."

I wanted to shout at Anwir, but he'd already gone, and Jeff was upstairs. It was all I could do to stop myself from hurling the Nokia at the wall, wishing I could watch with triumphant satisfaction as it shattered into pieces, falling silent forever.

Except I couldn't. Anwir had used another expression from my past. He knew what my father had said to me and my brother at bedtime. What had he done to get the information? Tortured Max? Extracted as many details from him as possible before tossing his body into a lake, like someone—possibly my dad—had done to Zachary Arlington?

Fingers still clenched, and with white-hot fury churning my guts, I vowed I'd get revenge for what Anwir was putting everyone through. Then I promised myself if Dad truly was a killer, I'd never speak to my father again.

"Stella?" Jeff's sudden voice behind me made me gasp. "Something wrong? Did I hear a phone?"

I slowly turned around, discreetly curling my hand and hiding as much of the Nokia as possible. "Yeah, mine. I ran down to get it, but it was a wrong number."

I thought I saw a frown cross his face as he said, "Want to watch TV if your head's okay? Take your mind off things?"

"No, but you go on ahead. I need to rest."

He gave me another look but didn't say anything. As he walked out of the room, muttering about forgetting his socks, I slipped the Nokia into my pocket. While I followed Jeff to our bedroom, I crossed my fingers, hoping he wouldn't spot my iPhone on my nightstand before I could get to it.

TUESDAY, AUGUST 5

CHAPTER 41

It's fascinating to watch you, Stella. To hear your conversations. Observe—from somewhat afar for now—how you're handling things. You're smart, and you know how to work your connections. Realizing the tattoo was the Aries sign was impressive indeed. Identifying to whom it could belong even more so.

I wish I could crawl into your brain. Have a good poke around in the places you hide your deepest, darkest thoughts and fears. We'll get there, eventually. I keep reminding myself to be patient. To bide my time.

You disregarded one of my rules yesterday evening. I knew you didn't have the phone close because I couldn't hear you. Possibly a genuine mistake so I decided to let it slide.

Do you think your husband suspects you of lying yet? He's such a solid, honest man. Caring and gentle. Always puts you first. Ever wonder why that might be? If he's compensating for a deeply buried piece of his past?

Looks can be deceiving, as you know. I wonder what will happen, what you'll do, when the rest of your world implodes. How you'll react when you learn you're not the only one who's warped the truth. I'd imagine you'll wonder why this is happening to you. You'll ask yourself why certain families, like yours, seem to have all the bad luck, plagued by tragedy after tragedy.

If you were here with me now, I'd tell you one of my secrets. I can see myself leaning in and cupping a hand to your ear. As the skin on your arms turns to goose bumps and the hairs on the back of your neck stand on end, I softly whisper, "It isn't always about luck, Stella. Sometimes it's entirely by design."

And in this case, I'm the architect of everything.

CHAPTER 42

STELLA

I was back in the studio Tuesday morning, dressed in my pajamas and ready for another round of research. Vivien would return the day after tomorrow, and I wished it wasn't so soon. Not only because I needed more time alone, but also because the prospect of a potentially explosive conversation with her kept turning my stomach into knots.

Bringing up how she'd failed to mention meeting Booker at Templetons and how she'd allegedly paid Dylan Firth to call *People of Portland*, instructing him to pose as Liam from Augusta, wasn't a conversation I relished.

As the last few days had passed, I kept wondering if Dylan had told the truth. My heart reminded me I didn't know him at all, really. Not in comparison to Vivien. Had Dylan fed me a bunch of lies? Was he Anwir after all? I still couldn't reconcile the possibility—he was Max's age, so surely he wasn't responsible for Fynn Baumann's disappearance twelve years ago. But could he somehow still be involved?

Then again, if Dylan hadn't lied, and Vivien had betrayed me for better ratings, it meant she was a snake. That prospect made me tiptoe away from the problem and turn to another. My father had been a murder suspect decades ago. I still didn't believe Dad was capable of harming anyone and wanted to smash all Hadad's theories leaning that way into infinitesimal smithereens.

Today, my focus would be on missing local men. Max was seventeen at the time of his disappearance. Fynn Baumann twenty-two. Kenji twenty-four. Armed with this information, I opened my laptop's browser.

Homing in on cases where the victims were men between the ages of fifteen and thirty, I headed back a little over three decades to include the time when Zachary Arlington had been killed.

For the next few hours, I scoured as many police websites as I could find, including those in surrounding states, and farther afield. Next I tackled other resources such as the FBI's website and NamUs, the National Missing and Unidentified Persons System, and other cold case podcasts, scrutinizing cases, cross-referencing dates, times, and geographical locations.

By midmorning, my eyes burned. There were so many disappearances and murders with multiple and unique sets of circumstances. I found it impossible to be certain which were linked, not without my own confirmation bias playing a significant role.

My thoughts became muddled as I tried to recalibrate what I was looking for, and I kept pushing away the nagging possibility that my father had hurt at least one person. And potentially my brother.

I hadn't spoken to Dad since our interrupted lunch on Saturday. Despite my leaving him a message, he'd yet to return my call. It was past ten now. Jeff was likely still asleep, but Dad would be up, probably at work. I grabbed my cell.

Before I could dial his number, a rush of emotions—love, anger, fear—flipped my stomach. I wanted to be a six-year-old kid again, the one who slipped her hand into her father's as he said he'd love and protect her forever and always. The one whose dad was her hero.

Dad and I had had our differences over the years, especially when I'd been a bigmouthed teenager with a snappy comeback for everything, but he'd always been there for me. He'd never blamed me for Max going missing. Never made me feel as if it was my fault. Not once.

Not once.

I balked again as one of Hadad's theories jostled for attention. Maybe Dad's refusal to blame me hadn't been out of the goodness of his heart but because he *knew* I wasn't responsible. Because *he* was.

No. I refused to jump head-first into Hadad's thorny, destructive vortex again. I had to speak with my father. He was my dad. I'd known him all my life.

I lifted my phone and this time hit Dial.

"Stella." Dad sounded quiet, dejected. "I meant to call, but I . . . I . . ."

"It's okay," I said, my heart crumbling. "Are you at work?"

"Took a few days off," he replied. "I can't face being at the office."

"Did you tell them what's going on?"

"Not yet. The cops haven't released any info, so neither will I. I said I was sick."

"Where are you now?"

"Fore River Sanctuary. Thought I'd try getting some exercise, but I can't face that, either." Dad's next words came out strangled. "I didn't hurt anyone, honey. I didn't kill Arlington. I promise."

"Did you park on Starbird?" I asked, not wanting to get into the rest of the conversation until I stood in front of him. When he said yes, I added, "Give me twenty."

I ran to the house and flicked on the kettle before creeping into the main bedroom, where Jeff was still asleep. He must've been exhausted, because he didn't move as I changed into leggings and a clean shirt before going to the bathroom to brush my teeth and tie my hair.

Five minutes later, I sat in my car with two thermoses of instant coffee. My heart thumped as I thought about meeting my father, what I'd ask him, and how I'd interpret the reactions of the man I'd believed I'd known so well.

Dad stood leaning against his car when I arrived. After easing into the spot behind his sedan, I got out, almost stumbling when I caught sight of his face. The dusky circles under his eyes had aged him a decade in three days. His thick graying hair stuck out like porcupine quills, and a bristly stubble peppered his cheeks and chin, a look I'd only witnessed when he'd been too ill to shave.

My mind spun stories, asking itself questions I couldn't stop or get a handle on. Did Dad look this rough because he'd been accused of a crime he didn't commit? Was it because he knew now that his prints had been identified on the arm, it was only a matter of time before he was charged?

"Hey, kiddo." Dad sighed as he pulled me in for a hug, which I almost had to force myself to reciprocate. "Thanks for coming."

I stepped back and passed him one of the thermoses before pointing to a bench by the side of the road. Once seated, I turned to him, unable to hold in my words any longer. "What the hell is going on?"

Dad winced and pulled a face. "I don't know. I have no clue how my supposed prints ended up on the arm you found. It must be a mistake. I haven't been anywhere near Bradley Hills in years."

"Are you sure?"

"*Yes*, I'm goddamn sure," he said, not far off shouting before running a shaky hand over his face. "Sorry, I didn't mean to snap. I keep expecting Peter Funt to jump out and yell, '*Candid Camera*.' The entire situation's absurd. I'd be in hysterics if my whole life wasn't on the line."

I decided to be as direct as possible in the hopes of getting a genuine reaction from my father. I turned to him, didn't blink. "Are you a murderer?"

"*What?* Stella, *no*. How can you think—"

"Did you hurt Zachary Arlington?"

Dad's jaw made tiny sinewy movements as he tilted his head to the sky. "If you're asking whether I punched the man decades ago, then yes, I did. And I don't regret it. At all. But did I bash in his head and dump him in a lake? No, I did *not*."

"Did Max know about this?"

"Why—"

"Did you hurt my brother?"

My father's mouth dropped open, and as he turned to me, tears flooded his eyes. "How can you ask me that? I love my son. I'd do anything to bring him home. Where's this coming from? Why do you, my *daughter*, think I could harm Max?"

Guilt coiled in my stomach, monstrous and vile, ready to eat me alive. I wanted to believe my father, but the rational side of me, the one that had worked on and read through so many criminal cases, knew those closest to us could do the most unforgivable, unspeakable things.

"Hadad," I said.

"Whoa. The detective thinks I hurt Max?"

"One of her theories is you killed Arlington, or hurt . . . whoever the arm belongs to. Max found out and confronted you, and then you . . . you . . ."

"Got rid of him?" Dad jumped up, his voice a hoarse whisper as he paced a few yards, arms flailing as he spoke. "Jesus, what next? Does she have me down for the Zodiac murders? Maybe she thinks I'm Jack the Ripper."

I got up, too, hands flying to my hips as I stared him down. I wanted to tell him my working theory about the arm belonging to Fynn Baumann to see what he'd say. Except he might tell Hadad, and it would get Talikha into trouble.

"How did your prints end up on a severed arm?" I asked.

"I already told you. I don't know."

"Then you're lucky they haven't charged you," I said. "In fact, you're damn lucky you were able to go home."

Dad stopped pacing. "I'm not naive, Stella," he said. "I know what the police are doing. They let me go, but they're trying to build a case against me. Except there's nothing to build. Never was, never will be. Because I *didn't* hurt anyone."

CHAPTER 43

STELLA

I wanted to believe my father. Desperately hoped he was telling the truth. Except I couldn't stop wondering if he'd lied to everyone, including me, for years. After all, both he and Mom had kept the fact he'd been suspected of killing a man buried deep.

While I understood why—he'd been cleared, wanted to leave it all behind to protect us and himself—it also demonstrated how secretive he was. The irony about apples and trees wasn't lost on me, considering my current predicament and how I was withholding the truth from everyone, including Jeff.

I needed to test another reaction, and while I'd managed to get away with whispering Anwir's name to Dylan, I didn't want to chance breaking that rule a second time. I pulled out my iPhone, created a new note, and wrote, *Who's Anwir?*

Turning to Dad, I covered the Nokia in my breast pocket with my left hand, hoping to muffle the microphone, and showed my iPhone to my father.

He leaned in, scrunched his face. "I don't get it. Who's—"

"Forget it," I said quickly, and was about to lower my hand when Dad spoke again.

"Why does that ring a bell?" He snapped his fingers. *"Dungeons & Dragons."*

"The game Max used to play?"

"Yeah. I'm almost certain it was one of their character names."

My heart thumped. Half expecting the Nokia in my pocket to ring because Anwir was furious at the muffled sound, I asked, "Do you still have Max's board games?"

"Everything's in his bedroom." Dad paused. "Waiting for him to come home."

"Do you think Mom would mind if I had a look around?" I asked.

Dad smiled and put his hand on my shoulder. "You don't need to ask. Our house will always be your home." He took his keys from his pocket, removed one from the key ring, and pressed it into my palm. "I've got to get gas. Let yourself in."

"You're sure Mom won't mind me showing up?"

"She went to work."

"Trying to ignore the situation, huh?"

"Can you blame her?" Dad said with a shrug. "Don't be so hard on her. Your mother was there for me when the police hauled me in after Arlington was found. She told them exactly what a piece of shit he'd been when they were together, and she stuck by me through it all. Not sure I'd have come out the other side without her, to be honest."

"Or the alibi," I said without thinking, watching as Dad's eyes narrowed.

"I didn't hurt him," he repeated. "Lord knows I wanted to."

"Best not mention that part to Hadad," I said. "Thanks for the key."

Not much later, I let myself into my parents' home. The smells of Pledge polish and Bounce dryer sheets greeted me like old friends. As I moved into the hallway, the familiar ticking of a cuckoo clock Mom's brother Bennett had bought for her on a school trip to Switzerland immediately enveloped me with a sense of childhood comfort. I wished I'd met him. Had often wondered how carefree Mom might've been if she hadn't lost a sibling at such a tender age.

I kept on walking through the house. There were such fond

memories of living here with my family. Decorating for the holidays, building blanket forts under the dining table. My parents' rowdy dinner parties with their friends.

On those nights, Max and I had been allowed to stay up late, watch a movie in the den with an extra-large bowl of popcorn. We'd turn the volume down, grinning as we listened to the grown-ups in the other room laughing, telling stories, and much to our shameless delight, dropping the occasional f-bomb.

I wasn't sure how often Mom had entertained guests after Max vanished, but I could probably count the gatherings on one hand. Did she suspect my father of being involved in my brother's disappearance? Had she known but stood by him again to protect herself because she'd seen him kill Arlington, and if she left, he'd implicate her? There was no way I could ask or allude to any of those questions without our relationship imploding entirely.

I headed upstairs. My brother's room was the first on the right, closest to the bathroom he and I had shared. When I'd lived here, Max had often darted to the toilet as soon as he heard me get out of bed. He'd slam the door and deliberately take his sweet time despite only ever brushing his teeth and wetting his hair, but he'd still tease me while I banged on the door.

Despite everything going on, the memory of me calling him a *dough-head* and him shouting back *fart-breath* unexpectedly made me grin. I'd have given anything for another of those petty fights now. Anything to go back in time and tell him on the night of the party that he had to follow Mom's rules and stay home.

I opened his bedroom door and stepped inside, the familiarity of all his things rushing to greet me. The LEGO car sets he'd patiently built and displayed on top of his dresser. A stack of high school papers on his desk, exactly how he'd left them. A soft green hoodie hanging on the back of the door.

My parents hadn't moved anything in six years. Mom meticulously cleaned Max's room every week, changed the sheets and duvet cover every two. It verged on the unhealthy. Then again, if they decided to rid the room of Max's things, I'd beg them not to. It would be too final. As if a definitive page had been forever turned.

My gaze landed on Max's bookshelf, which included *The Little Prince* and the *Asterix and Obelix* graphic novels Anwir had mentioned. The thought of him knowing anything about this sacred space made me want to punch the walls until my knuckles bled. Balling my fists, I stomped to the closet and pulled it open, searching for the reason I'd come.

It took me a while to find Max's *Dungeons & Dragons* game. As soon as I spotted it sandwiched between *Mouse Trap* and *Clue*, I pulled out the box and settled with it on the bed.

Along with figurines, multiple dice, cards, and rule books, I found copious amounts of Max's handwritten notes. Some of them contained character names such as Hagon Coldsong, Shu Moonfall, and what turned out to be Max's preferred pseudonym.

Anwir Regalflare.

I didn't have time to contemplate what it meant other than Anwir giving me proof yet again that he had details about my brother. When I flipped the page, I spotted another name I recognized. This one was real.

Dylan Firth.

A distant memory of Max, Kenji, and another kid—*Dylan*—playing in the basement rushed to the front of my mind. They'd been eleven or so, lying on the floor, zapping each other with pretend powers and debating the best strategy. I'd been fifteen, considered them annoying little boys because they believed drawings of hairy testicles and making fart noises with a hand stuffed in one armpit were the most hilarious things in the world.

Those boys had grown into young men. Max had disappeared. Now Kenji was missing, too. And Dylan had known them both well. What if he'd played me all along? His *poor little poor boy* routine, complete with ailing grandmother, could've been a ruse to throw me off.

Maybe he was Anwir after all.

I immediately reminded myself Fynn Baumann went missing when Dylan was only twelve. Could he really be Anwir? Unlikely, but not impossible. Could Dylan be Anwir's accomplice? A killer's apprentice?

I wanted to drive to Dylan's house or the radio station to confront him. Rant, rave, and demand he tell me the truth. Except... how did I expect him to react if I was right? Put his hands in the air, shout *you got me*, and wait while I called the cops? And all the while, Anwir could be listening and immediately disappear, meaning Kenji and the information about my brother would be gone, too.

The sound of a car in the driveway pulled me out of the impossible debate. I moved to the window, observed Dad getting out and opening the trunk. As I watched him, another vehicle arrived, parking directly behind my father and boxing him in. Hadad.

While she got out of her car and walked to my dad, I cracked open the window, hoping their voices would be loud enough for me to hear.

"Good morning, Mr. Dixon," Hadad said.

"Is it?" Dad asked, his tone terse as he immediately went on the defensive, making me ask myself again if his reaction was that of a guilty man. "It won't be if you're here to accuse me of whatever else I haven't done."

"Mind if we go inside?" Hadad asked. "I have a few follow-up questions."

"Here's fine," Dad replied. "I've got nothing to hide."

"Very well. I'll get straight to it. What's your relationship to Fynn Baumann?"

Talikha must've shared the information I'd given her with the detective. I didn't move, didn't blink as I waited for Dad's answer.

Finally he said, "Don't believe there is one. Not surprising, considering I don't know anyone with the name."

"You're sure you don't know this man?" Hadad held her

phone toward my dad, presumably with Fynn's photo. My father craned his neck, and I willed him to confirm he'd never seen him before in his life. Above all, I willed whatever he said to be true.

"Wait . . . maybe?" Dad said tentatively, and my stomach dropped. "Yeah, I might know him. He could be one of the volunteers at a shelter I helped with some IT stuff. It was years ago, though. I can't be certain. Why?"

"He's missing."

"I'm sorry?"

"Did you know Mr. Baumann was missing?" Hadad asked, moving closer.

When Dad spoke again, I hoped the detective didn't spot the worry in my father's voice as plainly as I did. "I had no idea. I barely knew him. What does this have to do with me?"

I didn't need to hear Hadad's reply. I already knew. Over the past twelve years, three men had gone missing: Fynn, Max, Kenji. My father had known them all. Like he'd known Zachary Arlington. And he knew Dylan Firth. Moments ago, I'd wondered if Dylan was a killer's apprentice. What if said killer was my father?

My trembling legs gave out from underneath me, and I slid to the floor. I didn't want to believe it, but the evidence was leading me to the same clear-cut conclusion.

At the very least, I was the daughter of a serial abductor. And quite possibly a murderer.

CHAPTER 44

STELLA

As I sat on the floor of my brother's bedroom, pressing my back against the wall, I couldn't stop wondering if Dad and Dylan were complicit. Worked as a team. But Fynn had disappeared twelve years ago, when Dylan was so young.

Perhaps Anwir and Fynn had been family, friends, or otherwise close. If Anwir figured out Dad killed Fynn, this could be his revenge . . . except my father's prints were on Fynn's arm. Why not just give it to the cops and let them take over? Why involve me first? I couldn't make sense of any of the possibilities, but one thing was certain—I wouldn't stay in this house.

I waited until Hadad drove away. Once I heard Dad come inside and head for the powder room, I slipped downstairs. Moments later I was in my car, head spinning, hands shaking. I drove a few hundred yards up the street and pulled over, yanking my iPhone from my pocket and dialing Jeff's number.

My call went to voicemail, but I needed to talk to someone before my head exploded. Dr. Graf didn't pick up. I couldn't imagine having a conversation with Vivien, and there was only one other person I felt I could trust. I hit Dial, shoulders sagging as soon as I heard the familiar voice say, "Hello."

"Charlene, it's Stella," was all I managed before an almighty sob escaped my lips.

"Sweetheart, what happened?" Charlene's motherly tone made me cry harder. "What's going on? Where are you?"

"Deering," I said, taking a big shuddery breath. "Close to my parents' house."

"Are you safe?"

"Yes, yes, I'm safe. I . . . I'm having a bad day." I let out a wry snort. "Understatement of the millennium. I'm sorry. I didn't know who else to call."

"Don't apologize," she said. "I'm at home. Do you want to come over? It sounds as though you could use a friend."

Once she'd given me her address, I whispered, "Thank you. I won't be long."

Dad called three times as I drove. I ignored him, burying my head so far into the proverbial sand, only my toes stuck out. When he tried again, I switched my iPhone to silent and stuffed it into the depths of my bag.

"Are you happy, motherfucker?" I said, lowering my chin to the Nokia in my front pocket. "You're a coward, hiding like this. I'm going to find out who you are. You'd better be ready when I come for you, you hear me? I'm going to make you bleed."

I willed the phone to ring, wanted Anwir to scream obscenities into my ear, lose control and finally give me a clue as to who he was. But nothing happened.

By the time I arrived at Charlene's house in the West End and walked up her front path, my pulse had somehow steadied itself. I pressed the doorbell, thinking the enormous redbrick Victorian had to be vast for one person, especially when I heard the chime echoing deep inside her home.

"Stella," Charlene said when she opened the door. "Come in. I have tea."

"Got anything stronger?" I said, trying—and failing—to make a joke.

"I'm sure I can make arrangements," she said with a dry smile as she ushered me inside and indicated for me to turn left, the *clunk-clunk* of her cane following me into a reception room.

I looked around. The building may have been old, but the renovated interior was fresh and new. Classic Victorian features such as crown molding and sash windows had been lovingly preserved, while a rich, dark blue wallpaper with delicate golden hummingbirds covered the back wall. In contrast to Dr. Graf's more clinical home, Charlene's was cozy, with heavy drapes, throw pillows, and a large watercolor painting of a lakeside cottage hanging above the period fireplace.

I sank onto the sofa while Charlene hobbled over, grimacing as she lowered herself into the love seat opposite me. Once she'd poured us each a mug of tea, her face filled with empathy as she patiently waited for me to speak.

It took a few tries to get the words out. Longer for me to arrange them into anything that made sense, and all the while I knew Anwir could hear every single word. I so badly wanted to tell Charlene everything about him, to unburden myself by burdening her. Except I couldn't.

Her mouth dropped when I mentioned I'd likely solved who the Bradley Hills arm belonged to before the cops. Next, I told her Dad's prints were on Fynn Baumann's remains and how they knew each other. Finally, I shared that my father had been suspected of killing Zachary Arlington thirty-two years ago, and Hadad's theory about him hurting Max to keep his secrets safe. Anwir surely knew all of this anyway, and I had to get the vile thoughts out of my body before they destroyed me.

"My gosh, Stella," Charlene said when I was done. "This is shocking. I can't imagine how you're feeling."

"Dad's adamant he didn't do anything to anyone," I said, swiping at the tears that wouldn't stop coming. "How can I believe him? The evidence . . ." I closed my eyes for a moment. "It's too compelling. It's only a matter of time until he's arrested, charged, and convicted of . . . *something*. There's no way even the best, most expensive lawyer can brush this all off as circumstantial."

"This is beyond intense. I'm struggling with what to say."

"Do you think I should believe him?" I asked, desperate for her to give me an emphatic *yes*.

She sighed, wavering before gently answering, "This isn't what you want to hear, but in my experience as a journalist, most of the time when all roads lead to Rome . . . you end up in Rome, although—"

"That's what I'm afraid of," I whispered. "My father's a liar and a murderer and . . . and he hurt Max."

"*Although*," she insisted, "from what I know about your dad, I can't imagine him doing any of this. Least of all harm your brother. What do you make of Detective Hadad's theory?"

"If you'd asked me a few days ago, I'd have been outraged," I said. "I *was* outraged. Now . . . I don't know. I can't get the thought out of my head. Maybe Max didn't find out about Arlington. Maybe it was about Baumann. Or both. What if . . . what if my father killed them all? Arlington, Fynn, Kenji, and . . . Max."

"But why?" Charlene asked. "Why would he do it?"

"Why do serial killers do the things they do?"

Charlene's eyes widened again. "There's no evidence to support he's a serial killer. You're speculating way beyond worst-case scenario."

"At this point, yes. But people like that go undetected all the time. When they're found out, nobody can believe it. Everyone insists they were stand-up citizens, pillars of the community, it must be a case of mistaken identity, blah, blah, blah."

"True," Charlene said. "Those who can hide it for years are masters of deception. They hold down normal jobs, lie to their family and their friends."

"The Golden State Killer," I said. "He went from burglary to assault to rape, and finally murder. He was married for years, had two daughters. Not even his family members knew what he was doing."

Charlene shuddered. "Thank goodness for DNA mapping and new technological advancements in forensics." She paused a moment. "Look, I don't know your father very well. What does your mother think?"

I sighed. "She's shutting down, not saying much. I . . . I'd talk to Jeff about all this, but . . . we're a bit distant right now."

Charlene waited for me to go on before saying, "Want to tell me about it?"

I hesitated as I decided how much to share. "It's about having kids."

"He doesn't want them?"

"No, uh, I'm not sure I do," I blurted.

"Oh, I see," she said. "It's a huge decision. One I could never make. Is that why you asked me for an ob-gyn the other day? Did you see her?"

"No, and . . . *shit*." I fumbled in my bag and pulled out the box of tampons. After removing my birth control, I cursed again when I saw I'd missed three days in a row despite the alarm on my phone. I popped a pill from the blister pack and chugged it down with a gulp of tea.

Once I was done, Charlene gently said, "Given where you're keeping those, I'm guessing Jeff doesn't know you're taking them."

Heat shot to my face, setting my cheeks on fire. "I . . . uh, well . . ."

"It's okay," she said. "These things can be complicated."

As I exhaled all the air in my lungs, I almost toppled over. I was so in the wrong. It was despicable. Jeff was my *husband*.

"Could you try talking to him?" Charlene asked, sounding a little like I imagined Dr. Graf would if I'd confessed this particular sin to him. "Don't you think he'd understand you're not ready to have a baby with everything else going on in your life?"

"He probably would," I said, although I still couldn't fathom how to tell him I never came off the pill in the first place. He'd never believe anything I said again. I wished I could share more with Charlene. Have an open conversation and seek her counsel properly, but I couldn't expose my festering secret to Anwir. It would give him something else to use against me.

"If you decide to talk to him, maybe don't mention that part," Charlene said as she gestured at the blister pack in my hands. When I raised an eyebrow, she added, "Nobody's a saint, Stella. Everyone has a skeleton or two in their closet, no matter how small. He probably does, too."

"Ha," I said. "Not likely. He's the most trustworthy person on the planet."

Charlene opened her mouth before closing it again. For whatever reason, it didn't appear she quite believed me.

CHAPTER 45

STELLA

Charlene and I talked for another hour as I steered the conversation toward neutral topics—movies and TV shows we liked, her love of fishing, and her work on *People of Portland*. While I didn't feel better about my father's situation, or Hadad's stubbornly persistent theories that I couldn't shake, at least I'd brought some of my raw emotions back under control. As Charlene accompanied me to her front door, I thanked her profusely for letting me visit and apologized again for interrupting her day.

"Not at all. That's what friends are for," she said, wincing as she shifted her weight onto her cane while reaching for the doorknob with her free hand. "I'm heading to the cottage for a few days, so I'll be out of town, but call me anytime you need me, Stella. Please."

Buoyed by her support and calm wisdom, I drove home. When my phone rang and Jeff's number flashed on the screen, I didn't answer. I was only a few minutes away from the house, and I needed them to ready myself for at least a partially truthful conversation with my husband.

However, when I saw Jeff's car in the driveway and I let myself into the house, those good intentions flew out the window as soon as I heard him in the kitchen, talking on the phone.

"I don't *know*," he said, his voice unusually terse. I stopped moving, staying out of sight as I listened. "No, I don't think so. We both agree she's been acting strange for ages. Weeks. No, it's more than Max's anniversary. Honestly, sometimes I don't recognize Stella at all these days."

I closed the front door behind me with a thud and walked to the kitchen. When I got there, Jeff sat at the table, his phone face down in front of him.

"Hey," he said, his expression innocent. "I tried to call you. How was your—"

"Who were you talking to?" I asked, trying and failing to keep my tone stable.

Jeff opened his mouth. When I raised an eyebrow and crossed my arms, he must've known he was busted. After a long sigh, he said, "Vivien."

"You were talking to her about me? Again? Why?"

He drummed his fingers on the table. "Because I'm worried about you. We both are."

"Seriously?" I let out a laugh. "With the amount of stuff happening, how can either of you be surprised I'm not doing well?"

"And your dad?" Jeff continued. "He called, too. Did you really accuse him of hurting your brother?"

"It wasn't *my* theory," I said. "It was Hadad's."

"But you thought it was a good idea to ask him if he killed Max? What the fuck, Stella? He needs you."

"Did Dad tell you he knew the guy whose arm was hacked off?" I asked, voice raised. "You know, the one his prints are all over? Did he mention that little gem?"

"*Yes*," Jeff replied. "He has no idea how it happened, and I believe him. So should you."

"Because he's my dad? Don't be so naive."

"Stella—"

"*No*. I know you've been desperate for a perfect family since your parents passed, and I get it, I do, but face it, Jeff. Whether my dad did something terrible or not, mine isn't perfect. The Dixons . . ." I looked away ". . . we're messed up. Broken. All of us. In fact, as far as I'm concerned, it's better if our branch of the family tree withers and dies."

Jeff stared at me. "Are we still talking about your father, or is that code for saying you don't want kids?"

"I never said I don't want a baby, Jeff," I offered, not ready to press the self-destruct button hovering over our relationship. "But with everything going on this past week . . ."

He got up and walked over. With his hands on my shoulders, he said, "I totally get it. I'm not an insensitive lump, but—"

"That's all it is, I—"

"No," he said with a firm shake of his head. "This has been going on much longer. You may not think I notice, but save for a day here and there, you've been distant since you came off your birth control."

"But I—"

"Vivien and I—"

"Vivien and you?" I snapped.

He took a breath. "We both think you've been . . . acting out of character. I figured it was the upcoming anniversary of Max's disappearance, but there's more to it. Tell me what's going on."

I stared at my feet. "Nothing."

"Stella, *please*." He put a finger beneath my chin and tilted my head upward. "Maybe I can help."

After removing his hand, I took a step back. "There's nothing to tell. I, uh, only popped in to change before my emergency session with Dr. Graf." I hated myself for lying again, but Jeff wouldn't continue this conversation if he believed it would make me late for therapy. "I'll see you later, okay?"

My husband's hardening expression wasn't one I'd often seen before. Turning away before he could say anything else, I muttered a quick goodbye and darted outside.

As soon as I was in my car, I searched for the details of the ob-gyn Charlene had given me. I plugged the address into my iPhone, deciding to make an appointment in person, hoping they might have an upcoming time slot so they could squeeze me in for a consultation.

As ludicrous as it felt, this was one problem I could act upon immediately and take back a smidgen of control. I didn't expect to be intimate with my husband anytime soon, but I knew not taking the pill for multiple days in a row put me at risk of getting pregnant when I eventually did.

Telling myself I'd first have a conversation about contraceptive options with the doctor before deciding, I eased out of the driveway and headed into town. I didn't want to lose Jeff. I loved him, knew I didn't deserve him, especially with the lies I'd told. He'd never treat me this way. The thought gave me a bigger sense of self-loathing than I'd thought possible.

I had to be done with this Anwir nightmare. Once it was over and I could tell Jeff the truth, I'd implore him to understand why I hadn't involved him before. He'd be angry, likely devastated, but I'd do whatever I could to make him see reason.

If I were being held captive, and my abductor engaged with Jeff the way Anwir was engaging with me, I didn't think my husband would go to the cops. He'd do whatever it took to find me and bring me home safe and sound single-handedly if it meant I'd be spared.

Things weren't any better or clearer in my mind by the time I got to the front steps of the clinic. As my fingers closed around the door handle, my iPhone vibrated in my bag. Stepping aside, I dug it out and saw it was my father. After letting the call go to voicemail, I was about to send him a message saying I needed space when I heard a voice behind me.

"Stella?"

I spun around. "Jeff? What are you . . . did you *follow* me?"

"Yes," he said before lowering his voice as a woman with a huge baby bump came out the clinic's front door, making us both take a few steps away from the entrance. "I didn't believe your therapy story. Clearly for good reason. What are you doing here? Why did you lie?"

I opened my mouth, trying to come up with an answer. I couldn't face telling the truth, but the thought of spouting more lies was worse. Desperation and humiliation surged, making me vulnerable and trapped.

"Is this a family planning clinic?" Jeff said, pointing at the sign in the window. "Why are you here? Are you . . . ? Oh shit. You're pregnant."

"No, I—"

"Now I get it. It's not mine, is it?"

"What? Jeff, *no*."

"Of course. Everything makes sense." He ran a hand over his face. "This is why you've been distant. You're involved with someone else."

"I'm not."

"You *are*. You have another phone."

"No, I—"

"Stop lying. The other evening you rushed downstairs to answer your phone when I was in the bathroom, but I could've sworn it was on your nightstand." He pointed at the iPhone in my hand. "You followed me upstairs and grabbed it before I could spot it again, didn't you? You have a second cell." Jeff squared his shoulders. "Who is he?"

"I'm not having an affair," I said, my mind spinning, trying to find a way to protect Kenji and preserve my access to whatever could lead me to finding Max. "I use the other one for the podcast. I give the number to people when I don't want them to have my regular one."

"*No*." The word exploded from Jeff's mouth. "You would've told me. Who *is* he?"

"I'm not seeing anyone. I promise, Jeff. I'm *not*."

"Then why are you here?" Jeff's raised voice filled with exasperation. "Explain why you pretended to have a session with your shrink. Again. What are you hiding? Tell me why you're here or—"

"I want an IUD," I shouted. "That's why. And it's the truth."

Jeff gawked at me, looking as if I'd punched him in the face. "Without telling me? After we agreed we'd try for a baby?"

"I'm not ready," I said, my voice nothing more than a whisper. "I might never be."

"So . . . instead of talking to me, your *husband*, you were going to get an IUD in secret?" He threw his hands in the air. "What did you think would happen? We'd try for a few years and give up? Were you going to fake not being able to get pregnant? What the actual *fuck*?"

"It's not like that . . ." I shut my mouth, because it was *exactly* like that.

"Did you stop taking your birth control, or was that another lie?" he demanded, and I bent my head. "Christ, I must be up for the most gullible partner of the century award."

I bit my lip, tears spilling down my face. "Please let me explain."

As I took a step to him, he put his hands up, palms facing me. "No. *No.* For months you've pretended to be sad whenever you got your period. You let me *comfort* you." His brow creased, face a mixture of pain and loathing. "I don't know what to say. All I know is that I can't be anywhere near you."

"We need to talk about this. I—" The sound of a phone ringing caused the rest of the sentence to die in my throat. When Jeff looked at the iPhone in my hand, its screen dark, the noise from the Nokia in my chest pocket created a chasm so vast between us, I couldn't imagine it would ever be bridged.

"I . . . I have to get this," I said, fingers fumbling.

"Of course you do," Jeff said, his sarcastic tone cutting deep.

"You don't understand," I pleaded. "I have to."

My husband, the man I'd thought would forever be the love of my life, stared at me, his eyes ice-cold. Turning around, he threw the next words over his shoulder, each of them another dagger to my heart. "Don't wait up."

CHAPTER 46

STELLA

"Hello, Stella." Anwir's voice dug into the depths of my bones as I stumbled farther away from the clinic. "That was quite the heated argument. I wondered if you'd hear the phone, what with all the shouting."

"Fuck you." The words slipped from my mouth before I could stop them. "I hate you. I hate your fucking guts, you *asshole*."

Unexpectedly, Anwir started to laugh, a deep belly sound filling my ears and my head, making me want to shout more. A second earlier I'd worried my outburst would provoke him. I hadn't expected him to be amused. He thought it was *funny*. I didn't know which was worse.

"My, my. Seems everyone's getting under your skin today."

I clenched the phone tight, gritted my teeth. "What do you want?"

He chuckled again. I wanted to put my hand through the Nokia and out the other side so I could wrap my fingers around his neck and squeeze. I imagined his face turning purple as he struggled for air. His hands clawing at mine, desperate for survival I'd never grant him.

In that moment, I understood how much hatred a person needed to be filled with to kill another human. Less than I felt now. Given a fraction of the chance, I'd make Anwir struggle for his last breath, and I'd take great pleasure in watching him die by my hand.

"Time to check your tone, Stella," Anwir said. "You've insulted me enough already. So, you're at a family planning clinic for an IUD after lying to your husband about taking birth control. Will you unpack this with our useless therapist, I wonder? I can't wait to hear how your next session goes."

A hand flew over my mouth. Even through my fury, I'd registered how Anwir had said *our* therapist, not *your*. Was this deliberate? Or had he finally slipped up and revealed a true nugget about himself I could perhaps use to find him?

I calculated if I should challenge him, demand to know how long he'd been seeing Dr. Graf to get a read on his reaction, maybe push him to slip up some more. It didn't feel right. Not yet.

Mind buzzing, I wanted to hang up and race to Dr. Graf's or send him an email with a bunch of questions about people he'd treated. Trouble was, he wouldn't break patient confidentiality. Perhaps he might if I told him what was going on, but that was a non-starter because Anwir would hear. And if I put it in writing, surely Dr. Graf would want to involve the cops. Also, *Anwir* wasn't my tormentor's real name. But if I could get access to Dr. Graf's files . . .

I had no clue how, but if I could break into my therapist's house, I'd be able to search the place. Maybe it would help unmask Anwir, and then, finally, *finally*, I'd be able to secretly write a letter to Hadad. I could text her. Tell her where I'd leave an envelope for her to find, especially if I could determine for certain that Anwir wasn't a cop.

In the meantime, unless this was all part of a ruse, I had to divert Anwir from the fact he'd made a mistake. I stood still, pulled back my shoulders, and when I spoke again, I injected all the loathing and disgust I could find into my voice. "Go. To. Hell."

"Now, now." Anwir tut-tutted, clicking his tongue. "As I told you, there's no need to be insulting. Kenji's fate hangs in the balance. Are you ready to figure out where he might be?"

"*How?*" I said. "You're not giving me anything to go on. I'm beginning to wonder if you have him."

Anwir sighed. "Perhaps the issue is that you don't care. Let's call it a day. Game over."

My confidence waned. "No, I—"

"I guess you never really wanted to know what happened to Max. Goodbye, Ste—"

"Anwir, wait." I hated the desperation in my voice, especially knowing he loved it so much. "Don't hang up."

He didn't answer for a few beats, then said, "For me to stay engaged, you'll need to demonstrate your commitment. Show you truly aren't giving up."

"How?"

"Never mind," Anwir said. "I'm not wasting more time. Of course, Kenji has no idea what's coming. Actually, he does. Poor lamb."

"*Please*," I insisted. "Leave him alone. Tell me what you want."

"So be it . . . but you won't like it. Remember on *People of Portland* you said you'd give *anything* to find out what happened to your brother?"

"Yes," I whispered. "I remember."

"And you know the expression about something costing an arm and a leg?"

"*What?*" I whispered.

Anwir chuckled, transforming my flesh into goose bumps. "Don't worry, I'm not *that* greedy. How about a fingertip?"

I almost laughed, too, the sheer absurdity of the request seeming wildly ridiculous. Except the image of Fynn Baumann's arm, and Talikha's words about his missing fingertips, meant nothing about this was remotely funny.

"You can't be serious," I said, words barely audible.

"I knew you wouldn't play," Anwir said, dismissive and indifferent. "You're weak."

"I'm not—"

"Show me. You have thirty minutes. Provide visual proof. Tick tock."

After the line went dead, I stood in front of the family planning clinic, my heart thundering. I tried to grasp Anwir's instructions. Was he joking? Was this a test? What would happen if I didn't comply?

I knew what. He'd painted Kenji's fate clearly. Time was running out, and that thought alone was enough to make my head kick-start the rest of me. I rushed to my car and gunned it down the street. As I drove, I told myself Anwir was playing with me to see what I'd do, but given what I'd found in the mine . . .

My stomach roiled, and more than once I almost pulled over to vomit. I forced everything down. There was no time for nausea. No time to think. Only to act. Get home. Decide on what to do next.

Traffic had picked up, and construction in my lane meant the cars in front of me were at a standstill. I pressed the horn, garnering glares from pedestrians and a cyclist, while the driver ahead of me gave me the finger, glowering into his rearview mirror.

"Come on," I whispered. "Come *on*."

We weren't moving. I took my chances and made a U-turn, much to the visible annoyance of the woman driving in the opposite direction. Going well above the speed limit, I zipped down a few side streets, hoping I wouldn't encounter any cops. If they stopped me, there was no telling what Anwir might say when—*if*—I spoke to him again.

Part of my brain urged me to slow down. If I didn't do as Anwir commanded, it meant Kenji would likely die, and I wouldn't get the information about my brother, but maybe my life would go back to normal.

Normal? I didn't know what that meant anymore. And because the guilt about Max's disappearance had nearly consumed me, I didn't think I'd survive Kenji never returning either, knowing I could've helped.

When I turned in to our road, I pleaded with the universe for Jeff not to be at the house. If he was, and he saw me in this state, I'd break down. I might confess everything despite my best intentions not to.

As I turned the last corner, a strange mixture of relief and anxiety flooded my body when I spotted our empty driveway. After dumping the car, I rushed to the kitchen while calling Jeff's name but was met with only deafening silence.

Twenty-two minutes had passed since Anwir had hung up on me outside the clinic, but now time slowed down, the next seconds stretching into hours. My gaze was automatically drawn to the wooden block by the side of the stove. As my eyes landed on the new chef's knife I'd bought, my knees buckled, and I had to put both hands on the counter.

Suddenly, most of me went into a strange and clinically detached state. Would the knife be the most efficient tool? Should I use garden shears? We had a pair somewhere. No, they were dirty and caked with soil. They'd take too long to clean. I gulped in air. Could hardly believe I was contemplating going through with Anwir's sick request.

The Nokia rang.

"Is it done?" Anwir asked. "Because I don't hear you screaming."

"I want evidence," I whispered, the cold determination in my voice surprising me.

"You're in no place to—"

"Prove to me Kenji's alive *and* you know what happened to Max. Prove it, you bastard, or we're done. *Done.* Do you hear me?"

"I've been expecting this request for a while now. As you wish."

Anwir hung up. I paced the kitchen, back and forth, back and forth as I waited. When I still hadn't heard anything, my body went into survival mode as I analyzed, calculated, and evaluated.

Slowly, I walked to the powder room and retrieved our well-stocked first aid kit from the cabinet under the sink. Back in the kitchen, I pulled out a plastic chopping board before cleaning it and the knife with sterile cotton balls soaked in rubbing alcohol.

Somehow, my hands and fingers held steady as I removed packs of nonstick pads, gauze, and a roll of medical tape from the first aid kit and tore them open. It almost felt as if I were having an out-of-body experience, nothing but an observer of this abhorrent reality.

Half an hour later, the Nokia chimed. I picked it up, trance-like, and saw a new message had arrived in the Whisperz app. When I swiped my finger across the screen, I let out a cry.

A photograph. Unmistakably Kenji, standing in a darkened room. He held a piece of paper with today's date and the time. His nails had been bitten down to the quick, cuticles red and raw, knuckles dirty. But the look on his face was what shocked me the most. Sunken eyes, tear-streaked cheeks, his mouth openly pleading with his captor to please, *please* let him go.

Scrambling, I tried taking a screenshot, but for whatever reason—privacy settings, I assumed—the app wouldn't let me. The image vanished, and the screen filled with a more disturbing picture.

Another man, curled up into a ball as he lay on his side, head down, knees pressed to his chest. I couldn't see his face from the angle the photo had been taken, but he seemed so frail, so emaciated and impossibly skeletal, I couldn't believe this was anything other than a corpse.

Before the second photograph disappeared, I already knew that while Anwir might have been a liar, he'd been telling the truth about at least one thing. He had information about Max, and I knew this because the *Simpsons* hoodie and the shorts of the man in the picture were identical to those my brother had worn the night he disappeared.

The howl escaping my mouth sounded more animal than

human, and as I sank to my knees, gasping in the middle of the kitchen, the Nokia rang with an incoming call.

"It's him," I whispered. "It's Max. Is he alive?"

"Put the fingertip down the garbage disposal. You won't need it anymore."

"Tell me."

"Do it, Stella. Email me a picture, or Kenji dies. He dies *today*."

Sobbing, I let the Nokia clatter to the floor and stood up. Without hesitation, I put my left hand on the chopping board. I curled my other fingers out of the way, leaving only the pinky, picked up the knife, and slammed it down. Hard.

Searing pain shot up my arm, and I dropped the blade. I screamed, my voice echoing around the walls as I looked at my hand. I'd severed my pinky clean through the middle of the nailbed. Blood gushed from the open wound, the tip an inch away.

Crying out again, I grabbed my iPhone and took a picture before throwing the tip into the garbage disposal. The blood was everywhere now. The chopping board. Knife. Floor. All over my hand. I swiped a set of the nonstick gauze pads, trying to apply as much pressure as I dared, but also knowing I had to send Anwir proof of what I'd done or it would all be for nothing.

Ripping the tape with my teeth, I wrapped my pinky as tight as I could bear before sliding my sticky fingers over my iPhone and emailing him the photo. Thirty seconds later, the Nokia chimed with an incoming Whisperz message.

Well done. Kenji lives to fight another day. I'll be in touch.

Before the message disappeared, the room began to spin, the floor rushing toward me.

WEDNESDAY, AUGUST 6

CHAPTER 47

Hearing you scream as you slammed the knife onto your hand was . . . satisfying. I wish I'd been there to witness it in person. Seen your face when you took in the self-inflicted damage.

You keep surprising me, Stella, because I didn't think you'd do as I demanded, truly I didn't. I expected you to lose your nerve and beg and plead. That's what all the others have done, but not you.

I wanted to see how far I could push you already. It's made me think more about what's next for you. What it'll take to break you. Once I've determined that point, I'll lead you to your precipice of fear again. I'll have you dangling from the ledge, holding on for dear life before I extend a hand and pull you back—just enough to give you a little respite.

And then we'll do it all again. And again.

Humans are fascinating creatures, and you'll be my most interesting project yet. One of the final pieces of a particular puzzle. I'm excited. Not like the kid in a candy store who's too overwhelmed by all the options and can't decide what to choose. No, I'm the child on Christmas morning, sitting patiently in front of the tree, so focused on one gift, the one they've longed and yearned for, the rest disappear.

You're my gift, Stella, and although you can't be mine forever—because nothing lasts that long—trust me when I say we'll be together for a very, very long time.

CHAPTER 48

STELLA

I'd sat in bed last night, propped up by a multitude of pillows and with all the lights on. My injured hand had begun to throb, and my mind zoomed back to what I'd done.

After regaining enough strength and composure to drive, I'd taken myself to Maine Medical's ER. Thankfully it hadn't been busy, and once I'd gone through the intake process, a kindly nurse had ushered me into a cubicle.

"I'm afraid we can't stitch this," the physician had said a while later, as I'd lied about what had happened, and she'd gently examined my wound. "I'll clean the injury, give you a tetanus shot and painkillers. You can take acetaminophen when what I give you starts wearing off."

"Will it take long to heal?" I'd whispered.

"A good few weeks," she'd replied. "Keep your hand elevated as much as possible. Change the dressing after forty-eight hours and then daily, and try not to get it wet. Make an appointment with your family physician in seven days. If there's any redness and swelling, or you develop a fever, see them earlier or come here."

Back home, I'd wondered if Jeff would arrive soon. He hadn't. Shortly before eleven he texted a curt *Staying at Owen's. Working on his renos tomorrow.* I could only imagine their conversations about my betrayal. Owen was a good, decent guy, much like Jeff, and his wife and young son were the most important things in the world to him.

At least Jeff had someone to talk to, but my husband would need a humongous amount of time to fully digest the discovery of my lies. Consequently, I'd answered, I understand. Sleep well. Love you xo

He hadn't responded.

Aside from the fact I sat alone in the house and jumped at every unfamiliar creak and groan, I was grateful for Jeff's absence because it gave me time. My mental state was becoming increasingly fragile, and I had to try to deal with the shock of what I'd done.

I'd already practiced the story—another lie—I'd provide Jeff. It was the same one I'd used at the hospital: I'd been angrily chopping vegetables, and the knife slipped. I'd been so frantic, I'd forgotten to take the fingertip with me to the hospital. As it turned out—and this was the truth—the doctor had said she couldn't have sewed it back on anyway.

Considering Jeff had seen multiple injuries caused by inattention, I thought I could make my tales work. I had to.

As the hours had dragged by, the pain had been a constant reminder of Anwir's demand. I'd barely snatched a few hours' sleep because of anxiety and discomfort, and because I couldn't erase the photos he'd sent via the Whisperz app from my mind.

Kenji was alive, or at least he had been yesterday. But the other man . . .

Max.

My heart wanted to believe it had been a current photo of my brother. That would mean, somehow and against all odds, he'd made it through the past six years alive. Except the man in the picture looked like a skeleton. A ghost. My head argued with my heart, reminding me to be careful what I wished for.

If it truly was Max, my brother would have been kept prisoner. I couldn't help the shudder hurtling through my body. The man in the picture had been starved. That much was obvious. What other atrocities had he suffered? What else had he endured?

Was the same thing happening to Kenji now? And what about Fynn Baumann? Talikha had said that judging by the state of the arm, he'd been severely emaciated. Was he dead? Had he been alive when his arm was removed? Where was the rest of him?

As dawn came and increasingly vile scenarios swirled through my head, each one more horrific and despicable than the next, I wanted to keep the curtains closed and sleep forever, safe and warm.

Safe?

As long as Anwir was out there, I'd never be safe again. Neither would Kenji and Max, or whoever was in the photo.

I thought back to Anwir's potential misstep, how he might have inadvertently given me my first tangible clue about his identity yesterday by saying Dr. Graf was our therapist. I had to grab ahold of this tiny detail and act, no matter the pain in my hand. No matter how much terror filled my veins. No matter if I thought it might be another lie. Another game.

Hunger eluded me, but I forced myself to eat a protein bar, stopping midway to take another painkiller. When the tears came, they weren't only because of my hand but fueled by frustration and endless hatred for Anwir, too. I needed to know why he was doing this. Maybe I wouldn't understand until I found out who he was. Identifying him remained my only priority.

An idea hit. During a therapy session, Dr. Graf had mentioned that he worked at a youth drop-in center every Wednesday morning. I googled the center and called, pretending to be a mom interested in the program. Once I'd established Dr. Graf would be there from nine until two, I grabbed my laptop.

After watching a few YouTube videos about how to secure a home from burglars—and thus how to break into one—I headed to the garage, where I retrieved a pair of gardening gloves, a hammer, and a slim screwdriver, feeling ridiculously unprepared.

I'd never broken into anything. Had no clue how hard it would be to slip inside my therapist's house. Or if I'd get caught.

Regardless, not much later I eased my car out of the driveway and headed to Riverton. After parking a hundred fifty yards away from Dr. Graf's home, I got out, pulled on one of Jeff's baseball hats, bent my head, and walked up the street with my shoulders hunched, trying to arouse as little suspicion as possible. When I approached my therapist's place, I glanced around but didn't see anyone.

As casually as I dared, I breezed up the path before disappearing into the backyard. This was an older neighborhood like ours. Decent lot sizes, plenty of mature leafy trees providing more than adequate cover from prying eyes.

Dr. Graf had created a little oasis here, with a stone patio, two cushion-covered chairs, and a sectional outdoor sofa placed around an empty firepit. I imagined him sitting here in the evening, relaxing with a glass of heady port. I liked Dr. Graf, and respected him. If only I could ask for the information I needed instead of breaking into the house of someone I trusted, and who trusted me.

I shook off the feelings and returned to the back door. For the next little while, I searched for a spare key everywhere I could think of. Underneath flowerpots. Behind the large barbecue. Around the windowsills and the patio door. Below stones in the rock garden. Nothing.

The desperate need to gain access to his files grew, and so I walked down the left side of the house, stopping when I reached the first of three basement windows. With a gloved right hand and the injured one tucked behind my back so I didn't inadvertently leave prints, I tried to slide the pane across. It wouldn't budge. The next one was firmly locked, too, although the third seemed promising.

Five minutes later, I'd barely made progress. This was hopeless. Whispering an apology to Dr. Graf under my breath, I walked to the back of the house again as I retrieved the hammer from my bag. After lifting the weapon into the air, ready to break the glass of the patio door, two things stopped me.

The first was the vague recollection of a keypad in the hallway opposite Dr. Graf's office. The next and more urgent one was the glimpse of someone moving about inside. Heart pounding, I ducked and darted around the corner of the house moments before the back door opened.

Crouching, I crawled behind a sculpted yew and snuck a glance. An older woman stood a dozen yards away, shaking out a rug, a plume of dust sparkling in the sunlight. When she turned, I pulled back, and once I felt certain she'd retreated into the house, I ventured another peek.

The patio door stood wide open. Seizing my chance, I crept forward, watching through the window as I saw the woman's legs disappearing up the main stairs.

I didn't know the layout of Dr. Graf's house well enough to be exactly sure of where I was going. Didn't have time to look around as I sped through the kitchen to what I presumed was a door to the basement, thinking it had to be the best place to hide.

As I softly opened the door, I heard footfalls coming back to the main floor. Panicking, I tentatively put a toe down, expecting the first tread of the stairs. The floor remained flat and even. With the woman fast approaching, there was no other choice. I stepped inside the room and pulled the door closed behind me.

After reaching for my iPhone and then the Nokia, reassuring myself I'd already set them to silent so I wouldn't be exposed by an incoming message or call, I switched on the flashlight. My heart sank. Neatly stacked shelves filled with furniture polish, toilet cleaner, dish towels, and laundry detergent. I'd landed in the supply closet.

I had to get out of there, but I could hear the woman bustling in the kitchen. It was too risky. However, if the woman I presumed was Dr. Graf's housekeeper opened the door, I'd have to make a run for it, hoping she'd be too startled to get a glimpse of my face. Except if that happened, I'd lose my chance to search through my therapist's files. And if she somehow apprehended me . . .

I spotted a large hamper. Hiding inside would be too dicey if the housekeeper was tasked with laundry. A tall cupboard seemed promising, but I quickly saw its shelves were placed too close together for me to climb inside.

Increasingly desperate, I spotted a large green plastic basket on the floor. I crawled behind it as fast as I could, lying flat on my side and stretching my legs behind a huge pack of paper towel rolls. The door opened the instant I'd positioned the basket in front of my torso, and as the housekeeper walked in, I pressed my back against the wall.

There'd be no escape if she noticed me. She'd have ample time to run from the closet, then slam and lock the door before I attempted to scramble out. My heart thudded as I watched her sneakers come so close, I could count the freckles on her shins, hear the muffled sound of Queen's "Bohemian Rhapsody" coming from what I presumed were her earbuds.

Just when I thought I might get away with hiding here, the green basket disappeared into the air. Expecting the woman to drop to her knees and peer at me with steely eyes, I tried, and failed, to come up with a suitable excuse about what I was doing.

But then she burst into a remarkably accurate impression of Freddie Mercury. She plucked a few supplies from the shelves, popped them into the basket, and disappeared from the room.

I thought my heart might explode, but there was no time to relax. After I heard the housekeeper heading upstairs, I slipped out of the closet and located the door to the basement. Once downstairs, I found the utility room, slid behind the gigantic furnace, and sank to the floor, knees to my chest.

It was too noisy to hear what was going on upstairs, so I waited. About an hour later I emerged, crept up the basement steps, and pressed my ear to the door. Minutes passed but there wasn't a sound, so I gently turned the knob, pushing the door open a crack and listening again. The house stood empty and quiet. I was the only person here.

Staying away from the windows, I sneaked into Dr. Graf's office. With the housekeeper gone, hopefully I had enough time to search through the files for any clues as to who Anwir might be, and get out of here well before my therapist returned.

I pulled open the top drawer of a metal filing cabinet. The hanging folders were sorted by last name and in alphabetical order, neatly labeled in Dr. Graf's tidy handwriting.

As I took in the dozens of patient records, the mammoth task ahead of me became clear. It would take days to comb through this amount of paperwork, especially since I had no real clue what I was searching for. I didn't have that long. It was already 11:00 a.m. If Dr. Graf came straight home from the youth center, it was only a question of hours. What about everything on his computer, too?

Nauseous, I removed the first file and skimmed through my therapist's crisp notes. The man in question had work issues, thought he was undervalued and underappreciated by his boss. The next patient hadn't been intimate with his wife in almost two years because of his fear of not being able to perform, and she'd suggested an open marriage. She loved him, but at forty-two, she wasn't ready for celibacy. He was considering it for the sake of their kids.

Could either of them be Anwir? How would I know? I wasn't trained in psychology. It wasn't as if Anwir would've self-identified as a serial abductor and confessed his crimes to Dr. Graf. Also, the basic description of *thirty- to forty-year-old white male* didn't help much. Too many of his clients could fit the profile, plus there were no photographs.

After another row of files, none of them helpful, and choosing to ignore my own, I chastised myself for thinking I could pull this off. I wasn't a detective, or a shrink. I was, however, a burglar. But as I tried to make up my mind if I should continue or get out of there, my eyes landed on another name.

Jeff Summer.

My husband.

CHAPTER 49

STELLA

I blinked three times. There had to be more than one Jeff Summer in the Portland area. When I'd told my husband about meeting Dr. Graf at the gym, and I was strongly considering him as my therapist, Jeff never mentioned talking to anyone with the same name. He couldn't have known Dr. Graf. Jeff would've said.

My fingers reached for the file as a distant memory flitted around my head. Jeff had attended a therapy session almost immediately after Max disappeared. For whatever reason—work benefits, I think—he'd switched to another therapist, whom he'd visited on a semiregular basis ever since.

As I opened the file, I immediately knew my gut instinct had been correct. This was *my* Jeff Summer. I also knew that reading a file about my husband was another huge betrayal on my part. That fact wasn't enough to stop me. I wanted to know what Jeff had said about Max's disappearance when it had still been so fresh in his mind. It was intrusive, another violation of his trust, but maybe I'd find a clue that would help.

There were only a page and a half of notes. Details about that night, how Jeff and I had waited for Max outside my parents' house before driving to the party. How we'd argued and I'd gone for a walk along the beach, leaving him behind.

I frowned as I read on. When I'd found Jeff, he'd been on his way back from the bathrooms. He'd said he'd had an upset stomach, yet while there was much detail about everything else, there was no mention of indigestion in Dr. Graf's notes.

Fair enough—gut trouble wasn't necessarily information you wanted to share with your therapist—but Jeff had spoken about us having an argument. Maybe Dr. Graf hadn't deemed Jeff's gastric problems necessary to jot down.

I kept reading, gasping at the next lines.

Follow-up note for next sessions: Jeff says he has "immense guilt" about the night of Max Dixon's disappearance. When prompted multiple times, he wasn't ready to divulge why. He shut down and wouldn't respond. He won't share what happened with anyone, including his partner (Stella, Max's sister). Said it was "a terrible mistake." Aim: help him vocalize what he's afraid of.

Vomit rose to the back of my throat. Jeff was hiding something.

Something huge.

Something awful.

What had he done? Had he hurt Max? If so, did it mean Jeff was Anwir? No. *No.* He loved me. We'd been together almost a decade. I knew him better than anyone—his heart, his soul, and especially what he was and *wasn't* capable of.

Didn't I?

I'm not sure how I got through more of the remaining patient files, but I didn't find anything useful. My thoughts kept returning to Jeff, and what he'd covered up for six years. I needed to know. I had to speak to him.

Ensuring everything in the office was back to how I'd found it when I'd arrived, I crossed the room and pulled the door open. As my eyes landed on the wall directly opposite, my immediate problem became abundantly clear.

The house alarm.

I hadn't imagined it. A green *Armed* button blinked fiercely, almost as if it were daring me to try and escape the house undetected. How long would it take for the cops to get here once I set it off? Pulling my baseball hat over my eyes might not help much if I was running for my car. I had no clue how many neighbors would spot me, and all of them could take photos of me and my vehicle. I could get arrested, thrown in jail.

There was no way I could disarm this thing. I wouldn't know which buttons to press and couldn't attempt guessing the passcode. Maybe I could slip past Dr. Graf when he returned, but it might turn out to be impossible, and what if he was gone all day?

I retrieved my iPhone, tried to google ways of disarming a security system, but it was hopeless. After more research, during which I desperately pretended to ignore the searing pain in my hand—and the fact the bottle of acetaminophen was in my car—I learned there would likely be sensors on windows and exterior doors. I walked around the main floor and spotted little white rectangular boxes on each one.

The windows on the second floor were armed, too, and the basement didn't provide an escape route either—sensible, considering it would likely be the first place a thief would attempt entry. I certainly had.

I'd almost decided to make a run for it out the back door when I remembered that from what I'd seen during my previous visits here, the house might have an attic space. Sure enough, I found a trapdoor in the ceiling of the upper floor. I grabbed a hook-like stick hanging on the wall, slid it into the eyebolt on the trapdoor, and pulled, revealing a set of folded stairs.

After putting the stick back, I brought down the stairs and climbed into the attic. The space was mainly empty, with a few cardboard boxes marked *Christmas* and *Party Decorations* dotted about. One of them had been placed a few yards in front of a little window on the left. The pane was small and had no alarm sensor. If it opened, it would be big enough for me to climb through.

Peering outside, I spotted the branches of an oak tree, close and sturdy enough for me to grab. Except with my injured hand, which throbbed worse than before, I didn't know if it would be possible.

Convincing myself I'd climbed out of my brother's window plenty of times, and ignoring that had been years ago, and his room was on the second floor, not the third, I pushed the window open, half expecting the shriek of an alarm. The house remained silent.

By yanking up the retractable stairs and closing the attic hatch, I knew I was effectively locking myself in, but I had little choice. This was the point of no return. Not wanting to waste any more time, I leaned out, reaching for the sturdiest branch I could find. After testing its safety as best I could, I climbed out.

The tree creaked as I turned back to push the window closed. I couldn't latch it again on the inside, but if I was lucky, neither Dr. Graf nor the housekeeper would notice it had been disturbed. If they did, hopefully they'd figure they'd simply forgotten to close it at some point.

Saying a few silent prayers to the tree gods, I moved as deftly from branch to branch as I could given my injury, inching closer to the ground. At one point I whacked my left hand on one of the branches and had to wrap my intact arm around the tree trunk to stop myself from falling.

Finally, mercifully, my feet touched the grass, and I sank to my knees. When I climbed into my car, I trembled as the throbbing in my hand reached explosive levels. But with Dr. Graf's notes about Jeff's session still fresh in my mind, my determination pushed away the pain.

I swallowed some pills and started the engine, ready to face my husband.

CHAPTER 50

STELLA

Not wanting Jeff to see my injury, I took my jacket off and draped it over my arm. It didn't matter in the end, because he wasn't at Owen's new place when I arrived.

"He stepped out," Owen said before leaning in, and gently continuing, "He needed a break and went for coffee. I hope you guys can figure stuff out, Stella. I've never seen Jeff this messed up."

After mumbling a thank-you to Owen, I fled, unsure if I could salvage my marriage, but knowing exactly where to find my husband. Angel's Café, a firm favorite of Jeff's where he insisted he could get the best cortado, was two minutes away. I got there fast, but when I pushed the door open, taking in the familiar smell of coffee beans and vanilla, I immediately saw Jeff wasn't around.

Outside again, I pondered waiting near Owen's for Jeff to return, then heard raised voices. I didn't see anyone on the street in a heated conversation, but as the shouting continued, I stood still and listened. Not only were the harsh-sounding words coming from the alleyway to the side of Angel's, but I could've sworn the voice was Jeff's.

I walked a few steps and peered around the corner. It *was* him—with *Vivien*—both facing each other and standing perpendicular to the main road, meaning they hadn't yet seen me. I watched as Jeff vehemently shook his head while Vivien put her hands on her hips.

"I'm telling her," Jeff said, and although he wasn't shouting anymore, the force of his words was unmistakable. He was a man on a mission. "I have to."

"No good will come of it," Vivien countered fiercely. "It was years ago. It doesn't matter."

"You don't understand," Jeff snapped. "She needs to know. She's my *wife*."

I couldn't wait any longer, had to know what was happening. I moved in, and when they turned and saw me, Vivien swore while Jeff's face turned red.

"First the secret phone calls, and now secret meetings," I said. "What's going on?"

Jeff took a few steps toward me. "Stella. What are you doing here?"

"Answer my question first," I said, staying firm as I challenged him.

He glanced at Vivien. "I, uh, we were . . ."

"Arguing over talking to me," I prompted. "What about?"

When Jeff's gaze dropped to my injured hand, his embarrassed expression was replaced with one of alarm. When I looked down, I understood why. Not only was the bandage dirty and gray from my exploits breaking into and climbing out of Dr. Graf's home, but blood had seeped through the material, turning it crimson.

He closed the remaining gap between us. "You're hurt. What happened?"

"Doesn't matter. Tell me what you were arguing about."

Vivien bit her lip and put her head down. "Nothing."

"That's not true," Jeff said, and as she tried to jump in, he added, "It's about the night Max vanished. It's about . . . it's about what we did."

"What you *did*?" A million thoughts appeared, the loudest

one shouting at me that I was about to hear Max was dead. This was what they'd really been talking about in secret. Jeff and Vivien were responsible for my brother's disappearance. They'd hurt him. Disposed of his body. Thrown Max into the ocean for the fish to feed on.

Had the murder been deliberate? It didn't make sense. It couldn't be possible. An accident, then. It must've been. This was what he hadn't been able to tell Dr. Graf.

I'd have turned and run if I'd been capable of moving, but my legs had transformed into immobile steel rods. And so I stood with my palms sweating as I waited for everything I'd believed to be true about my husband to shatter forever.

"Vivien and I . . ." Jeff said, tears filling his eyes. "We . . . we . . ."

"We slept together," Vivien offered, her voice small, apologetic.

"*What?*" I said, part of me thinking, *Wait, that's it?* It was an affair they were confessing to, not killing Max. With everything else going on, I almost laughed. "The night of the beach party? When?"

"After our argument," Jeff whispered as he stuffed his hands in his pockets. "I had a couple of beers, and I was angry. Vivien asked me what was wrong. We went for a walk, and . . . we ended up in the bus shelter, smoked a joint and . . ."

Shaking my head, I tried to dislodge the sudden and unwelcome images of my husband having sex with my best friend. A quick fumble in the dark. At the bus shelter. I wrinkled my nose. My suspicions about Vivien having a crush on my husband hadn't been misplaced after all. Her lying to me wasn't new. She'd been doing so for years.

"You . . . you cheated?"

"I'm so, so sorry, Stella," Jeff said.

"It only happened once," Vivien added. "We barely remember it."

"Why tell me now?" I asked, staring at Jeff. "Is it because of your *immense guilt?*"

His eyes widened again. "Of course I feel guilty. We both do."

Could this really be all Jeff was hiding? Sure, I believed he regretted cheating on me with Vivien, but the wavering in his voice told me to keep pushing. I moved toward him. "What else happened? What are you hiding?"

"Nothing," Vivien said. "We haven't—"

"I didn't ask you," I said. "And I won't believe anything you say ever again."

"What's that supposed to mean?" she asked. "I know sleeping with Jeff was a terrible thing. Being intoxicated isn't an excuse, but—"

I held up my hand. "Stop. Like this is the only instance when you've lied to me."

"It is. I—"

"You manipulated me into having lunch with Booker."

"I apologized," she said, voice stubborn. "I did it for the sake of the podcast."

"What about seeing her at Templetons the night Kenji disappeared?" I asked, getting the rest of my virtual barbs in a row, ready to fire. "Do you want to apologize for whatever scheming you were up to then?"

"It wasn't like that," she said quickly. "I ran into her at the club. She was with her wife and some friends. We had a chat outside about the upcoming lunch."

"To ensure you'd get what you wanted?"

"To ensure she'd listened to the show."

"And would offer to buy us out."

Vivien threw her hands in the air. "Yeah, okay, fine. That was my endgame. There, I've said it. But, Stella, we need her money to survive. You're too goddamn selfish to accept it."

"Hey," Jeff said. "You're out of line, Vivien, and—"

"*I'm* selfish?" I said, ignoring my husband. "How rich coming from the person who arranged for Liam from Augusta to call *People of Portland*."

"What?" Jeff turned to her. "No, you didn't, did you?"

"Of course not," she said. "I'd never—"

"Really? Let's call Dylan Firth and find out." I stared at the woman who'd been my best friend since high school as I pulled out my iPhone. Watched while her eyes darted from me to Jeff and back again, her face filling with panic.

Dylan had told the truth.

"Why would you do that to Stella?" Jeff asked. "What possible motive—"

"For better ratings," Vivien said. "That's why."

"You knew Booker might be listening," I added, my words clinical, matter-of-fact. I suddenly felt so tired. Too exhausted for more anger. "It was a selling feature."

"It was for *us*," Vivien whispered. "For the podcast's survival. You always insist you'll do whatever's best for our show. I'm no different."

"I stand by my statement," I said. "Clearly, what's best for *A Killer Motive* is for us to never work together again."

"But—"

"We're done, Vivien. Our partnership. Our friendship. They're over."

She drew a sharp breath. "You can't fire me."

"Majority shareholder, remember?" I said, sounding anything but triumphant.

"You need me," Vivien insisted. "There's no way you can do everything alone. You'll tank, and don't you dare take the Booker deal and cut me out. I'm the one who put it together. She won't be on board if I'm not around."

"In that case," I replied with the most nonchalant shrug I could muster, "you've got nothing to worry about. Now, if you don't mind, I want to speak with my husband. Alone."

Fists balled, Vivien looked at me, and then Jeff, who put his arm around my shoulder. Without another word, she stormed off.

As we watched her disappear around the corner, my bravado vanished. Our friendship and our business relationship were irretrievably broken. Panicking, I considered running after her and telling her I'd reconsidered, but the wounds from her multiple betrayals cut far too deep.

"I swear, I had no idea she did those things," Jeff said as I shrugged away his arm. "How did you find out?"

"Secrets have a habit of crawling their way to the surface," I said, knowing the same would be happening to mine soon, too.

Jeff closed his eyes. "About what went on at the beach . . ."

"No, Jeff, I—"

"Please, Stella, let me say this," he said, looking at me again. "I know you hate yourself for what happened to Max. It's the reason you're unsure about having kids. That's why I met Vivien today. I wanted her to know I was going to tell you everything, but . . ."

"She tried to stop you."

"Yes, but that's not all. Stella . . . I feel just as guilty as you about Max going missing."

"It wasn't your fault," I said. "You didn't convince him to go to the party. You didn't bail him out of your parents' home or let him stay longer, and—"

"I saw him," Jeff blurted.

"Wh-what do you mean?"

"After Vivien and I . . . after we . . ." His expression was that of a man begging for forgiveness. "She went to the bonfire to join the others, and I hung back so nobody would notice us together. I couldn't believe what we'd done. I was sick to my stomach."

"Did Max see you?" I asked, taking a step back. "Jeff, are you telling me you hurt him?"

"No."

"Don't lie," I said. "Tell me the truth or I swear I'll—"

"Yes, I hurt him, but not in the way you think," Jeff said, making my mouth snap shut. "After . . . after Vivien left, Max came down the sandbank."

"Alone?"

"Yes, and he was furious. He said he'd seen me and Vivien together and had decided to tell you immediately but changed his mind." Jeff ran a hand through his hair, rubbed the back of his neck. "Max said *I* had to tell you, not him. I knew I should . . ."

"But . . . ?"

"I was too ashamed."

"What happened next?"

"We argued. I begged him to keep quiet and give me time. He refused, and then . . ." Jeff closed his eyes for a few beats. "Max came at me. Hit me square in the gut. Hard."

"When . . . when I met you on the path, you told me you had stomach issues."

"I lied about the reason my gut hurt," Jeff whispered. "And when he went for me a second time, I moved out of the way. I hit him in the face. He fell. I told him to stay down."

"You punched Max?" I said, unable to believe Jeff had ever struck anyone in his life, least of all my brother. "Did he hit his head? Was he bleeding?"

"*No,*" Jeff insisted. "His jaw probably wasn't great, but I didn't break any of his bones. I told him to mind his own business, and I'd speak with you in my own time."

"Except you didn't."

"No, I didn't," he whispered. "When you saw me and said you couldn't find Max, I told you we should split up to search for him. I went back to where I'd left him so I could apologize. He was gone."

"Did you see anything?" When Jeff didn't answer, I asked him again.

"No, but I think I heard an engine in the distance."

"There was a car?"

"I—I'm not sure," he said. "The road curves, and it was dark. I figured it was someone leaving the party. I genuinely believed Max got a ride home."

"Did you tell the cops? Did Wade know?"

"Not directly—"

"I can't believe this. It's been six *years.* Why didn't you say any of this before?"

"Because I was terrified," he said. "I wasn't thinking straight. I cheated on you. Max saw it, and I hit him. I'd already lied when I told you I hadn't seen him."

"So you kept everything to yourself?"

"*No*. I didn't want to talk to the cops, so I emailed a reporter. Charlene."

"Thornton? From *People of Portland*."

"Yeah. When Max didn't come home, and Wade still seemed to think he'd gone to California, I sent Charlene an anonymous message saying she should get door cam footage from houses on the road leading to the beach." He paused. "Somehow, she knew I'd emailed her. She called and I agreed to meet."

"Which is why you recognized her when you got bagels the other day," I said, realizing it had been another lie. There were so many of them. "What did you tell her back then?"

"Not a lot," Jeff replied. "I asked her to get Wade to prioritize security footage, but not to tell him I'd suggested it. She promised she would."

"But . . . but when we asked Wade, he said the footage on the single video they'd obtained was useless."

"I know," Jeff said. "I guess it didn't matter in the end."

"Of course it did," I whispered. "How much time went by before Wade visited those houses? What if someone recorded over a video before Wade even got there because they didn't know it might be relevant to an investigation? What if he never asked the right questions?"

"With his incompetence—"

"Exactly," I snapped. "I could've used the information myself. You stopped that from happening."

"Stella—"

"We have to tell Hadad. Get her to review whatever they have on file, and to go door-to-door again. You'll tell her what you saw. A tiny detail could make all the difference."

"We can talk to her, absolutely," he said. "But I didn't *see* anything. It's another reason why I kept quiet. It wasn't—"

"No." I held up a hand. "You kept quiet because you're a coward, and I'm only just figuring out how much of one. Why didn't you tell me you'd had a session with Dr. Graf?"

"How did you—"

"Why didn't you *tell* me?" I shouted.

"I *did*," Jeff said. "You'd obviously forgotten by the time your paths crossed at the gym, because you didn't recognize the name."

"The decent thing would've been to remind me."

"Not when you seemed excited to see him," Jeff countered. "I didn't want the fact I'd spoken to him during one session to put you off. You need therapy. We both do. Perhaps as a couple we—"

"A couple? You think that's still what we are? And for the record, I meant what I said about me not having an affair. I haven't slept with anyone else."

"I believe you, Stella. Please, let's talk things through. I want to look at your hand. We can go home and—"

"No, stay at Owen's. I need to be alone."

I turned, leaving Jeff in the alleyway with his hands stuffed back into his pockets and his face grim. As I walked to my car, I couldn't stop the feeling that our marriage, and everything it was built on, had imploded entirely.

CHAPTER 51

STELLA

As soon as I closed the car door, I grabbed my iPhone and dialed Charlene's number. She hadn't even managed to utter a greeting before I plowed ahead with, "Jeff emailed you about the night Max went missing. You tracked him down. He came to your house."

Charlene calmly said, "That's right. I take it he never told you."

"No."

"I'm sorry I didn't mention it. Look, if you come over—"

"Tell me now how it all came about."

"Okay," she said, and I decided to keep quiet until she was done. "A few days after your brother vanished, I received an anonymous email. A friend tracked the IP and email addresses, which wasn't hard, apparently. They led to Jeff, so I contacted him. We met at my house. He told me about hearing a car on the road shortly after he'd spoken to Max by the bus shelter."

"And the argument between him and my brother?"

"What argument?"

"They got into a fight."

"Jeff never mentioned it. He said he felt the cops weren't doing a thorough enough job and thought a journalist sniffing around might light a fire under their butts."

"And you believed him?"

"It wasn't the first time I'd been approached by someone who insisted the police needed a shove to get things done."

"Did you talk to the cops?"

"I asked Detective Wade if he'd checked the houses on the road to Lighthouse Beach for security cameras. He said it was on his list to investigate." Charlene clicked her tongue. "Then he told me to stop interfering and let him do his job, which he didn't."

"What do you mean?"

"Well, when I followed up with him a few days later, he told me Max was likely living it up in California. So I decided to make inquiries with the homeowners myself."

"What did you find?"

"Two houses with cameras that captured part of the road."

"Two?"

"The others either didn't have any or were too far back. Anyway, I got the recordings. One was so dark and grainy you couldn't see anything. The other was better, and there was a car. I gave it to Wade on a USB stick. He must've mentioned it."

"No," I whispered. "Do you still have it?"

"Unfortunately not," Charlene said. "A pipe in the bathroom burst and flooded my office. Hard lesson. I keep everything in the cloud nowadays."

"Thanks, Charlene. I've got to go."

"Wait. Tell me what's going on. Can I help?"

"No, it's fine."

"It doesn't sound fine. *You* don't sound fine."

I had to talk to Wade about the footage he'd never mentioned, *today*. Having Charlene with me would help, but I couldn't drag her into this situation any further than I already had. It was too dangerous.

"I'd better go," I said. "Thanks again."

After hanging up, my mind turned to how I'd never trusted

Wade. Always detested how dismissive he'd been of Max's case. How he'd seemed to want to put in as little effort as possible to find him despite being a competent detective.

Now, six years later, I'd found out Charlene sent Wade additional security footage he'd never mentioned to me. Why? What if there was more to it than Wade getting lazy as he inched closer to retirement? What if it was something sinister?

One of the reasons I hadn't alerted Hadad about Anwir was that he might be a cop. What if Wade was Anwir? He certainly had the means, likely the opportunity. As for a motive? For some people, inflicting pain was all they needed. And his job would give him access to all kinds of things he could use in nefarious ways.

I had to obtain the missing video before I threw wild accusations around, and I discounted calling Hadad to ask if she could locate it. The conversation would be tricky with Anwir listening, and there was no guarantee the detective would give me what she had.

I needed the information now, so I called Talikha to see if she was available, thinking I could then send her a discreet text with my request. Her cell went to voicemail, informing me she was on vacation for the next four days.

As I was trying to think of who else I could trust enough to help me find the missing footage, my iPhone rang. Booker. I wasn't going to answer at first, but something inside me told me I should.

"Stella," Andrea said after I picked up. "I thought I'd check in to see if we're scheduling a day for your trip to Boston soon."

"Oh, no," I said. "I don't think that'll be happening. Vivien and I just parted ways."

"I see. May I ask why?"

"Creative differences."

Andrea took a beat. "Might this have anything to do with her Triple Crown ambush?"

"You knew I wasn't aware of Vivien's lunch plans?"

"No. I thought you'd both agreed to meet me, but I'm pretty good at reading people. You did an awesome job of hiding your surprise, but I could tell you weren't expecting me."

"No kidding. What else did she tell you?"

"You're running out of cash."

"Ha, of course she did. Why were you still interested in meeting us?"

"Because of *you*," she said. "It's a cliché to say I invest in people, but it's true. Your dedication to the podcast is evident. Your ethics, expertise, and know-how, too. It was all abundantly clear when you were on *People of Portland*."

"Thank you. I appreciate you saying so."

"Of course." She paused. "Once the dust settles from the fallout with Vivien and you have more clarity, let's reconvene. Continue exploring how we could work together."

"That's kind of you, Andrea," I said. "But without Vivien, in the short term at least, I'm not sure there's a future for the show."

"What if I help?" she said. "I'll send you an offer to run some advertising, which will give you a cash injection. Maybe you'd like access to some of my marketing and production people. Consider it a gesture of goodwill and the opportunity for you to try our service levels on for size."

"That's very generous of you."

"My pleasure. Is there anything else I can help with?"

I opened my mouth to respond but closed it again because I knew Anwir might be listening. "No, thanks so much," I replied. "We'll talk soon."

Immediately after hanging up, I switched my iPhone to silent and hurriedly started a text message exchange with Booker.

Me: Forgot to ask if you have contacts within Portland PD.

Booker: A few. Tell me what you need.

Me: Two door cam footage videos from the night my brother disappeared. I can only locate one. I need to know what happened to the other.

Booker: How urgent is this?

Me: Like, yesterday. Please don't tell them I'm the one asking. They absolutely can't know. It has to be discreet. Someone you trust completely.

Booker: Let me see what I can do. Might not take too long.

Unsure what else to do until I got her answer, and thinking Anwir might figure out I was the one behind the request anyway, I started the engine and drove home. By the time I parked my car in the driveway, my iPhone lit up with another incoming text, and I almost died when I saw Booker's words.

Only one video was entered into evidence by a Detective Wade. Which one do you have? Are you certain there's another?

Fingers flying across my phone, I sent a reply saying I must've got my wires crossed, but in reality her new information catapulted me to the same conclusion. There was a real chance Wade was Anwir. I thought back to the first email Anwir had sent me, which had included the last photo my family had of Max. We'd definitely given it to the detective. Not a doubt in my mind.

As I dropped my iPhone in my lap, tiny wings fluttered in my chest, as soft and gentle as a murmur. Not fear. *Hope.*

All I needed now was a plan.

CHAPTER 52

STELLA

I wanted to be more certain of my theory about Wade being Anwir, but even through my anger, I could see that confronting him wasn't the way to go.

If I could find evidence to prove my suspicions, I could hand it to Hadad, ask her to neutralize her former colleague and rescue Kenji. Max, too, if he was somehow still alive. If he wasn't, I might never find out what Anwir knew about my brother, and I didn't like the gamble, but I couldn't risk Kenji's life.

After heading into the house, I used my spy camera detector again, sweeping room after room and still coming up empty. It was midafternoon, and I'd already decided I wouldn't head out to snoop around Wade's place until after dark. I couldn't be certain he still lived in the same house where I'd confronted him in his driveway years ago, but I'd take a chance to find out.

The hours dragged on, during which I prepared food I didn't eat and switched the TV to a show I wouldn't watch, creating enough noise I hoped Anwir would think I was trying to distract myself from the ruins of my marriage. Frankly, I was surprised he hadn't yet contacted me to gloat.

Shortly before eight, when the sun had almost set, I headed upstairs. With the shower on and the Nokia on the bathroom countertop, I headed back to my closet and pulled on a black

T-shirt, long-sleeved jacket, and leggings. Next, I searched for an old iPhone in a drawer, relieved to see the Wi-Fi connection on it still worked. I opened YouTube, where I found a three-hour meditation for sleep.

Back in the bathroom, after switching off the shower, I pretended to dry my hair before climbing onto the bed fully dressed. I set the Nokia under the bed, the old iPhone with the volume up on my nightstand, and hit Play.

For the next little while, I pretended to toss and turn before settling down. When I couldn't wait any longer, I slid out of the other side of the bed and tiptoed to the door, softly closing it behind me. Leaving the Nokia here was a huge gamble, but Anwir—Wade?—could see my every move, so taking it with me wasn't an option.

Once in the driveway, I scanned the area for any indication that someone was watching. Nothing. No movement. No sound other than chirping crickets and the hoot of an owl in the distance.

I didn't know how long I might have before my ruse was discovered, so I got moving. Hopping into my car, I backed out and drove away. If Anwir saw my vehicle was gone, it would be over, but for now I refused to think about the possibility.

Wade's house on the outskirts of Scarborough was about twenty-five minutes away. When I arrived shortly after nine, the sky darkened further as the moon slipped behind the clouds, providing me with better cover.

I slowed down as I approached Wade's old bungalow. I remembered it was set around thirty yards back from the main road and a good distance from any of his neighbors. There'd been a large garage on the side when I'd visited, and as I got closer, I could see the faint outline of the white facade.

As I made a mental note to check if the garage was unlocked, I spotted a single vehicle in the driveway. A blue Chevy Silverado I recognized as Wade's. Light flickered from behind the sheer curtains in the front room. A TV.

He still lived here. And he was home.

After driving past and doubling back, I pulled to the side of the road twenty yards from Wade's house and parked behind the trees. There was no time to waste, so I summoned the courage to get out of my car and poke around the detective's home to see what I could find.

I crept up the driveway, staying low. Tiptoeing to the front of the house, I peered through the front window. I couldn't tell if Wade was lying on the sofa watching TV, but the two Barcaloungers were empty.

I kept going, often checking over my shoulder, expecting Wade to jump out at me or for him to press the cool steel of his gun against the back of my head. An animal snorted in the distance, and I cowered, but once it continued crawling through the brush, I forced myself to ignore it.

All the lights at the back of Wade's house were off, shrouding the backyard in complete darkness. I swiftly headed to the garage but found it was locked. Maybe he had a hook with keys near the back door, but there was no way I could venture into Wade's place without knowing where he was or if he'd come after me with a weapon.

If my suspicions about him were correct, my best bet would be to come back again and wait until he left before breaking in. Daylight would make it riskier if a neighbor saw me. I'd also need another plan for the Nokia, but I had a bit of time to come up with one that could work.

Dejected, I sneaked back through the yard. As I reached the side of the house, I heard a crash, and what sounded like a woman shouting for help inside. I turned around, breaking into a jog as I headed for the front door. When I got there, the door stood a little ajar, but now it seemed all the lights inside the house were off, including the TV.

I pulled the door open as quietly as I could, peering into the hallway. There was no more noise, not a hint of anyone being home. I slid my iPhone from my pocket and switched on the flashlight, holding it above my head. The room stood empty, but as I looked at the tiled floor, my heart leaped when I saw a large smear of blood, as if something—someone—had been dragged to the back.

I took another step, gasping when I noticed a shiny black stick lying askew in the living room doorway. Charlene's cane. All my senses went into overdrive, yelling at me to leave and get Hadad here as fast as I could.

I didn't see or hear the person behind me until it was too late. An arm went around my neck, and before I could move or cry out, something sharp pierced the skin below my right ear. I wanted to scream, but a burning sensation filled my veins as the walls spun.

Although desperate to fight, my body went limp, and my legs buckled. As my vision blurred at the edges, all I could think of was Max, and how I'd let him down again.

THURSDAY, AUGUST 7

CHAPTER 53

Are you ready, Stella?
　Because ready or not, here I come.
　Let the real games begin.

CHAPTER 54

STELLA

I'm not sure what stirred me first, the pain in my head, which felt as if it was being split in half, the otherworldly groan escaping my mouth, or the fact I couldn't stop shivering.

It took a few seconds for me to comprehend that I lay face down on a hard surface. Images flashed through my brain. Detective Wade's dark house. Someone attacking me from behind, what had felt like a needle being shoved into my neck.

I wiggled my hands and feet, which weren't bound. I shivered again. My attempt to sit up took a staggering amount of energy I didn't have. My sandbag-like limbs refused to move. They felt weak and heavy. Useless. The tiniest movement caused my headache to intensify so much, I thought I'd vomit.

When I tentatively opened one eye, I saw what could've been the moon, but as I pushed myself up, everything began to spin again. Although I did my best to stay awake, I gave in and let myself slip back into unconsciousness.

I don't know how much time passed before I woke up again. This time it was with a start as I gasped, my heart pounding. Dust filled my nostrils, the musty air tinged with damp. The floor beneath my fingers was rough. Concrete, or maybe stone. Not tile, and—

Wade had assaulted me in his hallway.

He'd drugged me.

Taken me to . . .

Where *was* I?

Wisps of thoughts slotted together, trying to form a more cohesive picture about my surroundings. A dripping noise came from somewhere to my left. Maybe a faucet.

The entire world was off, discombobulated, as if I'd stuffed my head and ears with cotton wool. I couldn't tell whether it was day or night, if I was underground or twenty stories above. I scrunched my eyes shut, tried to focus only on what I could hear.

Nothing other than the slow drip, drip of water. No animal noises or vehicles driving by, meaning I wasn't near an open door or window. Maybe Detective Wade's basement? No, instinctively I somehow knew that wasn't the case.

With considerable effort, I pushed myself into a sitting position and twisted my torso enough to glance over my shoulder. The faint outline of what seemed to be a heavy-duty chain-link fence was illuminated by the faint light on the other side of the enclosure—a single lightbulb hanging from the ceiling, which I'd mistaken for the moon.

Still groggy, I scrambled to my knees. An uneven concrete wall with blistered paint stood a few yards behind me, same on the left and right. If I stretched out my arms, I could probably touch both sides. The fence secured to a thick metal rod at the bottom went all the way to the ceiling and was topped with razor wire.

Swallowing hard, and unsure whether I'd collapse if I attempted to stand, I crawled forward. As my eyes adjusted a little more to the faint light, I looked up.

There! A gate in the fence. A way out.

After hoisting myself to my feet, I wrapped my fingers around the gate's handle and pressed down. I desperately pushed and pulled, but while the sound of rattling metal filled the air, the gate barely budged half an inch.

My eyes dropped to the thick padlocked chain holding it in place. I grabbed it and slowly threaded it through the fence, fingers fumbling for the lock as I searched for a key. Nothing. I was trapped.

Sinking to my knees, I pressed a hand over my mouth to stifle a cry. Where was I? What would Wade do to me? Immediately, the pictures of Kenji and the emaciated person in the second photo he'd sent caused waves of terror to crash into me. I wanted to yell, beg for help, but I forced myself to keep quiet as I sobbed.

I was going to die. Kenji was going to die. Max was probably already dead, and—

"Hello?" a voice whispered. "Stella, is that you?"

I wasn't alone. Hope grew as I crawled to the fence and peered through it. On the other side of what I thought was a long hallway of some kind was another person. They were on their knees, too. Eyes wide, face streaked with dirt and tears, fingers wrapped around their own metal enclosure.

"*Charlene*," I said. "Are you okay?"

"I—I think so," she replied, the fear in her voice audible, reigniting my own.

"What happened? How did you get here?"

"I went to see Detective Wade," she whispered. "I wanted to ask him about the security footage I'd sent him. He offered me a glass of water and I . . . I think he drugged me."

"I went there as well. I think he drugged me, too."

"But why?" she asked. "Why would he—"

"He's Anwir," I said, so grateful I could finally share the name with someone.

"Who?" Charlene whispered. "Anvil? What do you mean?"

"Doesn't matter," I said. "What's important is that Wade abducted Kenji. I think he took my brother, too."

"*What?* You can't be serious."

"It all makes sense," I said. "This is why he didn't bother investigating Max's case properly from the start. He didn't log one of the door cam videos you sent him into the system because he didn't want it there. Wade has been taunting me."

"I . . . I . . . Taunting you? How?"

"It's a long story," I said, my heart sinking. "But you being here, getting dragged into this situation . . . it's my fault."

"I don't understand," Charlene said. "Tell me how—"

She immediately fell silent when someone in the distance whistled the "Twisted Nerve" tune from the movie *Kill Bill*. Whoever it was sounded joyous, excited, sending ripples of dread into every cell of my body.

Charlene shrank back, ducking out of sight and disappearing into the shadows. I followed suit as my heart thumped, and I wished I could dissolve into the walls.

Lowering myself to the ground, I tried to recall what position I'd woken up in, hoping if Wade walked by and peered into my cage, he'd think I was still out cold. Maybe if he came inside, I could leap up and surprise him. Bash his head against the wall and knock him out.

While he was lean and fit, he was nearing sixty. Maybe I stood a chance if he didn't have a weapon, although the likelihood of that had to be close to zero. Anwir—*Wade*, it was Detective fucking Wade—was too smart to make a mistake so glaring.

As the whistling faded, I exhaled, trying to calm my racing pulse. When all remained quiet, I crawled back to the fence and tried to coax Charlene into talking to me again.

After I'd called out to her four times and she still hadn't answered, my eyes landed on another cage to the left of Charlene's, almost identical in width to each of ours. I squinted and leaned in as far as I could, pressing my face against the fence to get a better view.

Maybe it was the combination of shadows and fear making me see things that weren't there, but from the shape lying on the ground, it looked like another person. My heart leaped again. A third prisoner. Kenji? Max? Was the person unconscious, or . . . *dead*?

Terror threatened to surge, but I crammed it down, grasping the last slivers of determination that were willing me to *act*. I had to get us out of here. All of us. I couldn't let Wade hurt Charlene or whoever was in the third cage. I *wouldn't*.

Hoping Wade had moved far enough away to not hear me, I called out to Charlene again, a little louder this time. Finally her pale face emerged, lips quivering as she clasped the metal fence and gave it a shake, looking as if she might scream.

"Are you hurt?" I asked.

"I don't think so."

"We need to escape."

"I don't have my cane," she whispered.

"I'll help you," I said. "My gate's padlocked."

"Mine, too."

"We have to pick them."

"I can try." Charlene's voice filled with hope. "I've done it before."

"Really?"

"Ages ago when I mislaid a key. I need two thin, pointy pieces of metal. Sturdy wires a couple of inches each to slide into the lock."

She disappeared again, and I heard her moving around, searching the ground. I did the same, combing my cell inch by inch, crawling on my hands and knees. Suddenly my fingers brushed across something sharp.

"A nail," I whispered. "Will that work?"

"Throw it to me," Charlene said, but when I tried, it landed in the middle of the hallway, out of reach. "It's okay," she said. "It would've been too thick, anyway. Keep searching."

As I patted the ground, desperation rose while the lump in my throat threatened to cut off my air supply. I refused to let the tears fall. There was no time to break down, and I wouldn't give up. Wade couldn't win.

"*Yes.*" Charlene gasped suddenly. "A paper clip."

Hope filled my veins as I scoured my cell, but when the eerie whistling started again, I froze. Charlene let out a whimper. As the noise drifted away, she crawled to her fence.

"Come *on*," she said. "We need to find . . . *wait*. There. What's that? In front of your gate."

I scurried forward, saw a piece of copper wire on the ground half a foot away. The holes in the chain links were too small to push my hand through, but I was so close to getting Charlene what she needed, I had to try. I yanked on the fence. When it didn't move, I strained to wiggle my hand underneath, fingers stretching and reaching, the hard concrete scraping my palms.

Frustration built. I pulled my arm back, took a few beats, and tried again. This time, as I lay on my side pressed up against the fence, my fingertips grazed the piece of wire. Another minute went by as I painstakingly managed to bring it toward me a tiny fraction of an inch at a time.

"Throw it to me," Charlene said when I finally grabbed hold of the wire. "You've got this. You can do it."

I coiled the metal around my finger and flicked it to Charlene, hard, watched as it landed barely an inch from her. She slid her index finger through the chain link, and with a tiny bit more effort, managed to grab hold of the tool.

"It's perfect," she said, lighting a raging fire of brand-new hope in my chest. I had no idea where Wade had gone, or how long it might be before he got back, but if Charlene and I could get out of our cages, we might stand a chance, especially together.

Then again, she needed her cane to walk properly, and we couldn't leave whoever else was locked up here. I closed my eyes, realizing we'd have to. Escaping without Wade seeing us and trying to find help would be the only way for any of us to survive.

I watched as much as the dim light would allow as Charlene first unrolled the piece of copper wire before folding it in half. Next, she slid it a little way into the bottom of her padlock, holding it in place with one hand.

"There's tension on this wire now," she said, intense concentration on her face. "I need to insert the paper clip and jimmy the lock's pins upward, and . . . Oh my gosh, I think the first one's out of the way."

Neither of us talked as she wiggled the paper clip, swearing quietly when things didn't go her way. I kept expecting Wade to rush up to us with a loud bellow, smacking the wires from her hands, but all remained quiet. No whistling, no movement. Nothing until I heard the most satisfying click in the world.

"I did it," Charlene said, and moments later she'd undone the chain and pushed her gate open. "Now let me open your—"

The same eerie tune started up again, louder this time. Closer. Panic flooded Charlene's eyes as she peered down the hallway and stumbled to my gate. Once on her knees, she slid the wire into place and started working on my lock with the paper clip.

"Hurry," I said. "Please, Charlene. Hurry."

"I can't do this," she said, her fingers trembling harder when the whistling kept going. "I'm sorry, Stella. I can't." Before I could reply, she dropped the paper clip on the ground and stood. "I have to get out of here. I—"

"Don't leave," I begged. "Charlene. Please don't go."

Too late. She'd already turned and limped out of sight, consumed by the darkness.

CHAPTER 55

STELLA

"Charlene," I called out as loud as I dared. "*Charlene*. Come back. You're not safe." A second passed before I jolted into action, shoving my fingers underneath the fence again to grab the paper clip she'd left behind, but it was too far out of reach.

I needed a tool to help slide it to me, but I'd already searched my cell. Unwilling to quit, I examined the fence again, saw the bottom part was secured to the metal rod with pieces of wire.

Even if I loosened them all, I doubted I could push the fence far enough to crawl out, and it could take eons, but I had another idea. Kneeling, I tried to bend one of the wire ties. When it didn't move, I tried the next. The fourth had some give, so I kept wiggling it. Finally I had a sturdy, six-inch piece of wire tie in my hands.

My injured left pinky finger throbbed so hard, I wanted to throw up, but I had to keep going. Working faster now, I shaped the wire into a hook and slid it under the fence, barely able to believe it when it worked the first time.

I brought the paper clip toward me. With the precious object secured, I slipped the wire tie under one of the layers of the bandages on my injured finger, just in case, and focused on the padlock. Trying to recall what Charlene had said about applying pressure, I held the piece of copper that was still in the lock with my left hand and slid the straightened paper clip inside.

No matter how often I tried and how hard I worked, the lock didn't spring. I wanted to take a break. Couldn't decide between slumping to the ground or pounding my fists on the wall, but this was a matter of life or death, and not only mine.

I tried again, and again. At last something inside the lock shifted, and the shackle loosened a little. The glimmer of hope it provided almost made me drop the paper clip.

Closing my eyes, I urged myself to slow down, refocus, and renew my determination to escape. I visualized the steps. Copper wire in. Push to one side. Hold in place. Insert paper clip. Wiggle and press up. Retract a little. Wiggle and press up. Repeat. Again. Again. And again.

I'm not sure how many times it took. It might've been ten, could've been a hundred, but suddenly there was another click. The shackle released completely, and just like that, the padlock opened. Hardly able to believe what I'd accomplished, I removed it from the chain and lowered both to the ground as quietly as I could.

Pressing my hand on the gate, I pushed it open, wincing when it creaked. I stopped again and waited, expecting the sound of footsteps. Nothing. With my heart working its way up my neck and into my mouth, I stepped into the dimly lit hallway.

Glancing left, I saw a brick wall a dozen yards away, meaning the exit had to be in the other direction. At least I knew which path to follow, but if Wade arrived now, he'd see me. There'd be nowhere for me to go.

It didn't matter, because I had to find Charlene. Hopefully she was hiding somewhere in the building or had already managed to get outside. Maybe she was on her way to alerting the authorities. I took a step toward the way out but stopped. There was something else I had to do first.

Slowly, and ever so softly, I crept to the third cell. "Hey," I whispered. *"Hey!"*

The man lying on his side didn't move, but as I kneeled and leaned in to get a better look, I caught a glimpse of an owl tattoo on his bare shoulder. "Kenji." I gasped, tamping down the mixture of elation and panic encircling my lungs. "*Kenji*. It's Stella. Please wake up."

He didn't stir. Didn't blink. I thought I saw his chest moving, but I couldn't be sure. What had Wade done to him? Was Kenji still alive? As fear gripped me once more, I debated whether I should try to pick this padlock, too, so I could drag him to safety.

Guilt spun in my gut when I decided to leave him. For all I knew, Wade was around the corner, yards away. If he'd captured Charlene, no doubt he'd soon be back to make sure his other prisoners weren't on the loose. Plus, if I got into Kenji's cell, I wouldn't be able to carry him out of here while he was unconscious. And if he was dead . . .

I refused to grant the thought further entry into my brain and got up. My best bet, the way to save everyone, was to slip out of this building without alerting Wade, and find help. If Hadad arrived in time and made an arrest, maybe the crooked old detective really would give up the information he had on Max in exchange for a reduced sentence.

The whistling started again, but with my strategy decided, I wouldn't bail. I crept a little farther down the hallway. If Wade came my way, well . . . at least I'd be ready, and hopefully have the element of surprise on my side.

Although my heart kept telling me to bolt, I only moved a few inches at a time, hugging the walls as I passed what I now thought were livestock pens. Maybe I was in a barn of some kind. I hadn't noticed one on Wade's property. Then again, I hadn't looked that closely or been there in years up until last night.

The bulbs in the overhead lights seemed brighter, and as I rounded the corner, my heart leaped when the space opened, becoming almost cavernous. This *was* a barn, the beams of the wooden ceiling almost forty feet high, with small windows near the tops of the walls. I didn't know what time it was, but judging from the inky blackness outside, I figured it was the middle of the night.

I looked around the empty space, saw a pile of what appeared to be building supplies twenty yards to my left. My eye caught the faint outline of a door, and I got moving, exposed yet determined. Fifteen yards away. Ten. As I reached five, all I could focus on was the fact I'd soon be free . . .

Until the whistling started again.

I froze. This time, it was so loud, it sounded as if Wade stood next to me. I spun around, expecting to see him, but I was alone. It didn't make sense, not until I noticed a small black device and what looked like a wireless speaker on an upturned plastic milk crate.

Unable to believe what I was seeing, I hurried over, and as I reached the crate, the whistling stopped. I picked up what I now knew was a digital music player, and when the screen sprang to life, I saw it was Thursday at 4:23 a.m.

As the whistling sound of the *Kill Bill* tune emanated from the speaker sitting on the crate, I wanted to laugh. It was a recording. A deterrent to keep Kenji, Charlene, and me terrified and subdued. Hope batted its wings again. Perhaps Wade wasn't here.

This was my chance to alert the cops, locate Charlene, help Kenji, and bring Hadad back here—preferably in that order. Surely they'd be able to find Wade quickly, especially if he didn't know we'd escaped.

Sudden rage shot up from my stomach like lava—fiery and destructive. What if Wade couldn't be located? Finding the cruel bastard might be my only chance at knowing what happened to Max, and bringing him—whatever was left of him—home.

Depending on what was on the other side of the barn door, perhaps I could alert Hadad and then hide in the vicinity, so I could fight Wade if he came back. I had to protect Kenji. I'd never forgive myself if the detective returned and killed him out of anger at losing two of his captives.

One thing at a time. With my heart pounding so loud it had to be echoing across the building, I curled my fingers around the door handle. I was about to press down when I heard movement behind me.

"Where are you going, Stella?"

Anwir. *Wade.*

The sheer terror of his mechanical voice coming from the speaker on the crate almost dragged me to the floor. Where had he been hiding? Had he seen Charlene escape? Had he killed her? I turned around, fists balled at my sides, ready to finally face my persecutor.

Through the darkness, I saw Wade ten yards away, standing tall, clad in sturdy running shoes and camouflage-print pants, hat, and shirt. His presence was threatening enough, amplified further by the night vision goggles strapped over his hat and eyes.

He held a phone up to his face, obscuring my view of him some more. But it was the massive hunting knife in his gloved right hand that turned my stomach. The cold metal glinted in the faint light. Wade slipped his phone into his back pocket and approached, his steps fluid, almost graceful. I could hear his slow, steady breathing.

"Surprise."

This time, the voice coming from the person in front of me made me gasp as my mouth dropped open. He no longer sounded like Anwir, but it wasn't Wade either. This was someone else. Someone I knew. A voice I'd heard dozens of times, especially lately. I scrambled to accept the facts I'd been presented with.

My brain refused until Charlene removed the goggles and hat, her blond hair tumbling to her shoulders. "You should see your face," she said with a sparkling smile. "I should take a picture."

What was going on? I'd been locked up in a cage opposite her. Individual prisons we'd worked frantically to escape.

When? Why? *How?*

As a million questions swirled in my mind, I looked at her, saw unmistakable excitement glinting in her eyes. She pointed the hunting knife at me, and I shrank back.

"This will be another fun game," she said. "I call it *hide and go seek and destroy*. How about I give you a ten-second start? I might even close my eyes."

"What are you doing?" I said, finally finding my voice. "I don't—"

Charlene pressed a finger to her lips. "Shh. Don't spoil the hunt. It's my absolute favorite part." She leaned in and whispered, "*Run.*"

CHAPTER 56

STELLA

Scrambling, I bolted as fast as I could, all of my senses heightened while everything inside me screamed to move, move, *move*.

My mind refused to grasp, let alone believe, Anwir was Charlene. I'd known her for years. A former neighbor, a radio show host, and more recently, a confidante. Someone I'd trusted. She'd pretended to have been abducted by Wade. For fuck's sake, she was a sexagenarian who walked with a cane.

"Ten . . . nine . . . eight . . ."

While her voice rang out, I tried not to fall as I darted across the near-empty building, searching for another way out. I couldn't go back to the cells—it was a dead end. Charlene was too close to the only door I'd found, but there had to be another exit.

The image of Charlene in full camo gear hit me again, along with the knowledge she'd come here with night vision goggles. Ready to chase me down like prey.

"Seven . . . six . . . five . . ."

I took off toward the building supplies that turned out to be stacks of old lumber, piles of dusty bricks, and a few bags of mortar mix. Ducking, I darted behind it all, stumbling in the darkness as more questions peppered my brain.

How long had Charlene planned this? Did she take Max? What had she done to him? Could she, of all people, really be Anwir? Were she and Wade working together?

"Three . . . two . . . one. Ready or not, here I come."

The terror gripped my chest so hard, I didn't think there was room for me to take a breath. I could hear Charlene walking around slowly, methodically, not a hint of a limp. With the gear she had, hiding was near impossible, but so was trying to escape. I didn't know where to go, what to do. I had no clue how fast or strong she was.

Maybe my only chance was fighting her for survival, but she had a weapon, and I had . . . *bricks*. Heart pounding, I picked one up before sneaking a little to the left, cursing when my foot hit a stray plank.

"Oh, Steeee-lllll-aaaaa," Charlene sang. "Where are youuuu?"

I froze as I waited for the sound of her feet, any indication of her moving in the opposite direction. When I couldn't stand it any longer, I slowly peered around the side of the lumber. Charlene stood with her arms crossed, looking at me through her goggles, apparently waiting for me to make exactly this mistake.

"Didn't I say *run*?" she asked. "There's no need to make it easy for me."

I sped around the pile of building supplies, hoping to reach the only door I'd seen, legs and arms pumping, the brick still in my hand. Charlene gave a delight-filled battle cry as she came after me. When I glanced over my shoulder, I could tell she was barely slower than me.

Willing myself to speed up, my ridiculous, frantic plan became to throw myself against the door, hoping it would fly open. Because I wasn't paying enough attention, I stumbled on the uneven concrete and slammed face-first into the floor, the brick flying yards away, out of reach.

I cried out as my injured hand stung and throbbed from trying to break my fall, felt sick when the bandage on my finger turned damp. Ignoring it, I forced myself to get on all fours, telling myself to stand, find the brick, turn around, and fight Charlene with everything I had.

The force of her grabbing my hair and pulling me skyward almost lifted me to my feet. I twisted and turned, snarling at her to let me go. Fully aware Charlene's knife could slice into me, I took a calculated risk and donkey-kicked my leg.

When my foot connected with her knee, it was enough for her to loosen her grip for a split second. I moved quickly, taking a few steps to the left. I wanted to run, but turning my back on the hunting knife again wasn't an option. I needed to stand my ground. I wanted to survive.

Chest moving up and down, Charlene stood in front of me, knees slightly bent, arms open, almost as if she were inviting me in for a hug. Her grin broadened as she slowly took off her goggles.

"You're fast," she said, breathing hard as she dropped them on the ground. "But not fast enough. There's nowhere for you to go. Trust me."

I braced myself, waiting for her to charge. Two, three beats went by. Another smile lit up her face before she pounced, and I ducked and tried to roll.

It instantly became clear I'd made the wrong decision. Charlene planted a heavy foot in the middle of my back, shoving me down. I managed half a twist, saw her towering over me with the knife. I rolled over completely and then stopped moving, holding up my hands in surrender.

She slowly lowered herself, straddling me. When she pressed the tip of the knife against my throat, I tried to scream, but she put a finger to my lips.

"Shh," she said, her gesture almost motherly. "Shh, Stella, shh. I could say this will all be over soon, but that would be a lie, and I've told you so many of those already."

I tried to scramble away, but she was too heavy. I thrust out my arms, desperate to find the brick I'd dropped so I could use it to protect myself. My left knuckles brushed over something coarse but solid. Not the brick, but the plastic crate with the speaker.

"Why are you doing this?" I asked, aiming to distract her. "Where's Max?"

"Wouldn't you be glad to see him again?" she said. "I know you're desperate for a family reunion, and—"

Grabbing the crate, I lifted it and swung it full force at Charlene's head. It only caught her shoulder, but as she yelped, I heard the knife clatter to the floor. I thrust my hips upward with as much strength as I could find. She tipped over, and with another almighty heave, I pushed her off me.

I scrambled to my feet and turned, ready to grab the knife from the ground, but Charlene got there first. As her hand reached for the hilt, I lunged and brought up my knee beneath her chin. A bone or tooth crunched, and she let out a groan.

I'd underestimated her again. She charged me with such force, she knocked me onto my back, leaving me winded. This time she pinned down my arms with her hands as she sat on top of me, eyes ablaze.

My fingers scrabbled, searching for anything I could use. Without warning, the force of a slap stung my cheek, setting it on fire, but her attack had freed my left hand. I turned my head, could see the brick, but it was too far away. That was when I remembered the wire tie in my bandage.

"You're a feisty bitch," Charlene said, wiping her face as she picked up the hunting knife. "Your brother didn't fight half as much as this. It would've been more fun if he had."

"What did you do to him?" I shouted, trying to divert her attention from my fingers, hoping she wouldn't see how I was working the wire tie into the palm of my hand. "Where is he? Tell me what you did to him. Tell me if he's alive."

Charlene smiled. "He's been so lonely at the cottage. Apparently he's tired. Says he's ready to go."

"Go?" I pushed away my panic as I pretended not to understand what she meant. "Go where?"

"Shame you won't be together long. He wasn't happy when he found out you'd take his place." Charlene smiled again. "Do you remember telling me it's what you wanted? Maybe you should be more careful what you wish for."

She looked at the knife, seemingly pensive as she studied it. Eyes filling with glee, she whispered, "How afraid are you of pain, Stella? Tell me how terrified you are."

"Not as terrified as you should be," I replied.

Her expression turned into confusion, eyes widening when they darted to my right hand, which was empty. The fraction of time her surprise afforded me was enough to swing my left fist in the direction of her neck, jamming the sharp end of the wire tie into her skin as hard as I could.

It didn't go as deep as I'd hoped, but it was enough to make Charlene howl like an animal. Her hands grasped her neck, and in the process, she dropped the knife again. I shoved her off me, pushed her to the ground, and saw splashes of her blood splattering on the floor.

Charlene was on her hands and knees now, grunting as she held her neck, her backside pointing my way, ankles exposed. As I recalled Jeff's story about the guy who'd cut himself on the broken bottle in his garbage bag, I grabbed the knife.

Bringing it down through the air, I slashed the weapon across Charlene's heels, aiming straight for both Achilles tendons. The screech leaving her mouth sounded unearthly, and when she tried to stand, she only managed a step before slumping to the ground.

Breathing heavily, I pushed Charlene onto her back and straddled her torso, exactly as she'd done to me. Gripping the knife with both hands, I tried to stop them from shaking as I raised the weapon above my head, ready to deliver the fatal blow.

"Do it," she hissed. "Show me you've got what it takes to kill."

When I let out an almighty yell, wishing I could plunge the knife into her throat, she didn't flinch, didn't move. Her laughter echoed around the building, and I almost changed my mind about sparing her. Except I needed her alive, and she knew it.

I pressed the knife to her neck. "Max is at your cottage?" I asked, but when Charlene remained silent, unblinking, I screamed, "Where is he?"

She sighed, raising her shoulders as blood leaked from her wound. "No clue what you mean."

"You do," I hissed. "You'll tell the cops everything."

"Oh, you bet," she said. "Especially how you killed poor Detective Wade."

"I didn't—"

"You *did*. Your prints are all over the murder weapon they'll find at his house."

"What—"

"The knife you buried in the forest." She was gloating over the careless gift I'd left her. "I watched you. And a few other times when you were in your studio. Tonight, too, when you went to his house. As a true crime podcaster, you really should pay more attention to your surroundings."

"You can lie to the cops about whatever you want," I said. "They won't believe you. Kenji will tell them the truth. He's seen you."

"Has he?" she said before making a sad face. "He won't make it through the next hour."

She was messing with me again, and I couldn't let her lies get into my head. Holding the knife in my hand, and keeping it pointed at her, I unfastened her belt and pulled it off her. Without another word, I flipped her on her back as she kept talking.

"You called me ranting and raving, saying you were certain Wade had withheld evidence from the night your brother disappeared."

As I knelt on her back, keeping her in place, I stopped moving. "There was never a second video. You lied. You wanted me at Wade's house."

"Worked like a charm, and you're so easy to play," she said before changing her voice to sound so sincere, so genuine, I almost believed her next words myself. "I couldn't shake the impression that Stella might do something terrible, Detective Hadad. But when I got to Wade's house, it was too late. She . . . she'd already killed him."

"You're trying to frame me."

"Like I said, you make it *so* easy," she replied, and I wanted to grab her head and smash it nose-first into the floor. "I can manipulate you faster than a piece of Play-Doh. You gobble down everything I say. Like the apparent slip-up about Dr. Graf."

Realization dawned. "You were never his patient, but you knew Jeff had seen him."

"Of course I knew," Charlene spat as I got moving, tying her hands together with her belt, pulling it so tight she yelped. Good. "When we met, he told me he wanted to see a shrink, so I gave him a recommendation. I've interviewed Dr. Graf at his office for his expertise and insight multiple times. If Jeff saw him, I could get my hands on his file. Check what he knew about the night Max went missing. One mug of spilled coffee on the good doctor's prized chairs, and I had time to take a photo."

"You got me to break into my therapist's house," I said as I rolled her over again so I could see her face. "You wanted me to read the notes about Jeff. Why?"

Charlene smiled as she replied. "Call it part of an experiment. I'm wondering what it'll take to ruin your marriage. Although you and Jeff are doing a decent enough job at blowing it up yourselves. You're such liars, both of you."

"Shut up," I shouted. "Shut *up*."

She didn't. In her fake, innocent voice she said, "After . . . after killing poor Detective Wade, Stella brought me here, where she's been hiding Kenji. I think she was trying to turn the focus on Max because she's unhappy with the investigation. Maybe she suspected Detective Wade, but I can't fathom why." Charlene must've noticed my shocked expression because she smirked. "Seems you have a choice, Stella. Stay and be convicted of murder . . . or run."

"I told you to shut up," I said, patting her down and searching her pockets, where I found a set of keys and her cell phone. Her device had face ID, and once I'd unlocked it, I swiftly turned off the security setting to ensure I could access it again unencumbered.

I tried making a call. No service.

"Anyway," Charlene said with a shrug. "Who do you think they'll believe?"

I still didn't speak as I removed her shoes, ignoring her yelps and curses.

Heaving a restrained Charlene all the way to my former cage almost broke my back, but I couldn't deny my intense satisfaction when I tied her hands above her head to the chain-link fence using her shoelaces. Charlene swore as I clicked the padlocks from our cages—although I now doubted hers had ever been locked—in place with her trapped inside.

Using the keys from her pocket to open the lock on Kenji's gate, I finally got to him. Falling to my knees, I checked for a pulse. A faint beating. He was alive, barely. I tried to lift him, but he was too heavy, and I didn't see a way of getting him out of here without help.

And then there was Max . . . He needed me, too.

I turned and ran. After locating the key to open the barn door, I bolted from the building and kept running with the cell phone in the air, trying to get a few bars. Still nothing.

As I took in the tall, leafy trees swaying in the morning summer breeze, I realized Charlene had brought Kenji and me to the middle of nowhere. When I turned my head, I spotted her car.

Stumbling toward it, I finally got service and desperately searched for a contact who might be able to help, hitting Dial on the first one I found.

"Hey," Dylan said a few moments later, sounding groggy, which was no surprise, considering the time. "I heard you've been sick for a few days. I hope—"

"It's not Charlene, it's Stella."

"Stella?" Dylan said. "Why are you calling from Charlene's phone? Is she—"

"No time. She has a cottage."

"A what? You're breaking up."

"A cottage," I yelled. "Charlene has a cottage. Did she ever mention it?"

"No—"

"Would Izzy—"

"But I know where it is if that's what you need," Dylan said quickly. "Eastern side of Falcon Lake. Almost directly opposite the campsite."

"How do you know if she never mentioned it?" I said, wondering if I'd made a gigantic mistake and this was a trap.

"The painting in her den," he replied. "Why did you wake me for that?"

"Falcon Lake," I repeated. "You're sure?"

"A thousand percent. When I dropped some stuff off at her house, I recognized it from when I went canoeing there with my dad. It's quite a unique building. Log home."

"Thanks, Dylan," I whispered before hanging up.

My fingers sped across the screen as I frantically searched for Portland Police's main number, demanding they patch me through to Hadad immediately. It was a matter of life or death. As I waited, I opened the what3words website, and when Hadad came on the line, I barely let her get her name out before frantically shouting where I was.

"Get the emergency services here immediately," I said, explaining where she'd find Kenji and Charlene, not letting Hadad get a word in as I powered on. "Charlene Thornton killed Detective Wade with my knife. She abducted Kenji and me. She left Fynn's arm in the mine."

"Whoa," Hadad said. "Stella, slow down."

"No," I said as I got into Charlene's car. "Charlene's AL, the person who sent me those emails. She took Max. She's involved in everything."

"But—"

"Please, Najwa, get here quickly. Kenji's in a bad way. Hurry. Call my husband. Get the EMTs."

"Calm down and let's talk—"

"I said no," I yelled, yanking the car door open. "There's no time. Get your ass here, *now*."

"Wait," Hadad shouted. "Stella, where are you going?"

My spine, and my determination, transformed into titanium. "To find my brother."

CHAPTER 57

STELLA

The GPS on Charlene's phone told me Falcon Lake was a forty-minute drive, but with the empty roads I got there in thirty, just as the sun brightened the sky.

Google Maps showed six houses on this side of the small lake. *Cottage* seemed to be an understatement for the first one I arrived at. The huge structure built from logs, glass, and steel with wrought-iron gates and an intercom was a bona fide McMansion.

Dylan had called Charlene's place unique, and this certainly qualified, but from memory it didn't much resemble the painting I'd seen at her house. Nevertheless, I pressed the button on the intercom and waited, my heart pounding. Maybe they could help.

The person who answered sounded like a young girl. "Hello? Hell-oo-oo."

"Does Charlene live here?" I asked.

"Uh-uh. Sophie's my mommy, and my daddy's Tristan. I'm—"

"Who's this?" another older female voice demanded.

"My name's Stella. Is this Charlene Thornton's house?"

"No," the woman said. "Her place is two houses farther down."

I slammed the car into Reverse and got back on to the main road, heading past the next driveway and turning left into the second. And there it was, the pointy A-frame log cabin depicted in the painting hanging in Charlene's den. Instantly recognizable.

Her dwelling was older than the first two on this road—a generously sized home with a well-tended yard and an unobstructed view of Falcon Lake. Secluded. At least two hundred fifty yards away from the neighbors on each side.

The ideal place to hide someone. Potentially for years.

I got out of the car and darted up the porch steps, rattling the handle of the solid door. The fact it was locked did nothing to stop me from getting inside, but unlike at Dr. Graf's place, I didn't waste time searching for a key and instead rushed around to the back of the house. Moving quickly, I grabbed the first good-size rock I could find and launched it at the glass doors.

After the shattered pane fell to the ground, I stuck my hand through the opening, careful not to cut myself as I undid the latch before stepping inside. When I spotted a keypad in the hallway, I expected the sound of a piercing house alarm, but nothing happened.

It didn't make sense. If Charlene kept my brother here, surely she'd want a deterrent in case someone broke in and stumbled across him by accident. Maybe it was a silent alarm to alert only her. I didn't care. I needed to tear through this place.

"Max?" I shouted as I dashed through the open-plan living and kitchen area, barely taking in the modern glossy white cabinets, ash floors, plush area rugs, and sea-green sofa. I yelled his name over and over as I moved through the house.

Max wasn't in the living room, kitchen, or dining area. He wasn't in the first two bedrooms or en suite bathrooms I found, either.

Charlene had equipped the third and final bedroom as an office. A desk stood against the wall, and a large rectangular ottoman covered with throw pillows had been placed by the window. I backed out, checked the powder room and the pantry that was stocked mostly with canned food, dried pasta, and boxes of high-protein cereal.

Next came the utility area with a washer/dryer combo, and another storage closet filled with an ironing board and cleaning supplies. After combing through every square inch of Charlene's cottage, searching under the beds and inside wardrobes, and the mezzanine on the upper floor, there was still no sign my brother had ever been here.

"Max! *Max!* Answer me," I yelled as I returned to the living area, but once my voice faded, I was met with more silence. The realization Charlene had lied to me again hit me so hard, it knocked the wind clean out of me.

I slumped onto the sofa, tears spilling across my cheeks as I pictured her lying in the barn. Injured, yes, in pain, hopefully, but no doubt laughing at me for believing anything she'd said. What if her plan had been to get me to leave? Maybe she had an accomplice. She'd said Wade was dead, but I didn't know for sure. Perhaps it wasn't Wade. Maybe . . .

I shuddered. Dylan had given me this location, but he'd seemed bewildered by my phone call. I couldn't discount the fact that my father's prints were on Fynn Baumann's severed arm. Dad and Charlene had known each other for years, since she'd lived a few doors down from my parents. Maybe they'd met before we became neighbors. They could've easily stayed in touch after she moved to the West End.

Had my father and Charlene been working together? Had she double-crossed him by dumping Fynn's arm in the mine? Had she really killed Detective Wade? Or had he?

The desperation made my anger grow to levels I hadn't known existed. My fury had nowhere to go. With an ear-splitting yell, I got up, grabbed hold of a driftwood bookcase and pulled it over, letting out another primal scream as everything on it—books, ornaments, scented candles—fell to the ground. Not yet done, I stomped on a ceramic panther, crushing its belly before kicking some of the other items as hard as I could, wanting to destroy everything Charlene owned.

Two of the books flew into the air, and when one of them

landed, it fell open. I stopped moving when I saw this wasn't a novel, but a box disguised as a book, from which a set of keys had fallen out.

Bending over, I scooped them up and turned them around in my hand. They were similar to the padlock keys I'd taken from Charlene at the barn. Why had she hidden them here?

Peering through the window, I first spotted a tool shed at the back of the yard, and then a boathouse by the lake. Encouraged by the new places to find Max, I dashed outdoors.

I quickly discovered the neatly arranged shed smelled of gasoline, and disappointment hit when I saw only tools, a push mower, and a few bags of mulch.

The red boathouse next to the jetty was locked. The keys I'd found didn't fit, so I gave the door a hefty kick, and it sprang open. A small, cabinless motorboat bobbed in the water, the sound of gentle waves the only noise in there. I yelled Max's name, but there was no way Charlene could hide someone here. There was no space.

Desperation grew again. These keys had to be important. They *had* to be. I decided to call Hadad, get the authorities out here so they could assist with the search. When I reached into my pocket for Charlene's phone, it wasn't there. It must've fallen out as I'd torn through the cottage.

I sped across the yard and into the main house again, searching the ground as I ran. Back inside, I went into each room, trying to find the cell phone.

As soon as I got to the converted office, I spotted the device on the floor in the corner, next to the pillow-covered ottoman. I'd barely glanced at this piece of furniture the first time around. When I saw the hinges on one side, I realized it could be used for storage. Or hiding stuff.

When the pillows were in a heap on the floor, I lifted the ottoman's lid but only found a stack of fleece blankets. I rifled through the folds of soft material, pulling them out and tossing them aside. Still nothing.

In case Charlene had hidden something underneath, I decided to flip the seat. Grabbing hold of the corners, I heaved it toward me and turned it on its side.

At first, I thought I'd reached another dead end, but as I looked at the space where the ottoman had been, I frowned. A clear outline of a four-foot-by-two-foot rectangle—a little smaller than the ottoman—had been cut into the floorboards, with another padlock, and a set of hinges on the right-hand side.

I used one of the keys from the fake book to open the lock, but the door didn't budge. Fingers scrambling, I traced what I instinctively knew had to be a trapdoor, searching for a way in.

"Max," I yelled, pounding my fists on the wood before trying to use Charlene's keys as leverage to pry it open.

It didn't work, so I got up and searched her desk. Went through each drawer for a ruler, screwdriver, letter opener. Anything pointy to help me. Still, no matter what I tried, it didn't work.

Exhaling, I told myself I needed to calm down and use my brain. The trapdoor was cut into the floor. It had to withstand the weight of the ottoman plus anyone sitting on it, meaning the trapdoor itself would be sturdy, and likely heavy. Maybe Charlene had an easier way of opening it.

I searched her desk again, and when I got to the set of drawers, I crouched and peered inside. Something was attached at the very back, barely visible. Reaching, I grabbed the object and gave it a yank, my heart thumping as the Velcro strip made a distinct *trsschht* sound when it came loose.

It was a remote control. Two buttons. I pressed the first one and nothing happened, but with the second, there was a whirring sound and a soft click. The trapdoor slowly moved on an upward angle, finally granting me access.

Steep wooden stairs led into the bowels of the house, the smell of old dust filling my nose. I couldn't find a light switch, so I used the phone's flashlight, shining it on each tread as I took the stairs one at a time.

It was cold down here, damp, too, and when my feet touched solid ground again, I held up the phone to see better. The excavated concrete room was fifty square feet, perhaps, and empty save for an abandoned metal wine rack, and two unused shelving units facing each other on opposite walls.

My shoulders slumped as I finally admitted defeat. All this time I'd hoped to find my brother alive, but Max wasn't here. Kenji would be saved, hopefully, but if he hadn't seen Charlene, it would become a battle of wills, me against her.

I doubted she'd ever confess to what she'd done to my brother, not when she'd made her intention of framing me for Wade's alleged murder perfectly clear. The Nokia was still on my nightstand, but it wouldn't prove my claims. I'd left my prints all over Wade's house. I'd assaulted Charlene with a hunting knife, and she'd worn gloves. Who would the cops believe?

"Fuuuuuuuck," I yelled, the word echoing around the basement. "Fuck you, Charlene."

I was about to head upstairs but stopped myself from giving up so easily. Charlene had built a hidden trapdoor to conceal the access to her basement. What else might she have done down here to protect herself?

Three steps, and I put my hand on the first shelving unit, toppling it to the floor. Nothing but a bare wall. As I turned, I heard a noise. Searching the ground, I expected to see an animal scurrying away and hoped it was only a mouse, but I was alone. I stood still. Didn't move.

Another noise. Not a mouse. Not an animal. *A human.*

"Hello?" I said. "Is anyone there?"

Another muffled sound, and this time it resembled a sob. After rushing over to the second shelving unit on the opposite wall, I yanked it over, and my heart almost stopped when I saw a padlocked wooden door.

"Max?" I yelled, banging a fist against it before pulling the keys I'd found upstairs from my pocket, fumbling as I tried to stuff one into the lock. It didn't fit, and neither did the second or third, but the fourth slid in with ease. I pulled the door open . . .

Inside was the person from the photograph Charlene had sent when she'd called herself Anwir. They sat on a cot, cowering in the corner against the wall. With a single glance I knew their knotted hair hadn't seen a pair of scissors in years.

Trembling, the person brought their stick legs closer to their chest as a pair of impossibly skinny hands clutched a stained blanket wrapped around their upper body. As they made themselves smaller, burying their head between their knees, I saw a roadmap of scars crisscrossing their exposed forearms.

When I took a step, the stench of human waste hit me full-on, and my eyes dropped to the bucket in the corner. Ignoring the putrid smell, I moved closer as I held up the flashlight.

"It's me," I whispered. "It's me. Stella."

Slowly, ever so slowly, the creature lifted its head. And there they were. Those deep green eyes. The ones I hadn't seen in six years, and I'd feared I'd never see again.

Max.

TWO MONTHS LATER

CHAPTER 58

Abridged Transcript of *A KILLER MOTIVE* Podcast

Episode 129–The Truth About What Happened to Max Dixon

Welcome back to *A Killer Motive*, your East Coast true crime podcast, which is now a proud Booker Media Production. I'm your host, Stella Dixon, and ...

(Five-second silence)

Forgive me, this will be an emotional episode. I promise I'll do my best to get through it without crying all the time.

First, let me say that recording another episode about my brother was a tremendously difficult decision. The inaugural show of *A Killer Motive* was about Max's disappearance, and the backlash was so swift and brutal, I decided I'd continue my investigations about his disappearance privately.

However, since Max was found two months ago, the rumors, theories—conspiracy and otherwise—about what happened to him became so wild and extreme, not to mention incorrect, he and I decided to set the record straight. No, Max wasn't living in Arizona under a fake name and pretending to be missing as a publicity stunt, and he certainly didn't join a cult.

As a side note, we are in no way trying to benefit financially from this episode. In fact, a large donation has been given to a missing persons organization in Max's name to help those who haven't yet had as fortunate an outcome to their stories as we have.

What happened to Max Dixon? In this episode, I'll share what we've managed to piece together so far, including elements the police have agreed I can provide without compromising their ongoing investigation.

(Pensive music)

Let me start at the beginning. Max vanished a little over six years ago, a few days before his eighteenth birthday, from a beach party I took him to. He was found on August 7 of this year, after he'd been held captive in a secret basement at a cottage on Falcon Lake. This is Max's story.

(Pensive music)

Stella: How are you, Max?

Max: Overwhelmed. I can't believe I'm home. It's ... surreal. It's amazing.

Stella: Are you sure you're ready to talk about what happened?

Max: (Pause) Not all of it, no. There are certain things ... things she ... No, I'll never ... no.

Stella: Maybe we can start with the night of the beach party. What do you remember?

Max: Having a great time. Dancing, drinking a few beers. Maybe more than a few. If I'd known it would be my last night of freedom, I'd have emptied the keg (small laugh). Anyway, I needed the bathroom, so I headed to the bus stop because I remembered seeing a Porta Potty there (pause). Are you sure you want me to include this part, Stella?

Stella: Yes, it's okay, I promise. He and I talked about it, and we agreed.

Max: I, uh, I saw Jeff.

Stella: My then boyfriend, now husband?

Max: Yes, I saw him and (beep). They were, uh, they were having sex.

Stella: What did you do?

Max: Well, I was mightily pissed off. I wanted to go and tell you, of course, but I reconsidered because even in my drunken stupor, I knew it would hurt you. I stormed off and went for a walk away from everyone to clear my head, but I got angry again. After a while I went back to the bus shelter to confront Jeff and (beep), but he was alone. We got into a fight. I punched him. He punched me. Then he left and walked back to the beach.

Stella: Is this when the car pulled up?

Max: Yeah. It was our former neighbor, Charlene Thornton. She asked if I was okay, and when I said no, she said I was obviously upset and offered to drive me home. She was older, knew our family. I got into her car, and ... and ... (breathes heavily)

Stella: Take your time, Max.

Max: When I got into the passenger seat and turned to close the door, she injected me with ... I'm not sure what she gave me.

Stella: But you think it was a tranquilizer?

Max: Yes. I have flashes of us driving. Her helping me out of the car and inside a house. There's a vague memory of steep stairs. When I woke up, I was in a dark room.

Stella: The one I found you in.

Max: (Pause) Yes.

Stella: Did you have any idea where you were?

Max: No, none. I thought maybe her house in Portland, but I was wrong.

Stella: Did she say why she'd abducted you?

Max: She said people like me must be punished.

Stella: People like you? Did she elaborate?

Max: (Whispers) No, she never said. Not once in what you told me was six years (long pause). Six years. I can't believe I was gone for so long.

    (Pensive music)

Because of the ongoing investigation, and because Max isn't ready to share these details publicly, we won't divulge the horrific abuse my brother suffered during his captivity. What I'm allowed to share is that it wasn't sexual in nature, but involved isolation, extreme starvation, and frequent physical and psychological torture.

Max didn't leave his basement prison since Thornton took him there on the night he was abducted. When he was found ... (long pause, clearing of throat). When he was found, Max was so severely emaciated, the doctors at Maine Medical Center said if he hadn't been rescued, he'd likely have died from malnutrition within weeks.

(Pensive music)

Stella: Max, what do you know about Charlene Thornton?

Max: Not much, really. I knew she worked as an investigative journalist. I'd seen her at Mom and Dad's Christmas parties. We'd talked a few times. She was . . . *nice*.

Stella: No reason to believe she was going to hurt you when you got in her car.

Max: Not even one. I can't get my head around what you found out about her. I guess in some ways, what she did to me is starting to make some kind of sense. I mean, it has to. I've got to find a way to understand it all or I'm not sure I'll ever begin to get over it. I need to know *why*.

(Pensive music)

On *A Killer Motive*, we always try to get to the root of why people commit heinous crimes, and this case is no different. With permission from Detective Hadad from Portland Police, I'm allowed to share details about Charlene Thornton's background, providing I state all allegations against her have yet to be proven in a court of law.

Charlene Thornton, who is sixty-one, was born Camilla Turner in Falmouth, Maine. At age fourteen, she was the victim of a horrific home invasion when two men broke into her parents' residence. According to the details I obtained under the Freedom of Information Act, Charlene's twin sister managed to shove Charlene into a main floor closet, promising everything would be fine if she stayed quiet.

Unfortunately, that wasn't the case. Charlene's mother and sister were brutally murdered with a hunting knife, their slain bodies lying yards away from Charlene's hiding spot. She witnessed the killings. Terrified, she stayed hidden for almost twenty-four hours until her father returned from a business trip and found his wife and daughter lying in pools of blood.

The motive for the home invasion was established as financial. Money, watches, and jewelry were taken. According to Charlene's witness statement, the combination to her parents' safe was obtained by cutting off the tip of her twin's pinky finger, forcing her mother to reveal the code.

Despite Charlene giving descriptions of the attackers, men she described as white and somewhere between eighteen and twenty-five, no suspects were apprehended. The case went cold and to this day remains unsolved.

After her mother's and sibling's violent deaths, Charlene continued to live with her father. Unable to cope with the trauma of losing his family, he drank excessively and self-medicated, leading to an accidental but fatal overdose when Charlene was eighteen.

With the inheritance following her father's death, including the cottage set on five acres of land on the shores of Falcon Lake, Charlene was able to put herself through college and live comfortably.

Before graduating summa cum laude with a journalism degree, she changed her name from Camilla Turner to Charlene Thornton. She moved to New Hampshire for ten years, working as an investigative journalist, and then returned to the Portland area, where she has lived since. Five years ago, she became the host of the renowned WHMR *People of Portland* radio show.

Charlene's motive for abducting and torturing Max could stem from the home invasion and her witnessing the murders of her mother and sister, plus the tragic loss of her father four years later. Although I'll never forgive Thornton for what she did to Max, one can only imagine how much devastation and psychological damage the events she suffered have caused her.

Still, many questions remain. Why did she snap and abduct my brother? What made her decide to taunt me after I appeared on her show, and pretend to be a mysterious man called Anwir who had information about my brother's disappearance, information he'd only share if I did as he commanded?

I don't believe Thornton had any intention of letting me find Max. Abducting his best friend, Kenji Omori—who I'm delighted to say has physically fully recovered from his ordeal—was a way of forcing me to engage in her twisted games.

For me, one of the biggest questions of all is this: Has Charlene Thornton hurt anybody else? Initial forensic testing of her cottage and Portland home haven't revealed any clues to answer the question, but surely it would be unwise to hastily exclude the possibility for two reasons.

The first is that I believe she pretended to need a cane to walk for almost thirty years. Why? Finding someone to shed light on this question proved difficult. Thornton never married, didn't have a partner, and had no children.

I was, however, able to track down a few of her friends with whom she played soccer until she suffered a badly broken leg in her midthirties, which allegedly caused her long-term injury.

All of them, without exception, were shocked by the allegations of Thornton's involvement in my brother's, Kenji's, and my abductions, and the murder of retired detective Anthony Wade. Here's my conversation with a woman we'll call Jane.

(Pensive music)

Stella: How well did you know Charlene Thornton?

Jane: Really well. We played soccer together for about five years and saw each other almost every week, sometimes more if we were gathering socially.

Stella: What was your reaction when you heard of her arrest?

Jane: I couldn't believe it. I still don't. There's no way she could've done what she's accused of. Hurting someone? Torturing and starving them? Keeping a man prisoner for years? Murder?

Stella: You don't think she's capable?

Jane: No way. It's a mistake. Charlene's a kind and thoughtful woman. It was such a shame she had to quit the soccer team after her accident.

Stella: What if I told you she faked the injury's—

Jane: No chance. I was there. I saw the bone sticking out of her leg.

Stella: I meant the long-term effects. She doesn't need a cane to walk.

Jane: You think she faked her limp? Get out of here. I don't believe that, either.

(Pensive music)

After speaking with Jane, I asked Max about Charlene's disability.

(Pensive music)

Stella: Did you ever witness Charlene needing a cane?

Max: Not after she abducted me, no. It was all faked.

Stella: How can you be sure when you were locked in a basement?

Max: Because ... because when she'd come in with her ... with her knife, she never had a cane. She didn't limp. She had no trouble moving at all. She was vicious. Terrifying.

Stella: Did you ever try to escape?

Max: I wanted to. God, I thought about it every single day. But I think she drugged my food and water to keep me subdued, plus when you don't eat properly ... (audible sob) I was so weak, so tired. But no, she never needed her cane. It's all an act. *Everything* about her is an act.

(Pensive music)

The second reason I don't think Max was Thornton's first *alleged* victim is a mutilated body part she led me to find in the abandoned mines at Bradley Hills. However, it's also my belief that Thornton wasn't acting alone.

It's not at all uncommon for women to be groomed and coerced by men, in particular, into committing serious and violent crimes. In fact, it's entirely possible her partner's dead, which is why Thornton finally got caught. She lacked the discipline and expertise to work by herself. She got ... *sloppy*. The police are investigating this avenue and have asked me not to elaborate further for now.

Max and I have agreed we may make another podcast episode once Thornton's trial has concluded. Until then, I'll leave the last few words to my brother.

(Pensive music)

Stella: What got you through the past six years?

Max: Knowing you'd never stop looking for me. I felt it in my heart. It's what allowed me to survive. Sooner or later, I knew you'd find me.

Stella: And where do you go from here?

Max: (Long pause) Forward. That's the only way there's ever been.

(Pensive music)

This was episode 129 of the true crime podcast *A Killer Motive*. Produced by Booker Media Productions. Written and hosted by Stella Dixon. With special guest Max Dixon.

For further updates on this case and others we've worked on, please consider subscribing to our newsletter via our website. Until next time, thank you for listening.

CHAPTER 59

CHARLENE

My gut flutters with excited anticipation as I hobble into the prison's visitation room with my crutches and take a seat at the gray metal table bolted to the floor. It's mid-October, and the leaves on the trees I can see through the barred windows are a beautiful array of reds and golds, like twinkling gemstones in the midday sun.

I suppress my desire to get outside and feel the warm rays on my skin. It'll keep for later, when they allow us to exercise in the yard. I can't do as much as I want yet, but my tendons are healing. When the doctor said I may never walk properly again, I nodded gravely. It was probably wishful thinking on his behalf. They said the same thing when I broke my leg playing soccer, and I proved everyone wrong. Only nobody knew. This will be the same.

Although it doesn't bode well to have a limp in here. One of the women tried to take advantage of mine by stealing some of my commissary items. The new gap in her front teeth showed her otherwise. She hasn't bothered me since. Apparently I already have a reputation.

Good. If they knew the entire truth, they'd all be terrified. Prisoners and guards. Every single one of them. But I'm not willing to divulge my secrets to anyone. I've been playing the long game for years. In some ways, I'm only getting started.

The room fills with inmates dressed in jumpsuits identical to mine with MAINE STATE CORRECTIONAL printed in large black letters across their backs. They shuffle in, most faces expectant and hopeful, excited for whoever has come to see them.

When my guest arrives, on time, I can tell from the way she's holding herself that she's trying not to balk. As our eyes meet, she can't help her body from stiffening. She's still afraid of me. I love the little quiver this knowledge provides.

My gaze drops to Stella's left hand, and she immediately curls her fingers, tucking them into the sleeve of her sweater. No matter. Her pinky will have mostly healed by now, the thick bandages long gone. The missing fingertip will, however, always be a reminder of me. Nothing she does, no amount of therapy she has, will change that. I've scarred her forever. More than once.

Stella slows her stride as she approaches. When she gets closer, I can almost taste how much disgust and loathing she has for me. It doesn't quite mask her fear. That's her predominant emotion, and it fills my veins. Feeds my soul. It's an image I'll feast on for days.

She doesn't want to be here. Stella wishes she were somewhere else, far, far away. I knew she'd come. How could she not? I have what she needs. What she wants more than anything.

Information.

Insights.

The truth.

Once I sent her an invitation to visit—prison-approved, of course—it was only a matter of time before she showed up.

For a moment, she seems to focus on how different I look. Slimmer, leaner. More toned. Prison time and workouts will do that to you. Still, with my gray roots and my face devoid of makeup, most strangers wouldn't afford me more than a cursory glance if I were on the outside. They certainly wouldn't believe me capable of what I've been accused of, let alone the things I've done.

They never have.

Stella's at the table now. I chose the one farthest from any of the guards so we can talk undisturbed. I can tell she's searching my expression, wanting to know if I'm as unfazed as I seem by my incarceration. I'd be lying if I said it doesn't piss me off, but I've prepared for this. My activities require self-discipline and rules. One of the latter is to always have a contingency plan for this scenario, and mine is decades in the making.

As Stella lowers herself into the seat opposite mine, I give her a deep, courteous bow. "I didn't think you'd accept my invitation," I lie softly. "It's good to see you, Stella."

"Why am I here?" she asks.

I let my face fall, put a hand to my chest. "Is this how you greet a friend?"

"We're not friends."

After a slight chuckle, I lean in. "Don't you want to know how I am?"

Stella watches me, no doubt deciding whether she should play along. "How are you, Thornton?"

Good girl. She knows she must engage if she wants what she came for. Of course, I still have to decide whether to give it to her. "Very well," I reply brightly. "Thank you for asking."

I wonder if seeing me in the flesh again, instead of in the incessant news reports swirling since she rescued her brother, is much harder than she anticipated. I'll bet a part of her wants to run for the exit and never look back. But I know another piece of her, by far the larger one, is rooted to the chair. She wants me to answer her questions, which means she finds herself at my mercy despite the fact I'm the one who's locked up.

"I listened to your podcast," I say. "Good show."

"Was my theory accurate?" she asks.

I know what she means, but say, "Which one?"

She clears her throat. Sits back in her chair, feigning nonchalance. "You took my brother because he reminded you of the men who killed your mother and sister. You were trying to punish them by hurting Max."

I open my mouth as if I'm about to speak before pressing my palms on the table. Of course, everyone believed my story about the home invasion, and how sweet Penny pushed me into a closet to protect me from our assailants. It was exactly what my sister would do, considering she always looked out for others, constantly put herself last.

I can still hear her shock and devastation when she came home after school, the day I'd pretended I was sick, and she found my mother's lifeless body on the floor, covered in blood. When Penny saw me, she immediately thought someone had attacked us. She couldn't believe it when I shoved the hunting knife under her ribs, or when I cut off the tip of her pinky while her life ebbed away.

"Why?" she'd sobbed quietly. "Why are you doing this?"

Why? That was the ultimate question.

Oh, I'd already tried to ignore and push away my evil urges for years and years, but they'd been too strong. It wasn't the first time I'd watched someone die. That had happened the year before, when I'd been walking home from a babysitting job one night when I was thirteen.

Someone I didn't know, a young man a few years older than me, stumbled down the street, visibly drunk. As he fell in the middle of the road, chuckling and mumbling to himself, I hid behind some bushes, observing him.

When he didn't get up, my anticipation grew as I wondered what might happen if a car came along. I waited, and when headlights appeared in the distance, I didn't shout at the man to get up. Didn't do anything to stop the huge truck. Instead, I bit my lip as it drove straight over him, coming to a screeching halt thirty yards down the road as I slipped into the shadows, excitement rippling through my body.

A KILLER MOTIVE

Bennett Jackson was killed outright, according to the news. Mourned by his parents and his little sister, Erin. What did such devastation do to a family, I wondered? Would I feel anything if it happened to mine? I couldn't stop my fascination about finding out for sure.

I didn't have a terrible relationship with my mother and sister, although I knew Mom always favored Penny. But carrying out my experiment was easier at home. Safer. More convenient. More . . . relatable.

Months were spent working out my plan to the minutest detail. How I'd stage the perfect home invasion, timing it after a major basement renovation, meaning there were fingerprints everywhere.

I'd known the safe combination for years, but I figured out how I'd make the pretend robbery believable, including where I'd hide the things I'd take. The jewelry, watches, and cash are still buried in the woods at Bradley Hills, never to be found.

What shocked me the most wasn't how easy it all was, including the killing, but how the police never suspected me. Not once. I was a fourteen-year-old girl. Almost fully grown and relatively tall. A murderer. Right there, within their grasp. Except they couldn't see it.

Most of them still can't. Many don't consider women capable of calculated homicide, not unless their victims are the young or the elderly, the sick and ailing, and even then, it's met with utter disbelief. "She was angry, she reacted, she didn't mean to do it, she has mental health problems, she was *coerced*." And on and on and on.

Just look at the monikers women killers are given. The *Giggling Granny*. The *Arsenic and Old Lace Killer*. Cutesy names that say nothing of our brutality. Men, on the other hand, are stalkers, rippers, and stranglers—words to inspire utter fear and dread.

Women not capable of extreme violence? Torture? Cold-blooded, premeditated murder? Give me a break. But I will say this: never being suspected gives us the advantage of never being looked for, and in turn, never being found.

Almost never. I didn't think I'd be locked up in prison because of someone like Stella, that's for sure. I'd never lured someone in with bait, like I'd used Kenji when she wouldn't play. Turns out that wasn't my best idea, and I've prided myself on my ideas being resourceful and infallible for years. Still, with her little podcast and few years of experience diving into cold cases, Stella thinks she knows the kind of person I am. She has no idea.

"It's an excellent theory," I finally say, neither confirming nor denying Stella's suspicions about why I took Max, or how many others there were before him. Urges don't go away, but you have to pace yourself, be meticulous in your planning. You also have to figure out what you'll do as you age and still want to hunt. Have a plan for how you'll continue wreaking havoc, no matter where from.

"How's Jeff?" I ask, switching the subject. "You're not wearing your wedding ring. Did you split up?"

"None of your business," she replies.

From the sources I've tapped into, I know Stella moved into her own apartment a month ago, a place where Max often stays. Will the separation from her husband be permanent? After all, Jeff and Stella's mutual betrayal is so vast, it must seem insurmountable. How delicious.

I also wonder if since bringing Max home, Stella can finally see herself becoming a mother. Not with Jeff, I suspect. Too much damage has been done. Which is exactly the point. The ripples of my actions are almost endless, and they've been going on for a long time.

When I moved into the house near Erin and Howard, Erin didn't know who I was. But I knew her. It's why I'd chosen my new home in the first place. It had been multiple decades since her older brother, Bennett, had been accidentally run over by the truck as I'd watched. She missed him so much, she told me once when we had coffee together. Said she wasn't sure how they all got through the tragedy.

It hadn't broken her, and I wanted to continue my long-term experiment. See how much grief and pain a person could endure. And so I watched the family, pretending to be the perfect neighbor, observing my next prey. Obtaining evidence to plant on Fynn Baumann's remains, just in case his body showed up.

Given Max's age, he would soon be the perfect choice—like all the other young men before him. As always, if I got caught, it would mean giving the psychiatrists and forensic psychologists what they always looked for, what Stella constantly wanted to find: a killer's motive.

After a few years of living nearby and watching Max, time drew closer to me making my move. I was breaking one of my own rules. Typically I wasn't known to my victims, but taking Max and continuing with my destructive research was too good to pass up.

Torching my house deliberately hadn't been my original plan, either, but I feared I might have left some DNA evidence of Max's predecessor behind. Better to be safe than sorry, and that way I left the neighborhood before Max even disappeared. I removed myself from the list of possible witnesses and assumed my role of investigative reporter, which had always served me so well when I wanted to dig into some of the police reports of the men who'd gone missing by my hand.

I watched and waited for another while, and when I saw Kenji posting about the Lighthouse Beach party online, and Max commenting he'd go, all I had to do was wait for the perfect opportunity. Seeing him and Jeff arguing near the road was the proverbial icing on the cake, and I gobbled it down by the spoonful.

I wasn't planning to bring Stella into the game, but it's as I said—when you get older, you need to adapt to fulfill your urges. Besides, she irritated me so much when she said on the radio that she'd find whoever hurt Max with a single clue. No, she wouldn't, I thought. She'd never be a match for me.

I hadn't taken a woman before, not only because it didn't fit the motive I was building, but also because I always believed it would be too easy.

I was mistaken.

"Tell me why I'm here," Stella says, raising her chin. "Visits have an hour limit."

I take my time, sit back. "You got a few things wrong on your show."

"Did I?" She pretends to be bored, but the words came out too quickly. She's hooked. "Is this the part where you claim your innocence?"

I chuckle. "We both know I'll be convicted. Max's testimony will see to that."

"What did I get wrong?" she asks.

I smile again but don't answer her question. "You know, I could be a valuable resource to you. I can share insights into serial killers' minds, especially female ones."

Stella tries a dismissive wave, but her hand trembles. "I doubt it, Thornton. To be considered a serial killer, you need to murder at least three people, and with a distinct cooling-off period in between. Some even say it's four. You've only managed two. Wade and Baumann."

I bet my eyes flash, and I blink to regain control. "Did you know female serial killers often go undetected for years, decades, if not forever, because nobody can fathom a woman can commit such crimes?"

"I won't pander to your fantasies, so I'll ask again. Why am I here?"

"What would you say is the perfect murder?"

"Why am I—"

"Indulge me. For old times' sake. What's the perfect murder?"

She answers without missing a beat. "One the perpetrator gets away with."

I beam at her. "True, although I'd go a step further. It's a murder solved by having someone else convicted. The police close the file. It doesn't remain a cold case." I sit back, hold up my hands. "Now, isn't that the most perfect murder you've ever heard of?"

I can almost hear her connect the dots, leading the way to what I'm implying. Her father has maintained his innocence, says he knows nothing about Fynn Baumann's disappearance or remains.

No doubt the Dixons are all standing by him, and Max confirmed his dad wasn't involved in his abduction, but I'm sure Erin and Stella find it hard to trust Howard entirely. Another little shove toward their breaking point.

They'll never find the rest of Baumann. Never. I also know the police have been searching for a link between Howard and me for the past two months. They haven't found anything. Not a whiff of an affair or any sort of relationship other than us living a few doors down from each other for a few years. Which is exactly what it was.

Howard was one of my contingency plans, especially when I learned he'd been suspected of killing Erin's ex-boyfriend, a man I'd never met. There are more patsies out there, walking around without the faintest clue that I hold their fate entirely in my hands.

I knew if I ever got caught, I'd have many other men I could implicate in the same number of murders. Have them investigated, blow up their families, and watch my games play out from afar, including from prison. It's simple enough. Timed anonymous emails that will trigger from separate untraceable encrypted accounts if I don't log in to stop them.

Technology is incredible. Burner phones with spyware, laptops with VPNs, handheld Wi-Fi signal blockers to scramble a junkyard's footage—all of it hidden away in a secret location far from my house because the authorities have no doubt been turning my place upside down. Whoever thinks old dogs can't learn new tricks deserves to get bitten in the ass.

I'll share none of this with Stella, of course. She wants me to own up to framing her father, and I'll string her along. She'll get me on her podcast, and I'll make sure she brings the right cold cases—the ones I've manipulated—to me, so I get a front row seat to my handiwork. That will help satisfy my urges. For now.

"You know what would be great?" I say, as if the idea has just come to me. "If you were recording this conversation and included it in an upcoming episode."

"Tell me how my father is involved in the dismemberment of Fynn Baumann," she says, getting to the real reason she came. "Did he kill him? Did you murder him together? If so, why?"

I lift my chin. "People always want to understand the *why*. As if by knowing they can not only reconcile and make sense of what happened but also protect themselves from tragedy befalling them again. It's all about lightning supposedly not striking twice. Of course, it often does."

"Why are you destroying our family?" Stella says. "What did we ever do to you?"

This question sparks delight and excitement in my chest, and I whisper, "Remember what I told you? Why anyone does anything? Because they want to. Because they *can*."

My delivery is glacial, so utterly unrepentant she can't help the small gasp escaping from between her lips. I watch as she gets up and, without another glance in my direction, turns and walks away. She doesn't see me smirking as I look at the caged clock on the wall.

I start a game with myself.

Seven minutes.

I bet that's how long it'll take until she returns.

CHAPTER 60

STELLA

I know Charlene's eyes are on my back as I head for the door. Once I'm on the other side, the guard leads me to the private room where Detective Najwa Hadad waits for me.

"Good job, Stella," she says as soon as I walk in, her voice filling with empathy.

"She didn't give me anything," I say, shaking my head. "Nothing."

"Not yet."

Najwa hands me a glass of water. I think she pretends not to see my trembling hands. I hate Charlene's power over me.

"But your instincts were spot-on," the detective continues. "She likely summoned you here because you said on the podcast she was coerced by a man into hurting Max and got sloppy. The woman has one major ego."

Najwa and I have been working together for the last seven weeks, ever since she suggested us investigating and trying to piece together what Charlene has done, and to whom. So far, our collaboration has been surprisingly fluid, and she's an excellent cop. Smart, tenacious, an out-of-the-box thinker. Seemed I'd been too quick to judge her.

For example, I was intrigued to learn that for the thesis of her criminal justice degree, Najwa studied female serial killers. She explained how most people—as it turned out, this included me—attribute predatory behavior almost exclusively to men. Najwa calls it one of the most persistent myths she's encountered in her profession. And an exceedingly dangerous one.

"We both suspect Thornton has killed multiple times before," she says now, running a hand through her thick hair.

A lock falls over her forehead, and I resist the sudden urge to brush it from her eyes. I know I have that reaction because I don't have much human contact now that I live alone. Jeff and I are trying to figure things out, but I worry both of us already know it's a lost cause. Too many secrets and far too many lies. Way too much damage. The repercussions of what Charlene did will keep tearing our family apart, even if we try hard not to let them.

At least things are getting better with my mother. She cried so hard when I found Max, hugging me for the first time in six years. We've talked a lot since then, and while I don't think she'll ever truly forgive me, we've come a long way. I remain hopeful our relationship will be saved.

And then there's Max. Poor, poor Max, who cries out in his sleep, jumps at the slightest noise, and can't settle for the night without me or one of our parents being in his room. There's so much trauma, so many terrible, terrifying memories, I'm not sure he'll ever recover.

I refocus on Najwa, and the reason I'm here. "We have nothing to help us prove what Charlene has done. That's the problem."

"Not yet," she repeats. "We have to keep going."

She's right, and I have more ways to do so now. Since I bought out Vivien's share of A Killer Motive Inc. and it became part of Booker Media, Andrea has given me unlimited access to her pool of resources, and a ton of funding. She's as keen to get Charlene on all her crimes as Najwa and I are, although I told Andrea we wouldn't embellish things when we do. Not that I believe we'll need to.

"Did you hear what I said?" Najwa asks, and I shake my head.

"I got the approval to exhume Charlene's parents' bodies, and her sister's."

"Great news," I say. "Maybe we'll get lucky and determine she killed them."

"I'm not holding my breath," Najwa says. "There have been a lot of technological advancements, but we can't bet she made any mistakes back then. We need to work every angle we can think of."

"Any luck on finding out if the barn where she took me belonged to her?" I ask.

"No. Shell company after shell company and so forth. She knows how to hide."

"Then why did she keep Max at her cottage?"

Najwa shrugs a little. "Arrogance? I guess she was certain it would be safe. That she'd remain above all suspicion, forever."

"And she wanted to keep him close, somewhere familiar, in the long term."

"Yes. More than likely. We can't know for sure. Maybe she kept the others elsewhere. Or scrubbed the place clean each time she disposed of another of her victims. Hard to say."

My shoulders drop. "I'm going back in there to talk to her, aren't I?"

"Take another crack, Stella," Najwa says. "You're the only person she'll speak to."

"I'll bring her on the podcast." The force of my statement surprises me. No need to ask Najwa if she agrees because I already know she does. "She loves games. The more twisted, the better."

Najwa rubs her chin. "Be careful. She'll try to mess with your head. But if we can somehow find clues about what she did, and to whom . . ." She pauses. "You know I think she planted your father's prints on Baumann's remains, but we need to prove it. Otherwise, he'll have a humongous cloud hanging over him, no matter if we never charge or convict him. Thornton's got to talk, but on her own terms."

"Let her believe she has the power?" I say.

"Exactly. Eventually, she'll slip up and come crashing down."

I want to tell Najwa that Charlene never slipped up when she pretended to be Anwir. Every move was calculated, every phone call, every sentence. The red herring about her family, drama club, and the production of *Oliver Twist*. Her seemingly inadvertent comment about Dr. Graf. Her overtly and deliberately masculine behavior, although automatically assuming Anwir was male could've been my own prejudices clouding my judgment.

My guess is the only thing Charlene didn't expect was for me to fight back as hard as I did. Seems both of us underestimated what women are capable of.

A man—Detective Wade—died a horrific death, partially because of me. Najwa says it's not my fault, and I must do my best to not let the guilt crush me, but guilt and I . . . we have a complicated relationship, and it seems we're stuck like glue.

Shaking out my arms, I prepare myself for what's about to happen, for what I'm agreeing to do. Najwa puts a hand on my shoulder and gives it a squeeze before ensuring the tiny camera and microphone combo hidden in the button of my shirt is still working.

"You can do this," she says. "You're one of the bravest people I know."

I feel anything but brave as I walk back into the visitor's room. My brain's hollering at me to turn and run, but I don't. Charlene smiles as I walk to her. She expected this to happen. Before I arrived at the prison, I bet she knew, despite her circumstances, that she'd have the upper hand.

Or that's what she believes—and what I want her to continue believing. I hope she sees the sheen on my upper lip and attributes it to nerves, not the fingertip of water I dabbed on myself before I left Najwa.

I'm going to trick Charlene this time. I'll do everything I can think of. Najwa, Andrea, and I will be three steps ahead. Evaluating, calculating, recalibrating. Watching, listening, and learning as we observe her. She's the one locked up now, not me.

Charlene Thornton has no idea how deep my hatred runs. How it'll fuel everything I do. I never gave up on my brother, and I won't rest until I see her obliterated. Because I *will* obliterate her. I said I'd do whatever it took to find Max, and I did. It seems she's forgotten that.

The closer I get, the thicker the air between us becomes, the revulsion emanating from my body palpable. She waits a few beats, and I bet she thinks I believe I'm entering a pact with the devil when I finally look at her. The irony is, with the resources I have at my disposal, with the collaboration I've struck with Najwa and Andrea, Charlene's the one who should be afraid.

She's all alone. I'm not. Not anymore.

As I sit, I see the anticipation in her eyes, the intense, insatiable gluttony for power that will ultimately be her downfall. This time I'm the one who smiles and leans in.

"Let's do it, Charlene," I whisper. "Let's play."

★ ★ ★ ★ ★

AUTHOR'S NOTE (INCLUDES SPOILERS!)

I'm what you call a plotter in the writing world, meaning I outline my novels ahead of time. Each of my books starts with a general concept, followed by a loose idea of the protagonist and antagonist I'll drop into my fictional murderous mayhem.

When *A Killer Motive* was in its embryonic stage, I already had a certain amount of clarity on Stella, but her enemy eluded me for quite some time. After mulling over Stella's, Max's, and Kenji's journeys, I turned my attention to forming their opposition—and the villain immediately became a man.

As I outlined the story a little more, I asked myself why the antagonist had to be male. My instant reaction was, "Because women don't do these horrible things. They'd never keep someone prisoner for years, starve, torture, kill, and dismember them."

Instinctively, I had to challenge my preconceptions. The following books and article did exactly that, shedding an entirely new light on my understanding of and biases about female criminality, and in particular female serial killers. Thank you to these authors for providing such incredible and detailed insight, which helped me shape Charlene Thornton.

Nonfiction Books:
When She Was Bad: How and Why Women Get Away with Murder by Patricia Pearson
Just as Deadly: The Psychology of Female Serial Killers by Marissa A. Harrison
Murder Most Rare: The Female Serial Killer by Michael D. Kelleher

Article:
"The Last Frontier: Myths & the Female Psychopathic Killer" by Frank S. Perri and Terrance G. Lichtenwald

ACKNOWLEDGMENTS

Eleven novels, and penning this part is still one of my favorites. It means we're birthing another book together, and I can express my gratitude to the brilliant individuals and teams who've assisted during conception, labor, and beyond!

Starting with you, Dear Reader, has become tradition. There are a gazillion books available, and you picked this one. No matter if you read *A Killer Motive* in a professional capacity or for entertainment, I appreciate you. I hope you enjoyed this twisty ride.

Book reviewers and bookstagrammers—including Tonya Cornish and her outstanding Thriller Book Lovers–The Pulse team—you give my novels the most gorgeous, creative, kind, and hilarious shout-outs. Thank you for being an author's cheerleading dream.

Carolyn Forde, my astounding agent who's the best of the best—I *love* working with you! Your advice and guidance are second to none, and I'm so thankful for our friendship. Can't wait to see what we do next. A huge thank-you also to the Transatlantic Agency team for all the behind-the-scenes work. Thank you for having my back.

Dina Davis, my savvy editor—much gratitude for the input on *A Killer Motive* from plot to print. Your insights and questions always level up my stories. Thank you also for navigating us through the publishing process and answering my PITA questions.

This book wouldn't exist without the support of the amazing Harlequin, HarperCollins, HTP, and MIRA teams. Thank you to every single person who worked on this novel in some way, whether big or small. You are truly brilliant. Thank you also to my copyeditor, Jennifer Stimson—you have a tremendous eye for detail.

HarperAudio, BeeAudio, Carly Katz, and narrators Amy Hall, Bernadette Dunne, Carol Schneider, and Nick Thurston—you are fantastic, and I adore listening to you bringing my characters to life and making them your own. You are true talents!

Emily Ohanjanians—thank you for working through the outline for *A Killer Motive* with me, and for being such a trusted, wonderful friend. I can't wait to hold your debut novel in my hands and cheer you on the way you have me.

Karma Brown, Jennifer Hillier, Lynn McPherson aka Sydney Leigh, and Sonica Soares—my Oakville Women! What would I do and where would I be without you (pretty sure there's a song about that). Thank you for your unwavering support and friendship.

Fellow crime author and retired Detective Sergeant Bruce Robert Coffin—thank you for helping me murder fictional people . . . *again*! Same again soon, please.

Thank you to fellow crime author Steve Urszenyi, and to Lynne Urszenyi for your expert medical advice (and the stories that are as equally gross as they are fascinating).

To Dennis Russell—thank you for chatting with me about typical working hours for EMTs. You were very kind to share your expertise.

Laurah Norton, host of *The Fall Line* podcast and author of *Lay Them to Rest*—we met at Toronto's MOTIVE festival, and our discussion left a huge impression on me. Thank you for helping me shape Stella's podcast motivations, and for your wonderful words about this book.

ACKNOWLEDGMENTS

To the other authors who read an early version of this novel: Carter Wilson, Daniel Kalla, Heather Gudenkauf, Lauren Ling Brown, Rick Mofina, Robyn Harding, Samantha Downing, Sarah Pekkanen, and Sydney Leigh—thank you for being so generous with your time and giving me such lovely feedback.

I'm so fortunate to be part of the wonderful crime writing community. Sure, we get twisted on the page, but you are the funniest, warmest, and most generous people I've ever met. Thank you for your inspiration, wisdom, energy, and support.

Dad, Joely, Simon, Michael, and Oli; my in-laws Gilbert and Jeanette; and my extended family everywhere—thank you for sharing my work all over the world.

And finally, to Rob, Leo, Matt, and Lex, the best husband and sons I could've ever asked for. Thank you for all the love and laughter—and not being too weirded out when I share my latest research at the dinner table. I love you *beyond* the ends of the earth and back again, multiple times over. Thank you for being you. Thank you for making "us."

QUESTIONS FOR DISCUSSION (INCLUDES SPOILERS!)

1. A central theme of *A Killer Motive* is how women are underestimated (including by each other and themselves). Did you catch yourself doing this with some of the characters? If so, which ones, when, and why?

2. What did you make of Stella not being truthful with Jeff about her not being ready for a baby? Did you agree with her motivations and/or actions? What might've happened to their relationship if she'd been honest with him?

3. At one point Stella says, "The Dixons . . . we're messed up. Broken. All of us. In fact, as far as I'm concerned, it's better if our branch of the family tree withers and dies." Could you relate to any of their family dynamics? If you were Stella, would you have tried to mend the broken bond with your mother following Max's disappearance? If so, how?

4. If you were Stella, would you have told anyone about Anwir? How might you have handled the situation in order to find Kenji and get the information Anwir allegedly had about Max?

5. Did your allegiances shift during the story? Toward whom, why, and when?

6. What did you consider to be the most surprising scene in the book? What shocked you? What was your favorite scene?

7. A lot of the characters had secrets and told lies throughout the book. Which do you think were the worst? If any of those people had told the truth earlier, do you think Max or Kenji would have been rescued sooner?

8. Who did you think the antagonist was? Did your suspicions change throughout the novel? Were you surprised by the reveal?

9. How did you feel about the chapters written from Charlene's point of view, and their evolution? What did you make of her decades-old manipulation and subterfuge?

10. How did the book change your understanding and perception of female serial killers? Have you or will you read some of the nonfiction books and/or the article mentioned in the Author's Note?

11. What do you think might happen to Stella, Najwa, and Andrea versus Charlene Thornton now? Will this trio of strong women finally be able to take our cunning antagonist down?

A SPOILER-FREE CONVERSATION WITH HANNAH MARY McKINNON

***A Killer Motive* is a wild ride. Where did the inspiration come from?**
Typically, I can pinpoint where the idea for a book came from, but with this one it's proving to be a little more elusive. I remember wondering what a person might do if someone they deeply cared about vanished, and how that might affect those left behind years later. What if I pushed it further and the main character of my story blamed herself for the disappearance? How far would she go to find her missing loved one if she was given a clue? The story grew legs from there.

How did you develop your main characters, Stella and her antagonist?
Stella's psyche was relatively clear from the start, and I knew she'd feel responsible for Max's situation. I had no clue she was a true crime podcast host—that brilliant suggestion came from my agent, Carolyn Forde.

As with all my main characters, during the outlining stage I "interviewed" Stella, meaning I completed a three-page questionnaire about her. This always helps me get deeper insight about character background. I understand them more, and they become fully formed people as the story progresses.

As for my antagonist—who they were eluded me for some time as I noodled around the concept. However, once I had their identity, I put them through the three-page wringer, too. Like Stella, there was also a change in the villain's profession, although a little later in the process. This switch was thanks to my editor, Dina Davis, and I'm so glad because it works far better than my original idea.

You often say you're a "heavy outliner." Can you share what that means?
I'm very structured in my approach to outlining and follow a combination of *Save the Cat* by Blake Snyder and the Plotstormers course I took with www.WritersHQ.co.uk many years ago.

Essentially, I break my story into small steps, from beginning to end. While I don't come up with every single plot point or twist, I have the main beats, which help me move my outline from one chapter to the next. Along with my character interviews, I also build a photo gallery and a map of the area I'm dropping my characters into.

Typically, this outlining process takes around a month, depending on the book. I have been known to do this in as little as a week. Pretty sure that was a fluke and will never happen again.

So, do you know the ending before you start? Do your novels follow your outline exactly?
I like to say I *think* I know the ending. It gives me something to work toward, and a definitive character arc. For the last few novels, the endings have been very close to the ones I'd imagined, but that hasn't always been the case.

As for my novels following my outlines exactly, I'm never married to them. Things shift and evolve as I write, and sometimes better ideas emerge as the first draft and initial edits thereof take shape. Of course I then also rely on the input and ideas from my agent, editor, and the publishing team. It all comes down to what works best for the story.

How much research did you do in advance for this book?
That's a tricky question without giving too much away. Let's just say I read a lot about the type of person my antagonist is and leave it at that. For more info, please see my Author's Note. Be warned, it contains spoilers!

Can you describe a typical day of your author life?
I'm not sure there's a typical day, which is also why I adore this career so much. I might be walking around while muttering to myself about a new plot, pushing through the first draft of a novel, working on edits, designing graphics, interacting with readers on social media, asking people some seriously weird questions for research, or perhaps attending a conference. Most of the time it's a combination of any of the above. And I love it.

How did your corporate career help with your writing career?
My organizational and networking skills definitely come in handy, as does my head for business. In my corporate role, I often led different projects, e.g. building and implementing solid back-office policies and procedures from the ground up, opening subsidiaries in the Netherlands and Germany, leading due diligence for a company sale, or coordinating company mergers. I thrive being in new situations and figuring out how to work through them. This translates to my books as my new cast of characters is always in a brand-new scenario, and I have to help them get out of it (or not . . .).

Finish this sentence: "I can't write unless I . . ."
. . . have a tidy desk. For me, cluttered space = cluttered mind. It makes me jumpy, and I lose focus. I also need a huge jug of water and, if possible, a nearly empty inbox.

What advice do you have for aspiring writers?
Read as much and often as you can and listen to audiobooks. Write, even if you think it's terrible—you can't edit an empty page. Another tip someone suggested was to skip ahead if I couldn't figure out a chapter or scene, that I should focus on another part of the manuscript and trust myself enough to backfill later. It was revolutionary to think that although a book is read in a linear fashion, it doesn't have to be written that way. Finally, share your work. It can be scary, but it's the only way you'll get feedback and improve your craft.

Readers might be surprised to learn you've also recently written holiday romantic comedies as Holly Cassidy. Can you tell us more about that?
It's a bittersweet origin story. My mum passed away a couple of months after the pandemic hit, and I couldn't get to Switzerland to say goodbye. It was one of the most gut-wrenching, guilt-inducing experiences of my life. During that time, I worked on my sixth book, the thriller *Never Coming Home*. Although it's crime fiction, it turned out to be funny (dark and twisted humor, but humor nonetheless), and that happened because I needed to escape someplace where I could laugh when everything else felt so desperate.

I enjoyed writing the humor so much, I wondered if I could return to my romance roots (my first book, *Time After Time*, was a romance). I played around with a few ideas but didn't do much with them until my agent asked if I'd thought about writing a romantic comedy. Now, that's what I call serendipitous! *The Christmas Wager* and *The Christmas Countdown* were published in 2023 and 2024 respectively. It's been a delight to explore the lighter side of life in between my murderous ways.

What do you hope readers will take away from *A Killer Motive*?
I always say I hope to surprise readers, and that they keep thinking about the book long after they've finished the final page. My ultimate goal hasn't changed: it's to entertain, to provide people with a form of escape, something to unwind with, and to leave them satisfied, thinking, "I enjoyed that. It was time well spent! What else has she written?"

And finally, what can you tell us about your next novel?
I'm currently at the "noodling" stage with two very different ideas, so it's a little early to say. Both are quite the challenge, and I'm excited to develop them more and see where the characters and story take me.